THE

UNPLOWED

SKY

Daughter of the Storm
The Longest Road
The Island Harp
Home Mountain
No Roof but Heaven
Lady of No Man's Land
Texas Pride
So Many Kingdoms
The Heaven Sword
The Cave Dreamers
Mating of Hawks
Harvest of Fury
The Valiant Women
Daughter of the Sword
Bride of Thunder
A Woman Clothed in Sun
A Lady Bought with Rifles

THE
UNPLOWED
SKY

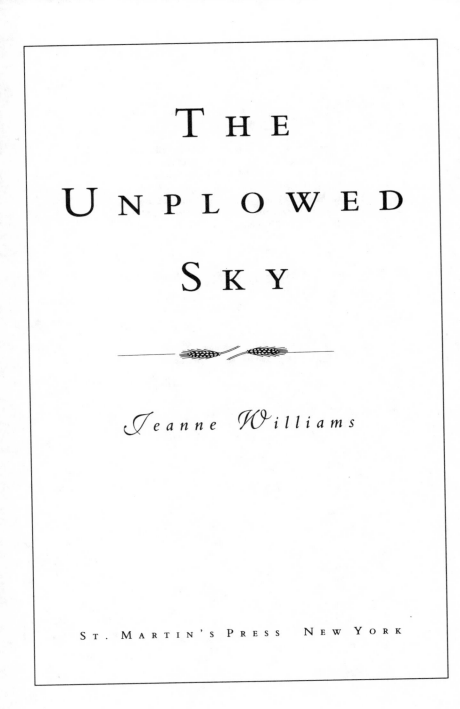

Jeanne Williams

ST. MARTIN'S PRESS   NEW YORK

Design by Judith A. Stagnitto

Library of Congress Cataloging-in-Publication Data

Williams, Jeanne.
The unplowed sky / Jeanne Williams.
p.   cm.
ISBN 0-312-11361-7
1. Young women—Kansas—Fiction.
2. Depressions—Kansas—Fiction.
I. Title.
PS3573.I44933U56   1994   94-19691
813'.54—dc20   CIP

First Edition: November 1994
10 9 8 7 6 5 4 3 2 1

This story is dedicated with love and appreciation to Uncle Lou, who worked on a threshing crew and helped build roads and railroads in No-Man's Land; to Aunt Dorothy, an indomitable spirit, who drove "Big Red" in the harvest fields; and to Alice Shook, my kissin' cousin, who has shared with me such vivid memories of life on the land and when the threshers came.

$\mathcal{E}$ven though they were no longer farming wheat, my grandparents and parents often spoke of those days, and Mother and Grandmother well remembered cooking for harvest and threshing crews. Half a century later, I'm sorry that I didn't listen better and ask more questions. Thank goodness, in the sixties, I did record considerable information from my father, Guy E. Kreie, who plowed virgin prairie near Dodge City when he was a boy and later grew wheat with my maternal grandparents and uncles near Elkhart, Kansas. I also have some treasured material from my mother's mother, Susanna Parks Salmon, and I wrote the book in view of a photo of my mother driving a tractor and my father on a header with my uncles and grandfather.

One might call these family memories the seed of this story, but I was lamentably ignorant about wheat farming when I decided to write this book about the period when the mighty steam engines that had revolutionized grain farming were being challenged by kerosene and gas-powered machines and the development of a practical combine that could harvest and thresh grain at the same time.

While reading *Bull Threshers and Bindlestiffs* by Thomas D. Isern (Lawrence, Kansas: University Press of Kansas, 1990), I was intrigued with the threshing outfits that traveled from farm to farm all over the plains. In the heyday of steam threshing, one hundred thousand men swarmed like migrating birds to a swath 200 to 300 miles wide that stretched from Texas into Canada. They harvested and threshed the fields that fed the nation and, during the war years, much of Europe.

Women usually cooked for the traveling threshers, whipping up huge, hearty meals in a small shack on wheels. There are countless photographs of women, many of them only seventeen or eighteen, standing beside their cookshacks, and managing to look pretty and neat in spite of their hard work. Many a romance bloomed as men vied to dry dishes for the cook!

The twenties saw dramatic changes in American life. Women got the vote in 1920. Radio grew from infancy to a medium as influential and widespread as television today. Henry Ford's production lines brought the price of a Model T to below $300. Prohibition fomented racketeers and bootleggers. Still, though flappers might smoke and dance the Charleston in the cities, on farms without electricity or indoor plumbing, women's work was laborious beyond modern imagining.

Fortunately for me, since I usually write about such households, I lived on my grandparents' farm in my teen years. It didn't bother me at all then to carry water from the spring for all our needs, scrub laundry on a washboard, read by kerosene lamps, and carry wood for heat and cooking. I'm glad I don't have to do it now, though.

Material for this book came from many sources apart from immediate family. I owe a tremendous debt to Dave Webb and Noel Ary of the Kansas Heritage Center in Dodge City, who lent me tapes and videos and suggested sources. Dave, a railroad enthusiast who lives in an antique depot, sent me many relevant articles and an invaluable taped interview with Hazel Moore and "Pat" Murphey who was a county agent in Greeley and Comanche counties. Also through the Heritage Center, I was able to view an excellent film on threshing that shows the old steam engines, *Steam Thrasherman,* Lloyd N. White of Colby, Kansas, adviser.

Naturally, I pestered all my relatives who experienced harvest and threshing firsthand. My cousin, Dr. Jack Salmon, videotaped his father's and mother's recollections. Later, when I visited them, they shared vintage photos and answered a lot of questions. Thank you, Uncle Lou and Aunt Thelma!

Alice Shook, my friend and cousin, wrote some warm, humorous and fascinating memories of life on an Oklahoma Panhandle farm. She also went to the trouble to send steam-whistle signals that she got from the kind people at the Antique Engine and Threshers Association at Bird City, Kansas.

My aunt, Dorothy Thompson, who has herself run a tractor at harvesttime, sent me a number of useful pictures, photos, and recollections. She has always been supportive of my writing, and I am glad I have filled a bookshelf for her.

George Scofield of Ponca City, Oklahoma, grew up in Elkhart, my birthplace, and worked at a drugstore. He sent me a wonderful account of life there in 1924, describing how he helped build a railroad across the Texas Panhandle, very much like the project Garth hires on for in this book. His spirited memoir yielded many interesting details about a work crew.

My neighbor, Sally Spofford, gave me some real licorice root and told me about that and other treats of the twenties. She also bore, as ever, with my travails.

Helen Brown, director of the Morton County Museum at Elkhart, gave me a special tour of that impressive and intriguing collection. It has everything from dolls to a windmill and a fine collection of machinery, including a marvelous old steam engine.

For Shaft's wonderful beard and kitten, I am indebted to friend and fellow writer Nelson Nye's nephew, Tom Johnson of Springfield, Kentucky. He told me about a small cat he had rescued and how it slept beneath his beard or draped itself shoulder to shoulder. No lover of cats could resist such a charming practice, and he kindly granted me permission to borrow his beard and cat.

Among books that helped in re-creating time and place were *Land of the Post Rock* by Grace Muilenburg and Ada Swineford (1975) and *Natural Kansas,* edited by Joseph T. Collins (1985), both from the University Press of Kansas, Lawrence, Kansas; *Kansas Bootleggers* by Patrick G. O'Brien and Kenneth J. Peak (Manhattan, Kansas: Sunflower Press, 1991) and *This Was Wheat Farming* by Kirby Brumfield (New York: Bonanza Books, 1958).

Robert L. Yates's *When I Was a Harvester* (New York: Macmillan, 1930) is the true story of a seventeen-year-old college boy who goes west to work the harvest. It was in his account that I read about Saskatchewan greyhounds. Carey MacWilliams's *Ill Fares the Land:* Migrants and Migratory Workers in the United States (New York: Barnes & Noble, 1967), has a concise and illuminating section on harvesters and threshers, showing how this work force differed from most migrant laborers.

Also useful were J. Sanford Rikoon's *Threshing in the* Midwest, *1820–1940* (Bloomington: Indiana University Press, 1988); *Winter Wheat in the Golden Belt of Kansas* by James C. Malin (Lawrence: University of Kansas Press, 1944); *The Grain Harvesters* by Graeme Quick and Wesley Buchele (St. Joseph, Michigan: American Society of Agricultural Engineers); *The American Farm Tractor* by Randy Leffingwell (Osceola, Wisconsin: Motorbooks International, 1991); and Jon Steward's *The Reaper* (New York: Greenberg, 1931).

A memoir I kept always at hand is *Pioneer Threshers* written and published by Joseph Dale Fry (Garden City, Kansas, 1993). Illustrated with a wealth of family photos and pictures of machinery and components, it gives a detailed, step-by-step account of threshing as his parents and family knew it, from 1884 to 1928. This is no dull textbook. It is a captivating story, full of humor, about real people and how they lived and worked. Mr. Fry kindly cleared up some of my perplexities by phone and letter. One of his prize possessions is a scale-model Case steam engine and separator made by his brother.

Another deskside reference was *Days of Steam and Glory* by Dana Close Jennings (Aberdeen, South Dakota: North Plains Press, 1968). Through drawings, photos, and vigorous language, it shows how the engineer cared for his engine, got it up to operating pressure, and what could happen if things went wrong.

Loving owners of the great old machines still get them out for threshing demonstrations throughout the wheat-growing country; and, once again, if only for a summer day, the giants belch smoke and whistle and thresh the grain.

JEANNE WILLIAMS
October 1993
Cave Creek Canyon

THE

UNPLOWED

SKY

I

$\mathcal{H}$allie stretched, opened her eyes, and smiled at the dawn. Then she realized that it glowed through a strange window in a wall papered with violets, and there was an unfamiliar warmth beside her. She turned, saw the curly black head burrowed into the pillow, and everything came back in a welter of confused feelings. Her main feeling was relief: relief that she had a job where she could look after her small half-brother while earning their living.

Her father had died of cancer a few days into that new year of 1924. Seven months later—just five days ago, but they seemed a lifetime—his widow Felicity had come to see Hallie, who was working her last week for the MacReynoldses. The childless couple who had been so kind to her had sold their dry-goods store and were moving back east in hopes that the climate would improve Fanny MacReynolds's health.

"I have a well-to-do childless cousin in St. Louis who is willing to adopt Jackie," Felicity said, as Hallie listened thunder-struck. "But since the child's your half-brother, I thought it only fair to see if you wanted to raise him."

Hallie's insides twisted. She looked at this small, pretty woman who had gotten rid of Hallie's mother's things as if they carried infection, who had made Hallie feel like an outsider with no place in either the house or her father's love. As she grew older, and especially since her father's death, Hallie had begun to understand a little of how difficult it had been for him and was sorry that she had coldly rebuffed his invitations and overtures after she had gone to live with the Mac-Reynoldses.

Now she stared at Daddy's widow, scarcely believing her ears. "The MacReynoldses are moving, and I'll have to find another job. I don't have a home, Felicity, no place to keep a child."

"Neither do I, unless I marry." Felicity's brittle tone took on an edge of desperation. "The bank foreclosed on the house. I have to be out by the end of this month. By the time I paid your father's hospital bills and gave him a decent funeral, I was destitute. Harry's waited all these years"—she touched her eyes with a lacy handkerchief—"he owns several drugstores and has done very well, but he says his life's been empty. I'm the only woman he ever wanted."

"But he doesn't want Jackie?"

Felicity snuffled. "He said he might have been able to adopt a little girl, but a boy who would remind him constantly that there had been another man—"

"Felicity, if you'll try to manage, I'll send all I can from my wages."

Felicity shook her stylishly bobbed head. Her new dress almost reached her knees. "There's no use looking at me like that! It might be noble to take in washing or slave in a restaurant to keep Jackie, but I'm not able to live without a man to love me and take care of me. I found that out while your father was in the hospital this last awful year. And Harry's waited so long! He wants children of his own."

"Then he'd better hope he doesn't die and you give them away."

"What a nasty thing to say!"

"What a nasty thing to do!"

The two women gazed at each other. Felicity's eyes dropped, but she squared her shoulders. "If you don't want Jackie, I'll take him to my cousin."

Remembering her own bewildered hurt when she felt that her father didn't want her, Hallie surrendered. "What in the world will you tell him?"

"That I'm sick, and in order to get better, I have to go live in a place he wouldn't like, a place where children aren't allowed."

"Just don't let him hope you'll come back," Hallie said. "That would be the cruelest thing of all."

At least she had a job. Mr. MacReynolds had found her a place with Quentin and Estelle Raford, a couple from the East. A few years ago, they had bought the largest farm in the county and had been adding small farms to it as mortgages were foreclosed. The price of wheat had fallen steeply since the hungry demands of the Kaiser's War. Most wheat farmers had bought more land and machinery on credit. Now many of them had been ruined along with the banks that held their mortgages.

Daddy had been an officer and shareholder in a bank that failed two years ago. Hallie wondered if the disaster, coupled with Felicity's bitterness, had brought on the cancer. At any rate, Mrs. MacReynolds had telephoned the Rafords about Jackie, and they had consented to let him stay with Hallie so long as she kept him under control. Mr. MacReynolds had driven them out the night before and slipped an extra ten-dollar bill in with her pay.

"You'll need it with the little fellow," he said.

"But Mrs. MacReynolds already gave me five dollars."

He grinned. "Did she? Good for her! The Rafords are out this evening. They said for you to go up to your room on the second story and have breakfast ready at seven-thirty."

Seven-thirty! Hallie had never heard of anyone sleeping so late. But she could use some extra time to get used to a strange kitchen—and she would fix them a breakfast that would make them glad they'd let her bring Jackie.

Poor little guy! How bewildered and scared he must feel with his father dead and his mother disappearing. He and Hallie scarcely knew each other, but he had clung to her last night when she tucked him in.

"You—you won't go away, Hallie?"

"No, sweetie!" She gave him a fierce hug. "We'll be together till you grow up. I promise."

"You won't get sick like Mama or die like Daddy?"

"Gracious, I hope not! Now, you cuddle up to Lambie and I'll be right beside you in a minute."

Looking very small in the big four poster bed, he hugged the faded raggedy terry-cloth lamb. He was asleep, tears dried on his cheeks, when Hallie finished getting ready for bed. How lucky to be at a farmhouse with a bathroom and electric lights! Plenty of houses in town didn't have indoor plumbing, though the MacReynoldses did.

Now, in the first golden morning light, Hallie propped her pillow against Jackie's back, hoping he would sleep till breakfast was over and she could devote some time to him. Hallie's thick black hair was depressingly, defiantly straight, and she braided and coiled it on top of her head. She had bangs, and when there was time, she liked to curl them with her curling iron so they fluffed over a forehead that she considered too high and softened a rather long face. She had no way to heat the iron in this room, but the Rafords would scarcely mind what she looked like if she cooked to their taste and kept the house pretty.

Hallie tied on her apron and hurried downstairs. Not that there was any hurry, except in herself. It was only six o'clock. She could start the laundry, though, churn butter, and set the bread to rising.

When the washing machine was chugging away on the long screened back porch, she set the table, laying her place near the door so she could speed to the kitchen for coffee or food. Then she set out enough cream for breakfast and biscuits before pouring the rest into the glass churn. As she cranked the handle, the paddles went around, swishing the cream at first, then turning more slowly till her shoulder began to ache and she changed to her other hand. Specks of pale gold began to form and clot together. When a mass of butter formed, Hallie poured the buttermilk into jars. Her mouth watered as she thought how good it would taste with a dash of salt and pepper.

Putting the butter in a stoneware crock, she worked it with a wooden paddle, carefully pressing out all the liquid till the butter was a firm, fresh-smelling mound. She scooped some into a cut-glass bowl for breakfast, glanced at the clock, and put the coffee to perk on the kerosene stove. What a blessing that would be! Fire on and off as needed without burning on the way a wood or coal stove did to make a kitchen a place of summer torment. She mixed biscuits rich with fresh cream, popped them in the oven, and sliced ham thin in a big skillet.

If she hurried, there would be time to cut some tiger lilies for the table. The morning air was as bright and fresh as the meadowlark's song. She felt sorry for anyone who was missing this finest part of the day—one could even say the only pleasant part in late June. The sun's heat increased as it rose. Farmers had already been in the fields for hours.

She was arranging the flowers in a blue-and-white pitcher when a deep male voice made her jump. "You must be Miss Hallie Meredith."

"Yes, sir." The man with tawny eyes and crisp grey hair gave the impression of filling the doorway. She had a ridiculous sense of being trapped, though when he stepped into the kitchen, she saw that he had a pleasant smile and was only average in height. "And you'd be Mr. Raford."

He nodded, still with that easy smile. "I'd like coffee, black, anytime it's ready. My wife will be down soon, but I have business in town, so I'll have breakfast as soon as you can fix it. Eggs over lightly. Should you break a yolk, fix another. Ham crisp. Toast"—he wrinkled his nose—"Do I smell biscuits?"

"Cream biscuits."

His gaze flickered to the crock of fresh butter. The practiced smile broadened to a grin. "It would seem I don't need to instruct you, Miss Meredith." He lazed away.

Pernickety. And if his wife had breakfast late, Hallie would spend half the morning in the kitchen. But they were paying her, and if that's what they wanted, they could have it—though sometime soon she'd have to see if Jackie was awake and give him his breakfast. It wouldn't do for him to feel abandoned again. Mr. Raford was studying some papers and only nodded thanks as she brought his coffee, but by the time breakfast was ready, Hallie heard a woman's high voice in the dining room.

Good! Hallie hadn't fancied sitting down with just Mr. Raford, though Mrs. Raford's tone had just a bit of a whine. How could that be, with such a nice home and a husband who apparently let her do just as she pleased? Hallie filled a tray with ham, butter, *his* eggs done just so, and the fluffy golden biscuits in a napkin-covered basket.

"Good morning, Mrs. Raford." Hallie smiled at the woman with stylishly bobbed blond hair and a flowing flowered dress that couldn't disguise raillike thinness. "How would you like your eggs? And do you want cream and sugar with your coffee?"

Mrs. Raford winced. "No eggs, thank you. Be a dear and make me some tea."

Could she have a headache? Or be expecting? Hallie brewed tea in a gold-rimmed pot and placed it, with a matching cup and saucer, on a small tray.

She set it in front of Mrs. Raford and was rewarded with a faint smile. "Wonderful biscuits, Hallie," Mr. Raford complimented. "I've always believed it took years to acquire such a knack, but you must have a natural talent."

"I've made biscuits since I was nine. With the lovely cream you get from those Jersey cows, it'd be hard to make a bad batch. Is there anything I can get for anybody?" She was ready to pull out her chair and begin to get acquainted with these people, though she already suspected that Mrs. Raford was going to be hard to please.

Mrs. Raford's violet eyes widened as they stared at Hallie's plate. "Oh, dear!" The woman's face went pink. She glanced at her husband.

He lavished butter on a biscuit and speared another slice of ham. He had inherited railroad money and was interested in scientific farming, though the actual work was done by tenant farmers. He said nothing. Turning even pinker, Mrs. Raford raised her hand in a delaying gesture as Hallie started to sit down.

"Hallie, dear—out here it may be different. I'm sure you mean no impertinence, but we don't sit down to table with ser—those we employ."

Hallie flushed till her body burned with surge after surge of pounding blood that also throbbed dizzyingly in her temples. "I—I—" The words clogged her throat.

She swallowed, and her eyes blurred as she stared at the Rafords' surprised faces. Could that be a hint of amusement—a sudden special interest—in the man's eyes? Hallie longed to take off her apron and let them know she wouldn't work for anyone who thought they were too good to eat with her. But she couldn't. She had Jackie.

Mrs. Raford said soothingly, "You're getting good wages, Hallie, and a nice room. And we let you keep your—your little brother. It seems to me that this should be a perfect situation for you."

Hallie's cheeks burned. She had never in her life been so hurt and angry. She wouldn't sit with them now if—if they begged her! "I do appreciate your letting me keep Jackie," she said and returned to the kitchen where tears came, despite of all she could do to choke them back.

Somehow Hallie finished serving breakfast, put the dishes to soak, and went upstairs. Jackie was just rousing. He swallowed hard when he recognized her and a few tears edged down his cheeks, but he didn't cry or make a fuss.

Hallie bragged about him because he could *almost* tie his shoes. He was an appealing little boy with their father's dark eyes and curly hair, which Hallie had so often wished she had inherited. Surely Felicity would change her mind, decide she couldn't live without him, and come back.

No, she wouldn't. Felicity looked out for Felicity first; and the less Hallie thought about her, the better. In the kitchen, Jackie and Hallie had a good breakfast from the plentiful leftovers. Jackie wouldn't put Lambie down, and he wouldn't go outside alone. He stayed in the kitchen while Hallie did the dishes and dogged her steps while she hung out the laundry, ran the Hoover over the downstairs carpets, dusted, and made preparations for lunch.

She had done these same things at the MacReynoldses'; happy to be useful, to cook food her employers enjoyed. Now, in her mind, was a hateful thrum: *I'm a servant. A servant. I'm their servant.*

The Rafords were polite. They complimented her on lunch, extolled the roast she fixed for dinner. And so it went for two days. Hallie was thoroughly miserable, though she tried to be cheerful with Jackie and entertain him as she worked.

He tagged her like a silent little ghost. She cursed Felicity and kept telling herself that he'd get over being so fearful once he could believe she wouldn't leave him. Still, though she could manage the work with ease, this was not a happy house. Most of the time, it was very quiet. She could see why Jackie didn't want to play alone in their room. The Rafords ignored him completely. He was a nuisance they put up with to have a highly recommended cook-housekeeper.

Jackie deserved better than that. He needed more than that—and so did she! When she had saved up some money—maybe by the end of summer—she would take Jackie to town and hunt another job.

Hallie didn't last the summer. She didn't last a week. On the fourth morning, hands closed on her shoulders while she was fixing breakfast. Before she could move, Mr. Raford swung her around. He kissed her full on the startled lips, smothering her cry.

Then he moved away and gave her that lazy, big-cat smile. "My wife has a headache. She won't be down for breakfast. I'd be pleased, Hallie, to have your company at the table."

She was already untying her apron. "I'm leaving. Right now."

"My dear young woman"—he reached into his pocket and handed her a gold piece—"will this sweeten your temper?"

"I'll take it for wages," Hallie said and marched upstairs.

She quickly packed the large suitcase with all she possessed. Patent leather dress-up slippers and her winter clothes were at the bottom, with the small cedar box with brass hinges and lock that held some favorite recipes and all she had of her mother's: a plain gold wedding band, two embroidered handkerchiefs, an ivory-handled manicure set in a green velvet roll-up case, and *The Book of Common Prayer,* handed down from the Episcopalian grandmother, Harriet Wilton, for whom Hallie was named. It comforted Hallie to read the prayers and offices though she'd never seen an Episcopal church, and its practices seemed as mysterious as those of the Roman Catholics.

On the bed, she spread out her pleated blue-green rayon best dress, her other two everyday ones of green plaid gingham and checked blue chambray, two nainsook slips, nainsook bloomers, a pair of satinette for best, two broadcloth brassieres, one pair of treasured silk stockings, two pairs of cotton lisle, two ruffled, flounced muslin nightgowns, and three white aprons. She wrapped her toothbrush in a clean everyday handkerchief and tucked it in the side, along with her comb, brush, and curling iron.

All the while, tears of angry humiliation dripped on her belongings, unless she smeared them away. How dare Quentin Raford! If Daddy were alive—

Jackie had waked and watched her with solemn eyes, hugging Lambie close. "You—you going away, too, Hallie?"

"No, honey!" She stopped and hugged him. "But we're going somewhere happier than this—somewhere you can play and be around nice people."

Beggars can't be choosers, especially not with a five-year-old along, but Hallie hoped she was right.

$\mathcal{L}$ook at the beautiful big trees, Jackie!" Hallie wiped the little boy's flushed hot face with her handkerchief and smoothed back the dark hair that was plastered to his forehead. "When we get to the bridge, we'll rest awhile and put our feet in the water. Won't that feel good?"

"Don't know. Are we goin' to find Mama?"

"No, honey." Hallie tried to keep her tone cheerful though she gladly could have wrung his mother's soft, dimpled neck. "She had to go away. It may be a long time before we see her again—"

Jackie dug his fingers into Hallie's wrist and his brown eyes, so much like their father's that they stabbed Hallie deep, were wide with fear. "She—she won't die and go to God-in-Heaven like Daddy?"

"No, goosie! Your mama's fine. But she had to go away and just couldn't take you with her." Not many men would want a five-year-old stepchild on a honeymoon. But to refuse to have him at all—and for that spineless woman to agree!

Hallie dropped her suitcase and Jackie's carpetbag beside the road, picked up the tired little boy, and carried him to the creek. Wetting her handkerchief, she washed his face and helped him off with his shoes so he could curl and uncurl his toes in the water while perching on the hull of an old cottonwood trunk.

They had walked perhaps three miles. It must be five more to town. As she gave Jackie the rest of their bottle of water, Hallie wondered whether they dare drink from the creek. She had expected to pass farmhouses, but the two facing the road had been deserted, the windmills taken away.

By some grace, the buffalo wallow they had just passed had escaped plowing even during the war, when thousands of acres of thickly entwined, deep-rooted prairie sod, graze first for buffalo and then for cattle, had been gashed deep, the ancient roots severed, and planted in the wheat that stretched in all directions except for this one haven of used-to-be.

This fringe of virgin prairie—buffalo grass, and blue grama spangled with orange globe mallow, purple coneflowers, thistles, and asters— stretched to the creek and extended westward as far as the eye could see. Along the creek, several giant cottonwoods reared eighty or ninety feet into the sky, dwarfing younger trees that had managed to thrust roots far enough down to withstand floods that scoured away weaker saplings and plants. These survivors cast the only shade for miles. Cottonwoods drank deep and thirstily, so they were usually cleared when land was broken to the plow. After all, it didn't put money in the bank for crows to chatter from the wintry limbs or for great horned owls to nest in hollows in the trunks.

Thank heaven the birds were left. To Hallie, whose grandfather had told her stories of how southwestern Kansas had been when he homesteaded after the Civil War, there was a strange, echoing emptiness about the broken prairie; a haunting absence of the buffalo that had once roamed there, of fleet pronghorns that died in snowdrifts along the fences they would not jump, of prairie-dog villages that had spread for miles, of the grizzly bears, wolves, and mountain lions that had culled the bison and pronghorn and deer. Where there were trees and mountains, it must be hard for man to completely wipe out native animals; but out here between earth and sky, there was no place to hide, though coyotes still chorused at night, and of course there were plenty of jackrabbits, kangaroo rats, and other rodents and now and then a grumpy old badger, skunk, or shadowy fox. Most of all though, there were birds and the sky no man could plow.

As they sat by the bridge, Hallie tried to enjoy wriggling her toes in the rippling current, but she was thirsty and hungry and as disgusted with herself as she was with the Rafords. Here they were, not even halfway to town, burdened with their belongings, and without even drinking water.

A fine mess she had made of it! If this was the way she was going to take care of Jackie, maybe he would have been better off with Felicity's rich cousin.

No! He was Hallie's brother. She knew their father would have wanted her to raise him if Felicity couldn't. Hallie just hoped that wherever Robert Meredith was, he didn't know that his wife had given his son away as if he were a unwanted puppy.

"Can—Can I have Lambie?" Jackie asked.

"Lambie's snoozing in your carpetbag, honey, and we've got to be going on. Why don't we let him sleep until tonight?"

"Well—if he's really asleep." Jackie's lip quivered. Hallie's almost did. Where would they sleep that night? At least she had some money—she hoped enough for room and board till she found another job.

A pall of dust rose from the road they had traveled. It formed a halo around the long lemon yellow Pierce-Arrow that slowed down and pulled up at the bridge. "Jump in," called Quentin Raford. "I'll give you a lift to town."

Just as if he hadn't ambushed her that morning, kissed her hard and brutally! And her first kiss, too. It made Hallie want to throw mud at him, mess up the vibrant gray of his hair and his smooth, unlined skin. His eyes were a hazel so deep they looked black—till he moved so the light struck them. Then they were like a hunting cat's.

Hallie kept her feet in the water and hoped she didn't look as tired and bedraggled as she felt. Safest to ignore what had happened though she burned with furious shame at the memory. "If you were going to town, Mr. Raford, why didn't you offer us a ride from your house?"

He grinned, showing the whitest teeth she had ever seen. "I thought a few miles on the road with the boy might put you in the frame of mind to consider a partnership."

"Partnership?"

"You're too pretty to spend your time in a kitchen."

"I have a living to make."

"You could manage my hotel."

"But I never have—"

"You'd learn. The salary would be twice what we agreed to pay you as cook-housekeeper. You could pick several adjoining rooms on the top floor and have them turned into living quarters."

It would have tempted her if he'd had suggested it before this morning. Thank goodness she wouldn't be led into another trap! "I'm sure you'll find any number of capable managers, Mr. Raford."

"I keep a suite in the hotel." His russet eyes traveled slowly from her mouth to her throat. She felt the frightened leap of her pulse, felt exposed as if he might tear her flesh with his teeth—or kiss it again. "When I'm in town, I'd expect your company."

"You know the answer to that!"

"Where can you do better? A nice place for you and the boy to live and a good salary?"

Still speechless, Hallie was able only to glare at him. He didn't look at all abashed. "I paid you the compliment of thinking you had better sense than to need seduction. After all, the proof that you're not a virgin is perched right beside you."

It took her a moment to understand what he meant. A rush of blood heated her face. "Jackie is my father's child, my half-brother!"

"A good story, my dear, but you can't expect anyone to believe that you'd hamper yourself with a child if he weren't your own little accident."

A dull rumbling that Hallie had scarcely noticed during the moments while her hopes soared high now growled like continuous thunder. A long, jaunty toot sounded over the reverberations, followed by a second long whistle and two short ones.

Hallie recognized the sound: a steam engine threshing outfit on its way to work. "Garth MacLeod!" Raford stared over his shoulder. "Now, why's he coming this way instead of heading for my fields?" Cold eyes ranged back to Hallie. "I'll just wait and talk to him. If you change your mind—"

"I won't."

Raford smiled. "I think you will, my dear, by the time you've piggybacked the boy to town and learned how hard it is to find work that'll allow you to look after him."

Hallie longed to bolt but there was no way she could lift her feet out of the water, let them dry, and put on her gartered stockings and shoes without exhibiting more of her legs than she wanted Raford to see.

Sudden hope filled her. Maybe the threshing outfit could give her a ride. Even a mile or two would be a big help with Jackie and their belongings.

The grumbling roar sounded like an earthquake. She could feel the earth vibrate as the machine lumbered into view. To her surprise, the steam puffing from the engine was almost clear vapor, not the dense black clouds she had seen the several previous times she had been close to an engine.

A man perched on a metal seat at the back of the engine, steering the tractor. When he saw Hallie, he grinned, tipped his wide-brimmed hat, and pulled on a cord. The whistle trilled a whole series of short little bursts, and the tall man in khaki work clothes riding on the separator called, "Best save your steam, lad!"

The huge separator that threshed grain was hooked to the engine. A house about eighteen feet long, mounted on iron wheels, was hitched to the separator, and a water-tank wagon was attached to the shack. The end of the procession was a coal wagon.

A gray-bearded older man and a boy of twelve or thirteen sat on the tank of the water wagon. The man held a gray kitten in the curve of his arm so that it was nearly hidden beneath his beard. Far enough behind this caravan to escape most of its dust was a shiny new Model T touring car with its fabric top folded back with the isinglass curtains. Behind it wheezed a much older version of Henry Ford's time-tested classic. Four men rode in one car and three in the other. Most were young. They looked curiously at Hallie. Several smiled and tipped their hats.

Uncomfortable at their scrutiny, Hallie turned and eyed the flimsy-looking bridge with misgiving. Could the threshing outfit possibly get across it? The separator must weigh a lot, and the tractor's great steel-lugged wheels looked as if they would mangle the rough planks that had been designed for nothing heavier than a team and wagon. The yellow Pierce-Arrow barred the way, but the engine didn't stop till it was only a few yards from the sporty auto.

"Where are you going with this rig, MacLeod?" Raford demanded.

The man on the separator stood up and pushed back a hat that might have been gray once but was now stained by dust and grease. Various tools protruded from his overall pockets. The wind-tousled hair was a curious shade between gold and silver.

"We're going to thresh Ed Brockett's place." There was a soft lilt to the English that made Hallie listen closely to catch the words. "We threshed him last a year ago. Now it's his turn to be first."

"*I'm* first."

"You were first last year."

"I give you more work than the rest of these two-bit farmers put together."

"All the more reason for them not to want their crop hailed or rained on. You can take a loss, Raford. Most of them can't."

Raford's heavy eyebrows jerked together above his broad nose. "You'll thresh my wheat first, MacLeod—or not at all."

"That's your choice. You have enough wheat to make it worth a thresher's time to detour off his usual run."

"But not enough for you?"

MacLeod lifted a broad shoulder. "You know how it's agreed among us neighbors. Whoever is first one year comes last the next year, unless the weather threatens. Then, so no one will lose his whole crop, I thresh a day for everyone before finishing the first neighbor's crop."

"That's a stupid waste of time! Look how long it takes you to get from one farm to another. That outfit can't make more than two miles an hour."

"Two and six-tenths."

"You're as out-of-date as your steam engine! And you've refused to sell me your farm for a lot more than it's worth." Raford's eyes narrowed in sudden decision. "I'm going to buy a gas engine, hire a crew, and run you right out of business in this part of the country."

MacLeod's eyes didn't flicker. "You can try." A threshing outfit was a big investment needed only for a short time each year. That was why most farmers preferred to pay a traveling thresher. But Raford wouldn't care about money. MacLeod nodded toward the bridge.

"It doesn't look like the county fixed this bridge the way you promised it would, Mr. Road Commissioner."

"Other projects were more important. If you obey the planking law, there won't be a problem."

"Planking law!" The young man on the engine gave a scornful laugh. His voice, too, had that soft music. Glancing from him to the man on the separator, Hallie thought they must be brothers, the engineer some years the younger. "As if stretching planks across a bridge like yon would keep it from caving in!"

"You'd better hope it does." Raford turned from the threshers as if dismissing them from his mind. His gaze enveloped Hallie; she felt it with shock, like a physical grasping. "Do you want a ride to town, Miss Meredith?"

"No."

He shrugged. "Well, when you get there, come to the hotel if you change your mind about that position."

The motor of the Pierce-Arrow roared as the long sleek vehicle crossed the bridge with a groaning of planks. Dust billowed back. "Why, that—" the engineer began, glanced at Hallie, and chuckled. "God bless him, I was going to say, miss. Is it a ride to town you're needing, you and the laddie?"

"What I really need is a job. Is that a cookshack behind the separator?"

"We've got a cook." MacLeod jumped down from the separator and began to unfasten some long planks about three inches thick and a foot wide from the machine. "Lend a hand, Rory. If a bridge ever needed planking, this is it."

The men in the Fords piled out and helped lay the planks across the bridge. Most wore overalls and blue chambray shirts but a few, including the engineer, had on khakis. Scratching the mite of a kitten behind its ears, the bearded man on the water wagon kept his seat as if the task were beneath his dignity. The boy, too, stayed in his place.

The bearded man watched Hallie with deep-set dark eyes that seemed benevolent. His mouth was too surrounded by mustache and beard for her to judge its appearance but the way he held the kitten made her think he was kind. "Are you a good hand with pies, lady?"

"I think so."

"Don't you know?"

The hope his question had roused in Hallie fused with determination. She threw back her head and looked him in the eye. "I make delicious pies. No one ever leaves a bit of the crust."

"Bread?"

"I've been baking since I was nine."

He grinned. "From the look of you, that wasn't all so long ago."

"I'm nineteen."

The man raised an eyebrow as he looked at Jackie. Hallie felt blood heating her face. Was everyone going to think what Raford did?

15

"Jackie's my brother," she said curtly and left off the "half." With their father dead and his mother gone, Jackie didn't need a half-sister. He needed a whole one.

The men had laid the planks. As MacLeod started to climb back on the separator, the bearded man shouted at him, "Garth, this young lady says she can bake pies."

The eight men paused beside the Model Ts. "Pies!" they cried in unison, every face lighting up.

"Besides," called the engineer, "she's a whole lot prettier than Shaft!"

MacLeod scowled at the older man. "I want my men to keep their mind on their work. That's why I hired you."

"And you said you'd hire me another helper after the last one quit to get married."

"I will. But—" Garth MacLeod looked above, below, and on both sides of Hallie, but not at her. His gaze lit on Jackie. "Listen, Shaft, how will you cook with the laddie underfoot?"

"That's not your worry. But you'll have war in camp if you don't get me a helper who can bake pies."

All the men nodded agreement. The stocky one with a patched and peeling sunburn and kinky hair bleached almost white glanced apologetically at Shaft. "Shaft makes the best sourdough this side of heaven, his biscuits are great, and his gravy's smooth. But a starved mule wouldn't eat his pies—and you know, Garth, we got to have pie!"

Garth MacLeod looked at Hallie then. She almost flinched at the pain and anger in his gray eyes. What in the world was the matter with him? "Are you sure you want the job?" he said, almost daring her.

"I want it."

"There's lots of ways for anyone, much less a child, to get hurt around a threshing outfit. The men must be tending their work, not the lad. You'll have to keep him out of the way."

Why was Garth MacLeod so hateful? Had she been alone, she would have told him to stick his job in one of his big ears. But she had Jackie, she believed she had an ally in Shaft, and she wasn't going to let Garth MacLeod threaten her out of a job that would let her take care of her brother.

Brother. She listened to the word inside her head. It sounded nice; balm on the ache of losing her father and the even crueler, earlier ache of being pushed out of her home by Felicity less than a year after her own mother's death. Felicity got rid of Mother's things and insisted on new furnishings as if Ellen Meredith's memory were an infection. Felicity and thirteen-year-old Hallie clashed often in private, but around Father, his new wife was all tearful innocence. Mrs. MacReynolds had been mother's friend. When she saw how things were, she had persuaded Mr. Meredith to let Hallie live with her and her husband and work as a daughter might to earn her keep. Hallie had seen her father often, but she had felt he wasn't really *her* father anymore. He was Felicity's husband and soon Jackie's father.

Now Jackie had only Hallie. She vowed to make that enough. Taking Jackie's hand, she looked straight at Garth MacLeod. "I'll be responsible for my brother."

The boy beside Shaft jumped up and confronted Garth, arousing an immense dog who rose from the wagon bed, stretched, and peered over the side at the strangers. He looked something like a Great Dane and something like a greyhound and was in between in size. His short hair was smooth and brindled gray except for a white breast, white paws, and white-tipped tail.

"Doggie!" Jackie cried. "Look, a doggie!"

"His name is Laird," said the bearded man.

The dog wagged his long tail and thrust his long, slender muzzle toward the child. His friendliness was a marked contrast to the expression of some of his humans, especially the boy. As overalls tightened over a long-sleeved blue shirt, Hallie saw the rounding of young breasts and looked more closely. In spite of cropped light brown hair this was definitely a girl, perhaps thirteen or fourteen, with dark-lashed blue-gray eyes that veered away from Hallie with passionate dislike. "Do we have to have a woman around, Dad? I'll bet I can make pies."

"You've never tried, Meg." Garth almost smiled, and his eyes softened. "You've got all you can do to hustle water for the engine. You ready to quit that and go to cooking?"

"No! But I—" The girl scowled at Hallie, who had no trouble

putting herself in young Meg's shoes. "I won't have somebody bossing me around—trying to make me act like a lady."

"Don't worry." Hallie realized immediately that she shouldn't have laughed. "I've got all I can do trying to be a lady myself."

Grudging approval showed in Garth's eyes. "Let's give each other a trial, then. Pay's a dollar a day and your food, of course."

A cheer went up from the men who piled into the Model Ts. "You can meet everyone later," Garth said. "I'm Garth MacLeod, that's my brother Rory on the engine, and you can climb aboard the water wagon with Meg and Shaft."

"I'm Hallie Meredith, and this is Jackie."

"Pleased to meet you." He sounded as if he weren't, but he did toss her suitcase and Jackie's carpetbag into the wagon. "All right, lad," he called to his brother. "Let's see if that bridge will hold us up."

The whistle shrilled. Hallie settled on the plank next to Shaft, Jackie on her lap, and hoped she had done the right thing. The tractor labored onto the groaning boards. Hallie shut her eyes. If they were going to plunge through the bridge, she would rather not know it. She held her breath till they were safely across and the men hurried to load up the planks.

"It'll be all right, Miss Hallie." Shaft smiled at Jackie, who ventured to pet the kitten shyly. "Garth's bark is a whole lot worse than his bite."

Hallie hoped that was true and grinned wryly. At least she wouldn't have to worry about his making offers along the lines that Raford had. Whatever else, it was a vast relief to be out of that man's reach.

I I

$\mathscr{I}$t was almost noon when, with a
spirited whistle, they turned up a lane that led past a small, unpainted
house with raddled screen doors and a big well-maintained barn. Several dogs ran alongside barking. Laird opened an eye and yawned but
otherwise ignored them.

Evidently the MacLeods knew the farm. Rory skirted a rickety
chicken house, malodorous pigpen, and a corral built around a creaking windmill and stock tank before the engine steamed into a seem-
ingly endless field. Grain waited in giant rows about fifty feet long,
twenty feet wide, and perhaps fifteen or sixteen feet high. The stacks
were only about eight feet apart.

"How does the engine pass between the rows?" Hallie shouted in
Shaft's ear. "It looks a foot or so wider than the space."

"It is. From wheel to wheel, the engine's nine and a half feet wide."

Hallie stared at the belching steam and thought of the fire and boiling water that caused it. "Can't the stacks catch fire?"

"Sometimes. 'Course the engineman closes all the ash-pan dampers
before he hauls the separator between the stacks."

Hallie's spine pricked at the thought. She had grown up in Hollister
but she really didn't know much about how grain got from the fields
into the bread she ate every day. The town depended on wheat and
she was accustomed to see the surrounding fields change from fresh

green shoots in early spring to tall stalks crowned with heads of grain. Many high-school boys earned good money working the harvest. During harvest and threshing seasons, the town swarmed with "hands" looking for work and farmers who needed them.

Like migrating flocks of birds, the workers followed the harvest north and some returned for threshing. Hallie often had seen men with their belongings tied in a bundle or stuffed into tin or cardboard suitcases spill out of each arriving train. A big change began about ten years ago when Henry Ford began turning out Model Ts on an assembly line—ten thousand a day, it was said—and the price was cut in half. Many traveling field workers now had their Tin Lizzies, Studebakers, or other cars.

Farmers hauled threshed grain to the huge iron-clad elevators rearing along the north side of the railroad tracks, where it was to be stored till it was sold and shipped away. The gleaming elevators towered much higher than any of the buildings in the little town on the south side of the tracks, higher than the two-story bank and hotel and even the spires of the Baptist, Methodist, and Presbyterian churches.

"Ed Brockett, the farmer, is showing Rory where he wants the straw stack so we can make our 'set,' " Shaft bellowed. "That locates the engine and separator in the right place. This is headed grain—it's been cut off without much stalk by a machine called a header. We'll thresh from the stack so our crew can handle the job." He squinted at the sun and then at a single large cottonwood tree that had been spared when the ground was cleared. "The minute the cookshack's unhooked under that tree, we'll have to rustle to feed the boys before they start work. Won't have to be a lot. They ain't done nothing but ride this morning, and they'll get afternoon lunch."

"Afternoon lunch?"

"Sure. Kind of work they're doing twelve hard hours in the heat, threshers need breakfast, morning lunch, dinner, afternoon lunch, and supper."

"That's a lot of cooking!"

"Sure." Shaft winked. "That's why I need a helper."

The engine puffed to a halt. The men were instantly on the ground, unhitching the separator from engine and cookshack, using spades to level the ground beneath it while Garth called out instructions. A bald man unhooked the coal wagon from the water wagon while Shaft and Garth released the water wagon from the shack.

Rory chugged around with the engine. "We'll get you into the shade, Miss Hallie!" he shouted. It was clear from the admiring laughter in his eyes that he didn't share his older brother's view of her as a nuisance.

Shaft placed his kitten and the Merediths' baggage in the shack, hitched his portable kitchen to the engine, and called to Hallie to jump inside. She clambered down from the water wagon with Jackie. He had drowsed off, cuddled against Laird as he sat in the bottom of the wagon on his carpetbag. Now he looked around with sleepy eyes, realized that he was being carried, and gave an imperious wriggle.

"Let me down, Hallie! I'm not a baby!"

"Of course you're not, but—"

Shaft hoisted him into the shack and gave Hallie a hand up. "You'll be able to play with Laird in a little while, son," the cook admonished. "But you've got to be real careful and keep away from the machines and wagons." At the disappointed droop of Jackie's lower lip, Shaft added, "Smoky's never been threshing before. It would sure help me if you'd keep an eye on her and make sure she doesn't try to play with the separator cylinder. I saw a man get caught in it once."

Jackie's eyes had gone completely round. "What happened?"

"He leaned in to oil the cylinder, got his coat caught on the shaft, and spun around and around before they could stop the engine. Poor guy's head and shoulders—" Shaft gave a mournful sigh.

Jackie hurried to grab the charcoal kitten and sat down with her on the linoleum floor while the cookshack was trundled into the heavenly shade. Even there it was hot, probably close to a hundred degrees. The men must need the rest they got during their morning and afternoon lunches at least as much as they needed the food. Some of them drove steel stakes near the four corners of the shack. To these they tied the stout ropes attached to each corner.

"On wheels and high off the ground as the shack sets, it needs to be tied down, 'specially when the wind blows," said Shaft. He put on a calico apron, produced a cord from his pocket, tied it around his beard, and fastened it to the apron band behind his shoulder.

"Praise be for kerosene stoves!" He lit burners and the oven, poured water into a gallon coffeepot, and set on a big enameled kettle. "Cooked beans last night so they'd just need betting up and fixed a big roast. How's about you making biscuits—about three dozen big ones?"

Hallie blinked. She was used to baking for three. Counting herself and Jackie as one mouth, there were thirteen to feed. So if she just multiplied ingredients by a little over four— No, these men were going to eat considerably more than frail Mrs. MacReynolds and Mr. MacReynolds who spent his days behind a dry-goods counter. Six times was more like it. She desperately wished she'd had time to look the kitchen over and find out where things were.

"I need to wash my hands."

Shaft glanced at his own and looked a bit embarrassed. "Why, sure. So will the boys. Washbasins, soap, and towels are in that box under the water keg stand. You can just fill up the basins and set 'em on the shelf that folds down by the door outside."

Hallie tied on an apron from the suitcase and hung three clean towels on nails above the shelf. Filling the water basins, she washed with a bar of Ivory and left Grandpa's Tar Soap and Lava to the tougher-skinned. Shaft had set a dishpan for her on the long table that clamped to the middle of the floor.

"Flour's in the biggest barrel. Lard's in the can beside it. Baking powder's on the top shelf." Slicing boiled potatoes into a big cast-iron skillet, Shaft chuckled. "Hey, I bet I know a boy who could set the table!"

"Who?" Jackie looked around.

"You!" Shaft said. "And then you can go play with Laird so long as you don't get near the machines and see that Smoky don't. Dishes are in the top cupboard drawer. We keep 'em there so they won't fall out when the rig's moving."

The man grinned at the boy, who seemed awed and overwhelmed at so many new things all at once. Hallie could sympathize. As she made a well of flour to hold the biscuit ingredients, she felt the same way. "Can you count to eleven, Jackie?" asked the cook.

He held up his hands. "I can count ten fingers!"

"Good. So just put on that many plates and add one more. Your sis and you and me will eat after the gang clears out. Knives and forks and spoons are in a box inside the drawer. Cups in the next drawer. Set them all at this end of the table. Easier to pour coffee that way."

As Jackie importantly counted out blue enamel dishes, Hallie cut lard into the mixed flour, baking powder, sugar, and salt. Praying that she had the proportions right, she added enough water for a stiff dough and kneaded it vigorously till it passed through the blistery stage and was smooth. She rolled the dough on a floured board and cut rounds a half-inch thick, hurried these into big pans and put them in the hot oven.

By then Shaft had carved a great platter of cold roast beef. Beans bubbled, potatoes crisped, and the aroma of Arbuckle's coffee filled the shack. If this was a light meal—

"You might open up a gallon can of peaches," Shaft suggested. "They're stored with other canned stuff in the bin under the shack, the one nearest the back axles. Bin at the front holds taters and onions. We've got to lift a trapdoor to get to the middle bin. That's where I keep cured hams, condensed milk, and anything the bugs can't hurt. Peaches'll have to do for dessert, but we'll have my special burnt-sugar cake and two kinds of pie for supper."

And there was afternoon lunch in between! Hallie's mind reeled, but Jackie looked so happy as he trotted about his chores that she resolved to somehow hold up her end of the work and not make Shaft sorry he had interceded for her. Besides, she wanted to prove her worth to that bewilderingly hostile Garth MacLeod.

Shaft handed Jackie a long-handled metal spoon. "Go pound that on the bottom of the washtub fastened to the porch wall," he said. "Bang hard so the men can hear."

Jackie complied with such ardor that Hallie clapped her hands over her ears. Shaft took advantage of the boy's absence to say, "Hope you don't mind my tellin' the little feller what to do, Miss Hallie, but I reckoned he might pay more attention to me if I cautioned him to keep clear of the machinery."

"I appreciate it," said Hallie earnestly. "Jackie doesn't know me very well. I've just had him with me a few days. I'm so glad to get a job where he can play with a kitten and a dog and I can look after him—"

Shaft gave her a searching glance. "If you want, I'd like to hear about it later. But you can count on me to help keep an eye on the tyke." He glanced out the window, one of four arranged opposite each other to create a cooling draft. "Here they come! Better take the biscuits out of the oven and get set to pour the coffee."

Laughter and good-natured joshing came from outside and flowed into the house with the men, abating as they saw Hallie. Most of them smiled and spoke. "Your kitchen's improved a hundred percent, Shaft," Rory teased. He beamed at her but his brother gave her only the briefest of nods.

Faces and hands scrubbed, hair slicked back, exuding the odor of pine-tar soap, the crew planted themselves on the closed-bottom benches on either side of the table and scooted around till each had enough room to ply his utensils. Their interest in the food was equaled only by their interest in Hallie, but they didn't stare at or appraise her as Quentin Raford had. Instead, they stole glances when they thought she wouldn't notice. The men helped themselves to the nearest bowl or platter and passed them. Hallie started the biscuits around—thank goodness, they were golden brown and smelled good!—and got a firm grip on the huge coffeepot.

"Boys, this is Miss Hallie Meredith," Shaft proclaimed. He set a hand on Jackie's shoulder. "This is her brother Jack. It'll take them a while to figger out which name goes with which of your ugly mugs, but we'll make a start. When Miss Hallie brings your coffee, I'll sing out your name and a little about you—what's decent to say in front of ladies and kids, that is.

"Jim Wyatt from Saskatchewan." Hallie placed a steaming cup in front of a well-built young man with straight brown hair, warm hazel eyes, and a large white scar blotching one side of his face and neck. "He had his own engine till the durned thing blew sky-high a few years ago. Jim was lucky. He lit in the straw stack. He lumberjacks when he's not threshing."

"Pleased to meet you, Mr. Wyatt," Hallie said.

"Likewise. But my pa's Mr. Wyatt. I'm Jim."

"Rory MacLeod you've met," Shaft continued. "Every outfit has a cross to bear. He's ours, but he's a dandy engine man."

In a stage whisper, Rory said, "I'll tell you the good things about me later, Miss Hallie." His grin was infectious. Hallie couldn't keep from returning it though she sensed the strapping golden-haired young man might like women as much as his older brother seemed to detest them. Look at that great stone face of his!

"Cotton Harris hails from Texas," Shaft said as Hallie placed a cup before a pale-haired man with faded blue eyes. He had one of those skins the sun burns but never tans, and his nose and cheeks were peeling where a hat couldn't protect them. "Cotton works in the oil patch when he's through threshing."

"Howdy, ma'am," Cotton drawled. "Proud to make your acquaintance."

Pat O'Malley from Colorado still looked like a boy in spite of his beanpole height. He worked as a hard-rock miner when threshing finished. Huge yellow-haired Henry Lowen helped with the big family farm worked by his father and older brothers when he wasn't on the road. He was so shy that he couldn't even look at Hallie and blushed when he was introduced.

"Now here's our perfessor, Rich Mondell." The thin, handsome man with curly black hair and green eyes looked up at Hallie and thanked her for the coffee with a friendly smile. "The perfessor ain't been fired from the college over at Lawrence," Shaft explained. "Says he just likes to change off from brain work and feel like he's earnin' an honest living for a while."

"I'm from a farm in the Flint Hills, Miss Hallie," said Mondell in a well-modulated voice that was pleasant to hear. "Never have been able to convince myself that teaching's really work."

"Don't sound like it to me, either," chuckled perhaps the oldest man of the group. He had red-brown hair and eyes and lots of freckles. "Though if it comes right down to it, I reckon I wouldn't swap my little hardscrabble eighty acres in Oklahoma for your classroom." He nodded appreciatively at Hallie. "Tip-top biscuits, ma'am. I'm Rusty Wells."

Next came a stocky thresher who was all one shade of light dust brown; eyes, hair, and skin. "Buford Redding can work at almost anything," the cook said. "Buildin' railroads, felling trees, swingin' a pick in the mines. Owns that shiny new touring car. But his real claim to fame is he's our onliest Wobbly."

"I'm sure not ashamed of it." Buford's dogged voice indicated that he was used to this kind of razzing. "The government's jailed our leaders and done everything it can to smash us, but it's not right for the guys on top to grind the rest of us, and you boys know it just as well as I do."

The bald man with coal black eyes and a walrus mustache sitting next to him snorted. "Ain't right for Wobblies to come in a boxcar and make everyone join, neither. Thanks for the coffee, ma'am. I'm Baldy Tennant from Oklahoma. I'm a fireman on the railroad when I'm not a fireman or flunky for a threshing outfit."

Buford said grimly, "What's right about railroad police with guns lining workers up, making the Wobblies buy tickets, and shipping them out of town the way they did me in Aberdeen, North Dakota a couple years back?"

"Huh!" derided the bald one. "Seems it was Aberdeen where about four hundred Wobs paraded down the streets hollering they wanted to abolish the whole wage system. They didn't just want an honest day's wage for an honest day's work."

"That's the kind of trick that's got folks saying IWW means 'I Won't Work,' " Henry Lowen put in.

"I'll work, and you know it," Buford retorted. "I don't hold with everything the IWWs done, but at least the union stood up for the hoboes." At Hallie's startled look, he said, "A hobo's not a tramp, miss. Tramps don't want to work, they just bum around. Hoboes travel from job to job. They work when and wherever they can. The state and federal employment services are a joke. Railroads and newspapers are always saying lots of men are needed in a certain place, but by the time a guy gets there, the jobs are gone—or they weren't there to start with. I'm sure glad I got on with Garth a few years ago."

"I'm glad you did, too, Buford." Garth spoke for the first time. "I'd sure rather know I can depend on my pitchers than hire just anyone who comes along."

"Shucks, you can have your pick of hands. Can't be anything fairer than the way you pay." Hallie passed another batch of biscuits, and Buford explained to her; "When a farmer pays us off, Garth and Rory take out a wage we all agree is fair for them and the machinery—six dollars each a day is how we figgered it this season. The farmer furnishes the team for Meg's water wagon, so she gets two dollars a day. The rest of us split up what's left."

"Believe you me," said Cotton Harris, "It's a sight more than the two-fifty a day pitchers usually get. That's promised us even if the MacLeods have to dig into their cut for it."

For all his dourness then, Garth had a good side. And he was clearly not the kind of man who wouldn't eat with his hired hands. "That's very generous," Hallie murmured.

"*You* get a straight wage," he said with a cool glance that brushed her face like a fleeting wind.

She felt her cheeks turn scalding hot. "I didn't expect anything else. Are you going to charge me for Jackie's board?"

"Hadn't thought of it, but—"

"Garth!" Shaft's tone was scandalized. "You know you wouldn't be so stingy! 'Sides Jack is goin' to earn his keep; I can already see that."

The boy looked anxiously at Hallie. Poor little kid! What in the world could he think with his world crumbled, his father dead, and his mother gone off to some mysterious place? Hallie darted a wrathful look at Garth MacLeod and gave Jackie a swift hug. "I'll keep you with me no matter what happens," she whispered in his ear. Straightening, she said, "You mustn't worry when Mr. MacLeod teases. Why don't you take Smoky outside, where it's cooler?"

Hallie was glad to see that Garth looked somewhat ashamed. He called after Jackie, "Laird's under the shack. Keep close to him, and he'll run off any rattlesnakes. He's real glad we've got a boy he can play with."

Rattlesnakes! Hallie hadn't even thought about them, but of course they could be a problem out in the fields. "Don't fret about the laddie," Garth said. It was as if he reassured her against his will from some kindly impulse he wished to deny. "Laird will keep an eye on him."

"Laird's my dog!" Meg claimed. She had eaten fast and furiously, keeping a pair of suspicious eyes fastened on Hallie.

"To be sure," her father said equably. "But you'd never grudge the wee lad his company while you're at your work?"

Meg looked as if that were exactly what she'd like to do. "How come we just have ole canned peaches?" she complained. "Now Shaft's got a helper—"

"Great glorious gollywoggles!" Shaft pointed a ladle at the malcontent. "Think we can cook while we're rattling over the road? Let's have none of your sulks, Megan Catriona Mairi MacLeod, or you can just attach yourself to the other end of a dish rag and help redd up the kitchen so's Miss Hallie and me can start some pies!"

"You're not the boss of me, Shaft Hurok! Is he, Dad?"

"He is when he's riled enough to give you all your names in the Gaelic," Garth said, rising and stretching. "Leave the kitchen to him, lass. He doesn't come out and tell you how to tend the water wagon. Come on, lads. Twenty minutes in the shade to let your food settle, and then we'd better get after it."

They left as quickly as they had come. Almost at once, the smell of tobacco wafted in. The men had either rolled their own or found a store that broke Kansas's ludicrous ban against selling ready-mades, though tobacco in all forms was legal. Hallie stared in amaze at empty platters and bowls, at plates wiped clean with biscuits.

"There's enough bread and roast left to make sandwiches for afternoon lunch," said Shaft as he planned, deftly sweeping up the plates on one side of the table while Hallie stacked those on her side and deposited them in the big dishpan. Shaft put a bar of Ivory on the plates and poured boiling water from the teakettle over it to make suds lively enough to cut the grease. "How about you doing the dishes while I whomp up some gingerbread and kind of show you where things are as I go along?"

Hallie was full of questions about threshing, the crew, and especially Garth MacLeod, but this was no time to ask them. Garth must be married—married young to have a child Meg's age—but it seemed strange that a mother would let a young girl go off for months with a threshing outfit even if her father was the boss.

That was another puzzle. Hallie knew that the owner of the machinery was the boss. Often he was also the engine man, though he might just keep a watchful eye over the whole operation. When there was no other boss, the engineer was in charge of overseeing the threshing. In this case, though Rory ran the engine, Garth had the indisputable authority that marked him as the true chief.

Such musings were pushed out of her head by the need to pay attention to Shaft as she washed, rinsed, and dried the dishes. The kitchen was organized for handiness and to keep things in place for traveling. "The tops of the benches lift up. Bedding and clothes are stored inside. You can put your things in one end, and we can stash your suitcase under them boxes of canned stuff in the corner."

"I don't have any bedding." Hallie wondered for the first time where she and Jackie would sleep.

"Plenty in the benches," the cook assured her. "The clean sheets are in the right-hand one, couple of pillows, too. Lessee, now. I can set my cot up outside and leave the shack to you. There's another cot you can have. Think Jack can sleep on the table if it's padded good with quilts?"

"The table should be fine," she said. "But I don't like driving you outside, Mr. Shaft."

"It's cooler. I usually sleep out anyway. We don't have misters! Anyhow, my real name's Milov Hurok. Bohemian. Shaft's a nickname, short for Deep Shaft."

"Please call me Hallie, then. You've got an unusual nickname."

"Earned it fair and square. I used to make the best Deep Shaft in the Balkans."

"The Balkans?" Hallie searched what she retained of her geography lessons. "You mean Bulgaria, Greece, Serbia, Albania, Montenegro— countries like that?"

It was his turn to look baffled. "Lord love you, no! I'm talkin' about right over in southeast Kansas, though I reckon them hills got their name because they was settled by so many folks from them places. Lots of Italians, too. Mostly work in the mines. But when Prohibition come along, a good many started bootleggin'. Includin' me."

"Oh."

Hallie had heard of bootleggers, of course, but had pictured them as machine-gun-toting Chicago racketeers. At her scandalized gasp, Shaft said defensively, "Well, most of us was raised Catholic and didn't see anything wrong in drinkin' wine or spirits at our tables or at parties. When the law came nosin' around, we hid our stuff in old mine shafts. Let me tell you, Hallie, girl, Deep Shaft's got a reputation that brings the highest prices all the way from Ontario to Mexico City. It sells for five dollars a pint in Detroit, though close to home a half-pint sells for two bits. Most of us made it just like we would for our ownselves."

Brought up in teetotal households, Hallie was fascinated. "How did you make it?"

"Well, you dump a hundred-pound sack of sugar in a fifty-gallon barrel, add rye or corn and two or three pound slabs of yeast—none of that fast-actin' stuff! Ruins it! Then you pour in water till the barrel's about three-quarters full and keep it warm so it'll ferment. Long about a week or more later, when it's ready to distill, you dip out the solid leavings of the mash. Good animal food, but I've seen critters get drunk on it. Even some geese."

"Is the whiskey ready, then?"

"Not by a long shot. It's got to be cooked in the still and then run through a copper coil in a barrel of cool water—have to keep changing the water to keep it cool. To make sure there wasn't no poison fusel oils in my batch, I'd filter it through an old felt hat half-full of ground-up charcoal. Pure and clear as spring water my Deep Shaft was. I never aged it in a Coca-Cola syrup barrel like some did to give it darker color, much less dumped in red rock candy. Al Capone hisself used to come buy five gallons at a time, which was all I'd get from distillin' fifty gallons of real fine mash."

"Don't people get poisoned on bootleg whisky?"

"Sure. The distillin' ain't done right, it can blind a person or cripple—even kill 'em. Hallie, I hope you won't ever drink, but if you take a snort, be sure it's not cheap likker that even a drunk has to lace with cherry syrup to swallow or that rotgut Jamaica Ginger that'll paralyze you."

Even Hallie had heard of jake and jakeleg. She forbore to ask Shaft why he advised her against drinking the brew he had described so pridefully. "If you were doing so well, Shaft, how come you're cooking for a threshing crew?"

Shaft sighed and fitted three big pans of gingerbread into the oven. "Well, my cousin's a deputy sheriff. Came on a raid with some federal Prohibition officers. They caught me sellin' a jug to some Tulsa fellers. My cousin had to haul my still and the rest of that run of whiskey into the county seat, but when he told me to get whatever I needed to come along with him, he gave me a long, slow wink. I grabbed what cash I had in the mattress, scooted out the back window into my old jalopy, and I ain't been back. Nothin' in the pen that interests me that much!"

"Does Mr. MacLeod know?"

"Figgered it was only fair to tell him. He allowed as how he didn't want me making any likker, but said his great-great-great grandmother distilled bootleg whisky on the Isle of Lewis—that's off the west coast of Scotland, he says. That's how she made her living while she was a widow. And that's how quite a few widows in the Balkans keep food in their kiddos' mouths, though more of 'em sell it than make it."

These fascinating disclosures were cut short by a motor wheezing to a stop outside the window. "Mr. Hurok!" shrilled a woman's voice. "You interested in some butter, milk, eggs, and chickens? We got more green beans and watermelons than we know what to do with. I'd be obliged if you'd use all you could. Hate to see food go to waste—"

She paused long enough for Shaft to say, "Howdy, Miz Brockett. If one of your kids could bring over a gallon of fresh milk after you're through milking tonight, it'll keep till morning. I can use four dozen eggs today, if you've got them, and three dozen tomorrow. Can you spare five pounds of butter? The men would sure appreciate the beans and watermelons. I can take about four chickens, providin' they're cleaned and plucked—"

The hefty broad-faced woman in the sunbonnet cackled, showing her wide-spaced teeth. "Don't like to wring their necks, do you? I recollect you got mighty pale when they were floppin' around without their heads!" She eyed Hallie and gave a disapproving grunt. "You don't look like you know how to gut a chicken, neither, much less singe off the pinfeathers. You want some real help, Mr. Hurok, my Sophie can wring a rooster's neck on the second twist, and her apple dumplings plumb melt away in your mouth—"

"Much obliged," Shaft said hastily, "but Miss Hallie's workin' out just fine. Got any beef for sale?"

"We knew you'd be along soon, so my man butchered a steer yesterday. Can you use a quarter?"

"Be about right. Can't keep it too long in this hot weather but what with lunches, the boys go through beef pretty fast."

Mrs. Brockett gave a nod so vigorous that it made her sunbonnet swish. "Fine. I'll send Sophie over with it and the other stuff soon as she cleans the chickens. We got electricity in this year, and I got a nice new washing machine, so if you want, Sophie and me'll wash up the men's clothes."

"Reckon that'll suit Garth 'cause the only washing I do is dish and hand towels."

"We can do them, too, lots easier than you can on the washboard. When Ernie brings the milk this evening, he can pick up the laundry, and we'll have it back to you tomorrow night. You've never seen towels as white as Sophie can get." The woman paused, then gave Hallie another look which was at once speculative and wary. "Mr. MacLeod got married yet?"

"Not as I know of."

"Time he did. Man without a wife gets all frayed and frazzled around the edges."

"Ma'am, I sure agree. Rory needs a good woman to settle him down. I'd bet your Sophie's the one who could do it."

"Rory! That feckless, reckless, rollicking, frolicking young hellion? He better not come hanging Sophie, or I'll send him off with a flea in his ear and a bee in his bonnet! The very idea!"

"Beg pardon, Miz Brockett." Shaft spoke contritely, but his beard didn't quite conceal his grin. "Now, ma'am, I kind of need them chickens if I'm going to fry 'em up for supper."

"If you ever tasted Sophie's cream gravy—oh, all right, Mr. Hurok, I'll get the things right over."

The Model T had a self-starter. After some whines and screeches, Mrs. Brockett wrestled it around and chugged toward the farm buildings. Though a mother's boasting could be discounted a bit, Hallie felt hopelessly inadequate beside what she had heard of Sophie.

"Shaft, if you'd like to hire Mrs. Brockett's daughter—"

He gave her a stricken look. "That woman would try her best to get Garth hitched up in double harness, and I don't want to see him smashed up the way he was when I first met him."

"He's been married?"

"His wife, back on Lewis, ran off with someone else while he was in the army. Guess that's one of the reasons he came to Canada to work in the harvest and wound up down here. Good grannies! It's already time to start to start fixin' afternoon lunch!"

So Garth had been married, but wasn't now. Did he distrust all women because of that? Hallie seethed with questions but sensed that Shaft was reluctant to discuss that private part of his friend and employer's life. Tossing the dishwater out the door, Hallie looked for Jackie, didn't see him at first, and got a little scared. She wasn't used to watching out for a child, but she had to learn fast. If he wandered over to watch the threshing and got in the way before anyone noticed—What if he got caught in that long belt stretched from engine to thresher or got in the way of the pitchforks wielded from both stacks to feed grain into the separator?

Her scalp prickling, Hallie started to call, then gratefully stifled the cry as she saw him. There he was, cuddled up against Laird in the shade between tree trunk and shack. Smoky, in turn, was curled up in Jackie's arms. Lambie, the little boy's threadbare companion, might lose some of his magic to the charm of these real animals. But if Jackie came to love them, wouldn't the parting be cruel when the season was over and Hallie had to find another job?

She'd worry about that later, much later. Right now she was relieved that Smoky, Laird—and Shaft—would fill some of the emptiness left by Felicity's desertion, that dreadful sense of abandonment that Hallie herself had felt when Daddy brought home a new wife to take Hallie's mother's place—and her own place, too, as it turned out.

No woolgathering! She had to prove to Shaft that he hadn't made a mistake in hiring her, especially when the formidable Sophie, who could wring chickens' necks without a qualm, would arrive at any minute. Hallie hurried inside and began to make piecrusts.

I I I

As she carried a basket of sand-
wiches out to the crew, two apiece with mustard spread on inch-thick
slabs of beef, Hallie wished for a sunbonnet. Her only hat, the straw
boater she had been wearing that morning, didn't have a broad
enough brim to shelter her face. Jackie trotted proudly along with a
pan of gingerbread, overshadowed by Laird, who stood inches taller.
In the fingers that weren't gripping the basket, Hallie carried a burlap-
wrapped crockery jug of water to replace the one stowed under the
separator.

At Shaft's direction, she had stirred a spoonful of oatmeal into the
water. "Cuts the alkali," the cook said. "Keeps the men from gettin'
the trots, which can be pretty inconvenient when you're threshing."
He carried the other pan of gingerbread, a sack of cups, and the gallon
coffeepot.

The steam engine gave them a rippling salute, followed by one long
blast. "That's the quittin' signal," Shaft said.

"Will the engine shut down?"

"No. Rory's injecting cool water into the boiler and shutting all
the dampers. That'll hold the fire and it won't take long to get up to
full steam again." Shaft squinted at the stacks on either side of the
separator. They were still higher than a tall man's head. "The boys

ought to finish this 'set' tonight and move on to the next stacks in the morning."

Pitchers, three on each stack and one working from the ground behind the separator, forked their last loads of headed grain onto the long extension feeder. This carried wheat spikes into the turning cylinder that separated grain from chaff and straw. On the other end, grain poured into a waiting horse-drawn wagon driven by Mr. Brockett, thin and wiry as his wife was buxom. The straw huffed from the long tubular blower into a growing pile.

"It must be hard to pitch over the belt like that." Hallie marveled at the distance the men could toss the spikes.

"It is, and you can see the wind's blowing chaff into their faces. That's why they wear bandannas over their faces and change sides pretty often and take turns pitching from the ground—the hole, they call it. Jack, plunk that gingerbread down on the corner of this oilcloth, will you? And get out the cups."

While Mr. Brockett drove off with his grain, the pitchers stuck their pitchforks in the stacks, scrambled down, wiped their faces with bandannas, and hunkered around the oilcloth. Rory and Garth examined their respective machines; but after Rory joined the pitchers with a pleased grin at Hallie, Garth was still tapping away with a hammer at the cylinder.

"Makin' sure the teeth are tight," Shaft explained to Hallie. "See, he's tightenin' one with a wrench."

"Garth'll always find something to fuss over," Rory said, pushing his hat up from the sweat-drenched golden hair plastered to his forehead. "The way he watches me on that engine you'd think no one but him ever ran one."

"Can't blame him for lookin' after a big investment," Shaft said peaceably. "He mortgaged his land to buy the tractor and separator four years ago, when wheat sold for twice what it does now, and he got fifteen to twenty-five cents a bushel for threshing headed grain, more for bundled. Prices busted in twenty-one. They ain't picked up. So this is the fourth year Garth's tryin' to pay on a two-bits-a-bushel mortgage with ten-cents-a-bushel fees."

Maybe that was why Garth acted like a bear with a sore tooth,

Hallie thought. Something she labeled sympathy tugged at her heart as he stuck the wrench in a clanking pocket and turned from the separator. He moved with easy, long-legged grace, broad shoulders narrowing to waist and flanks. As if on signal, Laird dashed to him and stood up on his hind legs, front paws planted on Garth's shoulders, white-tipped tail swinging back and forth like an ecstatic pendulum.

"Down, boy!" Garth commanded, but he gave the dog a lingering pat and soft word before he wiped face and hands on a bandanna and reached down for a sandwich. He muttered thanks as Hallie poured his coffee, but didn't look at her.

After a moment, he did. Their glances tangled. They both blushed before glancing away. Something like an electric shock radiated through Hallie, sang through her blood. Then Meg came driving the water wagon up to the engine. Still chewing on the sandwich, Garth went to help her drain the water into the engine reservoir. Hallie's eyes followed him. She felt her face redden when she saw that Rory had noticed.

"Like to see Cecil B. deMille's *Ten Commandments,* Miss Hallie?" he asked. "It's on at the theater in Hollister."

"Plannin' to get there on the tractor?" drawled Jim Wyatt.

"Why, no, Jim." Rory gave the former engineer a careless smile. "I figgered you'd lend me your Model T if I filled it up with gas."

Wyatt looked at Hallie, as if his answer was up to her. She had heard of the famous movie, of course, and had planned to attend a matinee. Then Felicity left Jackie with her and everything had changed—and kept changing.

"No, thank you, Mr. MacLeod," Hallie said quickly. Blushing again! She had to stop that. "I can't go off and leave Jackie our first night here. Besides, I think I'm going to be too tired to keep my eyes open."

"So would you be, Rory, if you didn't mainly stand around on the platform all day, lord of all you survey, while we break our backs." Rusty Wells, the Oklahoma farmer, delivered the barb in a good-natured tone.

"The engineer's job is the engine and keeping an eye on the whole picture," Rory retorted loftily. "If you toss your pitchfork in the feeder along with the spikes, as some have been known to do—"

Everyone looked at Rich Mondell and chortled. The handsome black-haired professor blushed beneath his sunburn but he laughed, too. "Well, boys, I only did it once."

"And you paid with nary a whine for fixing the cylinder," put in Garth, returning with his sulky-faced daughter. "It'll chew up a pitchfork, but can't digest one real well."

"Shucks, the perfessor's rich." Cotton Harris's nose was almost bloody from constantly peeling sunburn. "He just works for the healthy fresh air and exercise."

"If you saw my college paycheck, you wouldn't say that," Mondell retorted.

"You've gone and eaten all the crusty sides of the gingerbread," Meg accused, poking with a none-too-clean finger at the remaining center pieces.

"If they'd eaten the centers, that's what you'd have all of a sudden wanted." Shaft frowned at his boss's daughter. "Take that piece you've got your paws on, and see if it won't sweeten you up a little."

Meg scowled, but did as she was told. Rory eyed her warily. "You fall in the stock tank again?"

"The dratted board I had laid across the tank so I could dip water scooted out from under me." Meg shook the clinging legs of her overalls that were drying plastered to her skin.

"A bath might improve you," Rory teased, "but you'd better not have muddied up the water. You know what they say: " 'If you won't drink it, don't put it in your engine.' "

"Sure, worry about the engine!" Meg bit savagely into the roast beef. "You and Dad both care a lot more about your old machinery than you do about me!"

"You're cheaper to fix." Rory scrunched his nose at his niece. "And when you blow up, you don't send engines and cylinders and threshers flying everywhere."

"Not yet." Meg made a face at him and almost giggled. She took another chunk of the maligned gingerbread.

Now Hallie understood why a young girl was with a threshing crew, but she couldn't understand, any more than she had with Felicity, how a mother could leave a child—just go off and act as if the youngster had never existed.

Hallie had felt abandoned when her mother died though she knew, in her mind, that Ellen Meredith fought hard to live, that she hadn't wanted to die at thirty-two with so much life to live, so much love to love, with her daughter so young and her husband so distraught. Hallie felt abandoned by her father, too, though he had never intended that Felicity crowd her out. Hallie bitterly regretted now that she had probably caused him as much pain as he had caused her—though he'd had Felicity and Jackie for consolation.

Why did people who loved each other still hurt each other so much? And how much more terrible when there seemed to be no love—when a mother left a child who had come into the world completely helpless and depending on her. After that, how could either Jackie or Meg really trust anyone?

When the last sandwich and crumb of gingerbread were gone and the coffeepot was empty, the threshers rose and stretched, slouched their hats lower, tied bandannas over mouths and noses, and those who wore them pulled on their leather gloves. Baldy Tennant spread coal in the firebox of the engine, and Rory soon had the engine billowing steam.

"Can I go see the engine, Hallie?" begged her little brother. Awed by the rough-and-tumble jokes of the crew, he had sat very quietly beside Laird, who had lain down by Garth with his long muzzle resting his daintily crossed paws.

"Not now." The puffing engine, the long belt stretched to the separator, and the separator itself looked exceedingly dangerous to Hallie. She placed a hand on the boy's shoulder. "Jackie, don't you ever, ever come around the machines unless I'm with you!"

Jackie looked so crestfallen that Garth, to Hallie's amazement, smiled at him. "Reckon I can show you how the separator works some morning while Rory's getting up steam."

He frowned at Hallie's boater. She had saved for weeks to buy it and thought it quite becoming. "That's a useless hat if I ever saw one."

"Thanks for your kind opinion!" Why was he so rude, and why should she care? Hallie turned her back on him and began collecting cups.

They were scarcely back at the shack when the Brocketts' flivver churned up. Sophie was plump but slim-waisted. Her ruffled pink sunbonnet, tied in a flirty bow under her chin, shielded a rosily fair complexion.

She examined Hallie with Delft blue eyes as Shaft introduced them. Sophie gave her uptilted nose a further lift. "If you needed a helper, Mr. Hurok, I wish you'd have hired me. You know I can stand up to the work."

"Hallie's doing fine."

Sophie gave a scornful laugh. "Ma says you just hired her this morning! How do you know she'll last?"

Hallie came to Shaft's rescue. "Mr. Hurok felt sorry for me and my little brother, Miss Brockett. We don't have a home, and I was out of a job." She looked the other woman in the eyes. Those eyes had a curious hardness that made Hallie well believe she'd have no qualms at wringing a chicken's neck. Disturbed by that opaque expressionless stare, Hallie finished more emphatically than she had intended. "I'll do my best to make Mr. Hurok glad he hired me."

"Mmmph!" Sophie flounced around and began lifting food out of the backseat. Shaft put four big green watermelons in a tub of water beneath the shack and carved what looked like a twelve-pound roast off the beef which had come in a hundred-pound flour sack insulated inside two damp gunnysacks. He put the roast in the oven and hung the rest of the bagged beef from a limb of the tree. Hallie draped a wet towel over the crock of butter and set it in a kettle of water, trying to ignore the dishpan of plucked, headless chickens. She transferred the wet newspaper-wrapped eggs from Sophie's basket to a large crock that she placed in the coolest corner and put a wet towel over that, too. The MacReynoldses had an icebox and the Raford kitchen was equipped with a sparkling Frigidaire, but Shaft had explained that, except when the threshers were close enough to town to buy ice, they had to keep perishables cool as best they might.

"Here's the beans." Sophie almost threw the sack at Hallie. "Told ma she ought to charge for them and the melons, too, but she just said she couldn't stand to see food go to waste—and, after all, it was me that crimped my back picking the stupid things."

"Tell your ma we're much obliged." Shaft ignored Sophie's complaint. "If she'll keep track, Garth'll pay her when we move on, or subtract what we owe from the threshin' fee."

"You bet he will!" Sophie gazed out toward the threshers with mingled anger and what Hallie thought was frustrated longing. "Thresherman gets his fee even if that doesn't leave us enough money to plant this fall."

"Don't see how that can happen, Miss Sophie." Shaft's tone was patient. "Garth reckoned your pa's grain is threshin' out to around forty-fifty bushels an acre. That'll put some money in the bank."

Sophie's lip curled. "That'll pay on the loan we had to take out two years ago when wet weather made the wheat rust. What that and bugs didn't ruin, hail did. We got only about nine bushels an acre."

"Well, Garth didn't make anything either, since he takes every twelfth bushel as pay. Nineteen-twenty-two was a rotten year," Shaft commiserated. "But you folks ain't the onliest ones with a mortgage."

"I still don't think that thresherman's lien law is fair!"

"Well, Miss Sophie, the reason the wheat states and Canadian provinces passed some kind of lien laws is that quite a few farmers wouldn't pay up when the threshin' was over."

"Pa always paid!"

"Sure he did. So the law makes no never-mind to him."

Sophie climbed into the flivver, displaying plenty of shapely leg, and drove off as fast as she could. "Sure hope Garth stays clear of her," Shaft declared. "That's one mean female in spite of her soft look. Well, we better get to it, Hallie."

She peeled a dishpan of potatoes, strung and snapped a big kettle of green beans and baked three pineapple pies with juice oozing through the latticed crusts to turn golden brown. After Shaft took his luscious-smelling burnt-sugar cake out of the oven, she produced a heap of oatmeal cookies for morning lunch and mopped the floor.

Shaft tended two big skillets of frying chicken while Hallie chopped two cabbages into slaw and made biscuits and mashed potatoes. As if the success of the meal depended on him, Jackie held up fingers as he counted out plates, cups, and utensils and set the table. Hallie had scarcely filled the washbasins and put out clean towels when the whistle sounded.

It was 6:30, only about three hours since the men had demolished a big lunch, but they devoured chicken, biscuits, and mounds of vegetables as if they hadn't eaten in weeks. Conversation was limited to a terse "Please pass the smashed 'taters," or "Shoot the biscuits this way, will you?" It was only with chunks of pie, hunks of cake, and second or third or fourth cups of coffee that the men relaxed.

"Garth," said Cotton Harris, "reckon Quent Raford meant what he said about gettin' his own threshin' outfit?"

Garth nodded.

Cotton meditated while he forked up cake and pie in the same bite and announced the result with a blissful sigh before his brow puckered. "He's taken over a bunch of quarter-section farms along with his big one. That'll be a sight of bushels we won't thresh."

"Yep. As I recall we threshed out about thirty thousand bushels for Raford last year and it was a bad year, too."

"It'll hurt to lose that three thousand dollars."

Garth put down his fork and looked at Cotton. "Are you saying that because you men get a share of the profits that I should have asked you to vote on whether we knuckled under to Raford and threshed him first?"

"I vote to hell with Raford!" Buford Redding growled, his light brown eyes come to sparkling life in the monotone of his tanned skin and brown hair.

"I ain't a Wobbly," Rusty said in his deliberate manner. "But I don't hold with a man havin' it all his own way because he's rich."

"Fair is fair," Henry Lowen agreed. He spoke with a German accent. "Always it is the best way. The one threshed first one year in a neighborhood comes last the next year."

Jim Wyatt and Baldy Tennant nodded. Pat O'Malley frowned. "I'm saving up for a jalopy. I won't get it this year if we pass up crops like Raford's." He turned to Rich Mondell. "You teach eek—economics, professor. Is it good business to fall out with your biggest customer?"

"I think Garth's right," Rich said gently. "And evidently the rest of the crew does, too, except for maybe Cotton."

Cotton shrugged. "I guess we have voted. I'll go along with the crowd."

"Not that it matters," said Rory, "but for the record, I call it damn foolishness to lose that much money over an agreement that's not in writing and not enforceable." He flashed a defiant stare at his brother.

Garth didn't wince visibly, yet Hallie got the distinct impression that he had. After a long, baffled look at Rory, he said slowly, "Anyone who's not satisfied with how I do business is welcome to draw their share soon as we're finished here. The day my word's not as good as some contract a lawyer draws up and a court enforces is the day I quit making agreements."

Pat's thin young face was sullen. "I never made no promises."

"You didn't," Garth agreed. "I sure don't need a hand who thinks he can find a better job."

"I may just try." Pat turned to Rory, but the young engineer avoided his eyes.

Garth looked wearier than even a day's threshing should have made him. "If that's what you decide, lad, I'll give you your money and wish you luck as soon as we're through here."

An uncomfortable silence fell. Rich Mondell broke it by saying, "I wonder if Coolidge will go ahead and run in the fall election. He must be pretty broken up over losing his son."

"That was a shame," Hallie said. "The boy was only sixteen." Just a few days before Felicity left Jackie with her, the papers and radio had been full of the sad news that the president's son had cut his foot while playing tennis. Blood poisoning had set in, and doctors could do nothing.

"Oh, I expect Coolidge will run," Buford said. "After all, he just stepped in when Harding died last August. I bet he'll want to prove he can be elected."

"Seems like lots of the high and mighty are dyin' pretty close together," Cotton mused. "That Roosian, Lenin, that ran Russia after they killed their Czar—he died in January this year, and Woodrow Wilson passed on in the next month."

"Congress the same as killed Wilson when they wouldn't let the United States join the League of Nations," Buford said.

"Aw, that's a bunch of craziness!" Cotton blurted. "We ought to stay out of foreigners' affairs and make sure they stay out of ours!"

"That won't work, Cotton," Rich Mondell said. "Planes can fly around the world now. News flashes by radio and telegraph. We need foreign markets, and they need us. Like it or not, there's no going back to the way things used to be."

Cotton's heavy lips thinned. "Well, we'd better get rid of the foreigners that've dug into us like maggots, or this country is bound straight for hell!"

"I'm foreign born, Cotton," Garth said. "And so were your ancestors back along the line somewhere—unless you're an Indian."

"Indian!" Cotton snorted. "They're as bad as the foreigners! And you're not really foreign, Garth. You're from Scotland, like my granny."

"Watch your mouth about Indians, Cotton," Rusty warned. "My wife's half-Cherokee, and a finer woman never walked this earth."

"If she's half-Cherokee, how come you ain't rich from oil?"

"On account of a white man married her grandma and swindled her out of her land and some oil royalties—which weren't all that much to start with. It was another dirty deal the Cherokees got, after being rousted out of their lands in Georgia and the East and promised they'd be left alone in Indian Territory—what's now Oklahoma. It was chiseled away from them a hunk at a time in the Land Runs. Then, even though most of the Five Civilized Tribes didn't want to be part of what was going to become the State of Oklahoma in 1907, their old Nations, Cherokee, Choctaw, Seminole, Chickasaw, and Creek, was broke up. Common land was chopped into little allotments and—"

"Little!" Cotton sneered. "Every head of a household got a quarter section—a hundred and sixty acres! Single people got half of that. Plenty of white folks, like my ma and pa, are tryin' to scratch out a livin' on eighty acres!"

"You're tellin' me?" Rusty exclaimed. "Why do you think I'm workin' on this crew? Different Oklahoma tribes got different amounts of land, too, like the Quapaw hung onto two hundred acres apiece, and the Osage divided their whole reservation amongst their folks and didn't turn any of it over to white settlement. Anyhow, that quarter section wasn't much when you lay it alongside what the Nations had owned, much less what they'd had in the East. Most Indians weren't used to the idea of private property. Plenty got cheated out of their allotments, or were married for 'em, or murdered."

"Yeah? Then what about them Indians from around Ponca City and Woodward? I've seen 'em myself, drivin' brand-new Cadillacs and flashin' diamond rings."

"The Osages live up in that part of Oklahoma and there have been some big oil strikes on their lands. Everyone on the tribal roll shares in the royalties on account of the Osages agreed that the tribe owns mineral rights in common. The rights weren't split up with the land the way it happened in the other Nations."

"Osage-Smosage," Cotton grunted, "When I don't even have a flivver, no greasy Indian's got a right to a Cadillac or—"

Rusty loomed to his feet. He was halfway across the table when Garth laid a restraining hand on his arm and turned a cold gray stare on Harris. "Cotton, we don't talk that kind of garbage on my crew. If you can't keep your tongue from flapping, you can hunt another job."

The pupils of Cotton's pale eyes dilated. "I may do that."

"Suit yourself."

Young Ernie Brockett arrived just then with a crockery jug of fresh milk and the announcement that anyone who wanted clothes washed should leave them on the back porch that night. After the boy collected the basket of towels and things Shaft had gathered up, he went his way.

"Anyone wants a slug of milk to sleep on, hold out their cup," Shaft invited. Everyone did. When they had tossed off this innocent treat, Henry Lowen rose and stifled a yawn. "Brockett says we can sleep in his barn. Either of you fellows with cars heading that way about now?"

Jim Wyatt and Buford Redding both stood up. "Pile in, whoever wants a ride," Jim offered. "Mighty fine supper, Shaft, Miss Hallie. That pineapple pie was great and my own mama couldn't make that scrumptious a burnt-sugar cake."

The other men joined in with compliments that made Hallie glow. The work was hard but such heartfelt appreciation made it worthwhile. While the Fords chuffed away, Garth and Meg got cots and pillows from a chest in the corner and went outside.

"I hope Meg's not sleeping out because of me," Hallie said.

"Bless you, no." Rory's broadest grin made dimples in his cheeks. "She just likes to be in calling distance of her dad in case she wakes up. Her mother, you see, went off in the middle of the night and—"

"Thought you was goin' to town, Rory," Shaft cut in.

"Nope." Rory's grinned broadened even more. "I'm dryin' dishes for Miss Hallie, you old warthog."

"First time I recall your havin' an interest in a dish towel," Shaft said.

"First time you had a pretty helper."

"All right, bucko, you just jump to it." Shaft peered in the oven and took out the roast. "There. That'll do for morning lunch and dinner. Guess I'll whomp up some oatmeal-raisin bars."

"You could go to bed," Rory suggested, wiping industriously as Hallie washed and rinsed.

"I could, but I won't."

Rory shrugged and, with mirthful side glances at Shaft, regaled Hallie with yarns about bootleggers, especially those from the Balkans. Shaft whistled a tune, put three big pans in the oven, and added the mixing bowl and spoon to the heap of dirty dishes. He set the towel-covered milk in the pan of water beside the butter, wiped off the oilcloth table, swept up the crumbs, and when he could find nothing else to do, untied his beard, fluffed it, sat down on a box, and leaned back against the wall.

Jackie had been playing with the kitten, but the instant the cook settled himself, Smoky streaked across the shack, sprang onto Shaft's chest, and nestled under his beard, hind feet hooked to one shoulder, front paws and chin resting on the other. Jackie came over, bereft of his playmate, and peered wistfully up at Shaft.

"Smoky likes you better'n me."

"It's different, Jack. I raised Smoky on an eyedropper. She thinks I'm her mama."

Jackie winced at the word, and his mouth trembled. Without disturbing the cat, Shaft reached down and swung the boy to his lap. "You know, son, I've always wanted a boy. You're a mighty fine one. Reckon your sis will kind of share you with me?"

The child gave a happy bounce and hugged Shaft as far as his arms would reach. "Can I be Shaft's boy, Hallie?" he called.

"Of course you can." What else could she say, though she was worried about what would happen at the end of the season when the crew parted? That was several months away. She had enough trouble without borrowing ahead.

Because of Rory's amusing yarns, the formidable heaps of dishes and pans disappeared more quickly than Hallie could have imagined, but beguiling and handsome as he was, her thoughts strayed to his brother.

His wife had left Meg during the night, when Meg couldn't have been more than a few years older than Jackie? No wonder the girl clung to her father! Hallie resolved to try to make friends with Meg, though she knew from her own experience how difficult that would be. The best way was probably to be pleasant but not push, and hope that, in time, Meg herself would want to be closer.

Rory seemed inclined to linger when the last pan was dried, but Shaft got to his feet, setting Smoky down though he still held the sleeping Jackie. "Thanks for helpin', Rory. See you in the morning."

Rory threw up his hands in surrender and headed for the door, where he paused. "I promised your little brother to let him watch me get up steam in the morning," he said to Hallie. "Would you like to bring him over and see how it works yourself?"

She'd do anything she could to keep Jackie so busy and happy that he couldn't brood over Felicity. At some level, sometime, he would have to give her up, realize she wasn't coming back, that she was as lost to him as his father, but Hallie prayed that by then he could feel safe with her. Besides, Garth had offered to explain the separator, and she couldn't deny that she welcomed any chance to see more of him.

"Thanks, Rory," she said. "If I'm awake before Shaft needs me, I'll bring Jackie over."

"You'll be awake," Shaft promised. "Now take yourself off, Rory lad. I want to sleep even if you don't!"

With a last flashing smile, Rory vanished. Hallie made up a nest of quilts for Jackie on the table. Shaft helped her undress the little boy and pull on his nightshirt. Depositing Jackie on the bed, the cook said, "I'll set up your cot, Hallie, and then go smoke my pipe while you get settled. If you need anything, holler."

At last Hallie had a chance to unpack, though she decided to leave things she didn't need in her suitcase, which had her winter clothes at the bottom. She left her sprigged muslin best dress folded loosely around her one pair of treasured silk stockings and closed the suitcase.

Except for Lambie, which she tucked under her brother's arm, Jackie's things went into one end of a bench along with her everyday dresses and underthings. She went a little way from the shack to brush her teeth. Luckily, the tree was near the edge of the field, and she had relieved herself earlier behind a thicket of sandhill plums while watching out for snakes. Back from that nervous excursion, she discovered that a washcloth, Ivory, and a few cups of water in a basin could considerably freshen a sweaty face and body.

All the time, she was thinking of Garth and admonishing herself not to be drawn down what looked like a dead-end path with plenty of grief along the way if his wife's desertion had made him incapable of caring for another woman. Hallie found slivers of hope in his devotion to Meg, his affection for Laird, the way he had squelched Cotton's hate talk, and the fairness of his business dealings—charging the farmer according to the bushels threshed, giving the men shares in profits on top of a guaranteed wage.

She also admired the way he had stood up to Raford. Garth Mac-Leod was a strong man, the strongest she had ever met, but she didn't think he was hard. She liked Rory, enjoyed his outrageous blandishments and the way he made her laugh, but she doubted whether Rory would ever truly grow up.

Still, even as she was drawn to Garth and found bittersweet pleasure in enumerating his merits, Hallie didn't know if she could ever wholly trust a man, not after the way her father, as good and kind a man as could be, had married a woman who had robbed Hallie of her home.

Well, she'd have her own home someday. Meanwhile, she had to do her best to make Jackie feel loved and safe. He slumbered, with Lambie hugged tight against him, dark hair clustered about his face, lips parted in a smile. Thank heaven for that. Shaft was going to fill a lot of the emptiness Felicity had left, and so would Smoky and Laird. If Hallie could earn them a decent living, her little brother might be better off with her than with that childless cousin.

The windmill creaked and groaned, grated and screeched. How could the men in the barn sleep at all? Grateful that distance muted its racket, Hallie doubled a quilt on her cot, spread a sheet over it, tried to plump a discouraged chicken-feather pillow, and blew out the lantern.

IV

$\mathcal{T}$he eastern sky was a glory of rose and gold as Hallie and Jackie hurried through the stubble. It was almost as high as his head but he wouldn't let her carry him. The crew had threshed three sets yesterday and would start this morning at a new one. How huge the back wheels of the engine were! Higher than Rory, who strode eagerly to meet his visitors. Oiling the separator, Garth paid no attention to their approach.

It may take a while, thought Hallie, and it won't be easy, but I'll think of some way to make that big lummox look up and take notice when I'm around!

"A grand morning for a grand laddie!" Jackie didn't protest as the golden-haired young man hoisted him to one shoulder and threw a grin toward Hallie. The admiration in his eyes was balm for the sting of being ignored by Garth. "And a fine day for pretty ladies!"

"Every day's blarney day for Rory," Baldy Tennant grunted. He was breaking chunks of coal into pieces egg size or smaller, thunking a hammer against large chunks held in his gloved hand. "You'd think he was an Irishman."

"Close enough," Rory retorted. "The Scots came from Ireland to start with—that is, the smart ones. Now, laddie, you must know that Baldy and I get up while it's still so dark we can scarcely see. I cleaned the flues—those are long steel pipes that carry heat and smoke from the firebox through the water to the smokebox and out the smoke-stack."

"And I cleaned the cinders out of the grates and dumped the ash pan and got a fire goin' with some puny little sticks and bark I scrounged from under that ole cottonwood," Baldy grumped.

"Be glad there's a cottonwood," Rory said. "You're sure an old crank before breakfast, Baldy."

"That's on account of it's so dang long till breakfast," retorted the fireman. "Besides, we had that split flue."

"Lucky we caught it before the fire was going," Rory said. "Pulling a bad flue and roll-fitting a new one is a real dirty job when the engine's fired up, Miss Hallie. Baldy has to crawl into the smokebox to tighten that end of the flue."

"But I got a real nice even bed of coals goin' in the firebox, Jackie," Baldy said. "It's time to open the firebox door and chuck in more coal—see, I do it fast, but keep the coal spread out level to all four corners, not heaped up in the middle."

"See that boiler sweat?" Rory asked. "If it's just sweat—water vapor condensing on the tubes—it'll dry up as the boiler heats. If a tube's leaking, it'll get worse. Now, laddie, while the boiler heats, I'll oil the wheels and valves good and fill the grease caps with grease." He hoisted Jackie to the iron seat. "You sit up there and keep an eye on the water glass and steam gauge." He indicated a mark. "When the needle gets to that twenty-five, Jack, be sure and tell me."

Sobered at this responsibility, Jackie nodded and watched the gauge as if his life depended on it while Rory used his oilcan and grease. "Pressure goes up to fifteen pounds pretty fast," Rory said as he worked expertly. "That's just air driven out of the water. It bleeds off fast through the blower. The pressure will have to get up to one hundred forty pounds per square inch before we can thresh. It's a sixty-horsepower engine. Can you guess what that means, Jackie?"

"It's strong as sixty horses?" Jackie's eyes were big with wonder.

"Right you are—and it won't get tired like a horse or have to rest or get tormented by flies or have heatstroke—though the men may."

Jackie stroked one of the big levers in front of him and laughed. "Engine eats a lot of coal and drinks lots of water, though!"

"Right again. Meg filled the boiler up last night—it takes two hundred fifty gallons, which is an awful lot of water. A whole ton!"

Jackie yelled, "Mister Rory! The gauge says twenty-five!"

"Good lad! But you just call me Rory. Time to check the hand holes—we use them to wash the inside of the boiler. See, I just make sure the plugs fit snug and the gaskets don't leak."

A singing began like a giant teakettle coming to a boil. Baldy opened the smokebox and tapped the flues with his long reamer. When he nodded and shut the door, Rory climbed up on the platform and explained that he was opening the draft and the blower. A cloud of soot puffed out, and Hallie was glad the wind wasn't sending it her direction.

"Now, Jack," Rory instructed. "Keep your eye on that gauge, but you need to watch that tube of water even closer. It's what you might call my life insurance."

"Not that any company would insure you!" Baldy teased.

"Or you." Rory chuckled. "Now see, laddie, Miss Hallie, I have the water glass marked to show where the water in the boiler just comes over the crown sheet. That's the roof of the firebox, a five-eighths of an inch–thick chunk of steel. If water doesn't cover it, it'll get red-hot. The boiler explodes. If the flash steam doesn't kill you, a piece of the boiler or crown sheet will."

Hallie shuddered and thought privately that only men would invent anything so dangerous and exult in working with it. Every summer, the Hollister paper carried accounts of grisly—often fatal—steam-engine explosions.

Yet the power! Sixty horses. She closed her eyes and pictured that many huge, straining Clydesdales or Percherons. For one man to control that energy! No wonder Rory brimmed over with breezy self-confidence!

"The other mark on the water glass shows where there's an inch of water over the crown sheet," he went on. "The water drops real fast after that, so it's time to get more water in the boiler or get set to cool it off."

"Someday there'll come a thunder sound
And scattered far and near
O'er hill and dale and all around
Will be our Rory dear."

Baldy spread his arms wide as he sang the ditty raucously.

"I expect you'll scatter right along with me," Rory said. He dropped his hand on Jackie's shoulder, as if advising a fellow crewman. "If you have any suspicions about the crown sheet, the thing to do is stick your shovel in the firebox. If that crown sheet gives a red shine to the shovel, you better open the safety valve, close the draft, and quiet that fire down."

"I'd run!" Jackie said.

Rory shook his head. "Surest way to die next to injecting water onto a cherry-red crown sheet. Only chance you have is to cool that boiler down. Now, we're at fifty pounds of steam. So we'll just open this main valve real easy and crack the throttle a wee bit, start warming up the engine."

Uneasily aware that she wasn't being paid to admire Rory's skill and that Shaft must be busier than a one-armed paperhanger, Hallie said, "I'm really glad to know more about the engine, Mr. MacLeod, but I've got to help Shaft. Thank Mr. MacLeod, Jackie, and let's—"

The child's lip quivered but he started to clamber down. Poor kid, he was probably scared if he didn't mind slavishly, she'd desert him, too. "Look, I'm *not* Mr. MacLeod," Rory protested. He shot his older brother a devilish glance. "Not even Garth is, not while we're working."

"Then you'd best call me Hallie."

"Delighted." Rory bowed and then held Jackie on the seat. "Why don't you leave Jack here? He can help me get up steam and blow the whistle—"

"*Can* I?" burst out Jackie. "Blow the whistle?"

"Sure. If your sis says it's all right."

Dark eyes looked at Hallie so beseechingly that it was all she could do not to hug him tight and tell him how much she wanted him to be happy, that he could trust her, that she'd never abandon him. But Words wouldn't mean much to him. She had to prove her love. That would take time. But how lucky it was that Shaft and Rory were befriending him and that he had so many exciting new things to fill his mind.

"He won't be in the way?" she asked.

"No, because he'll stay where he's told and do exactly what I say. Won't you, Jack?"

"Yes, sir!"

"We'll be along for breakfast pretty quick," Rory assured her. He eyed Hallie as if seized by sudden inspiration. "Say, Hallie, how would you like to learn how to run the engine?"

"What?"

"You could."

"Oh, no, I couldn't possibly."

"It's all in how you think." He shrugged. "Quite a few twelve-, thirteen-year-old boys run engines for their dads."

"I'd be terrified of causing an explosion."

Why was she even arguing about such a ridiculous prospect? Maybe because Garth's shoulders and back, which he seemed to keep deliberately turned to her, looked all tensed up with disapproval.

Rory's eyes danced. "Shucks, you could explode that kerosene stove, too. Blow everything to smithereens."

"Thanks for reminding me!"

"You're welcome." He sobered. "Cross my heart, Hallie, with a good fireman like Baldy, you could learn to do everything else, learn to do safe—"

Garth set down the oilcan and swung around with a clank of the tools that stuck out of his pockets. "That's about the harebrainedest notion I've heard out of you, Rory, and I've heard some wild ones! Women just don't understand machinery. Anyhow, I hired Miss Meredith to cook, not be a blamed nuisance."

Hallie's face blazed. She glared at him, too angry and humiliated to speak without bursting into tears. She wanted to run the engine now, to make him eat his scornful words.

"Shaft wanted her to come have a look," Rory reminded his brother. "Besides, wouldn't it be handy to have someone who could run the engine in case I get bunged up?"

"Jim Wyatt can."

"Sure, but he thinks he'll have enough saved to pay down on his own outfit next year. Probably won't be back with us."

Garth's eyes brushed Hallie, chill and gray as a winter sky. "Who says Miss Meredith will?"

She shot Jackie a worried look and was relieved to see that he was so engrossed in watching the water glass and the steam gauge that Garth's sharp query apparently hadn't registered.

Rory drew himself out of his lazy stance and stared at his brother. Their eyes met almost on a level, Rory a fraction taller, Garth broader-chested, heavier-muscled, a man in his full prime. "I wouldn't blame Hallie for looking for another job next season, Garth, sour as you're acting."

Did his older brother redden? "A woman's got no business around a steam engine," he maintained stubbornly.

Hallie couldn't restrain a snort. "Your own daughter fills the boiler!"

"She's just a kid."

"Not for long," Hallie shot back. "So you'd better start trying to understand women a little bit instead of acting like you wish they didn't exist!" *That* made him blink.

Rory plunged on. "Garth, you know doggone well it's a good thing to have someone else trained to the engine. Hallie can't pitch grain or run the separator, but she could handle the tractor—and it might come in handy some day."

Defeated but unreconciled, Garth scowled at her. "Reckon I won't stop you if you're daft enough to try, so long as you don't shirk your cooking. But you can't wear skirts around the engine."

"More than likely Ernie Brockett's grown out of some overalls, the way he's shooting up," Rory said. "Miz Brockett's always glad to squeeze out an extra dime or two bits anywhere she can."

Hallie gasped. She didn't want to run the engine. She was scared of that hissing steam, the glowing fire, all those sixty horses she wasn't sure she could keep harnessed. But now that Garth had capitulated, she'd feel foolish to admit it. How in the world had she gotten into this predicament? She couldn't, though, just couldn't, let Garth have the satisfaction of thinking he was right about women's capabilities.

She took a deep breath. If twelve-year-old boys ran engines, surely she could. And if she succeeded—well, then she'd feel that she could do absolutely anything!

"Don't worry," Hallie told Garth in her frostiest tone. "I won't leave the cookshack unless Shaft says it's all right and I'm sure it is." She beamed at Rory despite the fear knotting her stomach. "It's kind of you to take the trouble."

"My pleasure." He laughed and jumped back on the platform. She started to hurry away.

"Wait a minute," Garth called.

Had he changed his mind so fast? Quelling her relief, knowing she had to conquer the engine or lose her self-respect and confirm this insufferable man in his woman-deriding beliefs, she paused. "Sir?"

"Wear this, Miss Meredith, when you're out in the sun."

He held out a ruffled blue sunbonnet figured with darker blue flowers. It looked brand-new. She gazed at it in such amazement that he colored beneath his sun-browned skin. "Miz Brockett just happened to have made a new one," he said. "It'll keep your face from blistering. A cook with a bad sunburn's not worth a hill of beans."

Of course. That was all he'd care about—that she didn't get in such a state that she couldn't work. But she did need it, and she knew the colors would become her. "Thanks very much indeed," she said starchily. "Be sure to keep what you paid for it out of my first wages."

She snatched the bonnet from him. Their fingers brushed—just a whisper, but a tingling shot up her arm as if it had been asleep and the circulation was returning painfully. Their eyes met with a shock that reverberated through her.

No man had ever made her feel like this. Hallie had gone to dances and parties and movies with carloads of other young folks she had gone to high school with, and she'd received several lighthearted, kisses but she had never kept private company with any man. The ones who had asked her out didn't make her heart beat faster, and the few who had that effect were courting other young women. Now Garth MacLeod turned away from her, stiffness in the set of his head and shoulders. She felt a wrench of her heart as if it strained to follow him.

"Be good, Jackie," she told her brother and hurried across the field. Though the sun was just tipping the boundless horizon and she didn't need the bonnet yet, she put it on anyway, because he had given it to her, because he had touched it.

Then she yanked it off and hurried along with it dangling from her fingers. This wouldn't do! Wouldn't do at all to moon around over a man who bore such a grudge against women.

Still, it was his somber face—not Rory's gay one—that kept rising before her as she stirred the big kettle of oatmeal, flipped thick slices of ham, and set the table.

"Now what about that old steam engine's given you such a frown?" Shaft demanded. He frowned himself, bristling his thick gray brows. "Rory get fresh with you?"

"No, he was real nice. He put Jackie up on the seat, and he's going to let him blow the whistle."

"Garth, then?"

"I don't know why he gave me a sunbonnet if he just detests the sight of me!"

Shaft sighed. "My guess is he likes the sight of you a heap too much for comfort, Hallie girl."

"Like it or not, he's going to see more of me. I—oh, Shaft, it's crazy, but he and Rory started arguing over whether or not I could run the engine, and somehow it wound up that I've got to learn, or that hateful Garth will say he knew a woman couldn't do it!"

"Well, well, well," Shaft murmured softly. "Well, well, well!"

"I won't throw my work off on you," Hallie quickly assured him.

"Bless your heart, I know you won't." Shaft grinned hugely. He put an eighth loaf of bread to raise in the warming oven and covered them all with a clean towel. "But it'd be almost worth doing all the work myself to see you set Garth back on his heels. He's so dadburned stubborn that he'll never look at a woman fair and square till he gets hit good and hard between the eyes. He's like a mule. You got to get his attention."

"But Shaft, I'm scared of the way the steam hisses, the fire burning right there—the dreadful things that can happen!"

"That's good." Shaft's tone held no sympathy. "Means you'll be careful. Hey, there's the breakfast whistle! Jack's really letting it tootle. If he don't turn out to be a boss thresherman, I'll miss my guess."

Hallie's eyes brimmed. "We're so lucky you talked Garth into hiring me."

"No, I'm lucky." Shaft himself blinked fiercely. "First time in my life I ever kind of felt like I had a family."

"Shaft! Really?"

He nodded, tied-back beard bobbing its limit. "Don't take it wrong, but it's just like the good Lord took pity on a run-down old bootlegger and sent me a sweet, smart, pretty daughter and hundred-proof son."

The men were pouring into the shack but Hallie gave Shaft's arm a squeeze. "There's no one I'd rather have for a kind of father," she whispered, and then passed golden biscuits and platters of steaming food.

*D*id you hear me blow the whistle?" Jackie kept asking each time he came in from playing with Laird and Smoky, who was still kitten enough to frisk and chase bits of string. "Didn't I toot real good?"

"Sure did, son," Shaft told him each time, never impatient.

"Rory says I can do it *every* morning!" Jackie would say next in an awed tone. Then he went out, imitating the whistle. "Whoo-eeee! Whoooo-eeee!"

It was wonderful to have him so contented instead of clinging fearfully to her skirt the way he had after his mother left him at the MacReynoldses. Shaft's words about family had stirred something buried so deep and long in Hallie that she seldom allowed herself to feel it. Did all grown-ups have that little ache of homesickness? Probably not, if they had grown up and left home in the ordinary way. But Hallie had lost her mother long ago, then her home and her father in any way that mattered, though he hadn't really died till that winter. She hadn't spent a full day with the crew, but already she felt more sense of home, of belonging, than she had in all her years at the MacReynoldses, kind as they had been. Wonderingly, she realized that some of that was because she had Jackie to care for, but a lot of it was due to Shaft.

"Let's see now," Shaft mused, slicing the last ham off the bone which he dropped into the simmering beans. "Bread's in the oven. So's a twelve-pound roast. That's a purty leaf pattern you made on them cherry and apple pies. They go in the oven soon's the bread comes out. You'll have them taters peeled by time to take out morning lunch. We'll give the boys ham sandwiches this morning, beef this afternoon, and I'll make hash tonight with whatever's left of the roast and taters. Stew a gallon of tomatoes with bread, heat up a gallon of green beans with bacon, make some rice pudding with plenty of raisins and cinnamon, and that's supper."

"Don't you ever wonder what to fix?" Hallie marveled.

"Not for long. Don't have a lot of choice. Taters every meal, fried, smashed, or boiled. Plenty of meat and bread. Beans cooked till they're juicy but still firm. Gravy that don't have lumps. A pick of canned tomatoes, corn, peas, green beans, and fruit. Slaw, if I can get ahold of fresh cabbage, stewed dried apples or peaches or prunes. The boys ain't fussy long as it tastes good, there's plenty of it, and they get their pie or cake."

Hallie had been peeling potatoes so long that her fingers cramped. She wiggled them, wondered how many tons of potatoes she would peel that summer, and picked up the knife again.

$\mathcal{R}$ory didn't give Hallie much chance to get cold feet. He disappeared after supper and returned as she was attacking the pots and pans. "Here you are." He dropped faded overalls and a shirt on the bench and took the dish towel away from Shaft. The instant the cook untied his beard and sat down, Smoky draped herself beneath his beard, spanning shoulder to shoulder, and Jackie scrambled up to nestle where he could stroke the kitten.

Just to see that was worth all the work Hallie had done that day, even if she hadn't been paid in money. Watching her brother in tender delight, she became aware that Rory was gazing at her. Something had changed in his eyes, in his manner which usually radiated young, almost arrogant masculinity.

"Looks like they're in pig heaven, the three of them," he said. "Hey, Shaft, I hope that beard of yours don't give fleas to the cat."

"I'll give 'em to you, young sprout, when I'm in a givin' mood," Shaft retorted, but he didn't even open his eyes.

"Now, Hallie," said Rory, "the best way to start you on the engine is when we make a new set. So you watch when it's time to bring morning and afternoon lunch. If the stacks are just about finished, put on your overalls, and I'll show you how to haul the separator to the next set and back the engine to where we can belt up."

Hallie cringed. She'd had time to regret that, caught between the brothers, she had let herself be pressured into attempting to control that monster of steel and steam. "Rory—" she began faintly. "I—I don't think—"

"Well, look who's got attached to the other end of a dish towel." Garth filled the door. Even by lamplight, Hallie could see the sardonic curve of his mouth. "Before you start helping out with cookshack chores though, laddie, it would be a fine notion to give your engine a going-over."

Rory flushed to the roots of his curly, sweat-damp golden hair. "Baldy takes care of the flues and firebox."

"You're still in charge."

"Doesn't seem much like it with you nosing around!"

"I'm the one paying the mortgage!"

The brothers' eyes clashed. Rory glanced away first. "I was going to check everything over good in the morning."

"What if something took a long time to fix and made us late starting?"

Rory swung around to confront Garth. "When it does—*if* it does—you can dock my share for what you're out of pocket."

Garth's tone grew more conciliatory. "No use having it happen in the first place, laddie. If—"

"Laddie! When are you going to quit treating me like a kid?"

"When you stop acting like one." Garth held out a mineral-crusted rubber ring. "You must have noticed this hand-hole gasket was leaking."

"Sure, but the boiler had to cool off. I was going to drain it in the morning."

"You'd have to be up long before Baldy to drain the boiler, take out the hand-hole plugs, and clean the holes and plate, oil the bolt, cut a new gasket to fit just right, and fill the boiler again before time to start the fire."

"I'd of done it!"

"You'll just have to pardon me all to blazes, but sleepy-headed as you are of a morning, I reckoned we'd better get it done tonight." Garth turned on his heel. "Boiler should be drained out by now. I've got a lantern rigged."

"Oh, for the love of mud!" Rory slung the towel at its hook. Half-way to the door, he paused, turned, shrugged, and laughed. "One of these days! But my brother's right, drat his hide! Sorry I can't finish wiping for you, Hallie. Be sure and remember to watch those stacks tomorrow!"

His whistling floated back, a bit too nonchalant, perhaps. Shaft removed Smoky carefully from beneath his beard and put her in Jackie's lap, depositing them both on the bench. He washed his hands outside and returned to take over the drying.

"Rory had that comin', but I sure thought he was going to punch Garth in the nose. Trouble is, Garth can't quit peerin' over Rory's shoulder, so Rory kind of expects him to do it, even if makes him madder'n a wet hen."

"It was mean of Garth to call Rory down in front of us."

"Job had to be done, and I reckon Garth wants to get to bed." Shaft slanted her a quizzical look. "Still, if you ask me, the boss is plumb, pure-dee jealous."

Hallie's cheeks warmed but she scoffed. "Jealous? Jealous of what?"

"I saw the way he watched you when we took out lunch and you wore that purty blue sunbonnet."

"Anytime I looked his direction, he was staring at the separator as if he couldn't wait to get back to it!"

"Sure. But his eyes were glued to you till you started to turn your head. 'Course you have that effect on most of the boys."

"It's just their food they're interested in," Hallie demurred, though she knew better. All the crew flirted a little, each in his own style, except for married Rusty Wells, and painfully shy Mennonite-reared

Henry Lowen. "Mightn't it be better if Rory got a job with another thresherman?"

"I get the drift that their mother didn't want Rory to come to America, too. Garth talked her into it, pointin' out all the better chances the boy would have. So I guess he feels bound to keep an eye on him, especially now both their parents are gone. Usually the lads get along, but this is the first time they both took a shine to the same young lady."

"If Garth's taken a shine to me, he's got a funny way of showing it." Hallie sniffed.

"He's out of practice, and he's fightin' it," said Shaft, setting the last kettle to be filled with picked-over beans that would soak all night. "All the same, I've been with Garth nigh onto five years. Seen quite a few women buzzin' around, but he's always dodged them like they were mosquitoes."

"He won't have to dodge me," Hallie vowed. "Not that I wouldn't like to sting him out of his notions about women!"

"You'll sting him pretty deep when you learn to run the engine."

Hallie shuddered. "How did I ever get stuck with that?"

"Just lucky," Shaft chuckled. "Say, we better get Jack to bed before he falls off that bench."

We. How good it was to feel she had help with the child, others who cared. As she washed Jackie's sleepy face and got him into his night shirt, she knew she *was* lucky, in spite of Garth's hostility. Even if the Rafords had been nice, Jackie was much happier with the threshers—and so was she though tomorrow she'd have to get up on the platform of that smoke-belching terror or be disgraced.

There was no way she would yield Garth that triumph. She would learn to run that beast. And she just hoped that someday that mulish, bullheaded *man* would have to be grateful that she could.

V

To Hallie's relief, morning lunch found the crew halfway through some stacks. But as afternoon lunch approached, the stacks diminished so swiftly that she set her jaw and went behind the cookshack to change into Ernie Brockett's shirt and overalls. She'd never had on trousers before. These were shapeless, and she had to roll up the bottoms.

"You look funny in those overalls, Hallie!" Jackie laughed as he trotted along with a pan of cookies. "Will the men think you're a boy?"

She grinned back at him. "Wouldn't it be fun if they did?" By the time they reached the set she was appreciating the fact that the wind couldn't whip her skirt around. Still, she was ill at ease in the strange garments and kept her gaze on the sandwiches as she passed them around.

Meg frowned at her and turned to Garth. "What's she rigged up like that for?"

"Ask your uncle." Garth shrugged.

"You may ask me." Hallie looked the girl in the eye and spoke in a firm, pleasant tone.

Meg's smooth, creamy brown skin went pink. When neither father nor uncle came to her rescue, she gave a toss of her head that made her brown curls jounce. "All right," she said with a dangerous sparkle in her gray eyes. "What are you doing in those clothes?"

"Rory's going to teach me how to run the engine."

Meg's mouth opened as if she'd been hit in the chest. She squeezed her sandwich till the bread crumbled and bits fell to the ground. She whirled to her uncle. "You wouldn't teach me! You said a girl's got no business on an engine!"

Rory squirmed. "Now, Meggie, lass—"

"You—you even said it was time Dad found someplace to leave me during threshing season—that I was getting too old to be a water monkey!"

"Well, you are! What kind of woman are you going to be if you never learn how to act like one?"

Meg's voice quivered with outrage as she jerked her chin toward Hallie. "I guess you think I ought to act like *her*?"

"Wouldn't be a bad place to start."

Meg gulped. For an awful moment, Hallie thought she was going to cry, but the girl sucked in a long breath before she spoke in a controlled but withering tone. "You won't teach me because you think I should start behaving like a woman—but because Hallie is one, you'll show her how to do a man's job. Sounds just brilliant, Uncle Rory."

"You've got your job, girl, and it keeps you busy. Reason I'm teaching Hallie is so she can take my place if we ever get in a fix where she needs to."

"The reason," Meg jeered, "is because you want to show off and have a chance to put your hand over hers while you teach her how to use the throttle!"

The men all laughed. Rory's sunburned face turned even redder. "Why, you little dickens!" He turned to his brother. "You going to let her wise off like that?"

"Sounds like the truth to me," Garth said with just the suspicion of a grin before he bent a stern gaze on his daughter. "There's no call to be rude and huffy to Miss Meredith even if you are upset with your uncle, Meg. Don't you think you ought to say you're sorry?"

Then the tears did brim over. Scrubbing them away furiously, Meg jumped to her feet. "I'm *not* sorry! I wish she wasn't here! And—and I'd rather die than act like her!"

"Meg!" Garth roared.

She pelted away, climbed up on the tank wagon, and called to the horses. She had been spiteful, but Hallie regretted Meg's humiliation in front of the men, all the more because it ruined any slim chance that in time the girl would accept her.

Hallie averted her face as she poured Garth's coffee. "I'm sorry," she muttered.

He said coldly, "No, I'm sorry. Meg was way out of line."

"She was disappointed."

He shrugged a shoulder. "That's life. She's got to get used to it." Yet he stared after his daughter with bewildered hurt in his eyes, and Hallie knew that whatever his mind said, in his heart he blamed her for Meg's behavior.

Hallie had never had a smidge of enthusiasm for tackling the engine. Now she positively didn't want to, but she couldn't retreat without earning Meg's contempt and probably Garth's. Rory polished off three sugar cookies at once and got to his feet.

"Ready?" he asked.

Hallie eyed the enormous wheels, the boiler that held such might and danger. "Ready as I'll ever be."

"Come along then, lass. We'll hitch up to the separator, and you get to haul it to the next set."

Hallie restrained a wail. "Wait a minute," Garth said. He went over to a box that held his oilcan and tools, and fished out a pair of heavy canvas gloves which he almost threw at Hallie. "Put these on and don't let me see you around the engine without them."

Protecting his cook's fingers? He barely nodded at Hallie's thanks. His eyes were on his daughter who was almost out of sight with the tank wagon. *I don't want to cause trouble between you. I understand some of the way Meg feels. I'd like to be her friend, but it won't help to let her walk all over me.*

There was no way to say that to this bitter, suspicious man. As she passed him, Shaft touched her arm. "You can do it," he whispered. "Show 'em all, Hallie, girl!"

Hallie tied her bonnet more snugly, pulled on her gloves, and approached the monster.

*A*n hour later, drenched with sweat caused by terror as much as the scorching sun, Hallie climbed down from the platform, her mind a whirl of Rory's commands: "Easy with the throttle! The gears are cast iron, but they're breakable as glass. . . . Keep an eye on that water glass—remember, the crown sheet's got to keep covered. . . . Right-hand lever is your clutch, left one's the reversing gear. . . . Turn on the injector!"

But she had steered the engine to where it could hook up the separator and had hauled it between the next stacks facing the prevailing south wind. Under Rory's guidance, she maneuvered the engine away from the unhitched separator and circled back to face it. "You're swinging too wide!" he shouted above the racket. "Reverse and cut in sharper!"

"You do it!" she begged.

"You do it."

On the third try, she lined the engine up with the separator. The men had already leveled the separator, taking a spadeful of earth here and there from beneath the wheels. Rusty Wells and Henry Lowen were stretching the belt from the drive pulley of the separator. The other men pulled the extension feeder around to the south end of the machine. The feeder was perhaps twenty feet long, the same as the separator.

"You did fine," Rory said in her ear as he took over the wheel. "Now watch how we belt up."

The engine crawled toward the belt. Rusty shoved the belt over the big wheel on the right side of the engine. Then he moved the reverse gear ever so lightly, backing away as the forty-foot canvas belt slipped and drew tight.

Rusty blocked one of the engine wheels and flashed Hallie a grin that was both surprised and admiring. Garth didn't glance her way at all. Busy squirting oil all over his precious separator, of course!

As she hurried to the cookshack, the searing wind parched the moisture from her clothes and skin. The tense lesson had drained her energy. She felt like collapsing in the shade rather than working over a hot stove.

Jackie ran to meet her, followed at a more leisurely pace by a yawning Laird while Smoky watched from the porch. "You drove it, Hallie!" Jackie hugged her legs tight and gazed up at her as if she had turned into somebody strange and wonderful. "You drove that big ole engine!"

"Well, sort of, honey." She bent to give him a hug. "At least nothing blew up or got mangled, but I'm a long shot from knowing how to run it."

"Can I run it when I get big?"

She ruffled his hair, black and curly like their father's. "That depends on if you decide to be an engineer." She wondered, with a twinge, where they would be when he was that old. For the first time, it struck her fully that she didn't just have the care of a small Jackie, but would be responsible for him as he grew up, as he became a man. She doubted whether she could handle that much better than Garth dealt with Meg's emerging femininity.

"I want to!"

"Then, if you want to hard enough, there'll be a way to do it."

"I'll want to real, real, real hard!" Jackie raced Laird to the cottonwood and resumed building a fortification out of sticks and long strips of bark. Hallie changed clothes, scrubbed her hands, and went inside where the shade of the roof was canceled out by the heat of the stove.

"You wrestled the durn contraption around like a reg'lar engineer," Shaft greeted her. "Bet Garth's steamin' more'n the engine. How'd you like it?" Nodding at a pan of boiled eggs and another of boiled potatoes, he added, "Want to put together some tater salad? The boys like plenty of sour cream, pickles, and onions."

Hallie started peeling eggs. "I'm all mixed up about that engine, Shaft. I halfway wish I'd never let myself get trapped into running it, but—well"—she took a deep breath—"it was really a thrill to turn the wheel or move the throttle and control all that power."

"Yeah. Must of felt kind of like Delilah did when she got Samson to help her spin." He shot her a sideways glance. "Garth say you done good?"

"He didn't say anything. Didn't even look, as far as I could tell."

"He looked, you bet. Nothin' goes on around that rig that Garth don't see. So, if he wasn't bellerin' at you, you must of done all right."

"He'd be the last to say so. Probably blames me because he had to call Meg down for being such a brat!"

"She was, war'n't she?" Shaft heaved a sigh. "She used to be a sweet little gal, but now she's turnin' into a woman while her daddy wants to pretend she's a boy."

Hallie made a baffled gesture. "That's not all of it, Shaft. I think she plain hates me."

He started to protest, then nodded slowly. "Maybe so. But even if she don't know it, she's got a mighty big need for a mama or big sister. Keep a steady hand on the throttle, Hallie. Don't crowd Meg, and I'm guessin' she'll come around."

Would Garth? Hallie doubted it. She vented her frustration on innocent potatoes by whacking them into cubes, two at time.

*T*he crew finished at the Brockett place so late Saturday afternoon that Garth let the men decide whether to move on to the next farm that evening or move on Sunday in order to start threshing early Monday.

"I say let's move tomorrow and go to town tonight," Rory said. "I'll buy gas, Jim, if we can go in your flivver."

"I'm ready for town myself," said Jim. "Need a haircut and new gloves. Many as can squeeze in can ride free."

"I'll take the spillover," Buford Redding offered. "I'm ready for some bright lights and ice cream myself."

"Lights better not get too bright for a married man," said Rusty. "But I sure would like a banana split with lots of hot fudge and nuts."

Into the chorus of agreement, Garth said, "All right, lads, I've settled up with Brockett. Won't take too long to figure out shares. You can take it all or however much you want."

"I want all of mine," Cotton said. He rubbed peeling skin off his splotched nose. His pale blue eyes flickered past Hallie. "Gonna hunt up a bootlegger and—"

"What you do when you're off is your business." Garth gave the Texan a hard look. "Just be sure come morning that you're sober and able to hold up your end of the work." He glanced around at the crew. "In case anybody's forgot, no beer or liquor's allowed while we're threshing—no bottles in the barn or haystack. If you need a toot, have it in town."

Cotton's bleached eyebrows furrowed. "It's plumb unreasonable that a man can't have a beer or two after work."

"That's how we voted at the start of the season; no drinking at all while we're on a job." Jim Wyatt touched the steam burns on his cheek and neck. "Enough can happen when a man's stone sober."

After supper the men disappeared to get cleaned up. While Hallie and Shaft did dishes, Garth came in with a battered notebook and sat down at the cleared table. A khaki shirt and trousers showed how the breadth of his shoulders narrowed to waist and hard-muscled thighs. Freshly shaved, he smelled of bay rum and pine soap. His hair, that strange blend of silver and gold, was darkened by the water with which he'd made a vain effort to slick it down. Nibbling thoughtfully at the end of his pencil while he worked at his sums, he had a scrubbed boyish look that tugged at an unguarded corner of Hallie's heart.

"Never saw you so shiny-bright, boss," teased Shaft. "Got a purty widder-woman tucked away in town?"

Even Garth's ears turned red. "I'm taking Meg to the movie. Gave Brockett a dollar to borrow his flivver." His eyes touched Hallie, then veered away. "Maybe you'd—"

Jackie burst in at that moment and grabbed Hallie's apron. "Hallie! Can we go to the movie? Can we? Rory asked us!"

"Clever cuss!" Shaft muttered with a wink and grin.

Hallie didn't think it was so funny. How could she disappoint Jackie? But, for pity's sake, why had Jackie hurtled in just when it seemed Garth was going to invite her? He said gruffly now, "If you and your brother would like to ride in the truck—"

And crowd in by Meg, who would be sulky as an out-of-patience mule? Anyway, crowded into Jim's flivver with half the crew and with

Jackie along at the movie, there was no way even brash Rory could consider this a courting occasion.

"Thanks," she told Garth, "but we'd better ride with Jim."

"And Rory!" said that young man, entering. Like his brother, he wore khakis and fairly sparkled from his ablutions. He shot her a look of laughing triumph. "Hop into some clean clothes, Jack. Wash up good, and I'll part your hair and lend you some of my Brilliantine."

Shaft wrinkled his nose. "That what it is? Thought a mouse had crawled into a corner and died."

Rory gave the cook's shoulder a playful jab. "You're just getting a whiff of yourself, you old polecat. When's the last time you had a bath?"

"Last time I fell in the creek." Shaft turned to Garth. "Reckon I'll stay here and enjoy my pipe and an early night, boss. Would you buy me a coupla bags of Bull Durham and a sack of Mail Pouch chewin' terbaccer and charge it against my pay?"

Garth frowned. "You starting to chew as well as smoke?"

"Naw." Shaft's tone was virtuous. "Chewin's a nasty habit. But nothin' cleans out your insides like eatin' half a sack of ole Mail Pouch once a month."

"You *swallow* that stuff?" Rory's eyes widened. "I'd think it'd kill you."

"Ain't done it yet." Shaft gave them a benign smile. "Keeps the breath sweet, hair from turnin' gray, cures the rheumatiz, and keeps me in a sweet and gentle mood no matter how aggravatin' you boys are." He gave a pull at Hallie's apron that undid the strings. "I'll finish up, girl. You get yourself ready. Jim's slow-movin' and soft-spoke, but when he climbs under that wheel, ever'body better be packed in solid and keep their heads down."

Hallie concealed clean underwear in her best cream-colored sprigged muslin, then recklessly added her silk stockings. No debate over shoes; she had only her best patent leather and her sturdy every-day ones. No time to use the curling iron. Anyway, she could scarcely heat it at the lamp and wield it in front of the men. Adding comb, hairbrush, towel, and washcloth to her things, she carried them to the rear of the shack, filled a washbasin, and did the best she could at getting fresh and presentable in the dark.

It was interesting to listen to the men as they came in for their wages. Cotton and young Pat O'Malley drew all their money. "Still of a mind to quit, Pat?" asked Garth.

"It just don't make any manner of sense to lose a big customer like Mr. Raford." Pat managed to sound belligerent and apologetic at the same time. "I want to work where I can make the money. It don't look like that'll be with you."

"Good luck," Garth said.

He counted out Pat's share. Cotton must have been watching because he demanded, "How come I didn't get the same as Pat?"

"Because you borrowed for gloves, a hat, and tobacco." Garth's tone was even. "See here? It's written down."

"Quite a bookkeeper, ain't you?"

"Do my best."

Cotton gave a disgusted grunt. "C'mon, Pat. Let's have a smoke. Buford won't let us light up in his car."

"Good for Buford," Garth said. "Remember, boys—don't toss away a stub till you can mash it to little pieces in your hand. This stubble would burn like crazy." As the acrid smell of cheap tobacco prickled Hallie's nose, the door opened and shut gently and Garth's voice warmed. "What'll you have, Rusty?"

Hallie could almost see the husky freckled man squinting as he did some calculations in his head. "Reckon a dollar'll cover tobacco and that banana split I been cravin'. Will you make my wife out a check for the rest, boss, so's I can just stick it in this envelope and get it mailed?"

"Your family in kind of a tight?"

"Well, our baby's had such bad earaches, he got mastoid and needed the doctor and lots of medicine. 'Course we run up a bill at the store durin' the winter in spite of tradin' in our butter and eggs. And we're still payin' on my daddy-in-law's funeral and hospital bill."

"Would it help if you drew some wages in advance?"

Rusty's breath sucked in. "Garth, you can't imagine how it'd ease my wife's mind if we could pay everybody a good hunk of what we owe. If you'll lend me a week's pay, I'd be tickled to pay some interest."

"No use in that." There was a pause while Garth must have made out a check and handed over a dollar. "You enjoy that ice cream, Rusty."

"It'll taste a sight better now." Rusty clumped across the floor, must have paused in the door and glanced back. "Garth, I sure am much obliged."

"Got to keep my best hands happy," Garth said with a chuckle. He *could* be nice, Hallie thought. But not to her.

She winced as she worked at a stubborn tangle. How would she look with bobbed hair? It certainly would be easier to take care of what with all the dust and chaff of threshing. She was afraid to lop it off herself, though, and no beauty parlors were open on Sunday, the threshers' day off.

Jim Wyatt drew a few dollars and said, "Not that I don't like working for you, Garth, but I sure hope I'll have enough saved by the end of this season to get my own outfit next year."

"I hope you do, too, Jim, though I'll hate to lose a good man."

"Give me five dollars, Garth," came Rich Mondell's pleasant, educated voice. "I'm going to get my raven locks shorn, buy *Harper's* and that new *Time* magazine if I can find them, have a chocolate soda, see the movie, and finish off with a strawberry soda."

"And a stomachache," Garth predicted. "Now, Henry, what'll you have?"

Henry Lowen was the only hand other than Garth and Rich who didn't either smoke, chew, or dip snuff, and Shaft had told her his religion forbade worldly amusements like movies. Back on the family farm in a Mennonite community, those strictures would be simple to abide by, but it must be hard for the serious, hardworking young man to go his lone way while his companions frolicked.

"I would like," he said in his careful English, for his family spoke German at home, "fifteen cents for licorice root and a tenth of my share to send home to our church."

"No ice cream for you, Henry?"

"I'm saving. I—I"—his voice dropped.—"a young lady there is I want to marry."

"She'll be lucky to get you. All right, Buford. What's your pleasure?"

Buford took ten dollars and didn't share his evening's plans. Baldy, too, drew all his pay and volunteered no information. The Fords were loading up when Hallie came around the shack. She still had some money, so she called to Garth that she wouldn't take any wages. Cotton and Pat stripped their cigarettes ostentatiously and swaggered to Buford's car. Pat stowed his cardboard suitcase on the floor so that Rich Mondell had to squeeze in.

In Jim Wyatt's flivver, the heftiest men on the crew, Rusty Wells and Henry, crammed the backseat. Rory helped Hallie climb into the front and settled an excited washed and combed Jackie on his scrunched-up knees.

Just then, the Brockett Model T chugged into sight. "Well, look who's driving!" breathed Rory. "I'm sure glad Sophie's after my big brother and not me! That is one determined woman."

Garth had come outside as Meg appeared from behind the rear of the shack. What a shame! Her denim overalls and shirt were clean but she should have had a dress for this gala excursion, and there must be some way to improve on her cropped hair, taper it so that it followed the shape of her head and framed her face with its broad forehead and pointed chin. As if she guessed and resented Hallie's dismay, Meg glared at her before turning the same scowl on Sophie.

All pink ruffles and flounces, Sophie smiled at Garth. "Papa forgot that he'd promised to take me to the movie," she bubbled, sliding over to give him the wheel. "I thought you wouldn't mind if I came along."

"It's your family's car," Garth said. "Let's stop back at your house and see if Ernie doesn't want to go."

"He—he doesn't have any money."

"I'll pay his way. Meg, you slide in the middle so I won't be bumping into Miss Sophie when I move the clutch."

"Didn't know Garth could think so fast," Rory murmured as Garth turned the Brockett car around and chugged away, followed by

Buford. "Putting Meg between them so Sophie can't get her legs in the way of his hand, and picking up her kid brother. You bet Sophie's gettin' up steam. Garth'll be lucky if her crown sheet don't blow."

"She's real pretty." Henry's tone was wistful.

"Take another look at that jaw," Rory said. He settled back and grinned at Jim. "To the town's finest cinema palace, my good man. Say, there's not much room up here, Hallie. Mind if I rest my arm along the back of the seat?"

"Not at all. I'll lean forward to give you all the space I can." She did, and the men chortled at Rory, who joined in the laugh and withdrew his arm.

*W*onder how they made the lightning flash like that," mused Jim. The usher had seated the threshers by scattered twos and threes in the crowded theater, but now they had collected at several marble-topped round tables at the rear of the drugstore near the soda fountain. Garth and Sophie had come in last, trailed by a pouting Meg and euphoric Ernie.

"Wouldn't it be something to hear the thunder?" Baldy Tennant asked. "Hear the dance music while them purty women prance around the Golden Calf and listen to Moses yellin' at them backslidin' Children of Israel?"

"They'll figger it out someday." Rusty savored a banana split that had hot fudge cascading over three kinds of ice cream. "Just like they figgered out automobiles and steam engines and radios."

"No end to inventions," Jim Wyatt agreed. "Some's good, but there's plenty we'd be better off without."

Cotton said derisively, "You want to go back to reapin' with a scythe and threshin' with a flail?"

Jim sighed. "No, but I can't help but wonder what it's goin' to be like when there's hundreds of thousands more people, most of 'em with cars, roads crisscrossin' the whole country, airplanes zoomin' over it, and several times the hurry-flurry-scurry than we got now which is sure more'n I like."

The debate continued, but Hallie was straining her ears to pick up Sophie's indignant voice. "—what's more, I'm a lot better cook than Hallie Meredith!"

"I believe in letting Shaft pick his help. Miss Meredith seems to suit him fine."

"And having that brat around a threshing outfit! If you ask me, it's mighty dangerous!"

"I didn't ask you."

"If you think he's really her brother—"

A white-hot blaze exploded in Hallie's brain. Was that what everybody thought, what everybody was always going to whisper? If she hadn't been trapped against the wall with Rory on one side and Jackie on the other, she'd have grabbed Sophie and called her a liar. Hallie clenched her fists under the table ran through the alphabet backward till she was calmer.

"Miss Sophie," Garth cut in. "Jackie's a dandy little boy. I don't care if Hallie found him under a cucumber vine."

"But—"

Garth stood up. "If your dad doesn't like the way I thresh, I reckon he'll say so. How I run my outfit is none of your business. Now I've heard what a tongue you've got, I wouldn't hire you if you were the last cook on the whole damn plains. Finish your sundae, Meg. Let's see if we can't crowd in some way with the others."

"You'll be sorry!" Sophie's voice shrilled. The men broke off their arguing and stared as she sprang to her feet and hissed at Garth, "Quent Raford wants me to manage his hotel, so there won't be any use your trying to hire me later!"

"I hope you'll like the job," Garth said.

The hushed crew watched as he strode up to pay at the cash register.

Then Quentin Raford strolled in.

V I

$\mathcal{H}$allie's heart stopped, then turned to a crushing weight that made it hard to breathe. Since joining the crew, she had been too busy to spend energy getting indignant about Raford's outrageous offer and had almost succeeded in banishing him from her thoughts. Now here he was, and she felt as threatened as if a dangerous beast had stalked in.

A trick of light made his eyes glow more yellow than green. Hallie fought to keep from shrinking visibly from their impact. He can't do anything to you, she told herself. But he could cause Garth trouble. And that, she realized unwillingly, meant trouble for her, ridiculous as it was to care about a man who treated her as if she harbored some deadly infectious disease.

It seemed a long time that Raford stared at her though it could have been only a few seconds. He smiled, then, gave her a slight nod, and swung back to Garth.

Even on that hot, sultry night Raford wore a perfectly tailored charcoal suit, starched shirt, and tie. "Ain't he the dude!" Rusty murmured. "Looks like a parson gettin' set to do the honors at a banker's funeral."

"More like a high-flyin' gambler," Jim Wyatt said. "Wonder what his game is."

Raford didn't speak loudly, but his voice was pitched so deep that it carried to the hushed threshermen. "I hear you're finished at Brockett's, MacLeod."

"You heard right."

"Then you can start on my farms."

"George Halstead's next."

"This is your last chance, MacLeod."

"What's the matter? Couldn't find another thresher?"

"MacLeod, it doesn't make any kind of sense to lose out on threshing my grain. I've got more than all the rest of the farmers on this run."

"I'll thresh it when your turn comes."

Raford gave a metallic laugh. "What you need to get through your head is that my turn is first. Always."

"Not with me."

The men stared at each other for a heartbeat. Then Raford said meditatively, "This is about more than turns. Isn't it, MacLeod?"

"What it comes down to is you're a suitcase farmer."

"What?"

Even Hallie echoed Raford's shock. Suitcase farmers bought or leased abandoned farms cheaply, came for a few days to plant wheat or had that done, and if the crop was worth harvesting, they came back for that. They didn't live on the land or take care of it by letting it rest or by planting cover crops like clover and alfalfa to hold the soil and restore nutrients. When their ruthless pillaging had exhausted the earth, they left it naked and barren to blow away.

"You don't live out of a suitcase," said Garth, "but that's how you operate. You came in here for quick profits, bought up land for next to nothing from folks who've gone broke. You've plowed up land that should never be plowed, that should stay in grass. You'll hope to make a killing as long as you can, and when bad years come, you'll clear out and let the dust blow. Dust is all you'll leave."

"You're crazy! Farming is for profit, just like any business."

"It's not."

"Then what is it?"

Garth hesitated. "It's being careful with the land," he said after he'd thought it out. "Careful, so it will feed the next generation and the ones after that—and the birds and animals, too. No matter what folks invent or how smart they get, they have to eat. In the long run, except for what we get from the ocean and rivers, all our food comes from the earth."

" 'Mother Earth'!" Raford mocked.

"You bet."

Raford turned away sharply. To Hallie's consternation, he strode toward her. "Good evening, Miss Meredith."

"Good evening."

"Now that you've found out what it's like to cook in that hot little shack all day I thought you might be more interested in that hotel job I offered you. It's still open."

"What hotel job?" Sophie demanded, her eyes narrowing.

Raford ignored her. "Well, Miss Meredith?"

"No."

"You should think of your brother. The heat, that dangerous machinery—"

Rory shoved back his chair and stood up. He was a hand taller than Raford, though not as broad. "Miss Meredith gave you an answer."

Raford gazed at the younger man and smiled. "Put a boy on an engine, and he thinks he's a man."

"Let's go outside and find out."

Raford shrugged, "I don't tumble around in the dust." His eyes rested again on Hallie. She felt her whole body tighten. "If you change your mind, Miss Meredith, I'll find a place for you."

"How about me?" Sophie cried, catching his arm. "You said I could manage your hotel! You said—"

"If you want the job, be there Monday morning for an interview."

"Interview?"

"I don't hire people without learning about their—abilities."

Sophie jerked her head toward Hallie. "You didn't tell *her* she had to have an interview!"

His smile included both of them. "Ah, but you see, Miss Brockett, I have already employed Miss Meredith. Briefly, yet long enough to know she could fill—admirably—the position I have in mind."

With a mocking inclination of his head, he moved away, ignoring

Garth. Pat O'Malley muttered a farewell, grabbed his suitcase, and hurried after Raford. His high-pitched young voice floated back. "Mr. Raford, you wantin' to hire a good hand?"

They passed outside. Sophie glared at Hallie. "I can't think of a blessed thing you can do that I can't do ten times better!"

"Very likely," Hallie said.

The admission infuriated Sophie even more. Her face swelled, and tears glittered in her eyes. "First Garth hires you instead of me! And now Quent Raford begs you to take a job that I've got to interview for!"

"Sophie, you can't blame Hallie for that," Rory interposed.

"I certainly can! Sidling around all prim and proper like butter won't melt in her mouth while all the time she's got her little bas—"

Without her willing it, Hallie's arm drew back. Before her palm could slap the rest of the evil word down Sophie's throat, Garth caught Sophie's wrist and fairly dragged her through the store and outside. "Come on, Ernie," Garth called to the gawky, miserably embarrassed boy. "Bring your sister's purse."

As the boy stumbled out, face a painful red, Jim Wyatt dropped a hand on Ernie's skinny arm. "Women are like that, son. Just see your sis gets home all right and don't worry about it."

Ernie gave the man a look of gratitude, mumbled incoherently, and fled. Hallie frowned at Jim. "Women *aren't* like that."

"Boys are."

"Yes, but you shouldn't put such notions in his head."

"Maybe not." Jim looked abashed. "Meant no insult, Hallie. I was just trying to get the kid not to take it so hard, his sis's throwin' a ring-tailed fit."

"We're going to need another pitcher," Rusty said. "Garth already told me he'd hire my brother-in-law if Pat sure enough quit. Jim, if I buy the gas, would you drive me down to get Luke tomorrow? He needs work, and we'd all be mightily obliged."

"Sure." Jim rose and stretched. "Be nice to see that green, hilly part of Oklahoma. We can leave before sunup and get back by night."

Buford surveyed the crew. "Pat's not riding, so we can put Garth in my flivver," he said. "Meg, you're skinny enough to fit in Jim's backseat with Henry."

"Skinny!" Meg bridled.

"Slender. Slim. Willowy." Buford turned up his hands. "Call it whatever you want, but let's go, folks."

$\mathcal{J}$im and Rusty left before daylight, fortified with Shaft's coffee and the leftover ham and potatoes Hallie fried for them. She also packed a basket with food that should see them through the trip and leave some good things with Rusty's family.

"Put in all of that gingerbread," Shaft instructed. "And the blackberry cobbler and walnut cake. We're not cookin' for the boys today, so I can catch up on bakin'."

"But it's your day off—"

"Sure, but I don't need to mannycure my fingernails. I'll play my fiddle—Smoky loves that—and have a nap and read the *Saturday Evening Post* Garth brought me." He winked at Jack. "Why, I might even give Jack a chance to beat me at chess."

"What's that?" Jackie inquired.

"A game. The boys play cards when they play anything at all, so I sure do need a chess partner."

Jackie's thin chest expanded. "I'll be your partner, Shaft."

"I hoped you would. I have a set my grandfather brought over from the old country, along with his fiddle." Shaft filled a box with canned goods, jam, a bag of sugar, and five pounds of coffee, jotting down figures. "I'm not stealin' from Garth," he explained to Hallie. "He told me to send the coffee, and the other stuff comes out of my wages."

"Oh, that's kind of you, Shaft."

He squirmed. "Shucks, it don't take much to keep me in tabaccer, and I never liked to keep money in a bank. Might as well give Rusty's kids a change of vittles."

Since it was Sunday, Shaft made pancakes for the rest of the crew; crispy golden stacks which fairly melted away along with bacon and fried potatoes. By the time the dishes were done and everything was packed securely for travel, Rory brought the engine over to hook up the separator, cookshack, and water and coal wagons.

"Get on your overalls!" he called to Hallie. "You can haul this whole shebang over to Halstead's."

She wanted to refuse but she caught Garth's skeptical look and stiffened her neck. He'd love it if she gave up on learning about the engine. Well, she *would* learn—and then there'd be one thing she could do that Sophie couldn't!

*R*ory, on the platform near Hallie's steel seat, tugged on the whistle cord as the engine chugged past George Halstead's big two-story many-eaved gray house. A person could walk faster than the caravan moved, so Hallie had plenty of time to judge where to bring the tractor in order to position the cookshack near several big black locust trees that had been left by a fence when the land was cleared. Their frondy leaves didn't create a canopy like Brockett's cottonwoods, but any shade was a mercy.

By then Mr. Halstead, a rangy leather-faced man with curly white hair, came to show them where he wanted his straw stack. "You take over," Hallie shouted to Rory.

"No! Good time to practice! No rush, we're not threshing today."

So, under Mr. Halstead's puzzled stare, Hallie maneuvered the engine while Rory repeat the warnings and admonitions of her first lesson.

Hallie's brain buzzed with things to remember. Forgetting could be costly, even fatal. Why had she let her pique at Garth propel her into this? Her palms sweated on the wheel. Even the scorching wind couldn't dry the sweat that beaded her eyebrows and soaked the back of her shirt.

Unlike the rows of long, high stacks of headed grain at the Brocketts, the grain in this field was bound in sheaves that were arranged in shocks. "Instead of the separator going to the wheat, the bundles will come to us," Rory yelled. "We'll go ahead and make our set facing the southerly wind. May have to change it in the morning, but you might as well get the knack of it."

Hallie steered the engine to where Mr. Halstead waited. The water and coal wagons were unhitched, and then she followed Rory's orders to place the separator where the blower would build Mr. Halstead's straw mountain.

"Now," Rory tutored as Garth and Baldy unhitched the separator, "take the engine out a way and then circle back to face the separator."

Hallie made the circle but swung too wide. "Reverse and cut in sharper!" Rory shouted above the noise.

"You do it!" she begged.

"You do it. You need to have the flywheel in line with the pulley of the thresher so the belt will run smack exactly in the middle of the flywheel."

On the fourth try, Hallie lined the engine up with the separator, which the men had already leveled.

"You did fine," Rory said in her ear. "Now we'll close her down and hope the wind's still blowing this direction in the morning, right into the firebox. If it's not, it could take four hours to get up steam instead of two. Always turn off this main steam valve by hand; a wrench will damage it. When the fire burns out, I'll clean the ash pan and cap the stack." He grinned, eyes blue and sunny as the sky. "If Shaft can spare you a little while after breakfast in the morning, you can watch us belt up."

"I'll see," Hallie muttered. What had she gotten herself into?

She stole a glance at Garth. Did he think she had done a creditable job for her first time? Probably he hadn't even noticed. He was tightening his dratted cylinder teeth with a wrench. Ignoring Rory's hand, she climbed down from the platform.

Except for Henry Lower and Shaft, the men had gathered around the engine with soap and towels. Piles of clean clothes lay on the tank wagon.

"Ready for your steam bath, lads?" called Rory. He said to Hallie, "I have to drain the boiler either Saturday night or Sunday so I can clean out the mud and junk that gets in no matter how hard we try to get clean water. When I open that main valve, a cloud of wet steam blows out. Dandy way to get a bath."

"It sounds like a dandy way to get scalded!"

"Well, you don't stand right up next to the valve, of course. A fellow can get just the temperature he likes by standing closer or farther away." His eyes twinkled. "If you want to try it, I'll save you some steam and promise not to peek."

"No, thank you very much! I prefer a tub—and privacy." She hurried to the cookshack and began to sweep and mop the floor.

Shaft got out shears, clippers, a towel, and an apple crate and set up his free barber shop. Jackie had a wonderful morning. He brought basins of warm water to the fold-down shelf and watched the men hone their straight-edge razors on whetstones, strop them to an even keener edge with razor strops, lather their faces, and bring the blades across their faces deftly without chopping off hunks of skin and flesh.

Since there were only two basins and two small mirrors hung on nails in the side of the cookshack, the men took turns with this ritual, getting their hair cut or washing out their clothes while they waited for a mirror.

Mrs. Halstead and her daughters would cook for the extra local men who would load and drive the bundle wagons so they'd have no time to wash for Garth's crew. Rather than carry dirty clothes with the clean ones in their suitcases, most of the men attacked their laundry with the stomper, a wooden-handled metal cone about ten inches long and eight inches around at the bottom. Inside the cone was another smaller metal ring with holes that allowed air to escape while the stomper was rammed up and down in the tub of clothes, soap, and water drained from the boiler. Rinsed in water that would serve to wash the next person's garments, the clothes were wrung out and draped over the fence. Hallie was amused to notice that the men hung their underwear beneath their shirts, evidently thinking she'd be scandalized at the sight of BVDs.

In between chores, there was a lot of teasing, especially of anyone who was wielding a razor. "Look at Rory," said Cotton. "Bleeding like a stuck hog! Guess Miss Hallie got him all nervous."

"The way your face peels, Cotton, it's a wonder you can grow a beard; but if you sprouted a full one, it would sure improve your looks." Rory rinsed his face, doused on bay rum and a dusting of talcum powder, and applied a bit of cigarette paper to a nick on his firm jaw. "Hey, let's see if Baldy can keep from cutting a jag in that fancy mustache."

"What you ought to do, Baldy," advised Buford Redding as he folded the celluloid handle of his razor to cover the blade, "is save your shavings and plaster 'em on top of your head. Maybe they'd sprout."

"They'd sprout before any of you got good sense!" Baldy finished stropping his blade and worked up a fluffy lather in his shaving mug. "Don't you guys have something better to do than pester me?"

"I'm going to town for a bath and real haircut—no offense to you, Shaft," Buford said. "Anyone want a ride?"

"I may not be artistic, but my clippers'll save you two bits," Shaft said.

"I'd be obliged," Henry said, beaming. "My Anna, she wishes to marry this fall."

"Sure, blame it on her," Cotton leered. "If she can't show you what to do, Henry, I'll be glad to help out."

Henry blinked. Then his large boyish face turned red. He grabbed Cotton, lifted him off the ground, shook him, and fairly tossed him away. "You will not talk like that about my Anna. Or say bad things where Miss Hallie can hear."

Cotton flipped open his razor. Crouching, he moved forward on his toes. "Stay inside, Jackie!" Hallie commanded as she ran down the steps. At the same instant that Rory kicked Cotton's legs out from under him, Hallie swung the dripping mop at his arm.

The razor went flying. Cotton lunged for it from the ground but Garth, who had come running from the water wagon, followed by a growling Laird, set his foot on the razor.

"That's it, Cotton. Get your stuff. I paid you last night, so we're square. Maybe Buford will drop you in town."

Wincing and cursing, Cotton got to his feet. "Should of quit soon as you sent Rusty Wells after that red-trash brother-in-law of his! I'm gonna hire on with a white man's outfit." He glowered at Hallie and rubbed his wrist. "You like to broke my arm, you—"

Rory stopped the word with a fist that sent the towheaded man heels over head. He rolled and catapulted to his feet, opening a folding knife with a five-inch skinning blade that he pulled from his pocket.

Shaft brought the apple crate down on Cotton's head so hard that it splintered. Cotton's knees buckled. He sprawled facedown. It all happened so fast that everyone stood dazed for a moment.

"I'd rather give a lift to a hydrophobied skunk," said Buford into the silence. "But I guess we have to get him out of here. Want I should turn him over to the law, Garth?"

"They'd turn him loose in a day or two. Just dump him at the depot. I don't owe him a cent, but I'll stick a few bucks in his pocket in case he's broke."

Jackie's muffled sobs reached Hallie. She hurried into the shack to console him. "I—I was scared Cotton was going to kill Henry and Rory!" he choked.

"He never had a chance, dear," she soothed, though she was beginning to shake from the reaction. "He's going away, so you can forget about him."

Jackie shuddered. "I won't forget that mean old razor!"

"Well, no," Hallie admitted. "I won't, either."

By the time Cotton groaned and pushed up from the dirt, nose and mouth caked with drying blood, his bedroll and tin suitcase were stowed in the backseat of Buford's flivver.

"Come on!" Rory ordered. He held a monkey wrench.

Cotton got in sullenly. Rory jumped in on the other side, and Rick Mondell crowded in by Cotton. Between the two of them, Cotton would have no chance to act up. Buford got behind the wheel, and Baldy climbed in beside him. What should have been a lighthearted trip to town had turned into the grim escort of a former companion who had tried to kill.

Shaft spat in the dust. "Meaner'n a sidewinder, that one. First time I ever saw a man go to carve on someone with a razor."

Henry said, "Garth, I am sorry—"

Garth briefly set a hand on the big young man's shoulder. A smile dissolved the taut lines at his mouth. "Better he's gone, lad. He might have got into something real ugly with Rusty's brother-in-law. Mr. Halstead's got a bunch of sons and in-laws. I'll go see if one'll take Cotton's place."

"I'll go with you, Daddy." In spite of the heat, Meg gripped her father's arm.

He turned to Hallie. He must have shaved before the rest of the men gathered for his tanned skin was so smooth that she longed to touch it, follow the taut stretch of it beneath strong cheekbones and jaw, smooth back the gold silver hair clustered damply on his forehead. The gray of his eyes was startling in his brown face. Something in their depths sent a sweet, fiery shock through Hallie; but when he spoke, his tone was cool.

"That was quick thinking, Miss Hallie, to hit Cotton with the mop. You probably kept him from cutting up either Rory or Henry." He hesitated. "I'm obliged."

Why was it so hard for him to say anything nice to her? Blinking back frustrated tears, Hallie flashed, "I didn't do it for you. For goodness' sake, don't thank me if it breaks your teeth!"

She picked up the mop and began to rinse and wring it. Garth stared at her. Meg tugged at him. After a moment, they set off for the house, Laird at their heels.

Shaft set the broken apple crate under the cookshack. "There's some good kindlin' for the engine. Park yourself on the step, Henry, and I'll save you two bits." The cook grinned at Jackie whose face was still tear-splotched. "How about a trim for you, son?"

Jackie nodded eagerly and settled down to watch. Hallie finished mopping the linoleum, glad to work out her fright and anger. Was it always this way with a threshing outfit, men quitting or getting into fights? It couldn't be easy for Garth, but why did he act as if she were some dangerous explosive he might set off if he so much as smiled or gave her a pleasant word?

Wiping her forehead on her apron, Hallie determined to thrust him out of her mind and thought longingly of the tub and buckets of water waiting behind the cookshack. These would warm naturally from the day's heat. How good it would feel to wash her hair, bathe, and put on fresh clothes!

She wrung out the mop and hung it over the porch rail to dry. Henry, yellow hair trimmed short, asked whether the floor was dry enough for him to sit at the table and write Anna a letter.

"Of course you can." Hallie smiled at him, confident because he was so shy. "Anna's a lucky girl."

"No, I am the lucky one." Henry's broad face spread in a smile. "Anna is sweet and kind and modest and pretty. She also makes good crusty bread and better apple dumplings than even my mother."

"For you to admit that, Anna is lucky," Hallie laughed. Collecting her bath articles and clean clothes, she went around the shack, on her way pausing to compliment Jackie's haircut.

She was sure that neither Henry nor Shaft would peek, but it was strange—almost frightening—to think of undressing outside and being completely naked, with no shielding walls. She worked up to that state gradually by leaving on her slip, brassiere, and bloomers while she washed her hair.

It took two latherings of coconut-oil shampoo to get rid of the sweat, smoke, chaff, and dust of the past days. She saved the last rinse water and put her clothes to soak with plenty of shaved-up Ivory.

By now she was enjoying the unaccustomed feel of the breeze and sun on her bare flesh. Hair wrapped out of the way in a towel, she luxuriated in sudsing herself with Cashmere Bouquet, scrubbing her skin till it glowed, then toweling dry briskly. She put on her green gingham and called Jackie for his bath.

He didn't grumble much while she washed his hair and scrubbed his neck and ears. She left him to splash, play, and perhaps scrub his knees and elbows while she did their laundry. When she hung it over the fence, she smiled at herself for arranging her underthings beneath her dress and aprons, but she did it anyway. She glanced up to find Meg watching her with narrowed eyes.

How long had she been standing there? Hallie didn't speak till she thought she could do so without sounding annoyed. "If you want to have a bath, Meg, Jackie's almost through."

"I'm going swimming in the creek. Want to come along, Jack?"

"Yes!" His delight changed to anxiousness. "Can I, Hallie?"

"*May* you," Hallie corrected automatically. "It's nice of you to ask, Meg, but are you sure you won't mind keeping an eye on him? I don't think Jackie can swim."

"I can dog-paddle some!" he cried.

"Except for the hole where I'll be filling up the tank, the water's not deep," Meg said.

"Please, Hallie!" Jackie begged.

She was glad that Meg had decided to be nice to the little boy but she was still nervous about placing so much responsibility on a twelve-year-old. As if reading her mind, Meg curled her lip.

"If Daddy can count on me to hustle water to the engine, looks like you could trust me with your kid brother for an hour or two."

It wouldn't be healthy for either of them to tie Jackie to her skirts and he had been good about playing near the cookshack and resisting the lure of the big machines. "All right," she consented. "But don't get in the deep water, Jackie. Watch out for snakes. Mind Meg and—"

"Holy smoke!" Meg interrupted. "We're not going on an African lion hunt!"

Jackie laughed and gave the water a gleeful splash. "No lions in the creek, silly!"

Shaft came around the shack, Smoky cradled in one arm. He puffed out a cloud of fragrant smoke and eyed Jackie from beneath bushy gray eyebrows. "Boys don't call their big sisters silly, Jack."

The child wilted. His lip quivered as his brown eyes came anxiously to Hallie. "Hallie not mad?" Behind the question she heard another: *You won't leave me like Mama did?*

Hallie swooped down to hug him in spite of his wetness. "Of course I'm not mad, honey! Maybe I was a little silly, but that's because I don't want you to get hurt. You'd better wear your clothes to the creek, but you can keep just your drawers on to play in the water."

They left him to dry off and dress. Garth was over doing things to the separator. It must be the most fussed-over machine in Kansas. "Lefty Halstead's going to work with us," Shaft said. "He'll make a good hand. His dad's had all those boys out in the fields soon as they could walk." The cook's gaze followed Hallie's as she watched Jackie trot to keep up with Meg. "Don't fret about Jack, honey. Meg'll watch after him." He stroked Smoky meditatively. The kitten swatted the side of his face lightly. "I'm kind of surprised she took up with Jack but since she has—"

"I think she wants to get him to like her more than he does me," Hallie said and hoped Shaft would contradict that.

"Could be. You've put Miss Meg's nose out of joint a couple of ways. Rory won't let her drive the engine, but he's teaching you. But the main rub, I reckon, is she's scared Garth may get sweet on you."

"He's barely civil!" Hallie unwound the towel, sat on the steps, and began to comb the tangles out of her hair.

Shaft grinned and put down the little cat. "Maybe he's scared, too. Say, would you like some music while you're drying your hair?"

"I'd love it!"

He went in the shack where Henry still labored intently over his letter, and returned with his grandfather's beautiful old fiddle. Cradling the mellowed wooden instrument as lovingly as if it had been alive, Shaft tuned the strings to his satisfaction and played. Smoky jumped up on the porch rail to listen.

Hallie had expected backwoods songs, barn-dance music. Instead, Shaft played tunes she had never heard before except for Johann Strauss's waltz, *The Blue Danube*. Swaying dreamily to the melody as she combed and fluffed her hair, Hallie said, "What are you playing, Shaft? It's lovely."

"What does it put you in mind of?"

"A river. A great, long, broad one with a current that sparkles and ripples and runs through fields and towns."

Shaft nodded. "A Czech named Bedřich Smetana wrote the piece about Bohemia's largest river, the Vltava or Moldau. Now let me play you my favorite, Antonín Dvořák. He used lots of folk music in his work."

Indeed, with her eyes closed, Hallie could almost see brightly clad young men and women laughing and singing as they clapped and danced. She leaned back and let the wind tug her hair, happier in a quiet way than she could remember being for a very long time, perhaps even since her mother had died.

Oh, she'd had some good times with the MacReynoldses and enjoyed parties and outings with her classmates, but she'd always been aware that she had no real home, no real family after Felicity claimed her father. Oddly enough, this traveling cookshack, so unstable that it had to be tied down with ropes, gave her a sense of home, of belonging. Jackie was an awesome responsibility but he truly was her family, and she his, with Shaft a kindly uncle. She was beginning to know the crew and relax with them. With luck, now that Cotton was gone, there would be no more trouble.

She was proud she was standing up to the work and surprised and proud that she knew a little about the engine. If Meg weren't so difficult—if Garth weren't so suspicious—

Something came between her and the sun. She sat up straight and opened her eyes. As if her thoughts had summoned him, Garth looked down at her.

VII

---

*F*or a charged moment, his eyes seemed warm and sunlit before they changed to thundercloud gray. "Hadn't you better braid your hair before it's all snarls and tangles?" His tone accused her of serious dereliction. She must have imagined that fleeting tenderness in his gaze.

"Since it's my scalp and my tangles, I don't see why you should care."

"Don't fuss, kids." Shaft wagged a finger so drolly that they both had to laugh. "Have a step, boss, and let some good Bohemian music soothe your savage breast."

"I just came for a cup of coffee, Shaft. There's been enough sand in the water to chew up the piston cup on the tank wagon pump. I've got to fix that and there's the boiler to clean—"

"That's Rory's job, ain't it?"

"He's in town."

"I noticed." Shaft's tone was dry. "None of my beeswax, Garth, but if your kid brother gets the fun of running that engine, and the good wages, then it looks like he ought to do the messy chores, too."

"Oh, he'd clean the boiler when he got home."

"But would he go around to both sides to flush all the settlings out of the bottom?"

Garth reddened, as if Rory had skimped this chore in the past. "He's young, Shaft."

"Not as young as you were when you were ducking bullets in France."

"I promised our mother to look after him."

"Till he's ninety?"

Garth was startled into laughing. Strange how much younger that made him look. Shaft pressed on. "Your mother would want you to look after yourself, too, lad. Have a little fun. Take it easy now and then, at least on Sunday." Shaft chuckled and swept the bow across the strings in a joyous ripple. "Drink your coffee sittin' down. Listen to some music. Watch a pretty girl's hair blow free, shinin' in the sun."

Garth looked at Hallie. For a moment, she thought he was going to smile, sit down with them, and share the morning.

Then his eyes veiled and his face hardened. "I've got work to do." He got his coffee and strode back to the machines, followed by Laird, who enjoyed this day when the engine didn't run and he could tag along behind his master.

Feeling as rejected as if Garth had slapped her, Hallie started to braid her hair, pulling the strands a good deal tighter than necessary.

Shaft's bow crowed another exultant trill. "Hallie, he sure does like you!"

She gasped in disbelief.

"Sure he does," the cook insisted. "You've got him on the run!"

"I'm not about to chase him."

"Don't have to. When he's plumb wore out, he'll fall over his feet. While he's layin' there in a heap, give him a smile, a hand up, and he'll be yours."

"I'm not sure I can stand that much good luck!"

Shaft eyed her severely. "The woman that Garth can finally give in to and love will be durned doggoned lucky. Don't you doubt that for a minute." Shaft sighed and nestled his fiddle and bow into their velvet-lined case. "Well, drat! Guess I can't put it off any longer."

"What, Shaft?" Concerned at the note of dread in his voice, Hallie thrust the last pin in her braided coronet and jumped up. "Can I help?"

His gloom disappeared in a broad grin. "Thanks, but I reckon you'd better not. I've got to take a bath and scrub my beard out so it won't give Smoky fleas."

"Why didn't you take a steam bath?"

"That's okay for them as is young and skinny, but when you got more flab than muscle, you're not so keen on friskin' around in front of everybody naked as a jaybird."

"Before you take over the bathroom, let me get my things off the fence. They should be ready to iron. You *do* have an iron?"

"Sure. My last helper, the one who quit to get married, made us buy her two of the iron do-funnies that you heat over a burner— sadirons I think they call 'em. Reckon ironin' all them ruffles on her aprons and skirts did some good 'cause she married the son of the second farmer we threshed. The irons and handle must be at the bottom of one of the benches."

Mrs. MacReynolds had an electric iron, of course, but once Hallie exhumed the heavy sadirons from the nethermost reaches of the bench from which she had to temporarily oust Henry, it was easy enough to figure out how to use them. The wooden handle was already locked into the top of the four-pound iron. She lit a kerosene burners beneath the irons, grateful anew that she didn't have to contend with a coal stove that took a while to get going and then radiated heat long after the cooking was done.

Folded sheets laid over one end of the table made a fairly good ironing board. Not that anyone could tell she'd ironed a dress or apron an hour after she put it on, but *she'd* know. One of the things she remembered about her mother was how perfectly Daddy's shirts and her own small dresses were starched and ironed right up to the time Mama hadn't been able to rise from her bed. It was too difficult to make starch here and go through all that extra bother, but Hallie found it was somehow a point of honor to iron her clothes and Jackie's as smoothly as she could.

"Am I in your way, Miss Hallie?" Henry asked, scooting his Big Chief tablet to the table's far end.

His face was as open and innocent as Jackie's. It was hard to believe his mild blue eyes had glittered with fury that morning.

"Of course you're not in the way, Henry." Hallie smiled at him and the pages accumulating under the tablet edge. "Anna will be thrilled to get such a nice long letter."

"I wrote her longer letters when I was in prison."

"Prison?" Hallie echoed. She couldn't believe her ears. Of all the crew, this bashful unworldly young man seemed the least likely to do anything to deserve jailing.

"My people do not believe in making war. I could not serve in the army." His clear, candid gaze searched her face. "Do you think I was a coward?"

"No." She had been only thirteen when the war ended, but she remembered the frenzied suspicion directed at Germans, even though their families might have settled in Kansas two generations ago. Anyone accused of hampering the war effort was feared and hated, "slackers" or "yellow-bellies" most of all. "I think it took more courage not to serve. But I thought men whose religion forbade fighting were given noncombatant duties."

"Some were. But is not driving a munitions truck helping make war? Cooking for soldiers? Writing out their paychecks? Even nursing them if they will return to the front?"

"Oh. That *does* make it complicated."

"I could not put on a uniform. So I was court-martialed and imprisoned at Fort Leavenworth. So were several hundred other Mennonites, Quakers, and Hutterites."

"Were you there long?"

"It seemed long. I was sentenced to twenty years, but was let go after the war ended." Henry stared out at a locust branch soughing in the breeze. "I was luckier than the Hofer brothers. They were Hutterites who were sent to Alcatraz and locked in solitary underground cells. They were beaten, starved, forced to sleep on the bare, damp concrete and got only half a cup of water a day. After five days, they were finally given a meal and allowed an hour's outdoor exercise once a week."

Hallie stared in shock. "Are you sure?"

"Too sure. After four months in Alcatraz, they were sent in chains to Leavenworth. Michael and Joseph were so sick, they died in a few days in spite of all we could do for them. David—well, when he was stronger, he was given a discharge and sent home to his parents in South Dakota. The Hutterites were persecuted so badly there that most of them moved to Canada."

"That's terrible!"

Henry gave a faint smile. "You have to remember that Theodore Roosevelt said we should be sent to dig trenches at the most dangerous front lines or be put on mine sweepers. He said we shouldn't be American citizens. Besides, we speak German in our homes and churches. That was the language of the enemy. And though we gave heavily to relief work and the Red Cross, we wouldn't buy war bonds."

"All the same—"

"If there is another war ever, which God forbid, it will be better. Our elders and those of the Quakers and other conscientious objectors kept going to Washington to try to work out an answer. In the summer of 1918, the Adjutant General ordered that objectors could be assigned to nursing soldiers who would not be fighting anymore. And other kinds of service were agreed upon." He nodded. "Yes. It will be better."

"You fought your own war," Hallie said. "I respect you for going to prison for your beliefs. But I do think a country must defend itself."

"We have always believed war—any killing—is wrong. That is why our people came from Russia, because the czar would no longer excuse us from military service. And we went to Russia in the first place because Catherine the Great promised that we would not have to be soldiers."

"You don't believe in fighting no matter what the reason?"

Henry grinned sheepishly. "I don't believe in it—but sometimes, like this morning, the Devil seizes me. The more shame because I had just read the Scriptures and prayed. I will study my Bible and pray more this afternoon. Next time I am tempted, I hope, with the Lord's grace to be able to resist. I should have admonished Cotton with love, not my fists."

The blond young giant meant it! Hallie frowned as she bore down on the iron to erase a stubborn wrinkle in Jackie's denim playsuit. "I don't think that would have done much good."

Henry ducked his head. "I provoked him to attempt murder. He might have killed or been killed. His soul is poisoned with hatred. No. I did a bad thing."

"It might have been worse if Cotton picked a fight with Rusty's brother-in-law."

Henry cheered up at that. "I am glad that Garth will hire an Indian. But, after all, he hired me, and he knew I wouldn't fight in that war in which he was wounded."

"Wounded?"

"Shrapnel is still buried in his shoulder."

Henry turned back to his letter. Betrayed into a rush of sympathy for Garth, Hallie concentrated on her ironing. How much like closed books the lives of other people were! And Garth seemed determined to keep his locked.

Had he loved his wife so much? Did he see her constantly in Meg, so the wound couldn't heal? When Hallie felt that sweet lightning flash between them, did he experience it, too, or was it only her heart that raced, her bones that melted?

Garth haunted her thoughts that day though now and then she had an ugly flash of Cotton's distorted face as he moved toward Henry with the razor. She fervently hoped he was on a freight train headed far away; but, like Pat O'Malley, he might try to work for Raford.

Raford. What was he willing to do to punish Garth for not knuckling under to him? Refusing to let him thresh Raford's fields and those he had bought from bankrupt farmers would seriously cut Garth's profits. But what if Raford set up a rival outfit, as he had threatened?

The thought chilled her. Raford apparently had enough money to do just about anything he decided to try. In Shaft's words, Garth was trying to pay off "a two-bits-a-bushel mortgage with ten-cents-a-bushel fees."

By taking a job with him while rejecting Raford's proposition, Hallie had undoubtedly magnified Raford's grudge. This made her feel a certain responsibility for the result, though there was no way she could work for Raford once he made his intentions clear.

She burned with humiliation. How could he have thought she'd accept? Jackie, of course. Did Garth believe that, too—that the little boy was hers? Still, it was small wonder that people had trouble believing that Jack's mother had abandoned him. Especially as she grew closer to the vulnerable child, Hallie could scarcely credit it herself.

Well, she wasn't going to get a copy of Jackie's birth certificate to wave at people. Garth seemed to want excuses to think ill of her. As for Raford, if he gave Sophie that "position" at the hotel, he might be so occupied with her that he would forget what could only be a whim.

Jackie was so happily exhausted after his "swim" that Hallie set up her cot for him between the shack and the locust trees. He devoured a thick slice of bread and butter and went to sleep with Lambie tucked against his cheek. His pale skin was starting to tan, and he had a few scratches, but he still looked like a small, dark-haired angel.

How, *how,* had Felicity been able to leave him? And how lucky he and Hallie were to have a place where he could be near her while she worked and have the company of Shaft and the other men, as well as Smoky to stroke and Laird to play with! Hallie shivered to remember Raford's hard, hungry mouth on hers.

A good thing he'd been blunt. Had he been kind to Jackie, had he pretended sympathy, been tender and patient— Overwhelmed by the sudden need to care for Jackie, still grieving for her father, her guilt at having treated him coldly mixed with anger that he had put Felicity in her mother's place, Hallie might have been an easy conquest for an experienced man who used the right tactics.

Yes, indeed! Thank goodness his cynicism led him into a frontal attack. Hallie glanced out to where Garth was working with Meg on the pump of the water wagon. Strange that what were probably similar assumptions about Jackie provoked Raford's advances but seemed to stifle Garth's. If ever he kissed her— For just an instant, Hallie let herself imagine what it would be like in his arms, feeling and hearing the sound of his heart, able to caress the strong muscles at the back of his neck, meeting his downcurved lips with hers . . .

No! She mustn't let herself dream, make herself miserable because he was cold. Such foolishness could ruin this haven, this safety, she had found for herself and Jackie. But if this were the way her fancies betrayed her when she wasn't concentrating all thought and energy on getting the crew fed, then she was glad Sunday came only once a week.

$\mathscr{T}$hrough the day, the hungry helped themselves to cold food. Toward sundown, Shaft sliced a platter of ham and began surrounding it with beet pickles, dill pickles, sweet pickles, green tomato relish, corn relish, chowchow, and piccalilli.

"I know I don't have to," he told Hallie as he set the coffee on. "But the boys'll be hungry when they trail in. Anyhow, it's prob'ly less trouble to set the grub out than clean up after they've rampaged through everything."

"What can I do?" Hallie asked.

"Open up some pork and beans and a gallon of some kind of fruit." Slicing bread, Shaft bent to peer through the window. "Drat and doggone! If Garth hasn't cleaned out that confounded boiler after he spent the rest of the livelong day workin' on the separator! There he is, helpin' Meg fill the pea-pickin' blue-eyed boiler while His Lordship frolics!"

"That may be why he cleaned the boiler," Hallie ventured. "Since it's empty, it'll take a while to pump it full. Garth couldn't want Meg to be doing that when she's tired and sleepy."

"Reckon not." Shaft appeared to gnash his teeth on his pipestem. "And Rory's a good lad, just thoughtless. Why should he think when he's got big brother to do the worryin'?"

Sure enough, as Buford drove up in the twilight, Rory was out of the flivver before it stopped, yelling at Garth. "I was going to clean the darn boiler! You didn't have to barge ahead and do it!"

"Sure!" Garth didn't shout, but the wind carried his voice. "You'd be banging around with lanterns when everyone's trying to sleep and expect Meg to stay up till all hours to pump that boiler full."

"If she can't do the job, she shouldn't have it!"

"That's what some might say about you."

"Is that what *you* say?"

"Oh, hush, Uncle Rory!" Meg's clear, thin tones rose above the deep ones of the men. "The boiler's clean and full, all ready to go in the morning. Let's eat."

Rory made a muffled retort, but before the wrangling could continue, another vehicle chugged up. "Hey, boss!" Rusty's hail was exuberant. "I've got a good hand for you. Meet my wife's kid brother, Luke Rogers."

"Any kin to Roy?" someone joked.

" 'Way far back," drawled a soft voice. "Sorry, but I can't do rope tricks, and I don't know any jokes fit to tell around a young lady."

He had to be referring to Meg. Hallie and Shaft grinned at each other. "Oh boy, oh boy, howdy!" Shaft murmured. "Get ready for Meg's first crush!"

The floor of the cookshack protested as the men poured inside. A slender young man with dark hair and green eyes held back to let Meg precede him. She swept him an astonished glance that changed to a look of wonder.

"Th-thanks, Mr. Rogers," she said.

"I'm just Luke, miss."

"Oh, I'm not a miss! I'm just Meg."

His smile was slow, sweet, and showed teeth that looked even whiter than they were because of his smooth skin. It wasn't rose, it wasn't gold, it wasn't brown, but a blend of all of these. He was— Hallie stopped at the word, but it came anyway.

He was beautiful. Could he do the grueling work of a pitcher? He must be able to or Rusty wouldn't have brought him. Rusty's affectionate pride in the younger man made Hallie wonder if his wife, in her woman's way, were as striking as her brother. If so, it was no wonder Rusty had crossed the racial line to marry her. As she was introduced to Luke and made a welcoming remark, Hallie was glad that Cotton Harris was gone. The washed-out pale-eyed Texan with his perpetually peeling skin would have hated Luke on sight.

With any luck, Cotton was bound far away. Hallie forced him out of her mind and poured coffee all around before she filled her plate and perched on the steps beside Shaft and Jackie. Rory followed, jumped to the ground, and went over to Buford's Ford.

"Miss Hallie, Cotton might have carved me up real artistically if you hadn't hit him with your mop. Here's a little thank-you."

"Little!" Hallie stared at the beribboned gilt box. "That's three pounds of French chocolates! It's too much, Rory."

"Not by the time you pass 'em around a few times," Shaft said. "Why, I could eat half that box myself just lookin' for my favorite kind."

"What's that?"

"Almond pecan raspberry caramel fudge."

"I've never tasted one of those."

"Me, neither. But don't it sound larrupin' delicious?"

Shaft looked so yearningly at the box that Hallie said to Rory in her demurest voice, "It's very kind of you, Rory. I'm sure the whole crew will thank you for the treat."

He looked dashed for the briefest moment, then threw back his golden head and laughed. "Just pass it to me first so I can pick out the toffees." He handed Jackie a small bag. "And here, lad, is something for you. *Two* somethings."

"For me?" Jackie squealed. He plunged eager fingers inside. "A likrish pipe! And a real one!"

"It's a corncob," Rory agreed, "but it's not Prince Albert. A little soap and water and you can blow the prettiest most perfect rainbow bubbles, clouds and clouds of them."

"I like to blow bubbles," Jackie said. His face clouded. "I—I had a bubble pipe but I couldn't keep it. Mama said I could keep just one thing—there wasn't room for more in my suitcase—so I chose Lambie."

Hallie would wager that Felicity had kept all *her* favorite clothes and jewelry. Parting with his familiar playthings must have added considerably to Jackie's distress. Thank goodness—and Shaft and Smoky and Laird, yes, and Meg—that he had so many interesting things to do that he couldn't miss his toys much.

"That's thoughtful of you, Rory," Hallie told him. "Blowing bubbles is a perfect way to spend a hot afternoon."

The light from inside cast his face into harsh brightness and shadow.

"The problem with bubbles is that they're only air when the rainbow bursts."

"That's all right," Jackie said. "I'll just blow more."

"Do that, laddie." Rory brushed back the dark curls from Jackie's forehead and went in to supper.

He took the men's joshing in good humor when Hallie passed the chocolates. "Good taste, Rory, my boy," said Rich Mondell. "Mmmm! Do I love cherry cordials!"

"Nothin' cheap about Rory," Rusty Wells agreed. "Here, Luke, take another Brazil nut. There's plenty more."

"Now I know how the man felt who accidentally dropped his pearls in front of a bunch of hogs," Rory grunted. "Never mind. I got all the toffees."

Though Garth took only one and Hallie thought he did that for sociability, the chocolates vanished almost as fast the bubbles Jackie was blowing. "That was the nicest candy I ever had," Hallie told Rory. "And the box is gorgeous. I'm going to save it to hold my sewing things."

"I'm glad you don't think you have to give it away," Rory said in a wry tone.

"Please, Rory. I can't let you spend your money on me."

He shrugged. "I can always lose it in the pool hall or rolling dice."

Garth was listening. Hallie wondered, didn't he feel like saying that if money burned a hole in his brother's pocket, it could certainly help on the mortgage? *She* felt like saying so but it was scarcely her place.

Jim Wyatt got to his feet. "Let's thank Miss Hallie and Shaft for setting out a supper when they didn't have to. I'll wash. Who'll dry?"

Everyone was willing, but Luke and Rich grabbed the dish towels first. In short order, as Shaft puffed contentedly on his pipe with Smoky purring beneath his beard and Jackie half-asleep on his chest, everything was put away and the kitchen readied for morning. With Cotton and Pat gone, the crew seemed almost like a family. After they called their good-nights, Hallie made up Jackie's bed on the table. He was already asleep, pipe in one hand, Lambie in the other.

"Rory means well," Shaft said abruptly. "But even if he is a couple of years older than you, Hallie, you know, don't you, that in some ways he's as big a kid as Jackie?"

Hallie stared at his furrowed brow and smothered a laugh. "Don't worry, Shaft! I certainly know better than to take him seriously! If I did, I'll bet he'd run a mile."

"I'm not that sure."

"Well, it won't happen, so there's no problem."

"*That* could be a problem, too."

"Honestly!"

He patted her cheek. "Don't mind me. It's just that I think a lot of both of the boys, especially Garth. I'd hate to see trouble between them."

"If there is, it won't be over me."

"I sure do hope not."

Hallie gave his beard an affectionate pat. "Don't look so solemn. Rory will fall for the next pretty girl he sees, and Garth will go on being Mr. Touch-Me-Not Grouch."

Hallie took her nightclothes and went outside to change and brush her teeth. A half-moon silvered the field and shocked grain into an enchanted world. A drifting cloud glowed spun crystal as it veiled the moon. Before Hallie could take off her apron, someone loomed beside her. She started to scream.

A hand closed over her mouth. "Don't yell," Rory whispered in her ear. "It's only me."

He took his palm away. She relaxed, but only a little. "Why on earth—"

"Shhh. I just want to thank you properly without the whole bunch flapping their big ears our direction."

"All right. You've thanked me. Good night."

He chuckled softly. "You owe me a minute for making such a joke of me and my chocolates. Let's just walk over to that nearest wheat shock." When she hesitated, he added coaxingly, "You wouldn't have to yell to bring the camp. Lifting your voice would do it."

"Snakes—"

"They want out of your way more'n you want out of theirs. Never heard of anyone get bit that wasn't trying to kill the snake or accidentally put a hand or foot on it." Hallie shuddered at the last provision. "Just step hard enough so they'll feel the vibration," Rory persisted. "They'll vamoose."

Agreeing seemed the fastest way to get rid of him. Besides, he had taken her disposal of his expensive chocolates with good grace. Placing her things on the lowest limb of a tree, she moved beside him toward the shock of bundled grain. Tomorrow these shocks would be loaded onto wagons which would be driven to the separator, where the bundles would be pitched onto the feeder.

"Does someone cut the binding twine?" she asked.

"Uh?" Rory blinked before he gave a mock sigh and shook his head. "You're supposed to be noticing how the moonlight shines on my hair, not inspecting the bundles. Before self-feeders were invented, band-cutters snipped the twine and men had to feed each bundle by hand into the cylinder."

"That sounds dangerous."

"It was. But now a revolving knife cuts the twines and a revolving rake combs the bundles apart to feed a nice even flow into the cylinder."

"Does—"

"Tomorrow you can learn more than you really want to know about threshing bundles." Rory took her hands in his and moved directly in front of her. "Hallie, I truly am obliged to you. Cotton could have sliced my throat. I owe you more for that than any box of candy."

"We're even." Uncomfortable with his solemnity, she tried to joke. "You gave Jackie rainbows."

"I'd like to give them to you." His tone roughened. His hands slipped to her wrists in an imprisoning caress. "Rainbows and stars and the moon up there."

"Moonshine for certain, Rory!" He was young and strong and charming. He delighted her eyes and she liked him. A beguiling warmth spread from his fingers, making her feel strange and lazy. But he wasn't Garth. She tried to slip from his hands. "You've thanked me handsomely. Good night."

Something pushed in between them. Wagging his tail, Laird looked from one to the other for a welcome. Rory dropped Hallie's hands and stepped back. "On the snoop, big brother?" he asked of the man who moved from the shadow of the neighboring shock.

"You never know when some crazy's going to set fire to a field."

Garth's voice was expressionless. "When I hear voices after dark, I'm sure going to have a look. Didn't mean to bust in on anything."

"We were just talking," Hallie said, and then felt like a fool. Why should she feel so guilty? She hadn't done anything. And even if she had, it was none of Garth's business.

"Don't let me interrupt." Garth's soft whistle took the dog away with him. Rory turned. Hallie fled.

VIII

$\mathcal{H}$allie glanced out as a loaded wagon rumbled past and an unloaded one pulled up among the shocks. The driver jumped down, tied his reins to the wagon frame, and helped the field pitchers load with three-tined pitchforks. They tossed the first bundles in at random but, as the rack filled, the men expertly built up the sides with straw ends facing out.

There were six bundle wagons in all. Two flanked the separator, where Garth's crew helped the drivers pitch bundles onto the feeder from wagons that were almost empty. Two loaded wagons waited their turn, and two were being filled.

"What are they doing at that other wagon?" Hallie asked. "Look at that man! He just tossed several bundles on at once!"

"Tryin' for a home run," Shaft snorted. "These young guys like to pretend they're Babe Ruth. One bundle is just a single. Two is second base, and three puts you on third. All well and good so long as they load 'em right. That makes a big difference to the pitchers feeding the separator."

"Six drivers and six field pitchers!" Hallie fluted the crust of a third blackberry pie. "Thank goodness we don't have to feed them!"

"Miz Halstead's got three daughters and a daughter-in-law to help," said Shaft. "The whole outfit's either sons, sons-in-law, or grandsons. Not a sloppy pitcher in the bunch. That's good 'cause Garth gets mad as fire if he has to stay on 'em to feed the bundles headfirst and one at a time so they overlap without bein' on top of each other. If that happens, it can clog the separator, and then Garth remembers quite a lot of language he learned in the army."

Garth hadn't sworn when he found her with Rory two nights ago, but the contempt in his manner stung worse than anything he could have said. Except for unavoidable commonplaces, he hadn't spoken to her since then. In particularly hurt and resentful moments, Hallie thought of quitting but it was never more than a thought. How could she take Jackie away from where he felt needed and liked, away from Shaft and Laird and Smoky? He had a new hero in Luke, who was teaching him birdcalls and animal tracks.

No, she would endure whatever Garth did short of firing her—and it wasn't just for her brother's sake. She didn't even want to think of the end of the season, when the crew would split up and she would have to find a new job.

Since the separator didn't have to be moved through rows of stacks, it was moved only once, when the wind changed and blasted chaff and grain into the threshers' faces. This was not helped much by the bandannas many of them wore tied beneath their eyes like bank robbers, so the set was moved and another mountain of straw started.

"We'll finish in time to move on to the Thomases tonight," Garth said at afternoon lunch. He looked past Hallie as if she weren't there, and she felt like sloshing hot coffee on his shins. "That make a problem for you with supper, Shaft?"

Shaft grinned. "Nope. I been keepin' an eye on the shocks and figgered we'd better plan on a move. Hallie's baked two cherry cobblers. There's beans left from lunch, and we'll make potato salad and slaw and slice a ham."

"I can always count on you." Garth flicked Hallie a glance that dismissed her as being definitely un-countable on. He reached for another butterscotch bar. "These sure are good."

"Hallie made 'em."

"Oh." Garth changed his reach into an elaborate yawn and stretch and got to his feet. Hallie longed to not only douse him with coffee, but swing the whole heavy enamel pot at him. She hurried to the cookshack and was banging around so wrathfully when Shaft joined her that he stared at her for a second before his eyes glinted.

"You have a dustup with Garth?"

"How can you have a dustup with someone who pretends you don't exist?"

"He seems to be pretendin' a little more since Sunday night."

"He's looking for excuses to think ill of me, Shaft!" Once Hallie started, it was a relief to pour out what had happened. "So, between Rory's flirting and Garth's suspicions, I can't do anything right!" she concluded.

"Which wouldn't matter if you didn't kind of like Garth, the big ign'rant lummox!" Shaft patted her shoulder. "The Thomases have a pretty brown-eyed daughter Rory took to a dance last year. Maybe he'll shine up to her again. That'd smooth Garth's feathers."

Sally Thomas's oval face was framed piquantly by short, curly hair, and she did glance at Rory from beneath long, dark lashes when she brought the milk, butter, cottage cheese, and eggs Shaft had asked to buy. She arrived after supper when Rory was drying dishes for Hallie.

"Sally, you just get prettier every time I see you," Rory said and smiled, but he didn't follow her out to the Thomas flivver. The next evening, her kid brother brought the dairy products.

"You got Sally riled at you, boy," Shaft teased Rory.

"She's too nice to kid along."

Shaft's jaw dropped. "Since when did you do anything but kid?"

"Since now." Rory's gaze rested on Hallie. She was glad that her face was so flushed from heat that her deep, slow blush was disguised.

Should she tell him straight out that she could never be serious about him? It might just make him more determined. Apparently Rory was famous for his butterfly heart, flitting from bloom to bloom. If she gave him absolutely no encouragement, Rory would tire of the siege. He was a boy, and when she fell in love, she wanted it to be with a man.

The Thomas farm was small, and the threshing was finished by mid-morning of the third day. Hallie, Shaft, and Jackie spread lunch under the locust trees. Jackie fanned away flies and ants, and the men ate on the run as they prepared to move on. Shaft and Hallie fastened down everything they could and were taking down the ropes at the four corners when a long yellow runabout sped up and stopped beside Garth, who was eating a sandwich while he made notes in his settlement book. That was where he recorded the details of each job: number of bushels threshed, expenses, the outfit's share, and how to divide it among the crew.

Hallie had to look twice to be sure it was Sophie Brockett in the passenger seat of the Pierce-Arrow. Bobbed hair peroxided almost white, slanted over one eye. Her pouting lips were red. Perhaps that gave them their swollen look. Rouge, powder, purple eye color— Hallie wished for the Brocketts' sake that Sophie had gone farther from home to imitate a flapper. She lit a cigarette and blew a stream of smoke straight at Garth.

Quentin Raford leaned back from the wheel. He didn't speak to Hallie, but his gaze moved slowly, appraisingly, over her, his eyes more yellow than green in the brilliant light. In spite of the heat, Hallie went cold inside. His eyes dwelled on her mouth, her pulsing throat. He smiled—just slightly—and turned to Garth.

"Thought I'd save you a trip, MacLeod. Jenkins won't be needing you."

Garth quit writing. Hallie could see the muscles ridge like steel in the back of his neck. "How would you know that?"

"Because my crew and brand-new gasoline tractor are already threshing for him."

As motionless as if he were paralyzed, Garth didn't speak for a moment. He closed his record book, put it in his shirt pocket, and stood up. "Pete Jenkins has always been satisfied with my work. But your bank holds the mortgage on his farm."

Raford nodded. "I don't hold a mortgage on Jonas MacAfee, but I offered to thresh for three cents a bushel less than your price."

"Well, that must have tickled Jonas. He's tighter than bark on a tree. You'll lose money, but I reckon you don't care."

"Oh, I'll raise prices—after I've run you out of business." Raford smiled. "There's one alternative: sell your outfit to me."

Garth smiled, too. "Reckon I can still break even."

"Can you?" Raford produced a small notepad and read off names. "Milt Jones, Stanley Ridges, George Cranston, Matt Bloodhart, Shelby Hughes. They've agreed to hire my outfit."

Garth controlled a wince at the first name. He listened to the rest with a face hard as granite. "There's still Mike Donnelly and Harry Crutchfield. Their farms aren't mortgaged."

"They soon will be if they turn down good business deals," shrugged Raford.

"Jim"—Garth, turned to Wyatt—"if you're packed up, will you take your bunch ahead to Donnellys? Tell them we'll be there in time to thresh at least one set before dark."

Raford frowned. "Sell your outfit and land to me and you can still live on the place and run your separator, have your brother on the engine. You can keep your crew. Why be a mule?"

"Must be I don't want to work for you. And I've told you before. I won't sell you my land."

Reddening to the edges of his thick dark gray hair, Raford said, "You're threshing two farmers instead of eleven in fields ten miles apart."

"They stuck by me. I'd thresh them if they lived at opposite ends of the county."

"With that kind of crazy thinking, it's a wonder you've lasted as long as you have."

"I like to live *with* as well as *on* what I do. Maybe you've got time to chat, Raford, but we've got to move along." He strode toward the machinery.

Raford swept a stripping glance over Hallie. "If you ever get tired of sweaty threshermen and hot stoves, come and see me."

The yellow runabout lurched in a circle, narrowly missing Luke Rogers, who was hurrying to Jim Wyatt's flivver. Meg, who had heard the exchange between Raford and her father, cupped her hands and yelled, "Blow a tire, you lousy skunk! Get stuck so deep in the sand you never can dig out!"

"Meg," said Shaft, "your dad don't want you screechin' names like that. Anyhow, it don't help."

"It helps me feel better!" Then Meg noticed that Luke was staring at her in amazed disapproval. She gulped and colored. "All the same," she muttered, "Raford is a lousy skunk."

"And an underhanded overbearing weaselly snake," Shaft agreed. "Now let's fold up these steps. Here comes the engine!"

*B*rawny redheaded Mike Donnelly, tagged by two small red-haired daughters, showed Rory where he wanted his straw stack. The cookshack had the luxury of three cottonwoods for shade. "Left 'em so the colleens would have a nice place to play," said Mike. He grinned at Jackie. "I'll hang up another old tire for you so you can all swing at the same time. Is it okay with you, Mr. Hurok, if Bridget and Kathleen stay and play for a while?"

"Sure, long as they don't get underfoot. Reckon Miz Donnelly has some extra milk and eggs?"

"All you want. And she just churned butter. We'll throw in watermelon, roasting ears, and green beans, if you'd like some."

"Would we!" Shaft told the young farmer what was needed and Donnelly left with a caution to his girls to keep out of the way.

Jackie was older than Bridget, younger than Kathleen. In short order, Kathleen was scratching the outline of a house in the earth near one tree while Jackie and Bridget dragged up fallen limbs and pieces of old bark for the walls. There was still plenty of kindling for the engine, which would please both Rory and Baldy. Laird stretched out near the "house" as if on guard, little knowing that he was now a mighty lion like the one the girls had seen at a circus in Kansas City when they went there to visit their grandmother.

As soon as the shack was in working order, Shaft asked Hallie to make some pies while he peeled potatoes. "Guess I'll make salmon loaf for a change," he said. "Now, if Miz Donnelly brings them good fresh vegetables, we'll be all set."

Mary Donnelly brought all her husband had promised and a basket of red tomatoes, ripe to bursting, and another of green onions. "There's not much lettuce," she apologized. "But if you wilt it with bacon grease and vinegar and serve it with scrambled eggs, there should be a bite for everyone."

"Wilted lettuce!" Shaft heaved a happy sigh. "My absolute top-notch all-time favorite! Though roastin' ears are a close second. Good gracious, Miz Donnelly! You can't give us all this stuff for free!"

"It'd go to the hogs otherwise. I've canned enough corn and beans to last us three years." Mary Donnelly was perhaps five or six years older than Hallie, pleasingly rounded, a dusting of freckles across her tilted nose. Her hair, more richly gold than red, was pinned up in a knot with many escaped ringlets. Her clear gray eyes met Hallie's. "Anyway, Mr. Hurok, we owe Garth MacLeod a lot. When the hail ruined our wheat three years ago, we got in debt so deep we thought we'd lose the place, but Garth loaned us seed wheat, and for two years he and Rory just charged us pitchers' wages—two dollars a day—instead of what the six dollars engineers and separator men get."

"Garth sure appreciates your staying with him," Shaft said.

Her eyes flashed. "You can't blame the ones with mortgages at Mr. Raford's bank. But I'm plumb ashamed of Jonas MacAfee, who's got more money than he'll ever use, and Matt Bloodhart and Shelby Hughes. They know Garth charges a fair price. What did he do to Raford, anyway?"

"He wouldn't thresh him first."

Mary Donnelly gasped. "So Garth loses by playing fair—by pro-tecting the turns of that ungrateful bunch! Serve them right if Garth *had* threshed Raford first and they got rained or hailed out!" She brooded. "Would it do any good if Mike went to talk to them? I'll bet Raford never said how come he was going into business."

"Like you said, the ones with a mortgage at the Hollister bank are in no spot to argue. The ones who switched for three cents a bushel would say Garth's a fool and deserves to lose his outfit."

"Will he?" The pretty young woman looked so distressed that Shaft forced cheer into his voice.

"The farther we get from Hollister, the less likely Raford's bank is to hold mortgages. If Raford does try to cut in on Garth's northern loop, I'd bet most of the folks will stick with the man they know has always done a good job and treated them square. 'Course, farmers are scared of rain and hail. If Raford's gang beat us to a farm and the weather looked bad, no one could blame that farmer much if he told Raford's crew to start threshin'."

"It's not right!"

"No, but your heart's right, Miz Donnelly. That'll mean a lot to Garth. And we'll sure enjoy the melon and roastin' ears and all."

The feast did raise the men's spirits in spite of the threat of clearing considerably less money than they'd hoped for. Ears of tender, juicy, golden corn dripping with fresh butter, crunchy green beans flavored with dill, sliced tomatoes on a platter with green onions. Cooled in a tub of water, the crisp red melon hunks seemed to evaporate. No sliver of Hallie's pie ever escaped, but Laird and Smoky got dabs of mashed potatoes and salmon loaf that night, the first time Hallie had seen leftovers.

Usually the men made for bed soon after supper; but instead of threshing ten hours today, they'd worked about six, and so they lingered. Perhaps, too, they unconsciously wanted to find out more about the two new hands, Lefty Halstead and Luke Rogers. While pitching grain into the feeder, a man had to shout to be heard. Conversation had to wait till appetites were sated at mealtime, and by then it was generally time to go back to work or hunt the coolest place to sleep.

"If I can get enough roastin' ears and butter, you're purely welcome to everything else—exceptin' Miss Hallie's pies, of course," Rusty said. "Remember 'meatless days' durin' the war? I was in the army, so it didn't bother me—all the grub was bad."

"Whooee, wasn't that a mess!" Shaft caressed Smoky, who had just draped herself from shoulder to shoulder. "Hoover was in charge of food in 1918, and he got the bright idea of two wheatless days a week, two porkless, and one meatless. On top of that, there was one wheatless and one meatless meal each day. And then the dratted influenza busted out!"

"Wheatless, meatless!" Rory whooped. "It sounds like a crazy song!"

"Yes, and then Congress gave us Daylight Saving Time,' Baldy grumbled. "As if humans can add one minute to the sun's shining!"

"It's like Will Rogers says; 'I don't make jokes, I just watch the government and report it,' " said Rusty.

"Will didn't like Hollywood." Luke spoke with the privilege of a relative, however distant. "He spent a year out there but now he's back twirlin' ropes at the Ziegfeld Follies."

"Funny place for an Oklahoma Indian cowboy," Lefty Halstead said.

"Oh, Will didn't have to be a cowboy," Luke explained. "His folks own a big ranch. He *liked* roping and riding."

"If he ever runs for president, I'll vote for him," Jim Wyatt said. "He's got a lot more sense than any politician up in Washington."

"Yeah, and he'd get every veteran's vote," Rusty said. "Did you see what he wrote about this measly bonus ole Careful Cal vetoed in May?"

Rich Mondell grinned. "Congress overrode him. Guess they heard from enough voters who thought it was fair to try to make up a little for the difference between what soldiers were paid and civilian wages during the war. A dollar twenty-five a day for overseas duty and a dollar for stateside service isn't a lot, but it helps."

From what Shaft and the men themselves said, Hallie knew that the young professor, like Jim and Rusty, had been in the war, though he had been mustered out as a captain while Jim and Rusty were sergeants. They were all infantry and had all shot and been shot at. None of them, according to Henry, had ever said a derogatory word about his refusal to put on the uniform they had volunteered to wear.

"Will compared the dollar twenty-five a day soldiers got with the twelve-fifty minimum shipyard workers pulled down," Jim said. When he laughed, the burned side of his face didn't move with the other half. Ironic that he'd gone through the bitter fighting along the Marne, including Chateau Thierry, without a scratch but had been almost killed on his own steam engine. "Will said statistics prove that the Germans fired an average of twenty-five bullets a day at each soldier, the same average number of nails a worker hammered. Will reckoned the pay of five cents per bullet was pretty stingy compared to fifty cents per nail."

"I liked his answer to those who claimed they didn't want to insult the soldiers' 'noble patriotism,' or that most of the men didn't want the bonus," Garth put in. "He said pay it to everybody, and let those that didn't want it put it in a fund for the disabled."

" 'Course they're not goin' to pay that bonus all at once," Rusty said. "Reckon they don't want us to spend it all in one place. The bonuses will be twenty-year endowment policies."

"But you can borrow up to a quarter of the face value from the government," Jim said. "I'm going to do that and put it towards my new engine."

"Another thing Will's right about," Buford said. "There shouldn't be any tax-exempt securities that rich people can use to dodge taxes—and that's what'll send the country to the poorhouse, not soldiers' bonuses."

"Quent Raford didn't go to war," Baldy said. "And the guy who runs the Hollister pool hall told me he'd heard Raford brag about not paying a dime of income tax for years."

"You can bet his threshing business is going to lose money this year," predicted Jim. "He undercuts Garth, tries to put him out of business, and gets a break on taxes for his dirty tricks."

As Rory went out to dump the dishwater, Shaft got to his feet, a slumberous Jackie cradled in his arms next to the little gray cat. "Bedtime, fellas! Let's not get into politics and dirty tricks, or we'll be up all night."

Rory lingered. "If you don't practice, Miss Hallie, you'll forget what you've learned about the engine. If we have a good chance tomorrow, you ought to learn to belt up."

"Oh, I don't—"

Garth said from the porch, "If she messes up that belt I spent hours lacing together, you can fix it, Rory."

Hallie's cheeks blazed. "If Shaft can spare me when it's time to move sets, I'll certainly come!"

"Great." Rory brushed her cheek with long brown fingers. Under his breath he said, "Good night, sweetheart." He was out the door swiftly.

"I saw quite a bit of gray smoke this evening," came Garth's voice. "So?"

"Generally means there's holes in your fire."

"I kept the steam up, didn't I?"

"Yes, but that fire needs to burn even from one end of the grate to the other. A hole lets a blast of cold air into the firebox. And it looks like you have a leaky flue."

"I'll fix it in the morning, for Pete's sake!" Rory's voice rose. "Say, how would you like it if I went poking around your damned old separator for any piddling little thing that wasn't quite right?"

"If you can find anything, I'd sure like to know it."

"Oh, hell, Garth! You're turning into a regular old grouch!"

"This isn't a game, Rory. Carelessness can get you—and the whole crew—blown sky-high. And everything I own is tied up in these machines. You bet I'm a grouch."

Rory didn't answer for a minute. When he did, his voice was so low that Hallie could scarcely hear. "Know what I think? That I wouldn't have caught a sermon about smoke or leaky flues if I hadn't asked Hallie to belt up tomorrow."

They moved down the steps. Hallie heard the crunch of stubble. If Garth made any answer, it was too soft to hear. She looked anxiously at Shaft.

He hunched a shoulder. "Reckon they're both right. And both wrong, too. Shall we wake your brother up or just undress him and put him to bed?"

$\mathcal{H}$allie's trial came after morning lunch. "Better get into your overalls," Shaft warned as they made sandwiches. He squinted through the window. "They've worked those stacks right down to the ground and fed in the grain that dropped on the tarp they keep spread in front of the separator. Hey, come look at this! Luke's showing off a little."

"Good grief!" Hallie stared fearfully at the lithe young man who was running toward the engine with his right arm wrapped around the moving belt. He was tugging at the belt, which, thank goodness, worked slowly. "Why doesn't Garth stop him?"

"Oh, it's a good enough way of getting the belt off the flywheel and it's kind of fun—for them as thinks it is. There! Belt dropped on his head. Generally does."

Hallie watched with misgiving as two men carried the belt to the belt reel in front of the separator. Surely Rory wouldn't expect her to fit that long, heavy weight of leather on the big flywheel! But somehow, whatever was expected, she would have to do it. To show Garth.

And Meg as well. Hallie was convinced that wooing Meg would earn only contempt. If she could win the girl's respect, liking might follow. Even if it didn't, there had to be respect. Since Meg took Jackie swimming, she had become his "hero," special because she was nearer to his age than the grown-ups and yet did a grown-up job. After all, he didn't know Hallie very well, and she was too busy to spend any real time with him except on Sundays. If he spent most of that day with Meg—

A twisting pang tightened Hallie's insides. It would only be natural if Jackie came to worship Meg, who could be both playmate and protector. Without trying, just by her attitude, Meg could influence Jackie against his sister.

It's not fair, Hallie thought again. Raford and probably Garth and who knows who else think Jackie's mine. It's not his fault. Not his fault I have to make us a living and can't pay lots of attention to him. But it hurts for him to think Meg's wonderful when she's such a nasty little beast to me.

So drive the engine. Make him think you're wonderful, too.

As soon as lunch was over, Rory opened the dampers and shoveled in an even layer of coal. The steam was quickly up to operating pressure. "It's all yours!" Rory shouted. "Steer over in front of the separator, and then haul it between the next stacks."

"There isn't room!" The giant stacks loomed sixteen feet high, fifty feet long, and twenty feet wide. The passage between these straw mountains was no more than eight feet, and the engine measured nine and a half feet from one huge front wheel to the other.

"Just keep to the middle. Of course you'll close the ash pan dampers while steering through the stacks. Don't want any sparks landing in the wheat."

"Oh, heavens, no!" Hallie spoke through her teeth. "Let's not do anything dangerous—just bring a white-hot fire through two straw stacks!"

"I've seen some fires, but none that started that way," Rory allowed cheerfully. "Hey, that's great! You're right in line with the separator."

Garth and Baldy swiftly hooked the separator to the engine. All the crew was watching, but Garth's and Meg's intent faces blurred the others. "Check that water glass," cautioned Rory.

Hallie did and saw the level showed that the water was only an inch above the crown sheet. Calling on her memory, she opened the steam valve on the injector and throttled so that water wouldn't go out the overflow. When the water glass showed almost half full, she shut off the injector.

As the engine crept toward the stacks, sweat dripped from her eyebrows and beaded on her chin. Under the slat bonnet, her hair felt plastered to her scalp. Her gloved hands fumbled as she closed the ash-pan dampers on the firebox. She gritted her teeth, fought the urge to duck and close her eyes, and sent the huge lugged wheels ramming between the stacks.

The wheels knocked loose masses of straw. Some fell to the ground, but other clumps came within inches of the firebox. It seemed an eternity before the feeder was even with the end of the stacks and Garth signaled for her to stop.

"Wasn't that fun?" Rory yelled.

Hallie couldn't answer. She hadn't knocked down the stacks or started a blaze, but only half the job of making a set was done. Steering away from the unhitched separator, she circled back to face it, swung too wide, and had to reverse and cut in sharper.

On the second try, she lined the engine up with the already leveled separator. Jim spread a tarp under the cylinder to catch and save the shattered grain. Henry and Rich pulled the extension feeder into place and got it ready. Rusty and Luke stretched the belt from the drive pulley of the separator, and Garth smeared it with his own belt dressing; pine tar mixed with linseed oil.

"Let's belt up," Rory called.

Hallie sent the engine crawling toward the belt as Rusty and Luke came forward. Rory tossed down the chocking block and Baldy wedged it in front of the drive wheel to keep the engine from moving forward.

"Get out there on the drive wheel," Rory directed. "Take hold of the outside of the belt with your right hand. Hang onto the brace support of the cab with your left hand and put the belt in place on the flywheel. Good! Now reverse real slow and easy so the belt will wrap itself around the wheel."

Hallie obeyed. Would the belt slip? Would it break? To her boundless relief, the canvas belt, guided by Luke and Rusty, tightened.

"Perfect! Stop!" Rory knew how nervous she had been. His eyes were admiring. "You lined the flywheel straight as could be with the separator pulley. Not only are you the prettiest engineer from Canada to Texas, you can be a darned good one!"

He gave her a hand down as Baldy blocked an engine wheel. The crew cheered lustily. Except for Garth and Meg. Garth raised the blower tube and quickly turned two crank wheels to swing it to the rear of the engine. The pitchers selected their pitchforks—each had a favorite to use through the season—and made running jumps at the stacks, using pitchforks to work their way up. Luke bounded up and stretched down his pitchfork handle to Rusty. The heaviest, oldest man on the crew, Rusty was a powerhouse on top of the stack, but it wasn't easy for him to get there.

Rory gave two long toots and pulled back on the throttle. The first grain spikes landed on the feeder. Chaff flew from the cylinder. Straw belched from the blower to begin a new mountain. Grain poured into the wagon Mike Donnelly would drive to his granary. Hallie walked to the shack, stripping off her gloves.

She had done it! Hauled the separator between the stacks, lined the engine up with the separator, and actually helped belt up! Of course she didn't know how to fire the engine or clean the flues or keep the steam at the right pressure. There was much she didn't know and would probably never learn.

But she *could* drive the engine; she *could* make a set. She was surprised at herself, and proud, no matter what Garth thought. Bridget and Kathleen, equipped with apples and oatmeal cookies, had already come to play with Jackie.

Blue eyes admiring, Kathleen said, "Mama drives the grain wagon. But she can't drive a steam engine. I don't even think my daddy can."

"They could if they needed to," Hallie said, but her heart swelled at the wondering pride in Jackie's face.

"You helped put on that big old long belt, Hallie! You drove the engine! Shaft says the engine man is the boss of the outfit!"

She gave him a hug. "I'm not the engineer, honey. And I'm sure not the boss!"

"Can I drive the engine when I get big?"

"I don't know about this engine but if you want to be an engineer, there's nothing to stop you."

"I'm going to have my own engine. And a separator! And Shaft will cook for us! He said he would."

"Well, then, all you have to do is grow up." Hallie took off her overalls and started cleaning husks and silk off the corn Mike Donnelly had dropped off that morning.

"Hallie, you done real good," Shaft said, putting six loaves of bread in the oven.

"Garth thinks it's all foolishness."

"Then he's a fool! When you stop to think about it, outside of driving the water or coal wagons, running the engine is the one threshing job a boy or woman can do. It takes a lot of strength to pitch spikes or bundles. I won't say a woman couldn't learn how to run the separator, but it's a job for an expert. Get someone on the separator who doesn't know what they're doing, and you wind up with grain in the straw stack. If Rory got hurt or sick, it could come in real handy for you to drive and help make a set." Shaft grinned at her. "So you just keep practicin'. One of these days old Garth may bless his stars you did."

"I hope so," Hallie said. "I don't want Rory to get sick, but I certainly hope his brother has to eat a good big wedge of humble pie."

"I guarantee he will. Later or sooner. Say, Hallie, do you know how to make corn fritters? They'd sure taste good with ham."

IX

$\mathcal{J}$ackie patted his tire swing good-
bye and let Shaft boost him up on the tank wagon. Rusty had yielded
his place in Jim's flivver to Hallie, so he climbed onto the separator
with Garth. Rory gave the two short and two long whistles that signaled they were moving on.

The Donnellys waved farewell. "See you next year!" Mike called.
Bridget and Kathleen echoed, "Next year! Next year, Jackie!"

"Next year!" he shouted back.

The procession rumbled away. The Model Ts took the lead. The
threshing had finished before dinner, and it was now early afternoon.
"It'll take the outfit a couple of hours to get to Crutchfield's," Jim
said. "But we should thresh a set before supper." He grinned at Hallie,
and she hoped any woman he might care for would look at his warm
hazel eyes and not care about the stiff white scars. "Did I see Miz
Donnelly give you some roasting ears?"

"And green beans, radishes, and green onions," Hallie said. "She
was afraid watermelons would jar to pieces but she packed half a dozen
cantaloupes in wadded-up newspapers."

"They are very kind people," Henry said.

Jim nodded. "I sure hope they never need a loan from the Hollister
bank."

"Or any bank," said Hallie. She and Mary had both been too busy

119

to visit but she had liked Mary immensely and enjoyed the little girls. Jackie would miss them, but already he was counting on seeing them next year.

Would he? Would Garth manage to survive Raford's underhanded attack? And if he did, would he hire Hallie again? For that matter, what was she going to do that winter? She cringed inwardly at the thought of how her small brother would miss Shaft and Smoky and Laird and the crew. And so would she.

          *F*resh vegetables, milk, and eggs were not to be had at the Crutchfields. Mrs. Crutchfield was an invalid, and the young woman who took care of her and the housework had no time for gardens, chickens, and cows. Harry Crutchfield, a gaunt, graying man with a surprisingly warm smile, drove one grain wagon, his hired man the other.

"Must be hard for Mr. Crutchfield to keep going," Shaft mused one morning as he and Hallie prepared dinner. "Only child they have is a daughter who married and moved to Oregon. There's no one to take over the farm and care about it the way he has. But I reckon he keeps planting and hoping and harvesting 'cause that's what he's always done."

When Sunday came at the Crutchfields, the threshers got their steam bath as the boiler drained. They had to do their own laundry here, so there was much shaving of bars of Ivory and plunging up and down of the stompers till the fence was spread with overalls, khakis, socks, bandannas, and BVDs covered modestly by shirts.

While they waited their turn at tub and stomper, the men shaved or patronized Shaft, who snipped and clipped his best for the men who either weren't going to town or were saving their money, like Rusty and Henry. After Jackie, wide-eyed, had watched all the men shave, Meg took him and Laird to splash in the creek that curved around the field. As water monkey, it was part of her job to know where the cleanest water was. If there was a swimming hole, she found it, too.

They were now closer to Blackwater than Hollister, so that was the day's destination for most of the crew. Luke gazed wistfully as the men scrambled into the Model Ts but shook his head when invited by both Buford and Jim.

"Rusty is writing to my sister, and I had better do that, too, so she can read it to our mother."

The older, heavier man rested a hand on his slim young brother-in-law's shoulder. "Luke's never been away from home before. His mama wouldn't turn him loose till he promised to write every week. And, as far as I'm concerned, the best way to keep my money saved for that team of good mules I need is not to go to town."

" 'When I was single, my pockets did jingle. . . ,' " Rory caroled.

"They don't jingle long," Rusty retorted. "If you bachelor boys can't get rid of your money in town, you lose it shootin' craps or playin' cards."

"To each his own," said Baldy, piling in Buford's backseat. The towngoers departed, and quiet reigned except for the distant whining creak of the windmill. Henry, Luke, and Rusty spread out at the table to wrestle with their letters.

Always and inevitably, Garth prowled around the separator with tools and oilcan. It didn't seem to Hallie that she would ever get to know *him* better on Sunday. Or anytime. She pounded her clothes and Jackie's with the stomper, wrung them, rinsed them, wrung them again, and hung them on the fence. Garth certainly didn't want to know her any better than he had to.

This bitter reflection couldn't spoil the pleasure of shampooing dust, sweat, and chaff out of her hair and bathing in sun-warmed water. Shaft's music, dreamy and spirited by turns, floated out of the shack. Hallie swayed to it as she toweled her hair. She dressed in clean clothes, brushed out her hair, and let it hang loose to dry.

The steps were partly shaded by a cottonwood. She settled there with her mending. Jackie had knocked the knees out of his overalls and lost buttons off his shirts. She had rips in two aprons and a dress and a small tear in her nightgown.

Behind her, the porch creaked. Luke's green eyes had a soft glow. His skin was really no darker than that of the sunburned men but his was smooth and even, with no blotches and peeling or that several inches of white forehead concealed by a hat.

"Your hair shines like a blackbird's wing, Miss Hallie."

"Why, thank you, Luke. That sounds like poetry." He truly was a beautiful boy. It pleased Hallie's eyes to look at him. Boy? He must be at least her age or older. But somehow, disagreeable as he could be, Garth had become her measure of a man. "Have you finished your letter already?"

His teeth flashed as he nodded toward the men hunched over the table, making much harder work of their pencils than ever they did of pitchforks. "I only needed to tell Mother I'm well and like the crew. Rusty has to tell my sister about his whole week and how much he misses her and the kids. And I never wrote to a sweetheart like Henry does, but that must take a lot of pretty words."

Hallie laughed. "You must be right. Henry spends hours on letters to his Anna, but it only takes him a few minutes to scratch a postcard to his parents."

The young man hesitated a moment. "Meg asked me to come swimming when my letter was done. Do you think I'm too old to swim with the kids?"

"Of course not. What's age got to do with cooling off on a hot day?"

He nudged his toe against the bottom of the porch railing. With a gulp of breath, he blurted, "Would Mr. MacLeod mind?"

"Garth? Why should he?"

Luke's face reddened. "I'm Cherokee. With some Scotch."

Hallie blushed, too, that anyone as graceful, hardworking, and courteous as Luke should have to ask such a question. "I know Garth won't allow any Ku Klux Klan sort of talk. The only man who seemed to have those kind of ideas got himself fired the day you hired on." Hallie looked up into the dark-lashed wide green eyes. "Garth brings his daughter threshing so he must think it's all right for her to be around the men he hires."

"But—swimming? Just me and the kids?"

"It's not far from the shack. I can hear them laughing. But some fathers wouldn't want *any* young man splashing around in the creek with a twelve-year-old daughter."

Luke's eyes went wider. "Oh, I wouldn't— She's just a kid!"

"Don't tell her so," Hallie advised. "Just to feel sure about it, why don't you ask Garth?"

Luke gasped. "I—I'm scared to!"

"Mmm." Hallie thought a moment. "Go tell him the cook—you don't have to say which one—wants to know if he'd rather have raspberry buckle or rice pudding for dessert tonight."

"But Sunday is your day off."

"Shaft and I are here." Hallie shrugged. "We don't mind setting out cold food and leftovers for supper or making an easy dessert. So find out what His Lordship favors. Then just say Meg asked you to swim, and you'd like to if it's all right with him."

Luke considered. "That's good. I can ask without making a big thing of it." He watched Hallie for a moment. "I—I wish you could swim, too."

You're just a kid. That thought was exactly what he had said about Meg. Could Garth possibly be thinking that she—Hallie—was too young for him? She doubted that had much to do with his coldness. She was female, therefore not to be trusted—even if she spent part of her free day making his choice of rice pudding or raspberry buckle.

Smiling up at Luke, she said, "There'd be so many of us no one could swim. Go along and enjoy yourself."

"If Mr. MacLeod says yes." Luke was still apprehensive.

"If he says no, it won't be because you're Cherokee," Hallie said briskly. "I'm sure it's easier preached than practiced, Luke, but I hope you'll try not to think that every turndown you get is because you're Indian."

"Lots of them are."

"Probably, and that's not right. But isn't your shirttail cousin, Will, the best-known, best-liked man in the whole country?"

"Sure. All the same, Miss Hallie, did you know it was only this June that all American Indians were granted full citizenship?"

"What?"

"Some tribes had held citizenship a long time, like the Wyandots and Kickapoos. The Indians in Indian Territory became citizens in 1901. But, till just a little over a month ago, all the others weren't."

Hallie tried to banter. "Well, Luke, women couldn't vote and therefore weren't full citizens till the Nineteenth Amendment was ratified in 1920—and even then, the women who'd worked so hard for the vote weren't allowed to witness the signing." Mrs. Mac-

Reynolds had been so indignant about the slight that poor Mr. Mac-Reynolds had apologized for all mankind.

Luke's smile was brief, but his sigh was long. "There are a sight more women than Indians, Miss Hallie. Now you have the vote, you should be able to change things."

"We can't change human nature." Hallie thought of Raford and Cotton, of an eighteen-year-old Henry Lowen imprisoned for his faith. "But we can work for what's fair. You'd better hurry, Luke, or you'll be too late to swim."

Returning from Garth, Luke said with happy eyes, "Mr. MacLeod says he'd appreciate my making sure the kids don't drown. And please, he'd like the buckle for supper." Luke frowned. "What *is* a buckle, Miss Hallie?"

"It's sort of a fruit pudding pie," she reassured him. "You'll like it."

He smiled and hurried toward the creek. Hallie began to plait her hair. How she wished that Garth would say it shone like a blackbird's wing—even a crow's! But he would only say she should braid it before it blew full of tangles.

Even braided, it got full of dust and chaff. If it were short— Well, why not? If Garth liked her hair long, she'd have endured it; but he clearly thought it a nuisance, to be pinned up as soon as possible.

She had never had it cut, even though Mrs. MacReynolds thought she'd look nice with a bob. For a moment, Hallie wavered. Then she thought of how much cooler she'd be, how much lighter and better her head would feel without the weight of the braids and tightness of pins. Before she could change her mind, she jumped up and went to the door.

"Shaft?" she called softly. "Your music's so beautiful I hate to interrupt—that was Dvořák, wasn't it? But I wonder if you could cut my hair."

The tune stopped with a discordant crash. Shaft got up so quickly that Smoky almost fell from beneath his beard. Judging by Shaft's expletives, the kitten saved herself by sinking in her claws. Soothing and smoothing the little gray cat, in spite of his own scratches, Shaft tucked Smoky under his arm and stared at Hallie, shaggy eyebrows drawn together above his long, crooked nose. "Did I hear right? You want me to cut your hair?"

"Yes, please." He looked as if she were urging murder, so Hallie said defensively, "It's so hot, Shaft! And I can't keep it clean. If my hair were short, I could wash it every day or two."

"Yes, honey, but your hair's plumb beautiful!"

All the wrong men thought so. "If you won't cut it, I will."

"Lordy-Lord!" Shaft appealed, as if a higher power might intervene. When it didn't, he sighed. "All right, if you're bound 'n' determined. But that hair took a long time to grow, and once it's whacked off, you can't put it back. Sure you wouldn't like me to just thin it some?"

"I'm sure I want a bob."

Shaft put down his fiddle. "It's your scalp. But let's spread a tarp so you can save the hair. You could make a coil or something to pin on when you get sick of your nice cool bob that looks like every other youngish woman's."

Hallie clenched her fists to keep from wincing when the first long, shining locks fell to the tarp; but as Shaft worked, squinting over each intended cut of the scissors, her head began to feel refreshingly light and free. She shut her eyes, enjoying the deft, gentle touch of Shaft's fingers. Now Garth MacLeod couldn't growl at her to pin her hair up out of the way.

"What in the world are you doing?" His voice made her straighten so abruptly that the scissors snipped dangerously close to an ear. "Maybe *she* doesn't know any better, Shaft," Garth seethed. "But I'd expect you to—"

"Expect him to what?" Temper rising, she stared into wrathful gray eyes. "You should approve! You didn't like the wind to blow my hair, remember?"

He let out an exasperated breath. "You had wonderful hair!"

"That isn't what you said!"

"Now you'll look like any city girl. I suppose the next thing will be to smoke, paint, and roll your stockings below your knees!"

"If I want to do any or all of those things, Garth MacLeod, it's none of your business!"

"Roll one cigarette, and you're fired!"

"Of all the nerve! I've never wanted to smoke, but you may just start me!"

"Children, children!" Shaft begged. "Boss, you're way out of line. Hallie's the best help I've ever had. Fire her and I go, too."

Hallie caught his hand. "Shaft—"

"Hell's bells!" Garth erupted. "Pluck out your eyebrows and make them over with a pencil! Wear clothes that make you look like a washboard instead of a woman! Ruin your breath and teeth with nicotine! Frizz the hair you've got left! I was beginning to think you had a little sense but this"—he bent to catch up and flourish a shimmering strand of black—"shows how wrong I was!"

He stalked away. "Damn him!" Hallie choked, blind with furious tears. "Double damn and drat him! First my hair's too long! Now it's too short! And he starts in on me for things I detest as much as he does!"

"Yes." Shaft sounded so happy that Hallie blinked and gaped at him.

"What made Garth act like that?" she appealed.

"My grandmother was a great one to read out of the Bible."

"Was she?" Hallie couldn't see where this was leading.

"Every night, three chapters before anyone could go to bed. Mighty tedious when we were stuck in the 'begats.' But I always liked the battles and angels. 'How art thou fallen from heaven, Lucifer, Son of the Morning.' I could shut my eyes and see Michael and Gabriel with their great wings all bright with power and glory. And somewhere it said that women should not uncover their hair because of fear of the angels—as if an angel could be snared in a girl's long hair, fall crazy in love, and plumb forget his heavenly chores."

"Yes, but—"

"I think Garth was scared of gettin' tangled in your hair."

Hallie's heart leaped, but she scoffed. "He's probably afraid I'll set Meg a bad example, though it's hard to imagine what kind of woman he'd think *is* a good pattern." Hallie looked down at the arm-length tresses and gave a rueful laugh. "It's funny, Shaft. It's lovely not to have all that weight piled up or tugging down. I feel light as a cloud. But I feel sort of naked, too, like a shorn lamb."

"You'll get used to it. And it'll grow out. Look in the mirror and you'll feel better."

Hallie peered into one of the mirrors hung above the washbasins.

Her hair still shone like heavy black silk. Oddly enough, since it wasn't pulled straight back, it framed and softened her angular face and high forehead. "Ohhh! I—I don't look too scalped, do I, Shaft?"

"You look fine. Instead of not seeing anything but that crown of hair, folks have to notice your eyes and mouth."

Would Garth? Both exultant and regretful, as if she were discarding some part of herself, Hallie located an old pillowcase and carefully folded her hair into it. This new, liberated Hallie could entertain scandalous notions; for as carefree shouts came from the swimming hole, she thought, Why can't I get in the water? I can't swim much but how heavenly it would be to cool off when I'm so hot after doing the supper dishes! Just play and splash by myself and not worry about getting my hair wet. I think I will!

$\mathcal{A}$s the men sat down to dinner, Luke eyed her hair sorrowfully but didn't say anything. Henry's broad, open countenance showed distress, as did Lefty Halstead's thin one, but they, too, held their peace. "It must be a sight cooler," Rusty said gamely though he looked dismayed.

"Why should women get headaches to suit men?" Jim Wyatt added.

"Why indeed?" Rich Mondell smiled at her. "But that braided coronet, Hallie, it really was your crown."

"Crowns are pretty uncomfortable in a cookshack," she told the young professor.

"It looks silly to have a flapper bob with plain old dresses," Meg said.

"Your hair's bobbed," Luke pointed out.

Color brightened Meg's tanned face. "That's different. I can't have a lot of hair getting in my eyes while I'm doing a man's job."

"Boy's job," Baldy corrected.

Meg scowled at him. Rory cocked his head and studied Hallie till her cheeks burned. "We-e-ell," he pronounced judiciously, "your eyes look enormous. I never noticed before how thick and long your eyelashes are, and how your eyebrows arch like wings. Say, have you always had that inside-out dimple in your chin? And your mouth—"

"That's enough!" Garth wasn't smiling. "What Miss Hallie decides to do to her hair is none of our concern."

Rich chuckled. "Seems it is, boss. Haven't known this bunch get so excited about anything since Cotton tried to carve us up. Miss Hallie, is there any more of that raspberry buckle?"

*A*t Rory's insistence, Hallie made a set early the next afternoon and got her hair full of prickly, dusty bits of straw. The rest of the day, she thought of the creek, of rinsing the chaff from her itching scalp, of floating on her back, unencumbered by any garment, as she watched the stars and the slender sickle moon.

Tomorrow they'd be moving on. There might not be a creek near their next stop, or if there was, enough water for a swimming hole. Meg said this one had a limestone bottom and was clear, unlike some silty streams.

Rory always dried dishes for Hallie but as soon as he took himself off and Jackie was tucked in, she was slipping down to the creek with a towel and her nightgown.

Perversely, since she had a plan, the crew got into an argument over whether Coolidge should be elected that fall and loitered over their dessert and last cups of coffee. Then Rory hung around till she made Jackie's bed and said pointedly how late it was getting.

At last her little brother was snuggled against Lambie and Shaft was having his bedtime pipe, sitting on his cot by the side of the shack. Hallie blew out the lantern, collected gown and towel, and went down the creaking steps. She waited till she could see a little in the frail moonlight and made her way cautiously along the fence toward the looming cottonwoods that marked the hole.

A great horned owl demanded eerily, *"Hoo-hoo-hoo?"* Had he already feasted on an unwary cottontail or jackrabbit? Hallie hoped he wouldn't get any bluebirds or cardinals, meadowlarks or gorgeous orioles, though of course he had to live, too.

Contrary to the widespread opinion that snakes liked to bask in searing heat, Jackie said Luke had told him they preferred to be cool and were thus abroad more on summer nights than during the day. Luke also said that rattlers sensed the presence of warm bodies through pits beneath their eyes and could feel vibrations from footsteps. Hallie therefore stepped as heavily as she could, alert for any warning sound or movement.

The creek murmured sleepily beneath the few guardian trees left when the field was cleared for planting. Hallie almost tripped over the huge stump Jackie had mentioned. Perching there, she took off her shoes and then her clothing, leaving her shoes on the stump but hanging her other things on a limb where she hoped they'd be less likely to attract and harbor spiders, scorpions, centipedes, and such explorers.

Hurried as her baths behind the cookshack were, she reveled in feeling the sun and breeze on her flesh. Now, as the strangeness wore off, standing naked in the darkness was even more delightful, spreading her arms to the wind that caressed her body. It seemed a little wicked, though. She sent herself into the water, dipping in her toes, standing where it flowed against her knees, then wading till the languid current rose above her breasts at the deepest place.

She had learned to swim—enough not to drown—in a sand pit on the farm of some friends of the MacReynoldses. Trifling as her skill was, she had no fear of water. Leaning back, she raised her feet from the limestone and floated, with water cradling her skull, lapping gently above her ears. No worry about her hair. Toweled, it would dry in a few minutes. She breathed in the rich odor of decaying wood and leaves and the fresher scent of grass and plants. The current moved her downstream slowly. Her heels struck bottom.

Turning over, she lazily dog-paddled back to the deep water and floated again. Pleasant as this was, when her feet grazed stone again, she'd better get out. Four in the morning came early. She never felt awake till she'd had a cup of Shaft's formidable coffee.

Her left heel dragged, then her right. She was coming to her feet in the thigh-deep water when she heard footsteps coming down the bank. She froze, crouching, then breathed again as she told herself it was too dark in the shadow of the trees for anyone to see her. She certainly couldn't make out the intruder.

Luke, taking another swim? The footfalls sounded too heavy for him. It could be any of the crew, even possibly Mr. Crutchfield's hired man who surely knew the place. Hallie wasn't afraid of physical harm. All she had to do was call out and ask the person to withdraw while she dressed and made her retreat.

But that would be embarrassing. Was there any way she could get her clothes and creep away without an encounter?

This hope shattered as Garth's voice came softly through the night. "Who belongs to these clothes?"

X

---

*T*hough she knew he couldn't see her, Hallie plunged into the deepest water. The current seemed to quicken and surge. It was hard to keep her feet planted on the bottom. The pounding of her heart filled her ears.

"You know those are my things, Garth MacLeod!"

"Enjoying your swim?"

"I *was!*"

"Well, go ahead. Enjoy. I'll stay at this end."

"You mean swim *together?*"

"Why not? It's dark as pitch."

"But—" In spite of the cool water lapping around her shoulders, Hallie felt consumed by a fiery blush.

He knew she was naked. How could he suggest they share the swimming hole? Was he that indifferent to her? Well, she wasn't that impervious to him! Even if twenty feet of water flowed between them, she'd be conscious that nothing solid was there—that the water coursing around her had just washed over him.

The splashing he made as he moved into the water almost panicked her. "Wait! I'm getting out!" She swam for the shallows a few strokes away.

"Seems a shame to run away from your first swim this summer."

"How do you know it's my first one?"

"Because I go in every night when we're close to a creek. Must be my selkie blood."

"What's that?"

"A seal. Folks used to believe they could take human form. Hundreds of years ago, a man of my family stole a beautiful selkie maiden's skin." Garth's tone resonated, mingling with the heavy beat of her own heart, traveling through her veins to reverberate in every part of her. "That MacLeod fisherman hid the selkie-lass's garment so she couldn't go back to the sea."

In the darkness, Hallie could almost believe the story. "What happened to the selkie-girl?"

"The MacLeod took her home and wed her. She could never go into the deep sea again. But they say as long as she lived, she would go to the rocks to swim with the seals. They would always come when she sang to them."

"It was cruel of the man to keep her."

"Men in love do cruel things—and women, too." His voice grew brisk. "Anyway, prairie creeks are nothing like the wide bay below my island village, but I still crave the water."

"Doesn't Rory?" Hallie had reached her clothes. She knew Garth couldn't see even her dim outline but she toweled hastily and pulled on her nightgown before she rubbed her hair.

"Rory would rather play cards or roll dice."

The disgust in Garth's words made Hallie ask, "You don't gamble?"

"All the time. Will it rain and slow down the threshing or ruin the grain? Will a farmer wait till I get to him or hire an outfit that turns up quicker? Will I clear enough to make the payments on the machinery?" He gave a rough laugh. "I gamble so much that I'm sure not risking a cent I don't have to. But Rory's a kid. He'll grow out of his crazy notions."

"Like teaching me to handle the engine?"

"That's his craziest stunt yet."

"Shaft doesn't think so! Shaft says it's the only threshing job a woman can do outside of hauling water or fuel."

"He's just trying to make you feel as if it's fine to leave him with your work while you get ready for something that won't happen."

"How do you know it won't?"

"Because I've already got a dandy backup engineer."

Squelched, Hallie thought and asked in a small voice, "Jim Wyatt?"

"Yes. He ran his own outfit for six years. By rights, he should be running my engine. But Rory hates pitching."

And he's too careless to tend the separator, and you want to keep him with you. "Didn't you hear Jim say he might be able to borrow enough on his veteran's bonus to put with his savings and buy another engine and separator before next season?"

"That's next year." Garth's tone was remote. "Did you plan to ask for a job then?"

Why, after being interesting and almost friendly, had he gone back to stiffness? "I—I hadn't really thought about it," she floundered.

And she had tried her best not to think about the end of the threshing run, when Jackie would miss Shaft and Laird and Smoky, Meg and the crew so painfully. She herself would wretchedly miss belonging, would miss Shaft's caring and wisdom. Most of all, she would yearn for this man who spoke now with explosive impatience.

"You'd better start thinking. You have your—brother to take look after."

"I know that better than you do!"

"He'll need to be in school winter after this one." Silence thickened the night between them. After a moment, Garth continued carefully, "Apparently Raford offered you a well-paid job."

"He hired Sophie to run his hotel."

"I expect he'd find a place for you."

Garth's tone was neutral, but somehow his words conveyed a slur. "If I'd wanted to work for him, I'd have stayed at his farm," Hallie retorted.

"Why did you quit? It must have been pretty bad to send you stomping out on the road with Jackie and your suitcases."

"It's none of your"—she searched for an expletive and borrowed one of Shaft's—"none of your blue-eyed cotton-pickin' business!"

"Could be his wife invited you to leave."

"She didn't!"

"However and whatever, you'll need a job this winter. Might not be smart to drop it to travel with a threshing outfit. You and the lad have to live all year. I thresh between sixty-five to eighty days a year, not counting travel, but the pay won't keep you all winter."

"Do you mean you don't want to hire me again?" In spite of a stern effort, her voice trembled.

"I didn't say that."

"You certainly didn't say you wanted to hire me."

"Far as I can tell, you do your work all right, in spite of fooling around with the engine," Garth said grudgingly. "Shaft thinks you hung the moon. But since you've got no folks to help you with the laddie or advise you, it seems you should start thinking about the winter."

"I'm having you save my pay," she shot back at him. "You know I've drawn only a dollar for that night we went to the movie, so you don't need to act as if I'm like that brainless grasshopper in *Aesop's Fables* who fiddled all summer and came begging to the industrious ant when it turned chilly!" She snatched her clothing off the limb and thrust on her shoes. "I suppose I should thank you for your concern, but I don't! You're insufferable. Good night, Mr. MacLeod!"

His next words stopped her in her tracks. "You could get married."

"So some man would support me?"

"Women do it all the time."

"Yes, and they often wind up sad and sorry." She thought bitterly of Felicity, who had gone straightaway to find another man to replace Robert Meredith, discarding Jackie. "I'll find some way to make a living. And I warn you, Garth MacLeod! Don't you dare try to find me a husband so your most peculiar conscience will be clear when you pay me off this fall!"

She stormed to the fence. A frightened nighthawk launched itself from a post as she climbed between the wires. As she hung her towel over the fence by the shack, Shaft called softly, "You okay, honey? Couldn't tell what was said, but I heard you and Garth hackin' away at each other."

"He—he the same as said he didn't want to hire me next year." Hallie choked with wrath, but kept her voice down so as not to rouse Jackie. "He warned me to plan for winter just as if I'd been squandering my wages—and he knows darned well I haven't! He—he even had the gall to say I could get married!"

"Well, I swan," Shaft mused. Which wasn't very helpful.

$\mathcal{T}$he caravan inched down the road next morning, passing two farms Garth threshed ordinarily. "A dog-gone shame," Shaft growled in Hallie's ear. "Garth's accommodated these folks, let 'em settle up after they sold their wheat when they was short on cash. But Raford gives 'em a cheaper deal, and they forget everything else!"

A Ford truck overtook them, churning dust as it veered around the procession and slowed down beside the separator. The driver pushed a straw hat back from his thin sandy hair. "Garth, can you thresh me?" he shouted above the noise of the engines.

"Thought Raford was going to."

The man's ruddy face turned redder. "That blame kerosene engine broke down," he yelled. "Needs a part out of Kansas City. When it does that the first day—well, if you'll come, I'd rather have you. I know you'll get the job done."

"I'm sorry, Chuck," Garth shouted back. "If I thresh you now that I've made other promises, I'd run late. That could mean someone who stuck with me might lose some of their crop to rain or hail."

"Rain or hail's what I'm scared of!" The farmer daubed his sweating dusty face with a bandanna. "Look, Garth, I'll pay an extra cent a bushel."

"Sorry."

"You can't pass up a deal like that!"

"I'm going to keep my word."

"You just want to get even!"

"You're the one who changed threshermen, Chuck."

The farmer glared and sputtered. When he saw no weakening in Garth's face, he lurched around and drove back the way he'd come. Hallie pulled her apron up to shield her face and Jackie's. Shaft tucked Smoky under his beard. When the dust settled back to the haze puffing up from the crawling threshing outfit, Shaft glowered at the receding billowing cloud.

"If Chuck Martin's wife wasn't such a nice lady, I'd wish it would rain enough to lay the dust he's raisin' even if it ruined some of his crop!"

"Shaft, you don't mean that!" The thought of wasted grain was terrible to Hallie, especially when she remembered the multitudes of starving during the war.

He shook dust out of his beard. "Guess I don't. But I'm glad Garth didn't let him bribe his way in front of the folks we're promised to."

"Will there be enough of them to make a worthwhile season?"

"I'd reckon so. As we head out of this country where Raford holds mortgages and can make farmers use him, what'll count more than his cheap threshing is who gets to a farm first."

Hallie nodded. No farmer breathed easy till his crop was threshed and hauled to the granary. Virtually the whole year's cash income came from that.

"Farmers need more cash, what with easy-payment plans and advertisements that make 'em want stuff they don't need," Shaft rumbled. "Used to be they grew nearly all of their food and could eat, whatever happened to the crop. Now there's a sight of 'em buying the cream, butter, and eggs they used to sell."

Even after Hallie's father warned her that the bank was in perilous condition and they needed to economize, Felicity was an ardent user of easy-payment plans. Unless it was a home or auto, Hallie didn't intend to ever buy anything she couldn't pay cash for.

Shaft allowed himself a little gloat. "If that kerosene engine keeps breaking down, no one'll let Raford thresh 'em. Word like that gets around fast."

"I wouldn't feel one bit sorry for him."

"No. But if Raford can't wreck Garth one way, I'm scared he'll try another."

"Like what?"

"I don't know." Shaft frowned. "And I hope we don't find out."

*C*ontending with Raford for jobs, sometimes ahead of him, sometimes behind, they threshed their way east and then north. Several times on Saturday night, Hallie went to town with the crew and attended a movie and bought groceries for the outfit. A few times when there were barn dances in the neighborhood, Shaft insisted that she go, but she was flatteringly looked after by all the crew who went.

Henry's religion barred dancing, Rusty wouldn't go without his wife, Luke didn't go because he was Indian, and Garth didn't because—because he didn't! After such occasions, he eyed her more grimly than usual. For his brother's benefit, Rory teased her in ways that implied they had more than simply danced together, and trying to squelch him made him flirt more outrageously. At dances, she never went outside "to get a breath of air" with Rory and avoided sitting next to him in the flivvers, but he was irrepressible.

The roads were still more suited to horses and wagons, of which there were many, than to cars and machinery. Perspiring owners of autos, mostly Model Ts, fixed flat tires, cleaned spark plugs, or waited for boiling radiators to cool.

Even main roads were unmarked, except for an occasional telephone post bearing the number of the highway. The only stretches of graveled road were those with a natural sandy bottom. Still, bad as dry roads could be, they were nothing compared to the muddy lakes, stretching from field to field, that low places of the road became during and after a thunderstorm.

"We've been lucky with rain," Shaft assured Hallie while they waited for one of these impromptu lakes to subside. "What we've had was just enough to give the boys a rest, but not enough to sprout the grain on the stacks. That plumb ruins it. It's a mighty sad thing to watch a family lose their crop after all the seedin', cultivatin', harvestin', and shockin' or stackin'."

Sad as it was for the family, it was also bad for the threshers, who weren't paid while they waited for the rain to stop and the grain to dry out. It was especially bad for the outfit's owner, who had to keep feeding his men if he didn't want to lose them. So far, though, by the time the men were tired of pitching horseshoes, playing cards and checkers, telling yarns, and listening to Shaft's fiddle, the sun dried the wheat, and the crew was threshing while a relieved farmer hauled the grain to the elevator or his granary.

Sometimes, climbing a hill, the steam engine's wheels would slip in the crumbly rock and sand, and the cleats would start digging holes. Then the men had to unhitch the engine from the rest of the caravan. Usually Rory could steer it to the top and pull the separator and wagons up by a long cable, but twice grinning farmers had to be summoned to bring their horses to rescue the iron monster that was steadily displacing them.

Near the Smoky Hill River, Jan Voltav, a prosperous Czech farmer whose wheat they had just threshed, smiled broadly as he hitched his great Clydesdales to the stalled engine.

"Them Clydesdales weigh a ton apiece," Shaft told Hallie, hoisting Jackie to his shoulder so he could see better. "Each can pull a ton at a trot. Mr. Voltav uses his for heavy hauling. Ain't they somethin'? All that power, yet they're kind of dainty. They don't have that heavy jowl most large breeds do."

"They have beautiful heads," Hallie agreed.

"Look at the little manes on their legs!" cried Jackie.

Silky long white hair or feathering did indeed ran down the backs of the legs to flirt around large hoofs. The blue roans—black with so many white hairs that they had a gray blue sheen—had dramatically muscled hindquarters and deep, broad chests to contain the mighty lungs and hearts.

"Out in Oregon and California," said Jim Wyatt, "I've seen twenty-six horse teams pulling those giant combines that cut grain and thresh it at the same time. It's really something! When gas and kerosene-powered combines come cheap enough for lots of farmers to afford them, it'll sure cut into the custom-threshing business."

At Mr. Voltav's command, the horses leaned into their collars. Their haunches bunched. The massive shoulders thrust forward. It was a hushed, straining contest between splendid animals of muscle and flesh and the weight of a machine of steel and iron.

Hallie's heart strove with the horses'. It seemed an hour—though it could have been only seconds—till the engine's wide front wheels rose from the hollows they had churned. When the engine was well beyond its place of defeat, Mr. Voltav stopped his horses. Sweat darkened them to the shade of gunmetal.

"There, my pretties!" He stroked and praised them, beaming with pride. "You showed the steam engine, didn't you? No one ever had to pull *you* out of a hole!" As Garth approached, the farmer added graciously, "Not but what the engine has its good points. With luck, it can make it to the top now." He waved a hand toward the rest of the outfit. "Shall I haul them up the hill, Mr. MacLeod?"

Garth estimated the distance. "Reckon you better. We don't have a cable long enough."

When the caravan was reassembled, Garth handed over a five-dollar bill, which Mr. Voltav smoothed carefully and tucked into an ancient wallet. "Must be a pretty good sideline, hauling cars and trucks and machinery up that hill," Garth said dryly.

Voltav's grin spread from ear to ear, and his china-blue eyes twinkled. "Yes. And when it rains, there is much hauling out of ditches and flooded places. But it isn't just the money." He tucked the wallet in his hip pocket and cupped the soft muzzle of the nearest horse in his hand. The horse pricked his ears forward attentively and nuzzled Voltav's palm.

"There's not an engine made can do that or run one minute on heart when it's out of fuel." The farmer caressed the horse's shoulder. "Anyway, I like to see the animals win."

Garth smiled. "Grand beasts they are, Mr. Voltav. My great-grandfather brought many from Scotland to sell in America. If this outfit has to be dragged out of its predicaments, I'd rather it was by some Clydes."

The farmer went down one side of the hill and the threshing outfit proceeded down the other. They were in the post-rock country, so called because early settlers had used the easily quarried limestone for fence posts.

"They used it for everything else, too," Shaft said. "Telephone poles, hitchin' posts, gateposts, tombstones, walls, and churches! Not many trees out here, and milled lumber costs money. Stone don't cost anything but work less'n you hire a stonemason."

The two-story Voltav farmhouse was of creamy stone, as were the barn, smokehouse, granary, and chicken house. Large hollowed-out slabs served as feed and water troughs. Even the privy was stone.

From her school history, Hallie knew that much of central Kansas extending north to the Nebraska line had been settled in the 1870s by Europeans escaping starvation or religious oppression. Settlers from the British Isles ranged from starving Irish and Highland crofters to younger sons of the nobility who gathered in towns like Victoria and Runnymede and coursed coyotes instead of foxes. There were Czechs, Scandinavians, and both Lutheran and Catholic Volga Germans, enticed to Russia by Catherine the Great with guarantees of religious freedom, then expelled by her grandson a hundred years later when they refused to become Russified.

None of these people, peasants or princely, chose to live in dugouts when quantities of stone could be crafted into anything from simple cottages and shops to cathedrals and three-storied turreted mansions. Hallie saw them all as the crew moved north.

Scot, Norwegian, British, German, Czech, these folk raised buildings varied and shaped by their heritage and means from the same limestone, the vast layers that formed benches and these flat-topped Blue Hills bounded on the west by the chalk cliffs and bastions of the Fort Hays escarpment.

"This was a huge shallow sea that at times stretched from Mexico to north Alaska," Rich Mondell explained one night at supper. "These shales and limestones were deposited when dinosaurs still roamed."

Jackie's eyes rounded and Rich grinned at him. "Can you imagine big reptiles flying around, hunting the fish and clams that were here then?"

Jackie moved closer to Hallie. "When—when was that, Mr. Mondell?"

"Oh, a good long time ago, son, ages before there were people; though scientists have found the proof of insects in fossils—rocks that hold the shape of something after it decays. Seventy million years, give or take a few million."

Henry Lowen turned red, but he spoke firmly. "I am sorry to dispute with you, Rich. You are an educated man, a professor, while I attended only primary school. But I think your scientists are puffed up with vainglory, and I do not believe them. The Bible teaches that God created the heavens and the earth in six days and rested on the seventh day."

"That's good enough for me," Rusty said. "Bring scientists into it, and they start arguin' that we descended from apes!"

"I think we probably did," said Rich gently, with a smile that robbed the words of any sting. "But I think apes might have more reason to complain of the relationship than we do."

Jim Wyatt laughed. "I knew an old Irishman who said he'd rather think we're a little improvement on monkeys instead of a dismal fall from the angels."

Henry frowned but, after a moment, a smile spread over his boyish face, making it seem even younger. "How good it is that we may talk this way—disagree without trying to make one another think as we do, or go to prison, or leave the country!"

They all stared at him. Then Hallie saw the connection. "Your people came from Russia, just like the Volga Germans!"

"Yes." Henry's clear blue eyes shone with the pleasure of discovering something wonderful. "But you see, Mennonites, who began in Holland and Switzerland, were persecuted till many fled. Those who went to Pennsylvania are now known as the Amish. Others found refuge of a sort in Germany, but were highly taxed and subject to rulers' whims. Being German herself, Catherine the Great knew Mennonites were excellent farmers. She needed reliable settlers in the wild borderlands. To us, as well as to other Germans, she offered tax-free land, exemption from military service, and freedom to practice our religions and have our own schools and language."

"So," Rich reflected, "over there on the vast plains of southern Russia, Mennonites were equal with Catholic and Lutheran Germans who had, in their own country, made life bitter for Mennonites."

The blond young man nodded. "Truly, we were equal in distress when Czar Alexander II revoked our privileges."

"And here you are in Kansas," Jim drawled. "Where, thank goodness, in spite of the KKK and such idjits, you can attend your churches and be full citizens."

Jim nodded. "Even if most of us don't believe a nation can last without making war, it's good for us to know people who believe in peace so strongly they'll go to prison for it, or even die." He considered for a moment. "Someday maybe enough folks everywhere will feel like that and wars will go out of fashion like a lot of other fine old customs—burning widows on their husbands' pyres, cannibalism, slavery, burning heretics and witches at the stake—all inventions that would put any honest monkey to shame."

"Amen!" Shaft left Hallie to cut and pass the pie. He got out his fiddle, tuned it, and the grandson of a Czech emigrant launched into a song they all knew, even Mennonite Henry and Cherokee Luke, for gradually everyone joined in.

> *"Goin' to lay down my sword and shield,*
> *Down by the riverside,*
> *Ain't goin' to study war no more . . ."*

As the crew traveled on toward Volga German country, little blue-stem thrived beyond the more arid region of buffalo grass and grama. Burnished tufts of its rich bronze set off the beginning of autumn's gentians and goldenrod along the road and in pastures that had not been broken to the plow where sleek cattle grazed.

Many of these were Aberdeen Angus, imported in the 1870s by the wealthy Scot, George Grant, who bought 70,000 acres of land from the railroad and founded Victoria as a center for what he dreamed of being a colony of aristocratic cattle breeders and gentlemen farmers.

"Instead," said Rich, who was telling the story while they threshed the fields adjoining Grant's splendid stone villa several miles south of Victoria, "those younger sons and remittance men put on their hunting jackets and chased their imported horses and hounds after plain old Kansas coyotes and jackrabbits. When Grant died, the gentlemen went back to England, and Volga German Catholics bought most of the land."

"Couldn't have been much more different settlers," Shaft chuckled. "One thing you have to say about the Germans, whether they were Lutheran, Catholic, or Mennonite, they stuck it out here through drouth and grasshopper plagues and blizzards that sent plenty of other folks scuttlin' back East."

The lusty young Volga German field pitchers spread their pitchfork tines wide apart so that two of them could attack a shock from opposite sides and throw the entire shock on the wagon at one time. If they dropped a bundle or two, these were tossed quickly on while the man on the wagon yelled reproaches in German and worked furiously to stack the bundles properly before the next whole shock sailed up to him.

The day Garth's crew finished threshing the old Grant place, Mrs. Baier, the farmer's wife, invited them to come up to the villa after supper for ice cream made with the farm's rich cream and peaches. The crew helped the family turn two big freezers packed with rock salt and ice. Emulating a Baier child, Jackie perched on one till his weight wouldn't hold the freezer still as the dasher labored through the thickening custard. Luke and Rory sat on the freezers, then, till husky Mr. Baier pronounced the ice cream done.

Of course it had to "ripen," packed with more ice, but as company, Jackie got one ice-cream-laden dasher to lick, and Meg the other. While the treat hardened, the Baier women, whose hair was yellow-brown as their grain and cheeks as rosy as their peaches, brought out bowls of the sliced golden fruit and almond and ginger cakes.

"Don't eat so much you won't have room for the ice cream," Mrs. Baier warned.

"Ma'am." Rusty beamed, as he took a proffered third slice of cake and covered it with the mellow fruit, "I'll have room for that ice cream if I have to run around your farm to shake down the rest of this!"

The family and crew finished every delectable scraping of the freezers. Hallie had never tasted anything so delicious, and she let the flavorful richness melt in her mouth, savoring each bite to the fullest. Even Garth seemed to be enjoying the luxury instead of stoking himself in a businesslike way for work.

"We will see you next year, then," Mr. Baier said as the abundantly feasted crew began to thank their hosts and hostesses. "You have never blown my grain into the straw pile, so I would not make a deal with the outfit that came a few days ahead of you, though the engineer said they would thresh cheaper."

"A banker's trying to run me out of business," Garth said. "I appreciate your sticking with me, Mr. Baier."

The stocky, sunburned farmer frowned. "When I wouldn't hire him, this engineer—he had cottony hair and a peeling face and sounded like a Texan—he said Germans had no right to be in this country, or Czechs or other foreigners, especially Jews. He said he used to work for you and quit when you hired an Indian."

"That's not exactly how it was," Garth began.

"Cotton—it must be him, Mr. Baier—he came at me with his razor," Henry put in. "Then he drew a knife."

Mr. Baier shook his head. "A bad man. The kind I would not want on my land if he were the best thresherman in the world."

"I'm sure he isn't that," Garth said. "He bragged about being an engineer, but I don't know anyone who had ever hired him as that. I'm kind of surprised Raford did. His first engineer must have quit, and Raford didn't take time to hunt for a good man because he was bound to get all my customers he could by beating me to their farms."

"Has he hurt you much?"

Garth raised a shoulder, then let it fall. "What with the contract I have with my home county for working the roads in the winter, I should be able to pay the mortgage. Could be when Raford sees I'm still in business, he'll get tired of losing money and raise his charges." Garth's eyes flicked briefly toward Hallie. "Or he may try to think of some other way to get even with me."

A chill fingered Hallie's spine as she thought of Raford, his devouring gaze, the way he seemed so sure that sooner or later she'd have to accept his offer. But that couldn't affect Garth, could it?

When she remembered that night at the creek, lightning played through her. Had she done as he suggested, had she stayed in the water at the other end, would anything have happened? Would he have taken it as an invitation? And then . . .

The lightning blazed, seized her till she couldn't breathe for a moment. If just the thought of Garth could affect her like that, what would his touch do? In the weeks since, she had swum after dark whenever they were near a creek or river, but never again had she encountered Garth.

Which was a good thing. She didn't want to confirm his apparent feeling that women were easily had, accessible to any man who appealed to them. She wasn't sure exactly what this feeling was she had for Garth, but she did know it wasn't just for an hour, a night, or a summer.

X I

The outfit swung into Nebraska and headed west for the High Plains, where harvest began so much later than in the central part of Kansas that it was possible to thresh both regions and work south, then east again toward their starting point. All the time they pursued or were pursued by Raford's threshers in this strangely deliberate, long-drawn-out contest. Hallie could make a set at first try most of the time now, and had learned a lot more about operating and maintaining the engine. It seemed that she had never lived another life—or that she hadn't been really alive—until she joined up with the threshermen.

They had journeyed three hundred miles, crossed all the rivers of west central Kansas, the Arkansas, the Smoky Hill, the Saline, and both branches of the Solomon. At twenty-six farms, over and over, stacks dwindled as bundles and grain spikes passed through the teeth of the separator to pour into wagons or build the straw stack.

Sometimes finishing a farm in one day or two, sometimes in five or six, sometimes running by moonlight when rain threatened, they threshed 70,000 bushels of wheat, 10,000 of oats, and a few thousand of barley. They were only one small part of the 100,000 workers who threshed a swath 200 miles wide and 1,000 long from Texas into Canada.

Hallie took satisfaction in feeding men who fed the nation and other countries, too. It was as elemental, as ageless, as planting seeds and tending crops; discoveries that let humankind remain in one place, that freed them from the ceaseless quest for game or wild foods that took up the time and energy of peoples who had no joyous harvest with its promise of winter sustenance.

And the slow miles and days spent in the open roused wonder and pride in Hallie at the vastness of plains and gentle limestone-crowned hills, of the great escarpment palisading the High Plains, all beneath the limitless, embracing sky that man could never plow. Transfigured in an instant, like desert and ocean, by sun and wind and shadow, this land was painted by the seasons with more lasting, gradual hues as grass and leaves changed from emerald to every shade of yellow, amber, copper, and plum or, when snow and ice glittered in the sun or took on blue or slate tones from a clouded sky.

The daisies, white and purple clovers, larkspur, purple coneflower, and wild roses that studded roadways and unplowed land at the beginning of the run gave way to flowers tall enough to thrive in the higher grass—scarlet globe mallow, cherry black-eyed Susans, and brilliant red-orange butterfly milkweed.

Meg's thirteenth birthday was the twelfth of August. Jackie gathered an armful of red and yellow Indian blanket, many sorts of asters, prairie phlox, creamy wild indigo, prickly poppies, purple-red thistles, and golden cinquefoil to make the bouquet that shared pride of place that evening with the three-layered chocolate cake Shaft had made. Meg was delighted with the heart-shaped locket from her father, Jackie's flowers, and a doe and fawn Luke had carved from a chunk of cottonwood root, but she thanked Hallie perfunctorily for the atomizer bottle of Lily of the Valley toilet water and didn't even sniff it.

I'll be glad to see the last of the wretched girl! Hallie thought. But that would mean seeing the last of Garth, too, and Hallie would not be glad of that. As summer waned, tribes of sunflowers grew higher than Jackie's head, goldenrod swayed gracefully in the wind, and spikes of brilliant purple gayfeather mingled with the rosier flowerlets of ironweed.

By the end of the first week of September, when nighthawks were starting south, the outfit threshed their last stacks and fed in the scattered grain including that fallen to the tarp beneath the cylinder. At

Rory's jubilant whistle, Shaft steered Hallie toward the door. "Come on, honey. You got to see this! Come on, Jack!"

The three of them hurried through the stubble and reached the set. A wild whoop went up as eleven stained, battered, frayed straw hats sailed into the feeder.

"It's the custom," Shaft told Hallie.

Rory called to her, "Want to toss in your bonnet? Celebrate your first threshing run?"

Hallie hadn't tied her bonnet strings. She gripped them tightly. True, the bonnet was faded, stained indelibly with engine grease, and needed patching. Garth had given it to her, though. It was precious. She didn't know what she was going to do this winter or whether she would ever see him again, but she would always treasure the bonnet. For its memories and because it was his gift.

The strings ripped through her fingers. Before she could snatch for it, the bonnet flew into the feeder. Meg's gray eyes sparkled maliciously. "Since you run the engine and make sets, you have to toss in your hat," she said.

Hallie fought the urge to grab the girl and shake her. To everyone else, it seemed a playful salute, even a generous admission that Hallie was part of the crew. But Hallie knew that the reason Meg destroyed the bonnet was that the girl's idolized father had given it to an intruder. Bits of chewed blue-and-white cloth blew onto the straw stack with the chaff of the hats.

Head atilt, Meg watched Hallie. *Hateful little wretch! It's just as well your father won't have anything to do with women. Being your stepmother would be the hardest job I can imagine.* Shoulders stiff, eyes stinging, Hallie marched to the cookshack and got on with supper.

It was the crew's last evening meal together, so she and Shaft made it an especially good one with mounds of fluffy sourdough biscuits and three kinds of pie with whipped cream.

Lefty Halstead and Henry Lowen were staying in western Kansas to work in the broomcorn harvest. Jim Wyatt and Buford Redding would drop the other men off in Hollister to catch trains home. Though the flivvers could travel a lot faster than the engine, Jim and Buford planned to stay in sight to help plank bridges.

"You don't need to do that," Garth said.

Jim laughed. "Doesn't really seem like threshing's over till the engine turns off down your home road and the whistle toots good-bye." He looked at Hallie as she filled his coffee cup. "Haven't heard you say what you're doing this winter, Miss Hallie."

"I'm not sure." She tried to sound more cheerful than she felt. "I'll look around Hollister for work that'll let me be with Jackie."

"Lumber camps always need good cooks. I'd be tickled to take you out to Oregon with me and help you find a job."

His hazel eyes were kind, and she knew—absolutely—that she could trust him. However, she felt desolate enough that she wouldn't be seeing Garth every day. Ridiculous as it was, she didn't want to go so far away that she couldn't hope for an occasional glimpse of that proud silvery gold head and perhaps a few words.

Before she could frame an answer, Rusty Wells said, "You and Jackie are sure welcome to come home with Luke and me, ma'am. We need a schoolteacher. Wouldn't be any trick for you to get a temporary certificate—that's all our teachers ever have 'cause they go to a bigger place soon as they have a regular one. My wife would sure make you welcome, and it'd be no trouble for her to look after Jackie along with the two of our kids that aren't school age."

Rich Mondell chuckled. "Let me put in my offer, Miss Hallie. I live with my aunt in our big old family home. We rattle around in it, and she's getting too old to run up and down stairs and do all the cooking and housework. You could live with us just like family, but of course you'd get a salary. I think you'd like Lawrence. There are lots of big shady trees and the university's there in case you want to take a degree and teach school or have some other career."

That was tempting. She was fond of the young professor who treated Jackie like an adult. Though Hallie had no burning urge to teach, as soon as Jackie started school year after next, it would give her the same hours he had. And she'd have summers free if—if Garth would hire her.

Stop that! she chided herself. You can't arrange your life in order to spend summers slaving for a man who has already hinted that you'd better find a steady year-round job. She didn't look at him, but from the corner of her eye, she saw the hard line of his jaw.

Rory's blue eyes caught hers with such intensity that a quivering shock lanced through her. He started to speak, glanced at his older brother, and got a stony gaze in reply. Narrowed in jealous disbelief, Meg's eyes had dwelled on each speaker in turn. She glared at Rory. He ignored her, brooding.

Shaft cleared his throat. "Hallie, you got some dandy chances here. Any one of 'em ought to work out fine for you and Jack. But Smoky and me don't rightly know how we can get along without our boy."

Jackie threw his arms around the cook's leg and hugged it tight. "I don't want to get along without you either, Shaft!"

Shaft hoisted him up to nestle against the tied-back beard. "Hallie, would you like for us to find a little house to rent in town? I can get a job cookin' at one of the cafés. Or we'll find jobs where one of us can always be home with Jack."

"But you—you always stay at our place!" Meg protested.

"I sure have appreciated that. But this year's different."

Hallie didn't have to deliberate. Jackie liked all the men, but he loved Shaft; and, as for her, he was, rolled into one, father, grandfather, and friend. The sense of being deserted—cast adrift alone with her small brother—melted at Shaft's warm smile. Swallowing at the tightness in her throat, Hallie looked around at all the men who had, except for Garth, become such friends.

"I don't know how to thank you, Jim. Or you, Rusty and Luke, or you, Rich. I can tell you've been thinking about Jackie and me, and I can't tell you how much that means. But I think you'll understand that Shaft's extra special to Jackie." She smiled at the man who had at first seemed so eccentric, but who had become so dear. "If you mean it, Shaft, we'd love to share a home with you and Smoky."

Shaft beamed. "Never meant anything so much since I told the deputies good-bye when I jumped out that window and hit the ground runnin'."

Everyone laughed. After a moment, Garth said, "I hope you'll cook for the outfit next summer, Shaft."

"I hope so, too, boss." Shaft looked straight at Garth and added slowly, "Reckon that depends on Hallie. She's the best help I ever had. Don't reckon I can manage without her—providin', of course, that she wants the job."

At last Garth could scarcely avoid meeting her eyes, but his were so veiled that she couldn't guess his feelings. "Do you want to work another run next summer?"

If I haven't found a better job, she should have said. *A cleaner, easier year-round place working for a reasonable human being who doesn't blame me for his runaway wife or have a daughter who thinks he belongs to her. I want to work for a man who won't think we ought to swim together in the night when he'll barely look at me by day or bawl me out for drying my hair in the wind and then act as if it were a crime to cut it off . . .*

But her heart swelled with gladness. She would get to be with him next summer. And who knew? Perhaps with a winter to think things over, he'd be in a fairer state of mind. "Yes," she said. She tried and failed to keep her smile from broadening into a happy laugh. "I want the job, please."

The men cheered. Jackie clapped, jumping up and down, but Meg cast Hallie a furious glance, swung off the bench, and rushed outside, letting the door slam.

Jackie scrambled after her. "Meggie! Aren't you glad? We're going to help thresh next year!"

"I'm glad *you're* coming, sweetheart," came her muffled voice.

Rory made a disgusted sound. He scowled at his brother. "If you don't get that lass straightened out about a few things, she's going to cause you more headaches than—" At the look on Garth's face, Rory swallowed his intended words. "She's going to cause you plenty of grief," he amended. "And herself more."

"You're a good one to talk," said Garth, "considering the white hairs you put in our mother's head."

"And of course you didn't!"

"Of course I did, but"—Garth controlled himself—"let's not wrangle. Meg's headstrong, but she's got a good heart. Look how she's taken Jackie under her wing."

Yes, to crowd me out, Hallie thought. But perhaps the winter would also improve Meg's attitude. At any rate, one more summer with Garth and these good friends was assured. Beyond that, she wouldn't worry.

"Since we have the cooks spoken for," Garth said, "do the rest of you want to make the run next summer? In spite of Raford's tricks, I can pay my mortgage, and I'm expecting to still be in business."

They all wanted to join the outfit again except for Jim Wyatt. Kneading his scarred cheek absently, he said, "If I can borrow against my veteran's bonus and get in a good season of lumberjacking, I hope I can be running my own engine next summer. If that somehow don't work out, Garth, there's no one I'd rather work with than you. I'll let you know by spring."

"Good enough." Garth nodded.

Hallie served another piece of pie to each man, sad at parting with them though she comforted herself that she'd see all of them but Jim next summer. Still, she was vastly relieved that she and Jackie would have a home with Shaft until threshing time. And though she knew it wasn't wise, she couldn't keep from rejoicing that, for at least one more season, she would see Garth every day, prepare his food, and help with his work.

$\mathcal{T}$he great cottonwoods on Garth's side of the creek gloried in the sun's last rays and beyond them, that breadth of unplowed prairie with its myriad gold and purple flowers and many-hued grasses was a different world from Raford's stubbled fields across the road, planted and harvested down to the ditch.

Raford's lands were indeed broken to the plow. As far as the eye could reach, there was not a tree, nor a thicket of sandhill plums, buckthorn, or chokecherry to gladden wild creatures. Along his side of the creek, even the low-growing willows had been chopped away. There were no tangles of wild grapes, elders, or virgin's bower to give food and shelter to birds and beasts. Raford, of course, would view foxes, raccoons, skunks, gophers, coyotes and porcupines as vermin, nor would he extend hospitality to grain-loving crows and blackbirds.

That Garth had not plowed that breadth of rich primordial prairie with its luxuriant creek fringe of trees, shrubs, and vines that gave sanctuary to wild things somehow made Hallie admire him more than anything else he had done, though she respected the way he had stood up to Raford, risking everything he owned, and the easy good nature with which he kept his crew and machinery running through searing sunup to sundown days. These things proved Garth a man of endurance and courage. But his sparing the most valuable land on his farm because it was wild and beautiful and necessary to other creatures showed a tender side of his nature that let Hallie dare hope a woman still might reach his heart.

The Model Ts rattled across the bridge. Hallie and Shaft had taken Henry's and Lefty's places in Jim's flivver. The engine, with its caravan, stopped at the bridge. Garth went to examine it, as he did every time they came to one. He made a grimace of disgust and shouted something to Rory that Hallie couldn't hear above the noise of the engine. Rory shrugged and made an impatient gesture.

"Raford's had the bridge worked on some but it still doesn't suit Garth," Shaft said in Hallie's ear. "Still, there's not much choice exceptin' to plank it unless Garth wants to leave his whole outfit on this side of the creek, which he don't. He'll need the engine to plant his wheat, and he always gets the separator under cover for the winter."

The men in the flivvers jumped out to stretch the planks across the metal surface as they had done so many times during the run. This was the last one. And it was on the other side of the creek, beneath Garth's cottonwoods, that Hallie and Jackie had been resting when they first heard and saw the engine and Rory had given that whistling salute.

He was giving it again, like a challenge to Raford; an announcement that the outfit was home after completing a run that would at least keep it in business. The engine clanked across the shrieking bridge. The separator followed, Garth on the platform. The cookshack bumped across. Meg was perched on her throne, the seat of the tank wagon.

The wagon was halfway across when the groaning planks cracked as the bridge beneath gave way. To Hallie's terrified eyes, it seemed to explode in a chaos of sundered metal and wood. Some fell with the wagon into the creek fifteen feet below. Other parts flew in a rain of splinters and metal fragments.

Rusty Wells screamed. He fumbled at a jagged shard thrusting from his inner thigh. Jets of blood spurted through clothing and his hands. Garth, Rory, and some of the men were already lunging down the bank to Meg, who had not made a sound since her first horrified cry as the wagon dropped.

Hallie and Shaft ran to Rusty who had either sat down or collapsed.

Luke bent over the big man, trying in vain to stop the bleeding with slender brown hands. Hallie ripped off the bottom of her slip. Shaft clutched a shattered piece of wood, took the cloth, and tied it around Rusty's leg. Bright arterial blood, pumped from the heart, still trickled through Luke's hands. Shaft slid the wood beneath the tourniquet and rotated it to tighten the cloth. The pulsing became a seep, but Rusty had lost consciousness and lay in a pool of blood, more than Hallie would have guessed to be in a human body.

"Pumped out fast through that big artery," Shaft gritted. "We got to get him to a hospital. And Meg, is she—?"

Garth and Rory, aided by the others, trudged up from the creek with Meg stretched motionless on the wagon's tailgate. The shallow cut on her forehead didn't amount to much but her breathing was fast and labored, and her pallid face was bedewed with sweat.

"I'm afraid it's her spine," Garth said. His face was white as his daughter's. His eyes were anguished. "Hate to jolt her over this road—"

Hallie ran for the shack. "Let's tie her in place with sheets and pillows and cushion the board as much as we can!" As she snatched bedding from the box-benches, she heard Garth command, "Buford, you go ahead with Rusty—go fast as you can! If you put him in back and prop that leg up, maybe Luke can squeeze in or lean over from the front and make sure the tourniquet doesn't slip. Tell the hospital folks we're coming."

Hallie's throat ached and she blinked back tears as she firmed pillows on either side of Meg's curly head. *Oh, let her not be hurt much! Let her be all right!* Overwhelmed by the helplessness she'd felt at her father's deathbed, Hallie marveled at how fragile people and life could be—Rusty hearty and well one second, bleeding to death the next, Meg whistling a jaunty tune till the instant the bridge gave way.

Meg didn't stir as they bound her and the padding to the board with torn sheets. Jackie whimpered and clutched at Hallie, but Rich Mondell scooped him up and took him off to "take care of Smoky."

Shaft heaped bedding in the backseat and crawled in on one side to steady and support the board that rested across the padded back of the front seat with Garth holding it from the passenger's side. Hallie got in back and gripped her side of the board. She knew that Rich and Baldy would look after her brother and probably soothe his fears better than she could.

Jim drove as carefully as he could, but the board seemed to jounce unmercifully and Hallie flinched with every bump. They passed the Rafords' imposing house, set well back from the dust of the road, the lemon yellow Pierce-Arrow gleaming from the garage.

With a bitter glance toward his enemy's palatial estate, Garth said, "I told Raford to fix that bridge. When I saw he hadn't, I shouldn't have gone across."

"What else could you do, boss?" Jim shot him a startled glance across Meg's swathed form. "Wait there till they put in a new bridge?"

"I should have left the machinery and wagons on the other side and then raised hell till the bridge was safe."

"Boss, if you start thinkin' like that, you'd never get out of bed. What is life except takin' one chance after another?"

"I had no business taking them for everybody else. If Meg or Rusty—" Garth's voice broke.

Hallie ached for him, but could think of nothing to say. Far ahead swirled the fog of dust churned by Buford's flivver. He could drive as fast as he could. Rusty had no injury except the one draining his life's blood. Rusty, who had laboriously scratched a letter to his wife each Sunday. Rusty, who had three little kids . . .

It seemed an eternity before they pulled up behind Buford's Model T at the back of the hospital. A gray-haired nurse came out at once, examined their first aid with a practiced eye, and said, "You've done a good job. We're short on attendants. You bring her in."

"The man who was just brought in?" Garth asked as he and Jim lifted Meg and went through the door. "Rusty Wells?"

The nurse shook her head. "I'm sorry."

"He—he's dead?" Hallie gasped.

"Dead when he got here."

Oh, Rusty! And poor Luke. How will he tell his sister? How will she tell the children? And poor Garth. Luke and Buford came down the hall, heads bowed. Suddenly Luke stopped and leaned against the wall, shoulders heaving.

Buford put an awkward arm around the younger man's shoulder. "Shaft, will you help here?" Garth gave his end of the board to the cook. Frightened as he was about his daughter, he hurried over to Luke. Hallie hesitated, torn between running to Luke or staying with Meg.

Deciding it was best to let Garth be with Luke for a little while, she followed Meg's procession into a small room. The men gently placed the board on a high, narrow bed and stood back, looking hopefully at the nurse.

"Please go to the waiting room," she told them as she took shears and cut swiftly through the ripped sheets and Meg's clothes, lifting them away as much as possible without moving the girl and draping her with a sheet. Meg groaned and lifted her hand. "Come hold her hands and keep her still," the nurse said to Hallie. "Are you a member of the family?"

"A friend." Meg and Garth might not agree with that and Hallie, as she clasped the girl's chilly hands, hoped Meg wouldn't be upset if she roused enough to know who was standing by her.

"Well, you may stay if you like. The doctor will be here any minute."

The white-coated doctor and Garth arrived at the same time. Hallie stepped back as the bearded young man applied his stethoscope to Meg's chest and abdomen and then examined her with searching fingers, checking her neck and spine and pelvis with special care.

She moaned and Garth stepped to her head and took her hands, talking softly. Her eyelids fluttered. "Daddy?"

"I'm here, honey. Just keep still." She obeyed, but her eyes moved. They widened as she saw the nurse and doctor.

"What—what happened?"

"Do you remember?" the doctor asked with an encouraging smile.

Meg frowned. Then her face twisted. "The bridge— I was so scared! I tried to jump and—and something hit my head."

The doctor and nurse exchanged relieved looks. "Now that you're back with us, young lady," said the doctor, "let's see how well your brain can boss your body around. Can you wiggle your fingers? Your toes?"

Assured that Meg was in no danger of dying, Hallie slipped out and found Shaft and Jim and Buford outside with Luke. "I'll take you home," Jim was saying. "Shall I go talk to the undertaker and see about having the coffin sent on the train? We'll get there before it does, but is there someone you want to telephone now?"

Luke shook his head. "I must be there when I tell my sister. Anyway, the nearest telephones are in town." He straightened his shoulders. "The undertaker will need money. I will talk to him."

Buford said, "We'll go with you, son. Undertakers generally try to talk a family into spending all they've got on a coffin, which is sure not what Rusty would want."

Shaft cut in, "Garth told me he'll pay for the coffin and everything. And we're all chipping in some of our wages for you to give Rusty's wife, Luke."

"You worked hard for that money," Luke said. "Buford, I know you are still paying for your Ford; and Jim, you have that engine and separator to buy."

"We'll be working this winter," Jim said. "We've got no one but ourselves to worry about. Rusty won't ever work for his family again."

"I'll work for my sister," Luke said.

"All the same, we want to help." Jim glanced around at the others who nodded agreement. "I'll give the collection to your sis if you won't, Luke."

Hallie took his hands gently in hers. "Think about her and the children, Luke, not your pride. We all want to help. Please let us."

His eyes glistened. After a moment, he said, "My sister will be grateful. So will I. Always."

The undertaker was just across the street. They all helped choose a coffin that was simple but dignified. Buford stayed to settle the bill. Garth came out of the hospital as the little group walked toward it.

"She can't move her legs," he said at their questioning glances. "She'll be in the hospital for at least a few more days." His haunted eyes rested on Luke. "Have you—"

Jim explained the arrangements. "We can drive all night. Don't reckon we could sleep anyhow. Guess we'll drive back for Luke's and Rusty's things and then keep going."

"I suppose that's best." Garth passed a hand across his face as if trying to clear his mind. "Luke, I told you I feel to blame. I'm going to send Rusty's family money till the kids are old enough to hold paying jobs."

"My sister—our family—won't want that."

"But—"

"If it was Rusty's time, it would have happened wherever he was, whatever he was doing. Threshing is dangerous. Rusty knew that. You must not let this eat at your heart, Mr. MacLeod."

Garth started to protest, but Luke raised his voice. "We don't need much cash money. We raise most of our food. Rusty saved enough this summer to buy a team of mules. I am going to buy another cow. Then we can sell cream and butter. And next summer I would like to work for you again."

Garth looked as if the breath had been knocked out of him. At the moment, he probably didn't feel like ever taking his outfit down a road again. After a moment, he put out his hand and shook Luke's. "You'll have a job with me as long as I have a rig. But let me pay for some more cows. I can see it's better for your sister to have income off her own little dairy than take money from me."

The younger man gazed at him, then slowly inclined his head. "If that is your wish. Is it all right for me to tell Meg good-bye?"

"I'll go in with you," Garth said. He paused, his face bleak. "I haven't told her about Rusty. Would you mind if I do that after she's better?"

"I'll just tell her to get well," said Luke. The two went in together. Hallie buried her face against Shaft's shoulder and wept. She couldn't believe that solid, kind, fun-loving Rusty was dead. And Meg! What if the girl was crippled? How would Garth endure that? Hallie's heart ached for him, ached that there was so little she could do, and ached even worse because she was sure he wouldn't accept even that little.

XII

$\mathcal{R}$ory had taken the machinery,
cookshack, coal wagon, and battered, splintered tank wagon on to the
MacLeod farm. When the Model Ts returned in the twilight, Rory,
with Baldy and Rich waited in and around an old Ford truck while
Jackie drowsed against the patient Laird with Smoky in his lap. The
back of the truck was heaped with the men's bedrolls and suitcases, but
the tailgate was covered with objects covered by a clean sheet.

In a tightly controlled voice, Garth told Rory what had happened.
"I'm going back to stay with Meg as soon as Jim and Luke get off," he
finished.

Rory looked dazed. Turning away, he swept the sheet off an array
of cold food. "There was plenty of stuff in the cookshack for supper.
Thought we could eat right here before the boys take off."

"Good thinking." Garth's drawn face relaxed slightly as he looked
gratefully at his brother.

"I'm not hungry," Luke said, but Jim handed him a thick sandwich.

"You've got to hold yourself together, kid."

Hallie forced herself to chew a little bread and cheese. She kept
thinking of Rusty, who had relished his meals more than anyone on
the crew, and who would never enjoy his food again. And Meg. She
must be frightened alone there in the hospital, unable to move her

legs. *Let her be all right,* Hallie prayed again with all her strength. She gladly would have stayed with Meg but was sure the girl would much rather have Garth and, failing him, Rory or Shaft. Anyone but Hallie.

There was a tug at Hallie's skirt. She looked down into Jackie's scared eyes. "Meg'll get all well, won't she?"

"We hope so, honey. She's awake now, and that's good. The nurse and doctor are nice. They'll take good care of her."

"Can I go see her?"

Hallie didn't look at Shaft. He might feel now that he should stay at Garth's to be of help. "You'll get to see her when she's well enough, dear."

Buford was moving around unobtrusively to collect money for Rusty's wife. Hallie reclaimed her purse from the flivver. On the way from town, she had calculated how much she and Jackie would need to live for several months if it took that long to find a job. She left that in the battered envelope and gave Jackie three ten-dollar bills to put in the cloth cap Buford wore since tossing his straw one in the separator.

There was a fat bundle of bills when Buford slipped a rubber band around them, and Hallie was sure few of them were ones. With Garth's donation for cows and Luke's and Rusty's wages, the family would have enough cash to get well on their feet. It couldn't assuage grief but it could prevent a lot of worry.

All the men shook hands with Luke and said they hoped to work with him next year. Hallie embraced him and kissed his cheek. Luke dropped to one knee to meet Jackie's fierce hug. He smoothed away the boy's tears and ruffled the hair that was black as his own, but curly.

"Remember, Jack. Find a place when the leaves fall where you can watch the prairie chickens boom and dance. Hunt for the same tracks in the snow that I showed you in the mud by the creek. Keep your eyes and ears open, and next summer you can teach *me* things."

Jackie clung to the slender young man who was really little more than a boy himself, though he was now the man of his sister's house as well as his mother's. "You will come back, Luke? Next summer?" No wonder he wanted assurance. His father had died, his mother gone away, and he had just seen a man fatally hurt and Meg injured.

"I'll come, Jack. When the wheat is harvested and the oats and barley are ready, I'll come."

The child could still not quite let him go. "Don't get old, Luke!"

"Well, I won't," said Luke in gentle puzzlement. "Not in one winter."

"I mean, you'll still swim with Meg and me, won't you? And show me how the compass plant works and who lives in what burrows and what plants are good for medicine and—"

"I won't get too old for that." Luke gave the boy a final hug and got in Jim's Model T.

They drove off amid a chorus of farewells, headlights wavering feebly. Buford, with Rich and Baldy, said their good-byes and were quickly on their way. Rich would catch a train home to that two-storied home in Lawrence and his university classes. Buford and Baldy were heading for the Oklahoma oil fields.

That left the MacLeods, Shaft, Hallie and her brother beside the truck parked where the lane to the MacLeod place ran into the main road that crossed the creek or led, the other way, to town. Shaft said, "Boss, if you want me to hang around till you know how Meg's going to be—"

Garth turned, his face a blur in the gathering night. "Hallie, would you and your laddie stay, too, for a bit? It's early yet to tell how much use Meg will get of her legs, but it's certain that we'll need a woman to help her for a while and run the house."

"Sounds like the best idea you ever had, brother," Rory said in a pleased, surprised tone.

Hallie's pulse quickened. In spite of the grief of that day and anxiety over Meg, she felt a rush of wondering gladness at the thought of being in Garth's home, of keeping it for him. But remembering how Meg had tossed her bonnet in the separator and the girl's unrelenting summer-long hostility compelled Hallie to shake her head.

"Meg doesn't like me. I'm afraid it would upset her to have me looking after her and doing things around the house."

"I expect a lot of her jealousy came from Rory's teaching you how to run the engine when he's never let her so much as toot the whistle."

Rory hooted. "That may be some of it, Garth, but the big cockle-bur in Meg's fur is that you've let her think she owns you."

"She sure likes Jack, though," Shaft put in. "If she's laid up quite a spell, he'd be a lot of company."

Jackie adored Meg almost as much as he did Luke. *That* gave Hallie some jealous pangs when she'd planned to spend Sunday time reading to him and he'd preferred to go off with Meg. He threw his arms around Hallie as far they would reach. "Let's stay with Meg, Hallie! I'll help lots and lots!"

Being with Meg and Laird as well as Shaft and Smoky would fill Jackie's cup to overflowing. And there would be no need to be away from him while she worked. Indeed, what work could be as joyful and rewarding as making Garth's home pleasant and setting good food before him?

It came to Hallie in a rush so powerful that it dizzied her that all she wanted from life, apart from rearing Jackie well, was to live with Garth—love him, share his work and dreams, one day have children that would give her the chance of loving him again in their children as he was before the war and his wife put him through the crucible. He had survived as a strong man, but Hallie longed to see the boy in him that stayed uppermost in Rory. If Rory were more grown-up and Garth were more boyish— But after this day's terrible accident it would be a long time, if ever, before his heart was light. She yearned to help him, apart from the benefits to Jackie and herself, but she feared Meg's rancor.

Garth spoke with an edge of desperation. "I can't make Meg welcome you, but I can promise she'll behave because I don't know of any other woman I'd trust with this job. If she won't give her word to act decent, she'll have to stay in town with a woman who takes care of invalids."

Rory whistled. "She'd hate that."

"She would. But that's her choice. You and I will be out plowing and planting and grading roads for the county, Rory. I'm not asking Shaft to stay here alone when I know he planned to be with Hallie and Jack this winter."

So Garth was thinking of her and hadn't wanted to leave her and Jackie on their own. Hallie didn't delude herself that Meg would be comfortable to live with. Short of overt insults and actions, there were plenty of eloquent ways to express dislike. The overriding thing was that Garth needed her. She could relieve his mind and ease his life. And he had amazingly said he trusted her with the care of his daughter and home.

Would he ever trust her with his heart? Hallie dared not hope for that yet, but she would feel blessed if she could help him through the months ahead. She let her hand rest fleetingly on his arm, wished she could gather him close and comfort him, and said, "I'll stay."

$\mathcal{R}$ory offered to drive Shaft, Hallie, and Jackie to the farmhouse before going into town with Garth, but Shaft said, "It's not far. You two go in and see our gal. I'll get Hallie and Jack settled in."

The truck wheezed off. Jackie got close enough to Hallie for her to suspect he wanted her to take his hand. "When will Meg come home?"

"I don't know, dear. Soon, I hope."

"She won't stay in the hospital forever?"

"No, of course not." What could she say to make him feel better that was true? Hallie tried to make her voice confident and cheering. "She'll be glad to have you keep her company. And you can help a lot by taking drinks to her and fetching things she needs."

After a moment, Jackie whispered, "She—she won't die, will she? She won't die like Daddy did?"

"Honey, I'm almost sure she won't. Meg's young and strong—"

"Rusty died!"

"That's different. He bled to death. Meg doesn't have any wounds like that."

"Rusty was a daddy, wasn't he?"

"Yes, honey. A good one."

"What will his little boys and girls do?"

"Luke's their uncle. He'll love and help them. But they'll miss their daddy. Just the way we miss ours."

"I don't have a nuncle?"

"No. But you've got me."

"Meg says you'll get married someday and won't want me."

Hallie froze, then battled a rush of anger. Meg really might believe that; her own mother had abandoned her. But it was a cruel thing to tell a child who had lost both parents. However that was, Hallie knew she couldn't hold the past against Meg if they were to get along.

Even though Jackie was almost too big for her to carry and usually felt himself too old for it, Hallie scooped him up and held him close. "Listen, Jackie, you're the only family I have. I love you. I'm going to take care of you till you grow up."

"What if you get married and the man doesn't want a little boy?"

"Darling, I won't marry any man who doesn't think he's real lucky to get a boy like you." She thought of Garth and sighed. "Anyhow, I may not ever get married. Either way, you don't need to worry about it."

"And you've got me, Jack," Shaft said. "I've always wanted a son or grandson, but since I never got married, you're my only chance. Look, here's Laird coming to meet us, and the lamp's lit in the kitchen. There's dust and cobwebs since we've been gone three months, but I reckon that won't bother us none tonight, fagged out as everybody must be."

Hallie had expected a small bachelor house. Instead, they passed through a screened porch that ran the width of the house and entered a roomy kitchen dominated by a Home Comfort range. That would be wonderful for winter heat, but Hallie was glad to see a small kerosene range against another wall. The lamp shone from a big, round table surrounded by cane-bottomed chairs. There was a large cupboard against one wall and a worktable beneath a big window.

What would it look out on? Hallie hoped it would face the stretch of wild prairie along the creek. At any rate, whoever worked there would have light and be able to watch the sky. As if to let her know they were there, an owl hooted and coyotes started yipping.

A washstand with several water buckets stood by the back door. Above it was a mirror and several pegs for towels. Beneath a film of dust, the plank floor looked well scrubbed. A high, wide row of open shelves proclaimed this was indeed a womanless house, for they were filled with canned fruits, vegetables, evaporated milk, and jars of store-bought jams, jellies and peanut butter, but not a solitary jar of home-canned food.

Except for a calendar advertising farm machinery, there was nothing on the walls, no hint of ornament. As if reading her thoughts, Shaft said, "Not much for purty, but everything's solid from foundation to roof. Bedrooms are upstairs." He smoothed his beard and caressed Smoky, who had strolled in from the dark of the next room. "Reckon Meg won't be able to climb stairs right away. She can sleep in the front room; there's a davenport there. I'll put you in her room. Rory already carried your things upstairs."

"There isn't a spare room?"

"No. Rory and Garth each have one. Meg's is across the hall and a lot bigger. A good-sized storeroom takes up the rest of the space."

There was no choice, though Hallie was sure Meg would hate having anyone use her room. Shaft lit one of several kerosene lamps that stood on a small table in the walkway between kitchen and what must be the front room. Stairs disappeared in a murk that lifted as Shaft led the way, but their shadows loomed on the wall, shifting as the lamp flickered, and assumed even more menacing proportions as they reached the upper hall.

"I don't want to go to bed up here all by myself!" Jackie whimpered.

Hallie was determined to wait up till Garth came home or there was more news of Meg, but that was likely to be a long time. "I'll tell you stories till you go to sleep," she told her brother. "And we'll leave a lamp on this stand outside the door."

Jackie still hung onto her. Shaft yawned prodigiously. "You know, I'm plumb wore out. Instead of tryin' to fight my way into my shack tonight, I'd like to bring up my cot and sleep here in the hall. Okay by you, Jack?"

The boy nodded. "Mighty okay, Shaft!"

"Good. I'll just get clean sheets out of the storeroom here. Maybe you could fix Garth's and Rory's beds while you're making yours, Hallie. I'll bring a cot from the cookshack for you, Jack, and put it next to the door so Smoky can visit back and forth. Come along with me and I'll show you where the outhouse is."

By the time they returned with the cots, Hallie had made the three regular beds. Hidden beneath the quilt tossed over Meg's four-poster was a faded, grubby rag doll. One button eye was gone, and the painted smile had faded to the faintest hint. The lumpy cloth body showed through a frayed sweater that Meg must have worn as a baby.

Such a beloved relic would be a comfort in the hospital, but Hallie suspected that Meg wouldn't want anyone to know about her cherished bedmate, so she leaned the doll against the mirror of the dresser, made the bed, dug Jackie's pajamas and toothbrush out of his carpetbag, and hurried downstairs. She was stirring hot cocoa when Shaft and Jackie came in. The cots were set up quickly and padded with blankets.

Since Shaft was going up with him, Jackie didn't demand his promised story. His eyes kept closing as he sat on Shaft's knee and sipped his cocoa. He sleepily scrubbed with his toothbrush, squinched his eyes shut as Hallie washed his face, neck, and ears, and Shaft bore him upstairs while Smoky streaked ahead of them. Hallie tucked her brother in with Lambie. Shaft kissed him goodnight and warned, "Now don't go bouncing around with Smoky, son, 'cause I can hear your teeniest wiggle, and I sure don't want to be kept awake. Hear?"

"Mmmhmm." Jackie smiled and patted Shaft's beard. "Look, I've got Smoky."

"So you have!" Shaft pretended great surprise though he had deposited the cat on the foot of the cot and she had stalked up it in a proprietary way before curling up near Jackie's chest. "Well, maybe she'll come see me later. Sleep tight, Jack."

"Mmhn."

In the hall, Hallie said, "I'll stay here for a while if you're not ready to go to bed, Shaft."

"I'm ready!" He added less vehemently, "Over the years I've found out people can handle trouble lots better if they get their sleep. So don't you stay up all night, honey. Tomorrow will be a rough day."

"I'll get some sleep." She hugged him and kissed his cheek. "Bless you, Shaft, you make a wonderful grandfather for Jackie! We're so lucky we met you."

"I'm the lucky one," he said gruffly.

Before she went downstairs, Hallie put out her nightgown and clean clothing for next day. She brushed her hair, still short and curving around her ears from a second cutting, and from the bottom of her suitcase she got out Grandmother Harriet Wilton's *Book of Common Prayer*. She needed it tonight.

*T*he clock above the stairway table showed eleven. Hallie had swept the downstairs and wiped dust off the furnishings. Now she read the labels of the canned foods, trying to think of something to fix for the men that would be nourishing and easy to digest. Lighting a lantern she found on the porch, she raided the cookshack for potatoes, onions, bread, butter, and the other perishables.

Glad that she didn't have to fire up the big range with the kindling and coal stored in boxes located a safe distance from it, she lit a burner of the kerosene stove and sautéed sliced onions in butter in a large kettle. When they were transparently golden, she added sliced potatoes and enough water to cover. After the soup simmered for a time, she added a can of evaporated milk and a little salt and pepper. With bread, it would make a meal, and she had found some tapioca and made pudding while she tended the soup.

It was midnight. Hallie sat down near the lamp and reached out with heart and spirit to Rusty's family, especially young Luke, who must take such a burden on his graceful shoulders. She thought of Meg, determined to be a hand on her father's crew, now unable to move her legs. And Garth. He would be in agony over his daughter and Rusty. Added to that was the guilt of thinking he should not have crossed the bridge. Of course, had he known what would happen, he'd have let his machinery and the wagons rust and rot. What were things compared to a life or crippling? Yet those machines were Garth's livelihood.

Hallie's thoughts twisted through an endless maze. She opened the small book with its yellowed pages and read the gospel for St. James's Day. "In my Father's house are many mansions—" Grandmother

Harriet had buried two infants and her husband. She must have read these same words, seeking comfort or at least acceptance.

The sound of a motor roused Hallie. It certainly wasn't the clattering truck, but it might be someone with a message from Garth. Hallie went out on the screened porch just as the door closed. The lamp cast a patch of light through the kitchen door but the person was beyond it and she couldn't see who it was. The visitor didn't speak, as would be usual.

With a twinge of fright, Hallie stepped out of the light herself. Then she could make out the heavy shape and Raford's eyes flickering yellow in the dimness. "So you're back, Hallie Meredith. I see you've cut off that wonderful hair. What else about you did the summer ruin?"

"Do you know a man was killed and Garth MacLeod's daughter badly hurt on that bridge he told you needed fixing back when the run began?"

"Repairs had been made. It's not the county's fault—or mine—if threshers don't lay planks."

"They did. But the bridge caved in."

"That's nothing to do with me."

"Garth thinks so."

Close as he was, Raford's physical presence was overwhelming. Not wanting to call Shaft unless she had to, Hallie retreated into the kitchen. Raford appreciatively drew in the smell of the soup.

"You cooked only one breakfast for me, Hallie. I've regretted that."

"I haven't. If you came to see Mr. MacLeod—"

"I didn't. He's at the hospital, very properly. I was in town and heard the news, so I guessed you were probably here."

"You're the last person in the world I want to see."

His strong teeth flashed and he chuckled. "Ah, but *I* want to see *you*. Now that the run's over, you'll need work and a place for you and your—brother."

"I've got a place."

The pupils of his eyes swelled, almost obscuring the glowing yellow. "Here?"

Her mouth was dry. She nodded.

He gave a jeering laugh. "I'm astonished that a woman with your puritanical standards would stay with single men. Two of them."

"Shaft will be here—and he's here right now, upstairs."

"How does that help? Three men instead of two. Your reputation won't be worth a cent."

"I'll be taking care of Mr. MacLeod's daughter. If people can't understand that, I don't care what they think."

He raised heavy eyebrows the same charcoal color as his thick, crisp hair. "Does that mean you expect one of the brothers MacLeod to make you an honest woman?"

"I *am* honest, and I don't expect a thing except my wages." Infuriated by his smooth hypocrisy, Hallie thrust, "You have a nerve to try to scare me with what people will think! How long would it have taken you to sneak in my bedroom if I had stayed at your house?"

That only amused him. "I'd have drawn it out when I learned how skittery you were. That's better fun. Your rapid decampment forced me into proposing that other arrangement at the hotel."

"Is Sophie still there?"

He raised a thick shoulder. "She's passable as recreation till I find something better."

Hallie repressed a shudder at his cold-blooded tone. Had she given in to him, he might be saying the same about her. It was a sickening thought. His gaze fell on the open prayer book. He started to pick it up. Hallie snatched it away, closing it, but he had glimpsed a page.

" 'From all deceits of the world, the flesh and the devil . . .' " he quoted. His voice mocked her, yet there was something different in his eyes. "I didn't know you were an Episcopalian."

"Don't you seduce Episcopalians?"

His laughter pealed. "Sometimes it takes a little longer."

"Well, I'm not one. My grandmother was."

"So were all the women of my family." He glanced around the room, his brow puckering, before he turned back to her. "So here you are, my dear. Having cleaned away the season's dust and cobwebs and prepared mouth-watering soup, here you sit mulling over prayers and, from your swollen eyes, you've been crying."

"Who wouldn't?"

"Multitudes."

"Go away."

"I enjoy your company."

"I don't like yours."

"How can you tell? You've never let me be nice to you." His voice deepened and the mockery was gone. "You're different, Hallie. I wouldn't treat you like the others."

"You won't get the chance."

This time the approaching vehicle, rattling and snorting, was unmistakably the truck. Hallie shoved at Raford. "For goodness' sake, get out of here! If Garth sees you right now—"

"If I know him, he'll come looking for me anyway." Raford instinctively touched the inside of his vest and smiled at Hallie's horrified look. "Of course I have a gun. I'll carry it till the MacLeods have time to cool down."

"You'll carry it a long time, then."

"Perhaps not."

"What do you mean?"

"I own all the rest of the land for miles on this side of the creek. It's an irritation, this section with all that mess along the creek sucking water and harboring varmints."

"You mean the trees and vines and old prairie?"

"They should be cleared and the land put to use."

"It *is* of use." Hallie thought of the great horned owls, coyotes, and other creatures living there.

"I want it put to *my* use."

"I hope it never is."

"MacLeod can't hold out against me. If you care about his welfare, you'll try to influence him to sell to me and go somewhere else. I'll offer him a good price now. If I have to spend more time and money breaking him, I won't be generous."

"Maybe you can't break him."

Raford laughed. "How can I fail? He gave me a race this summer, but he can't have done much better than break even. He can't afford that kind of run next year. And in a couple of years, he'll need new machinery. I'll get him. It's just a question of when."

The screen door opened and shut. There were swift footfalls. Rory came in. His eyes blazed at the sight of Raford. "You lousy son—" He gulped the rest of the name but closed the space between them and swung.

"He's got a gun!" Hallie cried.

Raford didn't reach for it. For such a heavy man, he sidestepped with surprising speed doubled his fists and brought them up beneath Rory's chin, almost lifting him off the floor. He kicked his legs out from under him. Afraid that the banker would hurt Rory badly, Hallie snatched a butcher knife from the slotted block on the worktable and started for Raford, who moved for the door with no apparent haste.

"My quarrel's not with you, young man," he said to the stunned Rory. "Good night, Hallie."

She dropped to her knees beside Rory, who moved his head cautiously as he sat up, feeling his neck and jaw. "Guess my head's still on"—Rory moved his legs—"and he didn't break my bones. That'll teach me to charge in like that."

"I hope so!" Rising, Hallie gave him a hand. "How's Meg?"

He started to shake his head, winced, and looked glum. "She's conscious, but she still can't move her legs. The doctor wants to keep her a few more days. I came home to get some sleep so I can stay with her and give Garth a rest." He rubbed his jaw. "That guy may be a banker, but he sure learned how to fight in an alley or saloon. What was he doing over here?"

"He wants to buy this place."

Rory stared. "He picked one helluvva time to do business!"

"He expects Garth to come after him about the bridge."

"He's right about that."

"Then Garth should know Raford's carrying a gun under his vest."

"I'll tell him when I see him in the morning."

"I'd be glad to stay with Meg, but I don't think—"

"You'll see plenty of her when she comes home." Rory sounded so grim that Hallie looked at him inquiringly. "Garth's told her you're staying," Rory said.

"And she didn't like it?" Hallie's heart sank, though she hadn't expected any different reaction.

"You might say the only thing she liked less was the notion of staying in town at an invalids' home." Rory hesitated, then blurted,

"She made Garth promise that you wouldn't sleep in her room. So he'll move a cot into my room and give you and Jackie his."

It was a slap in the face, but Garth needed her—and so, no matter how she begrudged that need, did Meg. Hallie thought of the tattered rag doll and suspected that Meg couldn't bear for her to know about it. "All right," Hallie said. "It'll be easy to move Jackie, and I've put clean sheets on all the beds."

Rory's nose wrinkled. "And made something that smells good. Do I get some?"

He had two bowls of soup and one of tapioca. "Meg loves tapioca," he said, "but she always scorches it." He rose and covered a yawn. "Better get your sleep, Hallie. Let me move the laddie for you."

"Maybe we can move him on the cot. It's just across the hall."

They accomplished this without waking Shaft who, far from rousing at Jackie's slightest rustle, had slept through the ruckus downstairs and was snoring heartily. Jackie, his cheek pressed to Lambie, didn't wake either, though Smoky jumped down till the cot was moved and then hopped back up, eyeing them reproachfully before she composed herself.

Through it all, Hallie kept a safe distance from Rory or made sure there was something in between them. When Jackie was settled and Rory moved toward her, Hallie backed into the hall. "Good night, Rory. Thanks."

He stopped farther away than his arms could reach and gave her a wry grin. "Don't be so jittery. You're our guest, in a way, and you're doing us a favor. I won't lay a hand on you." His eyes danced. "Unless, of course, you ask me."

Hallie got ready for bed and snuffed the lamp. She prayed again for Rusty's loved ones and for Meg and Garth before she started to get into Garth's bed.

His bed, his pillows. Her face burned as she fleetingly imagined his being there, welcoming her into his arms. Could that ever happen?

If it did, she would be the happiest, most grateful woman in the world. She was grateful anyway to have the chance to help him, though she would have given anything to have kept it from being necessary.

Hallie's body rested where his had left slight hollows. The feather pillow was modeled softly by his head. The sheets were clean, but man scent mingled with bay rum lingered in mattress and pillows. She had thought she couldn't sleep that night, but tension dissolved as she felt and breathed in his evidences. She would not even worry about Raford. Not tonight.

XIII

$\mathcal{E}$ither Garth or Rory was at the hospital till Meg came home the fifth day after the accident. She was allowed to sit up in a wheelchair and she had crutches, but Garth carried her up and down the stairs.

"Will she be able to walk again?" Hallie asked Rory. She couldn't bear to ask Garth in case the answer was no.

"The doctor thinks there's a good chance she'll get back the use of her legs. He showed Garth how to massage her legs and feet to keep them healthy."

Garth must have done that in Meg's room. Meg was grudgingly civil to Hallie but clearly intended to be as independent of her as possible. She wheeled herself to the water bucket for a drink and to the table for meals.

Meg's bedroom was equipped with an enameled chamber pot for use at night. The morning after Meg came home, Hallie set it behind the davenport in the living room. "If you'll just tell me when you need to use it, I'll help you," she said.

The girl's face turned scarlet. "I'll go to the outhouse."

"It'll be hard to get down the steps on crutches."

"I'll do it!"

"Meg, please! You could fall and hurt yourself a lot worse."

"I don't care! I—I'd just as soon die as have you—or anyone—help me on and off the chamber pot!"

"They must have at the hospital."

"That's different. Everything's different there. It's not *living*."

Hallie had never had to stay in a hospital, but she could sympathize with Meg's feelings. She pondered. "How about this, then? Use one crutch and lean on me a little going down the steps. I'll go ahead and open the door. Then you can use me as a crutch climbing the steps."

"I'd rather do it alone."

"I know you would, and I wish you could. But your father's paying me to look after you, Meg. I can't let you do something dangerous."

Dark eyebrows pulled together above Meg's resentful gray eyes. Hallie met the almost-glare steadily. How she wished the child would let her be warm and comforting! But she was sure that trying to force that would only completely alienate Meg. At least Meg had infinite tenderness from her father, her young uncle's teasing affection, and Shaft's heart though he was well aware of her faults.

"All right," Meg conceded. "But I think you're being silly." She spun her chair away. "Come here, Jackie. I'll give you a ride. We'll go in circles, just like a merry-go-round!"

She helped him clamber up. They went round and round as fast as she could turn the wheels. Jackie squealed with delight and Meg laughed for the first time since coming home. Then Meg sent Jackie upstairs for one of her books, Dinah Maria Mulock Craig's *The Little Lame Prince*.

Meg bore Jackie off to the front room and read to him in her high, clear voice. It had been one of Hallie's favorite stories. As she went about her work, she smiled ruefully to think that Meg, surely putting herself more than ever in the role of Prince Dolor, was as certainly making Hallie into the convict nurse who cared for the helpless boy only because that was her only alternative to prison. Hallie's smile faded as she thought of how wonderful the traveling cloak must now seem to Meg. *Let her walk again—please let her walk—and I don't care how hateful she is to me.*

In an hour or so, Meg wheeled into the kitchen. "I need you for a crutch," she said as she rolled to the door.

If turning Hallie into a piece of wood made it easier for Meg, that was fine with Hallie. Crutches don't smile, but Hallie ventured one. "Here's your crutch," she said, and took one of them while bending down to proffer her shoulder.

While Hallie waited, she surveyed the yard. Since there was no livestock to water, there was no windmill or tank, but a pump close to the back door. The cellar, at the other side of the door, used for coal storage and as a place of refuge during tornadoes, was solidly built with cement walls and floor. Its wood ceiling was mounded with earth, and the door was constructed of heavy boards nailed together and reinforced top, bottom, and crosswise.

The long storage building for the engine and separator had an extended metal roof which formed a shed, walled on three sides, to shelter the coal and water wagons and the truck. Garth had repaired the water wagon. Two wire clotheslines ran from the shed to two iron posts planted in cement. The house, never painted, had weathered to gray. Everything was built to last, but the ground was barren except for tufts of little bluestem and grama grass, a thicket of sandhill plums beyond the clotheslines, a black locust with leathery brown seed pods near the privy, and thistles and sunflowers, now gone to seed to the gratification of this morning of sparrows, goldfinches, and a pair of cardinals.

What a difference some hollyhocks and tiger lilies would make! Planted where they'd catch the runoff from the roof, they wouldn't take much water. A bush of fragrant lilacs might be coaxed to shield the privy. Why hadn't Garth planted a few fruit trees that would give both food and shade? The answer to that was the same as why he didn't keep milk cows. Anything needing regular care would die while he was off threshing. But some hardy perennials— Meg came out and Hallie closed the door.

After that, Meg wheeled to the door and called, "Crutch!" when she wanted assistance. Maybe she pretended it was like Prince Dolor's magic word that ordered the cloak to carry him out of the tower window to soar among the clouds and birds.

"What kind of manners is that?" Rory growled the first time he heard it.

Hallie said quickly, "We've made up a game." Garth, who had raised his head and looked ready to rebuke his daughter, relaxed visibly.

As Hallie supported Meg down the steps and handed her the crutch, Meg paused for a moment. "I'm glad you didn't whine to Uncle Rory and Daddy."

"I don't want to do that any more than you want me to."

"I guess you don't want Daddy to think that you can't handle me."

"I don't want to worry him." At the jeering look on Meg's face, Hallie demanded, "Do you?"

"No, but—" Meg stumped the crutches around. Her head lowered and her shoulders heaved. "I want to walk!"

"I hope you will."

Meg sent a baleful glance over her shoulder. "*Do* you?"

"Of course!"

"Then what excuse would you have to stay here and make over Daddy?"

Before Hallie could summon an answer, Meg swung off for the privy. Too hurt and angry to speak with calm, Hallie hurried to open the door. No good response came to her while she waited. She blinked at the sting in her eyes.

Spiteful little cat! Meg was set on thinking the worst of her and didn't appreciate one bit Hallie's efforts to be patient and spare her pride though she knew perfectly well that she had to either get along with Hallie or stay at a home in town.

When the girl emerged, Hallie had still not thought of anything to say that might not turn into a flood of bitterness. A crutch, she thought. Fine. I'll be a crutch!

She closed the privy door. At the steps to the house, without a word, she took the crutch and offered her shoulder. Meg's grip on it was urgent.

"Are you going to tell Daddy?"

"I don't want to worry him. He has enough troubles." Just as she had feared, once she spoke Hallie couldn't restrain herself. "I won't put up with that kind of slur from you, though, Meg. I'll just quit and not say why."

They had reached the top of the steps. Hallie handed back the crutch. Meg caught her arm. "I don't want to stay at that awful place in town!"

In spite of her anger, Hallie pitied the girl, but she had no intention of listening to such accusations. "Where you stay is up to you," she said in a level voice.

Meg's face crumpled. She stared at Hallie from frightened eyes. Slowly, she opened her lips. Hallie relented. "You don't have to say you're sorry, Meg. Just don't do it again."

She held the door open to let the girl pass through. Far from being pleased at facing Meg down, she felt discouraged and defeated. She could all too well imagine the girl's venom sealed up and boiling within her. She'll never like me now, Hallie thought with a pang. I was a fool to hope she might. But at least I can stay while Garth needs me. I'm just not old enough or wise enough or good enough to let her say whatever she wants to and go on as if it doesn't matter.

$\mathscr{G}$arth went to see Meg's teacher at the country school three miles away and came home with seventh-grade schoolbooks and assignments. "Miss Howell said to send the written lessons in when someone's going that way," he said. "She'll send tests you can take under adult supervision. When you go back, you should be able to fit right in."

Meg regarded the stack of books, the new notebook, tablet, pen, and pencils without enthusiasm. Hallie didn't think it was the right moment to suggest that she'd be glad to help. Aimlessly, Meg reached for the top book, a geography. She flipped it open with a grimace.

"Look!" Jackie cried. "There's a camel! Wouldn't it be fun to ride one? Can you read about him, Meg?"

"Climb up and I will," she said. "And then we'll see how much you remember." She laughed up at her father who was looking relieved. "Wouldn't it be funny if Jackie knows seventh-grade subjects before he starts first grade?"

"Miss Howell may be a mighty surprised lady," Garth said. His eyes met Hallie's in mutual relief.

Meg had to do her arithmetic and diagram sentences on her own, but Jackie loved her history, geography, science, and reader. By pretending to teach him every morning for a few hours, she seemed, from what Hallie observed, to be quite satisfactorily teaching herself.

By the end of September, the MacLeod brothers had plowed the fields and planted all the land to wheat except for what Hallie thought of as the Old Prairie.

"Garth's keeping away from Raford because he's afraid he couldn't keep from getting into a fight," Shaft told Hallie. "It'd make him feel better to punch Raford around, but Raford's the sort to file assault charges, and Garth doesn't need time in jail or a big fine. What he did do was raise so much Cain with the county officials that they didn't dare buy another of Raford's tin bridges. They're putting in a concrete bridge that'll hold up to heavy machinery."

Garth paid a price for his victory. He went to the courthouse, expecting to sign the usual contract for maintaining county roads that winter and was greeted with the news that Raford had been awarded the contract.

"I asked the county commissioners if it wasn't shady to give the contract to the Road Commissioner," Garth said at the supper table. "Seems Raford has resigned to devote himself to campaigning for the state legislature."

"Who's the new commissioner?" Rory asked.

"Pete Jenkins."

Shaft let out a disgusted sigh. "He'll do whatever Raford wants, just like he let him thresh his wheat."

"Can't blame him much," Garth shrugged. "Raford's bank holds Jenkins's mortgage."

"So what'll we do without the road work?" Rory demanded.

"We bought the corn sheller last year to take care of those German farmers on the Arkansas River who grow so much. I drove on over and talked to them. They'd like us to come again. They'll supply a crew and board us. I'll take the truck so we can come home weekends."

"So there's maybe a month's work."

"Have us another little job, too. Mr. Thomas wants us to move a house he bought for his daughter and her husband out to his farm."

Rory stared. "Sally got married? Pretty brown-eyed Sally?"

"Guess she decided it'll be a far day till you settle down."

The younger brother's eyes flicked toward Hallie. "I'm not so sure about that."

Garth's face tightened. "There's always work for an engine. We'll get by."

"We could set up a sawmill."

"Sure, if we want to travel to where there's a lot of trees."

"There's enough trees right here to keep us busy this winter."

It was a moment before Hallie understood what he meant, and it seemed to be seconds before Garth understood. "I'll never cut those trees or break that sod."

"Not even to keep our land?"

According to Shaft, Garth alone had put money into the land and machinery. His smoke gray eyes met Rory's blue ones. "If I have to sell out, I'll try to sell to someone who feels the way I do about leaving some land wild."

Rory grated his chair back from the table. "You say I'm your partner, but you sure do exactly what you want!"

"I have to live with what I do."

"Well, let's just hope you figure out a way to live on it, too. If you'd threshed Raford at the start of the run, we'd never have had all this trouble."

Garth didn't wince openly, but Hallie saw the hurt in his eyes, and then the anger. "No one had to stay with me. You could've quit, like Pat O'Malley."

"You're my brother!"

"Don't let that worry you if you see a better chance."

Rory made a disgusted sound and got to his feet. "Hallie, want to go to town for a movie? Douglas Fairbanks in *The Thief of Baghdad* sounds pretty good."

He knew Meg needed her to get to the outhouse. Anyway, Hallie didn't want to give him any encouragement. "Thanks, but I can't."

"Won't, you mean. Well, I'm for town!" He gave his brother a challenging look. "That is if I can use the truck, boss."

"You know you can." Garth sounded weary.

As the truck gasped, coughed, and finally started, Shaft said, "He's just young, Garth."

"Sure." But Garth refused his favorite deep-dish apple pie.

"I wish *I* could go to the movie," said Meg. "I'm sick and tired of this old chair!"

"Honey, I know you are." Garth leaned over to squeeze his daughter's hand. "Does it seem like you can put more weight on your legs, like they're moving better?"

"Maybe a little. It's hard to tell. I'd like to burn the old crutches and this chair, too!"

"Hey!" Garth pleaded in mock horror, "Won't it be okay to just turn them back in to the hospital and go to the movie and soda fountain with the deposit?"

Meg laughed reluctantly. "I guess so." She sobered. "Daddy, how do you suppose Luke is? And Rusty's little kids?"

"I have to think they're getting along as well as they can without Rusty. Luke promised to write once in a while, especially if there was any big problem."

"Could I write to him?"

"I expect he'd like that. Just don't be disappointed if he's slow in answering. Lots of people love to get letters but never get around to writing one."

"I want to draw Luke a picture of Meg's wheelchair," put in Jackie. "I like to go round and round in it."

"Yes, that's fun as long as you don't have to use the darned thing," Meg retorted. "But you draw a good picture, and we'll mail it with my letter."

They were just completing this project a few days later when, as if Meg's question had summoned it, a letter came from Luke addressed to Meg and Garth.

"Doesn't he have the most beautiful handwriting?" Meg said, admiring it and even deigning to pass it to Hallie. "It runs so smooth and pretty. And look, Jackie! He's drawn a picture of the new mules! Daddy, Luke's an artist!"

"He's got a knack." Garth smiled as he passed the picture to Shaft, who nodded. "You can see the one mule's feisty and the other's as hard to stir up as froze molasses. Mind reading the letter, Meggie?"

She did, swallowing hard and scrubbing away tears when she read the parts about how Rusty's wife and children had taken the terrible news and how much they missed the big, fun-loving gentle-spoken man.

"They will be all right, though," Meg read through her tears. *"Our neighbors are helping, and with the mules, I can plow in return for things we need. We bought four cows with calves and sell enough cream to pay for what cash stuff we need. Our mother has seen much trouble. She comforts us all and reminds us that we were lucky to have Rusty as long as we did. My sister does not blame anyone for the accident. She says it was Rusty's appointed hour. She thanks you all for the collection that bought the mules and four cows and paid for the funeral, and she wants you to know that Rusty's wages are safe in the back of the big clock on the mantel."* He had earlier asked Meg how she was, and he ended by saying, *"I hope you were not much hurt, Meg. Please let me know. Tell Shaft I miss his music and sourdough biscuits. If you see Miss Hallie and Jack, say I think of them often and tell Jack I expect him to remember the difference between skunk and raccoon tracks. I hope I will see all of you next summer."*

"He's a fine young man," Garth said. "I'll never forgive myself for crossing that bridge, but I sure feel better to know that Mrs. Wells doesn't hate me. Meg, before you seal up your letter, let me put in a note."

"Guess I'd like to scratch a few lines," Shaft said.

"So would I," said Hallie. Maybe you can't think of what to say to bereaved folk, but you can at least say you're sorry.

Jackie looked alarmed. "Is there gonna be room for my picture, Meg?" He was beginning to ask her about things more often than he did Hallie. Glad though she was that the two were such excellent companions, Hallie felt increasingly excluded and hurt. *I took you when your mother didn't want you,* she sometimes felt like saying when, at Meg's summons, he sped past her without a glance. *Raford and probably Garth and goodness knows who else think you're my baby, not my brother. I know you're only a child, but I wish you could understood that I have feelings, too.*

She couldn't say any of this, of course. Maybe this was how her father felt when she begged to go live with the MacReynoldses, when she made no effort to see him for weeks on end. But that was because he brought Felicity home! she defended herself to herself. *He loved you and took care of you for twelve years, not just a few months. Now you have this chance to do something for him, take care of his little boy. Let's have no whining out of you.*

Now, at Jackie's anxious question, Meg gathered him to her in a hug. "Of course there'll be room for your picture! Just make it a good one."

The next day, with a very fat letter to mail, Garth took the truck and Rory the engine and corn sheller, a four-wheeled contraption with chutes, a funnel, and a much smaller power wheel than the separator. They would be working along the fertile bottoms of the Arkansas River about twenty miles north.

The night before, a sullen Meg allowed Garth to show Hallie how to massage the girl's legs and feet. "When we get back from shelling corn, I'll take you to the doctor," Garth told Meg. "We want to be able to say we did what he prescribed." Meg was so stiff, though, under Hallie's ministrations, that it was hard to believe the rubbing did much good.

While Meg held school with Jackie, often with Laird and Smoky in attendance, and Shaft mended fence—that perpetual task of farmers and ranchers—Hallie vented some of her frustration with Meg by undertaking an autumn "spring cleaning."

The house was neat, except for Rory's room, that looked like a tornado had passed through; but the woodwork needed washing or polishing, the windows were dingy inside and out, quilts and bedspreads needed washing, and the floors would benefit from a thorough cleaning followed by several coats of wax. The wallpaper, the same beige and olive stripe upstairs and down, was murky around the downstairs ceilings from coal smoke. Hallie had several times helped the MacReynoldses hang paper. She yearned to buy patterns suited to each room and get Shaft to help her put it up, but that would be presumptuous without Garth's approval.

It bothered her, though, not to have curtains, at least on bedroom windows, and in the kitchen, where the family spent most evenings. Raford had driven up once after dark. She hated the thought of his being able to look in and watch her. Yes, especially with Garth and Rory away, and Shaft sleeping in his little shack, she felt justified in insisting on at least some curtains.

Closets and storeroom yielded nothing that would work and she had no sewing machine, so she resorted to the Sears, Roebuck catalog. She pored over the curtain and drapery pages for a long time. Though this wasn't her house, this was the first time she'd been in charge of one, and she was spending her own money, so she was determined to choose something that would look pretty and not earn MacLeod disapproval. After scowling at the offending wallpaper that limited her choices, she settled on gold crinkled Austrian cloth for the kitchen and dusty green tapestry for her bedroom.

Would Meg like curtains? It was hard to believe any teenage girl wouldn't. Just then, Meg's peremptory call of "Crutch, please!" came from the screened porch. On the way to the outhouse, Hallie said, "I'm ordering some curtains for my bedroom. Would you like some for yours? There's some lovely damask—"

"I don't want any. Curtains get dirty and keep out the light."

So do dirty windows, Hallie thought. "You might at least have a look."

"I'm not going to squander Daddy's money."

"Neither am I. It's fair enough for me to pay for curtains since I seem to be the only one who misses them."

"That's not your bedroom, either," flashed Meg.

"No, but I'm sleeping there. I'm willing to pay for the curtains. When I leave, if they're not wanted, I can certainly take them down."

Meg's face twisted. "Well, you just remember that it's our house, not yours! We like it the way it is." She clumped into the privy.

Hallie counted to ten twice, but was still seething. Hateful brat! Try to do something nice for her, and get this kind of thanks! A faint honking sounded above. Hallie looked up to see a high, shimmering skein of wild geese flying south.

How would the house, the farm, even all of Raford's land, look to those high, far travelers whose thoroughfares were unmarked sky above a series of watering places where they descended to rest year after year? In the shining air, they called to each other, and perhaps the sun and wind. Human disputes and boundaries were nothing to them so long as their age-old resting places were not drained.

If they saw Hallie at all, she would be a tiny speck, nothing as visible as a cottonwood tree. Somehow, trying to imagine the earth from their lofty sweep calmed Hallie, made her take a long view, consider her ultimate purpose in being here.

That was to free Garth from worry about his daughter as he went about making a living and to make it possible for Meg to recuperate in familiar surroundings rather than go to the feared and detested invalid home. Ranking close to that was having employment that provided a good home for Jackie and allowed her to look after him.

Wonderful as it would be to win Meg's affection and trust, that was not Hallie's reason for staying. She couldn't keep herself from imagining how welcoming and pleasant she could make the austere house, and she would clean it thoroughly and wax the floors, but that was not her main goal, either.

So she would try to think of the high, wild geese next time Meg provoked her, and hold to her intention as the geese pursued their winter haven above the changing and divided earth.

When Meg came out, she darted a belligerent half-shamefaced look at Hallie. Hallie smiled and closed the door. "The geese are starting south."

Meg gazed up. The crutches seemed like skewers clamping her to the ground. "It must be wonderful to fly—to not even need a traveling cloak like Prince Dolor."

So the girl did escape with the lame prince and soar over the wide, wide world on his magic cloak. Hallie could not stay cold to her. "You probably will fly someday in an airplane."

"That's not the same."

"No. But I'd love, at least once, to watch the world spread out below the way the wild geese do."

Immediately, Hallie regretted confiding the wish. She braced herself for a jeering remark or withering glance, but Meg only looked at her in a puzzled fashion and swung along toward the house. Helping her up the steps, Hallie ventured a suggestion.

"I broke my ankle when I was about your age, Meg. It took it a long time to get strong again, but I got around by pushing a chair in front of me. That way I could put as much weight on it as was comfortable, but have support when I needed it."

Meg considered. "I might try it. I'm sick of these old crutches."

As soon as they were in the kitchen, Meg got next to a chair and leaned her crutches against the wall, gripping the high back. Gingerly at first, leaning heavily, then with increasing confidence, she shoved the chair along the floor.

"Why, I can use my legs better!" Her cheeks glowed with happy color. "I don't have to hop like I do on the crutches, but I can rest when I need to! Oh, I'm glad you broke your ankle, Hallie!" Hallie's shock must have been clear for Meg hastily added, "I mean, I'm glad you found out how to do this!"

Jackie watched a minute and asked, "Can I push a chair, too, Meg? We could run a race!"

Meg had the grace to look at Hallie. "*May* you," Hallie corrected and smothered a sigh as she relinquished her dream of a resplendent waxed floor. That wasn't a goal, though. It was only a wish. She brushed back her brother's curly dark hair. How he had grown since Felicity left him, and how brown and healthy he looked! She smiled and said, "Yes, Jackie, you may push a chair but I think you'll have to do it by the seat."

"Race you to the end of the front room!" cried Meg, and they were off.

Hallie watched them scoot out of the kitchen, more hopeful of friendship with Meg than she had ever been. Then she got the catalog and began to fill out her order.

XIV

$\mathscr{W}$hen he came home that weekend, Garth was so pleased that Meg was pushing around with chairs and getting more use of her legs that it stung only a little that Meg didn't credit Hallie for the idea. *Pretend you're a wild goose* had become Hallie's watchword for the high, long view. It did help.

The postman left the curtains and wax package in the big mailbox at the turnoff to the MacLeods on the same day that he brought a letter from Luke. "His writing's as beautiful as—as he is!" Meg said. "Look, Jackie, he drew you a picture of the cows and their calves!"

Her expression changed. Her fingers clenched on the paper before she handed it to Hallie and began to read the letter aloud. The sketch must have been done from memory. Hallie, in her sunbonnet, was at the controls of the engine while the belt ran to the separator. Garth and the pitchers on the stacks were defined by a few swift strokes but Hallie was drawn carefully, even her shadowed face. Meg, driving up with the water wagon, had her back turned.

Peering over her shoulder, Shaft whistled. "The boy's good! You can almost see that old belt whirrin' and the chaff spitting out."

"I like the cows and calves better," Meg said. "Now, Shaft, if you don't mind, I'd like to read this letter."

"Yes, ma'am, Miss Meggie." Shaft bowed low.

Luke was sawing up logs he and Rusty had cut and trimmed the year before, and splitting them into firewood; one size for the kitchen range, bigger chunks for the fireplace. They had slaughtered a hog, rendered out the lard for cooking, and Luke's mother and sister were making sausage and headcheese while hams and side meat cured in the smokehouse.

At night, while the women patched clothing, or worked on a quilt, Luke and the older children picked meats out of black walnuts or shelled corn. Mrs. Wells—Vinnie, Luke called her—usually popped a dishpan of fluffy corn and poured melted butter over it. Luke's mother told stories, or they sang songs, or just talked. *"Tell me what all of you are doing,"* Luke concluded. *"Send me another picture, Jackie. Meg, we all pray every night that you will soon be walking."*

Meg's voice wavered on the last sentence. "They—they're praying for me!" she choked, scrubbing at her eyes. "When you couldn't blame them if they hoped I'd be crippled forever!"

"They're not that kind of folks, honey." Shaft patted her shoulder. "But if you've got any dolls or toys or such you've outgrown, you could send them to the kids."

"I won't send them old stuff. Daddy saves my wages for college or whatever I'll want to do, but he'll get me a money order for Sears, Roebuck. Jackie, bring the catalog here, and let's pick out something nice for each of the kids."

While they were absorbed in this exciting task, Hallie swept and mopped the front room. As soon as the wood was dry, she began to rub in the wax with a soft rag while she knelt on an old doubled towel. The dry wood soaked up the wax thirstily, but the grain showed mellow and pale gold. Garth might not take much care of his floors, but he had bought expensive oak.

When this coat dried, she would buff it and put on another. Polished to a sheen, that ought to keep this seldom-used floor looking nice for a long time. She'd have to do the kitchen after everyone was in bed.

She had opened the front door in order to let the floor dry faster. Something blocked the light. She glanced up. The man seemed to fill the door. The sunlight spilling around him obscured his face, but she knew it was Raford.

"Stay outside," she ordered. "I don't want anyone tracking up the floor."

"Such hospitality!"

"You shouldn't be here at all."

"Oh? In that case, I'll just go my way and return this letter the MacReynoldses wrote you."

"Give it to me!" Hallie scrambled up. She opened the screen door and reached for the envelope.

He caught her hand, held it easily in spite of her efforts to withdraw it, and examined the wax-stained fingers and nails. "My God, Hallie! You'll ruin your hands!"

"They're my hands." She couldn't break free without attacking him with kicks, scratching, and teeth. He'd enjoy that. She willed her her hand to be lifeless in his, as a wild creature plays dead. "Give me my letter."

"MacLeod has a nerve to expect you to slave on your knees like this!"

"He doesn't expect it. He doesn't know I'm doing it."

Raford sucked in his breath. His eyes glittered like sunlit amber. "That makes it worse! You *want* to break your back for him!" He dropped her hand and caught her shoulders. "You're beautiful and special, Hallie. You belong with a man who would know how to take care of you."

She fought down panic at being gripped in those merciless iron fingers. "I'm not a horse or machine. I can take care of myself. Give me the letter."

His eyes flamed. His grasp tightened. Something in her expression checked him. He muttered a few words beneath his breath and let go of her so abruptly that she had to catch herself against the door.

"Why, when I finally love a woman, does she have to be a fool? Tell me this: are you warming his bed?"

Without thinking, Hallie slapped him as hard as she could, so hard her palm hurt. His arm drew back. She thought he'd hit her back, but after a moment, he laughed with relieved exultation. "He hasn't had you yet."

"You—you—"

"Can't think of anything bad enough?" Raford chuckled. "You

missed your only chance to be rid of me, my dear. If you'd blushed or looked ashamed, given away that you'd been with him, I'd have made myself leave you alone. I won't have MacLeod's leavings."

"You thought Jackie was my child."

"I could forgive a slip that happened when you were little more than a child yourself. But I've had a letter from the MacReynoldses, too. They confirm what you told me; that the boy is your half-brother."

"What can I do to make you believe me? There's no way on earth I'll ever—"

She couldn't even say it. He smiled. "Never say never, Hallie love."

He gave her the envelope and sauntered toward the Pierce-Arrow that was parked some distance down the road. So he could come up quietly, take her by surprise. Hallie began to tremble. She sat down on the front step to read the MacReynoldses letter.

As she read, slow anger burned in her. It was clear that Raford had given them a dire picture of her circumstances. They wrote that she and Jackie were welcome to come live with them in Maryland, though their house was small and it would be a little crowded. They could look after Jackie while Hallie worked in an office or store.

"Though," Mrs. MacReynolds admonished, *"it really sounds as if you should go back to the Rafords. He's baffled as to why you left but is willing to give you another chance."*

I'll bet, Hallie thought grimly. She had written the MacReynoldses a few times that summer but explained there was no way they could answer till the run was over. She had, in fact, got off a letter a few days ago, but they wouldn't have it yet.

Maybe what she told them would allay their worries over whatever Raford had passed on, but they had been kind to her and she didn't want them troubled. That was why she hadn't told them why she'd left Rafords, only that it seemed like a way to keep Jackie from missing his mother so much.

Tonight, while thanking them for their concern and kindness, she would set them straight on that and any other lies Raford might write them in future. She didn't even consider going to Maryland.

$\mathscr{S}$haft put up rods for the curtains and helped Hallie hang them. They looked even better than she had hoped, emphasizing and framing the outside views and brightening the colors of the wallpaper. Would Garth like them?

Meg didn't. "They'll just get dirty," she said with a curl of her lip when Hallie stepped back to admire the transformed kitchen windows.

"Then I'll wash them."

"They make it dark."

"How can they? Look, I ordered the rods long enough so the curtains cover the woodwork but don't shade the window at all unless they're closed on purpose."

Meg shrugged and smiled at Jackie, who was wriggling with impatience. "Do you want to show Shaft and your sister what we ordered for Rusty's kids?"

Nodding, Jackie opened the catalog on the table to the first marker. "We picked out this dump truck and this locomotive." He flipped pages to the other things. "And Tinkertoys and a blackboard that makes into a desk and paints and this big teddy bear and a uke-uke— well, a uke! And look! A red wagon like the one I used to have, and Meg's ordered one for me, too!"

Hallie's conscience smote her. Why hadn't she thought of that? Toys would have been in the way during the run, and they had never stayed in one place long enough for Jackie to exhaust the natural possibilities. Now that they were settled, of course he'd miss the toys he used to have.

"I want to pay for the wagon," Hallie said. It cost $5.98, a week's pay for being in the cookshack from four in the morning till supper dishes were done about nine in the evening. "And I'd like to help buy the other things, Meg."

"No. I want them to be from me." Jackie looked crestfallen. Meg gave him a hug and added, "And from Jackie, of course." The girl stared at Hallie above Jackie's dark head. "I want to give him the wagon. You can get him something else."

Don't let this turn into a contest, Hallie warned herself. It wouldn't be good for her brother to sense that he could manipulate them. Jackie's birthday was a few days before Christmas. She would replenish his toys then. Now she forced a smile and said, "That's very generous of you, Meg."

After the others were in bed that night, Hallie waxed the kitchen floor by lamplight. The drawn curtains made her feel safe and protected—as much as she could with Raford living three miles up the road.

He had left no mark on her wrists and hands, yet they felt bruised. Why was he so set on her? It must be because he wasn't used to being refused, and he found her provocatively different. Also, just as he coveted Garth's land, he would want any woman he thought Garth might care for—not that he had that reason in her case, Hallie thought. She rubbed the wax vigorously.

It was past midnight when Hallie polished the second coat by sliding around the room on part of an old sheet. Panting and exhilarated, she surveyed the shining floor and gold curtains. It looked beautiful—an entirely changed room—and she had done it, mostly by hard work.

Garth would be home tomorrow night. Surely, surely he would like what she had done.

It was hard to tell whether he did or not. Rory whistled when they entered the kitchen and went back on the porch to wipe his feet on the mat. Garth had wiped his feet well the first time. After kissing Meg and greeting the rest of them, he glanced about the room.

"You'll tell me the cost of the curtains and whatever you used on the floor," he said. "I'll add it to your wages."

Reminding her that she was hired help, that it was presumptuous of her to do anything without his permission. Hallie felt blood heat her face, but deep as the humiliation was her disappointment. She didn't speak till she thought she had her voice under control, but it betrayed her by fraying a little.

"Waxing the floor makes it easier to keep clean and take care of. *I* like curtains, but since I seem to be the only one who does, let's just consider them mine. I'll take them with me when I leave."

"They look spiffy," Rory approved. "Guess us heathens just never thought about having any. Or waxing floors."

"It does look different," Garth said. His face was unreadable, and whether he meant his remark as a compliment or a complaint, Hallie couldn't guess.

Very early the next morning, she found him gluing felt rounds from a dilapidated hat on the bottom of the chair legs and tables. He blushed, as if caught at something shameful.

"No use you spending all your time on floors." His tone was gruff, but his words were sweeter to her than all of Rory's blandishments. "This'll keep the wax from getting scratched so easy."

"Thank you, Garth."

He slanted a half-grin at her. His hair was tousled, as if he hadn't combed it yet. She had an almost irresistible urge to bury her hands in the silvery gold mass and let her fingers trace the contours of his head, smooth away the lines at his eyes, and mouth. The mouth she longed to feel on hers.

"It's for me to thank you, Hallie. Even an old bachelor like me can see this place looks a sight more like a"—he searched for another word, couldn't find it, and said doggedly—"like a home."

He bent to his work. Hallie wished she were brave enough to put her arms around him but she was afraid of being repulsed. Better just be grateful for what he said, the care he was taking to protect her labor. But someday— Someday, maybe.

*M*onday had been washday at the MacReynoldses, and Hallie resumed the custom here. She might have lamented the MacReynolds' electric machine more if she hadn't had a summer of washing with the stomper and wringing by hand. After that, it seemed luxury enough to simply turn the lever that propelled the rotating apparatus in the High Speed Wizard that had a corrugated lining inside its wooden outer tub. It could wash six sheets at a time. Hallie ran the laundry through the hand wringer, drained the machine through the drain cock at the bottom, filled it up with water from the pump, rinsed white things twice and coloreds once, and hung them out on clotheslines that ran from the machinery shed to two steel posts.

She was battling a flapping sheet when she heard a motor. A hacking one, not the smooth purr of Raford's Pierce-Arrow that could scarcely be heard from a distance. Subduing the sheet with more clothespins, Hallie turned as a roadster churned up to the house. Cotton Harris got out.

Hallie froze. She was sure he hadn't forgotten how she'd swung the mop in his face. Shaft was fixing fence on the north boundary. Except for the children, she was alone. She glanced around in vain for a handy weapon. The willow clothes basket wasn't formidable. There were lots of tools in the shed, but she didn't want to show her fear by running in search of one.

She started for the house, heartily wishing for a butcher knife, hammer, or any such defense. Her only comfort was that if Cotton was working for Raford, or hoped to do so again, he would know of Raford's interest in her and be afraid to do her any real harm.

"Does my heart good to see a woman doin' woman's work." Cotton's twisted grin revealed tobacco-stained teeth and though the summer was past, he still was sunburned. "It was a plumb disgrace, the way you wore overalls and drove that engine."

"What do you want?"

His pale, pink-rimmed eyes slid over her. "What I want and what I'm here for are two different things. Reckon you know Quent Raford's running for the state legislature."

"I'd heard that."

"You aimin' to vote?"

"I can't. I'm not twenty-one."

He spat in the dust. "It's a scandal women can vote at all. But Mr. Raford's hired me to go find him votes, so I thought I'd be neighborly and stop by."

"You know no one here would vote for him."

"Plenty will. Sophie Brockett's organizin' ladies' meetings and socials and such." He tilted his head—he hadn't removed his sporty felt hat—and squinted through narrowed eyes. "Mr. Raford can charm females, and we'll sure take their votes, but I'll promise you one thing. Bein' in the legislature is just a leg up toward runnin' for governor."

"Mr. Raford's plans are none of my concern."

"They will be." Cotton drew himself up but he was still only a few inches taller than Hallie. "I have his solemn word that he'll make it so hot for Catholics and Jews and niggers and red niggers like your friend Luke, and draft dodgers like Henry Lowen that they'll be glad to get out of Kansas alive."

Hallie's scalp crawled at the hatred in his eyes and voice. "You *do* belong to the Klan, don't you?" she whispered.

"I do, and I'm proud of it. Just a few years ago, there weren't hardly any of us, but now we're everywhere and gettin' stronger." He crossed his arms. His slow appraisal was an insult. "We're goin' to make America decent again. Down in Texas, I've helped whip women who divorced their husbands or voted or cut off their hair or wore face paint or men's clothes. One gal who led me on and then tried to play righteous and pure, we fixed her good. Mr. Raford's told me he's got plans for you, but if that ever changes, I'll make you sorry you ever swung that mop at me."

"I don't want to tell Garth MacLeod you've been here, but I will if you don't get off this place and stay off."

"Got no reason to stay. But I'll just leave you a handbill." Hallie wouldn't take the yellow poster. He swaggered to the door and thrust it in the screen.

Raford's likeness smiled at her. A PATRIOT WHO DARES TO SAY AMERICA'S FOR AMERICANS! trumpeted the lines above his head. Beneath was lettered: A NEW DAY FOR KANSAS.

Hallie tore the offending handbill from the door and crumpled it. Cotton just laughed. "You'll get what's coming to you," he called as he got into the roadster. "I hope I get to give it, but one way or another, it'll come."

He drove away, tires flailing up dust. A Klansman! One of the hooded cross-burning hate group that lynched blacks and etched their victims' foreheads with KKK or a cross. Hallie had seen them on newsreels in their white sheets and peaked hoods. If they weren't so scary and horrible, they'd be ridiculous.

Shaken and dizzy, Hallie leaned against the door. Cotton's eyes had glued themselves to her in a way that made her feel slimy, soiled. That poor girl down in Texas—what had he done to her? The idea of someone like him judging and punishing was such a travesty that Hallie wanted to believe it couldn't happen—but she knew it could.

That night after the children were in bed, she got Shaft to promise not to tell Garth or do anything himself, and then told the cook about Cotton's threats.

"Do you think there's a chance Raford could get elected by catering to the Klan?" she asked. "If there are any of them around Hollister, I certainly never heard about it."

"That no-account Cotton could be starting groups wherever he finds some likely prospects." Shaft's bushy eyebrows met above his crooked nose. "The Klan's spreading. It's not just in the Deep South."

Hallie nodded. "Yes, last year, the governor of Oklahoma called out the National Guard to control Klansmen. When he lost the election a few months later, most people believed it was because he stood up to the Klan."

"Yeah, and remember this July when they found a minister dead in Michigan with KKK branded on his back?" Shaft's voice thickened with disgust. "And in August, about the time Henry Ford was praisin' the KKK as patriots, six Illinois folks got killed in some kind of Klan uproar."

Hallie shivered. "Cotton said he'd helped whip women down in Texas."

"He'd get a kick out of that. But Texas has outlawed masks, and Ma Ferguson, who's running for governor, sure gives the Klan the devil."

"Coolidge won't say where he stands, though." Hallie worried.

"No, but folks like his "Silent Cal" act, and they're sorry for him because his young son died. He'll win."

"It's so awful! If Cotton had his way, he'd kill people like Henry Lowen and Luke, or run them out of the country. And what he'd do to women!"

"He's a mean one, but too ign'rant to swing much weight except with his own kind. I doubt if Kansas has too many of 'em since so many folks came here from other countries less than fifty years ago. It's the smooth customers like Raford that we have to worry about."

Shaft tugged disquietedly at his beard. "I sure don't like that varmint comin' around you, Hallie. Maybe I better forget the fence and work close to the house."

"I don't think he'll be back. If he is, I'll tell Raford." At Shaft's puzzled look, she explained. "Raford evidently told Cotton that he's got plans for me and not to do me any harm."

"I don't like the sound of that!"

"Neither do I. But, after all, he's not a robber baron who can kidnap me. I don't see that he can do much."

"If Garth knew—"

"He mustn't! The last thing Garth needs is more trouble. If he got in a fight with Raford, *he's* the one who'd wind up in jail or fined for assault."

Shaft heaved a long sigh. "I'm afraid you're right."

"I'm sorry," Hallie repented. "I shouldn't have told you, either, and got you upset, but I—I just had to talk to somebody."

"Aw, honey, you can tell old Shaft anything. If it makes you feel better, I'm at least good for somethin'."

"You're good for a lot!" Hallie gave him a quick hug. "I just can't tell you, Shaft, how glad I am you spoke for me that day we met and got Garth to hire me. It was the luckiest day of my life, and Jackie's, too!"

Shaft's rough old hand caressed her cheek. "I hope you'll say that a year from now, Hallie girl. I reckon I was in luck the day my deputy cousin let me go out the back window and again the day Garth hired me on, but the luckiest day of all my born days was when you and Jackie turned up to be my family." He looked into her eyes, as if searching for answers. "If Garth wasn't so blamed scared of women! You be patient with him, honey."

"I have to be."

When Shaft looked a question, Hallie met his gaze and said, blushing, "I—I love him."

Shaft caught in a delighted breath. "So you finally admitted it!"

"Not that it helps—"

"He'll come around."

Hallie grimaced. "Even if he does, I don't think Meg ever will."

"Maybe not. She's mighty used to having Garth be all her own.

Love's like picking blackberries, honey. The fruit's sweet and juicy, but you get a lot of scratches." Shaft gave Hallie a level stare. "Can you wait five years? Till Meg's old enough to make her own home?"

Five years! It seemed forever. But again, listening to her heart, Hallie said, "I don't have any choice."

XV

$\mathscr{S}$himmering clouds of white-breasted, black-bibbed, dusky-backed horned larks with their plaintive tinkling call and bolder fluting yellow-breasted black-necklaced meadowlarks rose from or descended on the stubbled fields. White-crowned sparrows trilled as they hopped briskly in search of seeds and goldfinches in gray-brown winter plumage swayed thistle stalks as they fed and sweetly called *per-chik-oree* as they flew. Shaft tied chunks of tallow to the naked black locust tree. This attracted several gossipy long-tailed magpies, mockingbirds, and flickers. A pair of cardinals, the male jaunty crimson, the female duskily modest, devoured the last of the dried sandhill plums. Red-tailed hawks soared above, sometimes circling before plummeting down for a rabbit or mouse.

Jackie's wagon arrived, shining red with balloon tires. He brought coal from the cellar, though he got to pull it only about fifteen feet before loading it into a bucket to carry inside. He hauled the mail home from the mailbox, and foraged the Old Prairie for dried yucca stalks, which made good kindling.

"There was a St. Louis company bought them soapweeds for a while," Shaft remembered. "They made rope and cord and soap, but the freight cost so much that the company couldn't make a profit. In the spring, when the soapweed shoots are nice and tender, they're good eating. Boil 'em and slap on butter and a little salt and pepper."

At the end of October, Garth and Rory finished in the Arkansas River bottoms and brought the engine and corn sheller home. They moved what would soon be brown-eyed Sally Thomas's home from Hollister to her parents' farm and returned to the MacLeod farm with Rory tootling exuberantly on the whistle as the engine chugged up the lane.

"We're going to help build a railroad across the Texas Panhandle!" Rory shouted as he jumped down from the platform. "It'll keep us working till spring at good pay. They wanted us to leave tomorrow, but I said this is my first year to vote, and I sure aim to do it. Want to see William Allen White get in as governor and don't want old Careful Cal to be president."

William Allen White was the longtime editor and owner of the *Emporia Gazette*. When Hallie was in school, her class had studied his famous 1896 editorial, "What's Wrong with Kansas?," which brought White national fame and was used by the Republican campaign to help elect McKinley.

"My feelings exactly," Garth said. "I doubt if White can win, but he's sure waked people up to the danger of the Klan's taking over the state. We'll stop by the schoolhouse, vote, and head south." His step was springy despite a hard day's work, and the lines etched his at mouth and and eyes didn't seem so deep. "There's a job for you, Shaft, if you'll cook." Garth's eyes came to Hallie. "If you're willing to stay—"

It took her a moment to absorb the fact that he would be gone all winter, and another moment to comprehend that if Shaft went, too, she'd be alone on this farm with two children, one of them hostile, and with Raford and Cotton too close for comfort.

Hallie's face must have betrayed her dismay. Garth shrugged and said, "Can't blame you for not wanting to be stuck out here alone. Of course I'd fix it for folks like the Crutchfields and Donnellys to stop by every week or so and see how you're doing and what you need from town. Donnellys' oldest little girl starts started school this fall, and Mike or Mary drive her. I'm going to ask if they can take Meg when she's able to go back. Till then, they've already offered to pick up her assignments and take them to the teacher every week." He looked at Meg. "I'll take you to see the doctor tomorrow, honey. Maybe—"

Meg whirled her chair around and wheeled into the front room, but not before Hallie saw tears and quivering lips. Poor Meg! Trapped in the house by her lameness, and her father gone till spring! If Shaft went, too, she'd really feel like Prince Dolor, locked up with his criminal nurse.

It'll be pretty awful for me, too, Hallie thought. Months without seeing Garth, having to put up with Meg's balkiness. But I can't leave her even if she is hateful. With Raford cutting Garth out of the county road work, he really needs this job. Only how will I manage without Shaft? His music and jokes and his—yes, his love. It makes my heart warm deep down where it froze when I was mad at Daddy and thought he didn't love me because Felicity shoved me out.

Hallie hadn't known exactly when Garth and Rory were coming home, but she had baked apple dumplings that day and the kitchen had a good smell of cinnamon, crust, and fruit. Beans flavored with onions, tomatoes, and hot peppers were simmering gently. While the brothers cleaned up, Hallie made cornbread and set the table, scarcely knowing what she was doing.

Till now she hadn't realized just how much she had looked forward to seeing Garth almost daily that winter, preparing his food and sharing it with him, having his home comfortable for him when he came in from work, knowing he was asleep just down the hall—almost being a family.

Now there would be none of that. If Shaft went, too, how would she bear the loneliness—Meg's as well as her own? Shaft didn't need to earn wages that winter. He got his food and little shack for working around the place. She would ask him not to go, even tell him, if she had to, about Raford's visits. Garth must not know about them. He might get into more trouble with Raford, who already wanted to cause Garth all the grief he could.

Rory and Shaft did most of the talking at supper. Meg's eyes were red, and she barely nibbled. Hallie, when no one was watching, tried to fix a picture of Garth in her mind so vividly that she could call it up during the once anticipated winter that seemed now to stretch ahead endlessly.

She loved the angles of his face, the thrust of jaw, the way he held his head, the straight mouth that softened when he looked at Meg.

She loved his hands, shapely though muscular, with long, blunt-tipped fingers. Those dark gray eyes were startling in his brown face, like the mass of fair hair that fell across his forehead though he'd slicked it back with water. He smelled like salt and earth and grain—like a man, her man. She closed her eyes to breathe in and hold the scent of him. It filled her, permeating the center of her body, till she felt possessed by him.

Hallie opened her eyes to find his fixed on her. Sweet, tremulous lightning flowed between them, ran through her veins. Could he guess what she'd been feeling? As if seared, he looked away. She blushed and was amazed to see heightened color stain his face and throat to the opened collar. Did she have an odor for him—a special one, as he did for her?

The thought seemed not quite nice; one of those deceits of the world, the flesh, and the devil from which the prayer in Grandmother Harriet's book asked deliverance. Hallie couldn't ask to be delivered, though. She hungered for his touch, for the feel of his body, the knowledge of his mouth. Men were supposed to want such things more readily and imperiously than women, weren't they? Her senses clamored that Garth did want her even if he didn't love her; but when she dared glance his way again, he was watching Meg with such a fiercely protective expression that Hallie's brief elation died.

Meg was Garth's first concern, his first allegiance. Hallie could accept that, at least while Meg was still at home. Hallie wished her own father had felt that way, or at least considered her more before marrying Felicity. But in spite of the lightning and the way she yearned for him, Hallie wanted more than the physical loving which seemed to her so rapturously awesome and mysterious. She wanted to live with Garth the rest of their lives, to share days and work as well as passion.

Would he ever allow that, even when Meg was grown? *Can you wait?* Shaft had asked. Hallie placed this season against the years till Meg was eighteen and tried to take the long view—capture the sweeping vision of the wild geese—but she was mortal, earthbound, and all she could see was winter.

$\mathcal{H}$allie was washing the men's clothes next morning while Rory readied the engine for the long journey south and Garth took Meg to the doctor. That afternoon he would clean and oil the separator which would stay in the shed till spring. Shaft came in the porch and took over turning the lever.

"Hallie, I can tell you don't like the notion of staying here alone with the kids. Are you scared of Cotton Harris?"

"Not that he'll do anything. Raford's evidently told him not to try to get even for that mop I swung in his face. But I don't feel too comfortable knowing he's around."

"I'll stay if you say so. But I hope you'll decide you can manage. I don't need the money myself, but Garth may. He's runnin' on a mighty thin edge, even with this railroad job. I'd like to be able to help him if he needs it."

So would I, Hallie thought. And he does need it, so I just have to make myself be able. From somewhere she dredged up a smile and fended Shaft away from the lever. "You'd better start getting the cookshack ready. We'll be all right."

When Garth and Meg returned from the doctor, their faces told the results of the examination. "Doc says to just keep up the massage," Garth said. With attempted cheerfulness, he added, "He says Meg's muscles have stayed supple and—"

"But he didn't say I'll ever walk again!" Meg cried. Swiftly, she pushed her chair into the other room.

Garth looked helpless. Then he turned and went outside.

For the next two days, Hallie treasured every moment she could watch Garth or be with him, hoarded them for the months ahead. She cooked the foods he liked and mended and sewed on buttons for all three men. At supper and afterward, talk centered on the election.

"It's plumb disgraceful that Coolidge won't come out against the Ku Klux Klan," Shaft growled as he sipped his coffee. "I'm sure votin' for John W. Davis, but lots of people are scared of disarmament and the League of Nations."

Garth nodded. "Being for them may cost the Democrats the election, though you'd think Coolidge would just have to sink from having all the Harding administration scandals tied around his neck. I'm worried about Kansas, too, but mighty glad White's been pouring it on the Klan."

"Wouldn't be too healthy for guys like Henry Lowen if the Klan gets strong here," Rory said.

"Or for me," Shaft rumbled. " 'Cordin' to that bunch, I'm a bohunk." He snorted. "They don't like Indians, but everybody else, including their families, had to come from somewhere across the water."

Rory fired up the engine before daylight next morning. It was already hitched to the cookshack, coal, and water wagons. Garth would be the fireman, and they would hire a water monkey in Texas. They were taking the truck since they would need it for getting around, and Hallie wasn't eager to drive it.

Hallie woke as Rory went downstairs and could not go back to sleep. Her heart was too heavy to allow her to enjoy a last luxurious snuggling into her pillow. She dressed and went to the kitchen. It was chill enough to make a fire in the big range welcome. She got one going and started cinnamon rolls. While the dough raised, she put on coffee and got water boiling for steel-cut oats that were so chewy and delicious.

She heard quiet steps on the stairs and turned as Garth entered the room. "A fire feels good these mornings." He came to stand by the stove. There was still a sleepy look in his eyes, a young vulnerability in his face. He sniffed appreciatively. "Cinnamon rolls! You're seeing us off in style, Hallie. Is the coffee ready?"

She poured him a cup and one for herself. This was how she had hoped it would be all winter. It was achingly sweet to be alone with him in the snug room with mellow lamplight and curtains still drawn against the darkness.

"Garth—I'll keep up Meg's massage—do my best for her."

"I know you will." His eyes touched her. "Your hair's growing."

"Yes. By the time it's long enough to braid, I'll have to cut it off for the threshing run. Right now it's too short to braid or put in a French knot, and too long to fly loose."

"I like it loose. My grandmother used to sing an old Island song I thought was beautiful. '*Oh, girl with the sea-gray eyes, your hair has captured me like ropes of silk, like a net of black silver . . .* ' "

Rory banged the porch door. Meg called from upstairs. Garth drained his coffee and went up to get her as his brother came in, followed by Shaft. Hallie thrust the cinnamon rolls into the oven and gave the oats an irate stir.

What would Garth have said if they had had just a few more private moments? At least he had noticed her hair. And that song was lovely, even if he had only been reminiscing, rather than using it to speak to her.

After breakfast, Rory put more water in the boiler and closed the dampers. "That ought to hold it till we're back from voting," he said to Hallie. "But maybe you'd check the pressure once in a while. If the gauge shows less than sixty, you could open the dampers and put in a little coal."

The men drove the truck to the schoolhouse and voted as soon as the polls opened. "Cotton Harris was hanging around," Rory said. "He had a flivver parked a hundred feet from the polls behind some cottonwoods. He was handing out drinks from a red fifty-gallon Coca-Cola barrel but if it wasn't Jamaica Ginger, I'm a monkey's uncle."

"It was jake. I could smell it," Shaft grunted, wrinkling his crooked beak. "Ninety percent alcohol, the kind of rotgut that's blinded lots of folks or given 'em the staggers. Not like the prime stuff I used to make."

"Cotton's friends wouldn't know the difference," said Garth. He frowned. "They more than likely drink plain old Alcorub they get at the drugstore. We've got the secret ballot, thank goodness, but I'd reckon everyone with a mortgage held by Raford's bank is going to vote for him along with the ones Cotton buys with whiskey and his hate talk. Raford's too smart to peddle that line himself. He'll fool a bunch of respectable folks who think he's just patriotic."

"Have some coffee and a cinnamon roll before you leave," Hallie urged, clutching at every minute with Garth. "The pressure's fine, Rory."

Meg, Jackie, and Hallie sat down with the men for the last small meal. The rolls, just out of the oven, were fragrant with cinnamon and sugar, but Hallie barely tasted hers. Her stomach knotted in a tight, sick ball, and her throat ached. Garth was leaving. All of the men were. Soon she would be alone with the children, be alone for months.

"Are just you three gonna build the railroad?" Jackie asked.

"No, lad. There'll be dump-wagon drivers and Fresno operators, and I don't know what all," Garth smiled. "We'll meet the rest of the crew down in Texas, at the town where we'll all start building the roadbed."

"How do you do that?" pursued Jackie.

"Guess we'll level off the hills to fill in the valleys."

Jackie's eyes grew round. "Will you lay the tracks, Garth?"

"No, laddie. We'll just haul the grader. It has a plowshare that digs up dirt and throws it on a conveyor belt that raises up high enough to dump the load into horse-drawn wagons traveling alongside. The Fresnos—those are big machines hauled by horses—will be moving earth, too. When the bed's solid and level and the cross-ties laid, a crane will pick up a rail and lay it on the ties. Then tracklayers move it in place, bolt it to the last rail, and drive in spikes to hold the rail to the ties."

"Do the spikes ever come loose?" Jackie worried.

"Let's hope not. That's why the road has to be done right, so there won't be trouble later. After enough track is laid, a locomotive chugs along pushing flatcars of rails to the end of track. A crane is mounted on the lead car to swing the rails to the ties, like I said before. So the locomotive follows the new track till they lay the rails to where they join up with the main Santa Fe line."

Jackie pondered. "I'd like to move the hills to the valleys and toot the whistle."

"Maybe you will someday."

"*I* just wish I could come along and be the water monkey," Meg burst out. She caught her father's hand. "Daddy! Won't I be able to drive the wagon next summer?"

He drew her head against his side and stroked her curly brown hair. "Sweetheart, I doubt an hour passes when I don't pray for that. You keep on walking with the chair and building up your legs. If you get well, I'll never pester God for anything else."

She clung to him. Hallie realized Meg was still more child than young woman and felt a wave of sympathy. She—Hallie—dreaded the winter, but for Meg, unable to run or walk or play and missing her beloved father, it must be much worse.

"Please come home for Christmas, Daddy," she begged in a muffled voice.

"If it's anyway possible, we will, Meggie."

He kissed her good-bye, shook hands man–to–man with Jackie, and turned to Hallie. "This is putting a lot on you. Would you feel better with a shotgun?"

"I'd feel worse. What if I got scared at some noise and shot one of the children or a neighbor?" She forced a smile though her heart cried *Don't go! Don't leave me.* "We'll be fine. I'd rather have Laird than any gun."

"And Smoky!" put in her brother.

"And Smoky," Hallie laughed. Truly, she was glad that the huge dog was staying at the farm—not only for protection but for his benign company.

"You take care of my cat, son." Shaft knelt to put an arm around the boy. "Maybe I should say *our* cat, since she sleeps on your bed all the time." He chuckled. "If you had a nice thick beard, I'd really lose out with her!"

Jackie giggled at that. Even Meg smiled. They all went outside, Garth helping Meg down the steps. He patted Laird, spoke a few soft words, and got in the truck. Shaft gave Hallie and Meg the same hug and peck on the cheek before he got in the other seat. Rory tousled Jackie's hair, kissed his niece, and turned to Hallie.

She put out her hand. He ignored it and took her in his arms. He kissed her hard and hungrily, hurting her mouth, but so swiftly that by the time Hallie started to shove him away, he was already stepping back. "Remember that when you're lonesome, Hallie," he said beneath his breath. His blue eyes were somber and for a moment he looked like the man he would become in a few years. "Remember that I love you. I know that now for sure."

Then he was the old reckless teasing Rory, laughing as he climbed up on the tractor and sounded the whistle. Hallie caught a glimpse of Garth's shocked face, saw it turn tight and grim as he put the truck in gear and steered around the engine. Shaft waved till the truck was out of sight, and Rory blew several short, jaunty toots but it was Garth's closed face that stayed in Hallie's mind as she helped Meg up the steps.

Any hope she'd had that Meg wouldn't think much about Rory's kiss vanished when the girl almost jerked away from her at the top of the steps. "Are you Rory's girl?"

"No!"

"Then why did he kiss you?"

Hallie's face burned and she knew she looked guilty as sin. "He was just kidding. And saying good-bye."

Meg scowled. "He said he loved you."

Her accusing tone exasperated Hallie. "I can't help what he said, Meg. He's never kissed me before. I'm his friend, but not his girl-friend."

"That's not how it looked," Meg said with a sniff. Then her frown eased. She said with malicious satisfaction, "I bet that's not how it looked to Daddy, either."

Hallie was sure of that. After what he'd said about her hair, she'd hoped he was starting to be less wary. Now Rory's prank—or deliber-ate action—would stir up all his older brother's fears and suspicions.

To add to the muddle, Rory was in love with her—or thought he was—probably just because she hadn't fallen for him as most women did. Hallie could have wept. She wouldn't put it past Rory to hint to Garth that there'd been more between them than lessons on the en-gine and a few trips to town shared with other crew members.

Refusing to respond to Meg's last dart, Hallie went upstairs and began to strip the beds where two strong young men had slept last night and that would now lay empty till Christmas, at least. Almost two months. It seemed forever, yet the hope of those few days with Garth and Shaft in the deepest part of winter were all that strength-ened her now. She wished fervently that Rory would find a girl in Texas and spend the holidays with her.

Garth's pillows smelled of him. She drew his scent deep into her, closing her eyes. Her body still remembered Rory's arms, her mouth his kiss. She made them into Garth's instead, tried to pretend, but that didn't work so she buried her face in the pillows. *I love you, Garth. Know that. Don't believe Rory.*

She changed his sheets, put the pillows she carried to her room, and put them on her bed. His scent would fade in time, but she could press her cheek where she thought his head had rested—and dream that someday, maybe, if she had the best luck in all the world, he would sleep beside her.

To live with the one you loved! The immensity, the wonder of it overwhelmed her. How could anyone ask for more than that? But you had to ask and strive for that because without it, there would always be a cold place in your heart.

XVI

$\mathcal{M}$ike and Mary Donnelly stopped off with Meg's graded papers, her assignments, and the dismaying news that Raford had won a seat in the Kansas legislature, William Allen White had lost the governorship, and Coolidge had defeated Davis two-to-one.

"Ugh!" Hallie said. "If I could have voted, it wouldn't have been for any of the bunch who won! Rory's going to be mighty disappointed with the first election where he could vote."

"Voting's still real special to me," said Mary. "I've voted for county and state officials before, but this was my first chance to vote for a president." She grimaced. "I guess women just have to be glad we finally can vote."

She cast such a look at Mike that he grinned and shrugged his broad shoulders. With their red hair and freckles, the two looked enough alike to be brother and sister. "Now, darlin', you know I voted for women to get the vote—and just remember while you're snortin' at me that if *men* hadn't given you the vote, you still wouldn't have it!"

"Horsefeathers! We had the right to vote from God himself—"

"Herself?" Mike teased.

"But you rascals stole it from us!" Mary swept on, shaking a finger in his face. "And it took till four years ago for you to get enough ashamed of yourselves to make things the way they should have been to start with! Don't expect me to thank you for my rights, Michael Terence Donnelly!"

"Sit down and have some cocoa and cookies," Hallie invited.

While Kathleen showed off her schoolwork to Meg, Jackie, and her small sister, Bridgie, Hallie made cocoa and set out crispy oatmeal cookies she had baked that morning.

"White ran only so's he could show up the Klan for what it is," said Mike. "He did that. So you could say that in a way, he won."

"But Raford's winning is dangerous," Mary worried. "We've heard his bank's foreclosing on any loans to Catholics and foreign-born people even if they're citizens."

"I guess the Mennonites don't owe him money," Mike said. "And there aren't any Jews or Negroes or Indians in the county, so far as I know. But he's makin' do with what's he got."

The Donnellys had to get home to do their chores, but they promised to stop for a grocery list the next time they went to town. Mary bent to give Meg a hug. "Your teacher hopes it won't be too long till you can start back to school, honey. But she says you're keeping up with your class, so not to worry."

When the flame-haired Donnellys were gone, the kitchen seemed lonelier and even colder, despite the warmth thrown out by the range. Thank goodness, Meg didn't seem to feel it. She was going through her returned assignments and proudly showing Jackie her good marks. "A-pluses, Jackie! That's the best grade you can get. I only got one B."

Jackie admired the red letters. "Do you think I can make big red A-pluses when I go to school next year?"

"Of course you will. I'll help you." Meg patted the seat. "Come on and I'll read you my history lesson."

He got up beside her. Laird lay near her chair, and Smoky was curled up in her basket in its cozy place behind the range. Feeling closed out, Hallie stirred the potato soup they would have for supper and went upstairs with a load of socks and underwear that she had washed and mended after the men left.

Rory's drawers were a mess. She fished out odd socks, most with holes, buttonless union suits, and tattered bandannas. Sorting these into piles of unredeemable rags and things that could be rescued with thread and needle, she organized the wearable clothing and opened the first of Garth's drawers.

A few pair of socks were matched and folded neatly. Except for what Hallie had just brought up, he must have taken all his underwear with him. A sweater knitted of heathery blue wool filled one corner. She was sure his mother or grandmother had made it. How soft the wool was, how springy and resilient!

Hallie picked it up to better admire it. Something dropped from its folds to the bottom of the drawer. A lock of long black hair!

Could it be his wife's? Hallie scarcely dared believe her eyes, but she had to trust her fingers as she smoothed the tress and then felt her own hair. It was the same. The same color, the same texture.

Somehow he had filched this strand when Shaft cut her hair. He must have kept it hidden through the threshing and then tucked it away in this garment made by other women who loved him, women he had loved.

Hallie's heart swelled. She pressed the sweater against her, praying for a blessing from the ones who had made it. *I love him, too. I'll take care of him just as you did. Please help him realize that.*

She folded the sweater the way it had been and slipped the lock inside. Descending with Rory's dilapidated things and her sewing basket, she sat near the window to work. And dream.

*P*ostcards from Garth came every few days, postmarked from little western Kansas towns. Then, as the men headed south across the Oklahoma Panhandle, almost as bare of people as it was of trees, there was nothing for four days and then, postmarked Borger, Texas, half a dozen cards came in the same mail. Apparently Garth scrawled one every day whether or not he could mail it.

These were addressed to Meg. When Jackie came trundling back from the mailbox with his wagon, Meg was waiting on the porch and took possession of the cards immediately. She read them to Jackie so Hallie learned that the engine had got stuck in sand and had to be pulled out by horses. "Didn't that old farmer laugh! He charged us enough to feed his horses for a month, but we were glad to pay it." Shaft was keeping them well fed, except for pies. How was the homework going? Was Laird staying husky on rabbits?

Garth always concluded with "Tell Jackie 'Hi!' My regards to Hallie and love to you." Meg emphasized the "regards" and "love." She didn't leave the cards lying around, so Hallie never got to hold one and study the slant of the bold handwriting. Still, it was heartening to know he was well, and Hallie comforted herself with the secret of that lock of hair folded into his Island sweater.

Meg wrote to him every day at Borger in care of the contractor building the railroad and invited Jackie to send Shaft drawings of Smoky and anything else he wanted to draw. She never asked Hallie whether she wanted to send a note or a message, and though Hallie longed to write to Garth, she felt that he should show he wanted to correspond by writing to her first or at least tucking a note into Meg's letters. Now the men were working dawn to dark, the cards stopped, but Garth wrote a fat letter every Sunday.

Hallie had to content herself with writing to Shaft now and then. To her surprise, his written English was better than his spoken. His handwriting was round and careful, like a child's. Luke wrote every few weeks and composing an answer occupied Meg and Jackie for several days. Meg gave Jackie a sketch of himself with Laird; the rest of Luke's art was tacked to her bedroom walls. Except for that drawing of Hallie on the engine which Hallie had put away in her dresser.

One afternoon Jackie brought in the day's mail importantly and identified the letters by their penmanship. "Here's one from Garth." He handed it to Meg. "One from Shaft." That went to Hallie. "One from Luke!" He held on to that himself, since Luke addressed letters to both him and Meg and she let him open them. "And here's a newspaper."

Garth didn't subscribe to any, though he got *Capper's Weekly, The Saturday Evening Post,* and *The American Thresherman.* With a condescending glance at Hallie, Meg opened her father's letter and began: *"My dearest daughter—"*

Hallie listened avidly, but to disguise her hunger for Garth's news, she opened the newspaper. Quentin Raford, fist upraised, laughed triumphantly from a photo that took up a quarter of the front page of what was called *The American Patriot*. It was published in Topeka, the state capital. A box in the center of the front page proclaimed in bold letters:

THE PATRIOT'S GOALS

PROTECT THE RIGHTS OF 100% REAL AMERICANS
LIMIT FOREIGN IMMIGRATION
GUARANTEE THE SOVEREIGNTY OF STATES' RIGHTS
PROTECT PURE WOMANHOOD
COMPEL MORAL BEHAVIOR
SUPPORT THE ORDAINED SUPREMACY OF THE WHITE RACE
STRIP OF CITIZENSHIP ALL WHO REFUSE TO SERVE IN OUR
ARMED FORCES

The headline screamed: POPE TO EXCOMMUNICATE SOLDIERS! The story said that the pope was expected to issue an encyclical that would threaten with excommunication any Catholic who bore arms outside of his own country. "We are not against Catholics who do their American duty," the article ran. "But no man can serve two masters. We demand that anyone enjoying the blessings of this country put America first, above the commands of a foreign churchman."

There was more in this vein, with half the page given over to Raford's election and what he meant to accomplish in the legislature. Hallie opened the paper and looked for the name of the editor. He was a stranger. The address for subscriptions was Topeka, but the publisher was Quentin A. Raford.

She crumpled the paper and stuffed it into the stove. It blazed up, almost singeing her hair, but collapsed to fluttering bits of ash. She could only hope that Raford's influence would do the same.

The only good thing about his election was that once the legislature convened next year, he would spend most of his time in Topeka. Hallie hoped devoutly that he would move there and take Cotton with him. For the first week or so after the men left, she kept the doors locked even in the day and was unutterably grateful for the heavy curtains. When it began to seem that Raford was going to leave her in peace, she locked only the kitchen door at night, though if she heard a vehicle turn down the lane, she hurried to turn the key and didn't unlock it till Donnelly's flivver rattled into the yard, as it did several times a week.

Mary and Mike brought Meg news of her schoolmates and visited with Hallie, letting their girls play with Jackie for a while. When they stopped on the way to town for Hallie's grocery list, they always brought a jug of milk and some butter, a wonderful change from evaporated milk and margarine. Apart from mail, these drop-ins were almost the only contact the strange little household had with the out-side world. Hallie always had gingerbread, cookies, or some other treat on hand.

"I can't tell you how much I appreciate your coming by," she told Mary one afternoon while Mike was playing bear with the shrieking children. "It would get so lonesome—"

Mary squeezed her hand. "You don't have to tell me, dear. We got hailed out two years in a row, and Mike had to work the broomcorn harvest to keep us from going broke. I was alone with the babies. One fall they got whooping cough. Next fall it was measles. Mike didn't get home till Christmas. You bet I understand."

It must have been scary with the babies sick, Hallie thought. I guess I'd better be grateful—and I am—that Jackie and Meg have kept well. But Mike was yours; you knew he'd come back and someday, with luck, he'd never have to be away from you another night. If Garth were my husband, or if I knew he would be someday, I think I could stand this better.

The Halsteads stopped once to leave some apples from their small orchard, and Mr. Crutchfield dropped off a stack of old *National Geo-graphics* for Meg, but the Donnellys were Hallie's salvation as autumn faded into winter and Thanksgiving loomed.

"I can't be very thankful when I still can't walk and with Daddy away," Meg grumbled one day as Hallie massaged her legs. "You might as well quit this—"

"I won't," said Hallie. "It's all we know to do. So we'll do it."

The glumness lifted at a proposal of the Donnellys. "Why don't we have Thanksgiving here?" Mary suggested. "We'll bring a stuffed chicken and cranberry sauce and—"

"That'll be plenty." Hallie glowed. A festive holiday for the children after all—and for her, too. "I'll make pumpkin and mince pies and rolls and an applesauce spice cake."

"And I'll bring piccalilli, and chowchow, and some of my sweet pickled peaches, and green tomato relish," Mary added. "And some thick cream to whip, and fresh butter."

It was agreed that the Donnellys would come before noon; so, deep in her baking, when Hallie heard a motor approaching, she thought they were arriving a little early. She hurried to finish the lattice crust of the second mince pie, popped it in the oven, and wiped her hands on her apron as she went out on the porch to greet them.

Instead of the Donnelly's old Model T, an elegant silver Cadillac was parked near the house. And instead of laughing red-haired Donnellys, a woman in a sealskin coat and matching cloche and muff was coming up the steps.

"Felicity!"

"Aren't you going to ask me in?" asked the woman who had been Hallie's stepmother. Blond bangs curved artfully from beneath the cloche. Her eyebrows were slim, surprised pencil lines, and her eyelashes were thick with mascara. "Don't just stand there with that stupid look on your face, Hallie. Where's Jackie?"

Hallie stayed in the door. "You haven't seemed to care about that these past six months!"

"Things are different now." A tear caught on a painted lower lash and made a black runnel down the powdered cheek. "After all the years he waited, poor sweet Harry only had a few months with me. He died last month of heart failure." She dabbed at her eyes. "At least he died in my arms. I tell myself that was a comfort to him."

"I'm sorry. But I still don't see why you've come."

Felicity stared. "I've come for Jackie, of course. Come for my baby."

"He's not a baby." Hallie's rising, smoldering anger erupted. "I can't believe you have so much nerve, Felicity! You threw him away. How do I know you won't do it again if you meet some man who doesn't want a child around?"

"Oh, that's all taken care of," Felicity said eagerly. "Milford thinks it'll be wonderful to have a son who's already out of diapers and through the messy baby stage."

"Who is Milford?" Hallie wondered whether she could believe her ears.

"Harry's cousin and business partner. The dearest, kindest man! Utterly devoted. All he wants to do is take care of me."

"Has he waited for years, too?"

Felicity looked reproachful. "Of course not. I didn't meet him till after I married Harry."

"I see. He waited a few months."

Felicity crimsoned. "Shame on your nasty spiteful tongue, Hallie Meredith! Milford never said a word till on the way home from the funeral. He was trying to comfort me, and it all came out. He's never loved anyone before and had thought he would just suffer along, watching our happiness—"

"It's convenient. He won't have to hunt a new partner."

"If you're implying—"

"I'm not implying anything." Hallie pondered. "I really don't want to let you see Jackie at all, but in case he still loves you in spite of everything—"

"Certainly he loves me!" Pink spots overshadowed Felicity's rouge. "I'm his mother."

"You gave him away!"

"Don't you have any heart? Any compassion?"

"More than you, I think."

"I demand to see him!"

"I suppose you should." Hallie stepped aside, but her gaze held Felicity's. "You'd better understand this, though. If Jackie wants to go with you, fine. But if he doesn't—"

"That's absurd! Of course he'll come with me."

"Not if he doesn't want to."

"The law—I have rights!"

Hallie shook her head. "With children you have responsibilities, not rights."

Felicity's light blue eyes narrowed. "Any judge in the country would give him to me."

"Maybe not. The MacReynoldses would testify that you left him. The people I worked with all summer know you never wrote or came to see him. You just—vanished."

"I was still distraught from your father's death. I wasn't in a normal state of mind."

"Maybe you aren't now, Maybe you're distraught over Harry's death."

"I left Jackie with you, his own sister. I knew you'd take care of him."

"I think it's called desertion. Maybe abandonment. I don't know what tale you told Milford, but he may not think too much of you if the whole story gets plastered all over the papers."

"You've always hated me!"

"I did once. But that's not what this is all about. This is about what's best for Jackie."

Felicity shot her a glance of pure hatred and sailed into the kitchen the instant Hallie opened the door. "Jackie, darling!" she cried, swooping down on him as he sat playing checkers with Meg. "Look, it's Mama!"

She kissed and embraced him, but he sat as if made of wood. When she moved back, he stared at her wonderingly. "You're not dead."

"Of course not!" Her eyes shot daggers at Hallie. "Did your sister say that?"

"No. But you said you had to go somewhere to get well, some-where I couldn't go."

Felicity colored. "I did, honey. But I'm fine now."

"I thought you had to be dead." Jackie's simplicity was terrible. "You didn't write to me. Luke does. Shaft does."

His mother's blush deepened. "I wanted to, angel, but I thought it would just make you miss me more."

"I thought you were dead, like Daddy."

"You can see I'm not, you funny little bunny!" Felicity's attempt at gay laughter sounded brittle. "And I'm well now and have a beautiful home for you. There's a basement where you can have an electric train with a town and farms and an e-normous yard with big trees where you could keep a pony."

"A pony?"

"That's right." Felicity sent Hallie a smug look. "You can pick him out, Jackie, and give him his name and take care of him."

"You gave me my name, Mama. But you—you didn't take care of me!" Some of the baffled anguish Jackie must have felt when his mother left sounded in his voice, showed in his eyes and quivering lips. "Hallie did."

"Yes, I know how she dragged you all over the country with a threshing crew!" Felicity shuddered. "All that dangerous machinery! It's a wonder you weren't killed." For the first time, she acknowledged Meg's existence with a wave of her hand. "Or you could have been crippled like your poor little friend here!"

"I'm not poor!" Meg's eyes flashed. "And I'm going to walk again!"

"I do hope so, my dear." Felicity's tone was placating, but Meg swept on.

"We take care of Jackie! We all do. Laird won't let a rattlesnake get near him. Shaft's just like his grandfather, and I—I wish he was my brother!" Grudgingly, she added, "He *is* Hallie's brother. So, Mrs.— whoever you are—I think Jackie's better off with us than you."

"You impudent girl! I'm his mother!"

Meg gave a short bitter laugh. "That doesn't mean much unless you live it. My mother left me when I was four, and Daddy was in the war—it started quite a while before the Americans joined in, you know. I cried a lot then. I missed her something awful. That's about the earliest thing I remember, asking Gran when she was coming back." Meg's face hardened. The contempt in her voice was so savage that Hallie winced for Felicity. "Do you want to know something, lady?"

"Not particularly." Felicity adopted a superior air. "I'm sorry about your bad experience, but I *have* come back." When no one spoke, she threw up her gloved hands. "For heaven's sake! It's only been six months!"

"I thought you were dead," said Jackie.

"My mother did die," Meg said. This was the first time Hallie had ever heard her mention her mother. Hallie had believed that Meg couldn't remember that loss, but clearly it had left a wound that still ached beneath the hard scar tissue. "She got tuberculosis. Someone in the Glasgow hospital where she died found Gran's address in her purse and wrote to us." Felicity watched Meg as if hypnotized. "Do you think I cried?" Meg asked with derision that still echoed with pain. "Lady, I didn't cry a bit. I'd already done that. As far as I was concerned, my mother died when she left me."

Jackie jumped up to hug Meg. "Oh, Meggie! Don't feel bad!"

"This isn't fair!" Felicity rounded on Hallie. "I haven't had a chance!"

Meg sobbed on Jackie's small sturdy shoulder. Maybe she hadn't cried when she learned of her mother's death, but she was crying now. Hallie wanted to comfort her, but knew Meg wouldn't accept her sympathy at this moment, maybe never. Anyway, Jackie seemed to be the person Meg needed. Probably she had never wept like this in front of her father.

Hallie drew Felicity into the front room, which was heated today for the gala. "I think you'd better go." Felicity looked so dazed that Hallie felt a twinge of pity. "Listen. Jackie's made himself a new family. I doubt that he'll ever want to live with you again. He can't trust you. But you could make friends."

"Friends!"

"That could be a lot better than nothing—for both of you."

The red mouth twisted. "And how do I make *friends* with my only son?"

"Write to him. Send him presents. Maybe when he's older, he'd like to come stay with you for a month or so." Felicity looked so appalled that Hallie searched for a way to make her understand. "You can be like his aunt."

"While *you're* his mother, I suppose?"

"No. I can't be that. Until you left him with me, I wasn't really his sister. But I am now."

"I've got his room ready. Milford helped me pick out a lot of new toys."

"Maybe you can have a baby," Hallie said though she hoped not, unless Milford was a steady man fated to live a long time. "Or you could adopt a child."

Felicity caught Hallie's hands. "Let me take him home. I swear that if he's not settled down and happy within a month that I'll bring him back."

"Ask him."

"You know he'll say no, especially after that stupid girl's outburst."

Hallie shrugged.

"What a Thanksgiving!" Felicity wailed. "It took Milford and me two days to drive to Hollister, and he's ordered a special dinner in our hotel suite. How am I going to tell him—"

"You'll think of something."

Felicity cast her a furious look and rushed into the kitchen. Meg had quieted and was wiping her eyes. "Jackie!" Felicity cried. "Mama's leaving, Good-bye!"

He kept his eyes on the floor. "G'bye."

"Don't you want to come with me?"

He put his hand in Meg's. "I want to stay here."

"Do you know that means you'll probably never see me again?"

"I didn't think I would." Jackie looked miserable. "I thought you was dead, Mama."

"At least kiss me."

Jackie endured her embrace, but he didn't return it. She walked out quickly and didn't look back. "I hope you're satisfied!" she said to Hallie. "Milford and I would give him a lovely modern home and a college education. If he stays with you, he'll likely be a hired hand breaking his back for board and thirty dollars a month."

"He wants to be an engineer," Hallie said. "And he'll go to college if he wants to." She hesitated. "I hope you will decide to try to be his friend."

Felicity got in the Cadillac and slammed the door. "I'll never be your friend!" she almost screamed. "And if you get pregnant by some threshing hand or that Garth MacLeod people have told me about, don't crawl to me for help!"

She drove off as fast as the bumpy lane allowed. Hallie stayed on the porch till she stopped trembling from anger and tension. Then she went inside and got a cold wet cloth for Meg to press to her eyes.

"I was scared she'd make me go," Jackie sniffled.

"No. She won't do that. When she has time to think it over, she'll be glad you're happy here."

Jackie still looked doubtful. Meg gave him a fierce hug. "Don't worry, Jackie! No one's going to take you away. Now go wash your face. The Donnellys will be here any minute."

Indeed, at that very moment, the familiar chug could be heard. Hallie put more coal in the stove and began to set the big oval table in the front room.

That had been an awful row with Felicity, but Hallie was beginning to be glad it had happened. Jackie had a chance to choose today. He hadn't been a helpless child to be disposed of like an inconvenient puppy. In a way, it cleaned the slate.

It was easier to understand Meg's jealousy of Garth. She must be terrified of losing him, too. Even if Garth ever got over his distrust of women, Hallie was afraid Meg wouldn't. *Take the wild-goose view,* thought Hallie, and went to welcome the Donnellys, a flame-haired tide, who swarmed into the house and filled it with laughter, greetings, and savory food.

XVII

$\mathcal{W}$hen the men left for Texas it had seemed forever till Christmas, but with Thanksgiving over, the days flew. *"We'll only be able to stay a couple of days,"* wrote Garth, *"but we'll be there unless a blizzard piles up ice and snow we can't get through. It'll be great to see my girl, Meg. I hope your legs are stronger and you'll be able to walk before long."*

"I don't know why I can't," Meg said angrily. "When I push the chair around, it doesn't feel like I'm putting much weight on it. But when I try to take a step—" She bit her lip, and tears glinted in her eyes.

"You *are* better," Hallie encouraged. "Keep your legs strong, and maybe all of sudden you'll walk before you know it."

Meg gave her a withering look, then sniffed and asked, "What's that you're making?"

"Coffee caramels in one pot, butterscotch in the other, and gingersnaps and another fruitcake in the oven."

"Daddy always buys our Christmas candy."

"Yes, but homemade is fun. Besides, I want to make up a nice box for the Donnellys and a big tin each for Shaft, Rory, and your father to take back to Texas. Wouldn't you like to send Luke and his family a box of goodies?"

"Yes!" Meg cried, but then looked glum. "It's not much fun if I can't help make things."

"Oh, I think you can. Candy takes an awful lot of stirring. You can sit on the stool to do that, and you can mix up batter if I bring the ingredients to you."

Meg started to protest as she automatically did at any suggestion of Hallie's, but then she thought it over. Her face brightened. "I can do a lot, can't I? Will you let me look at your recipe book and pick out what to make for Daddy and Luke?"

Hallie passed it over. "One thing they'll all like is sugared almonds. I had the Donnellys buy twenty pounds of them, and filberts and walnuts and peanuts, too."

"Then we can make peanut brittle," said Meg, scanning the pages. "I know Luke likes that. Can we make fudge?"

Hallie nodded. "Pfeffernusse are good, too. They're crunchy ball-shaped German cookies that keep for weeks. We need to make them now to have them ready for Christmas."

"I want to help!" Jackie begged.

"Wonderful! We've got peanuts to shell and nuts to grind. And when the pfeffernusse are baked, you can roll them in powdered sugar."

The kitchen was full of good smells, and working together took away some of Meg's prickliness. "Maybe I could send some candy to Miss Howell," she said. "She's been nice to write out my homework assignments and take so much trouble grading my papers."

"We're going to have a dozen kinds," said Hallie. "When they're all ready, you could make a box with some of each. I guess Rory has a sweet tooth. There are lots of nice empty chocolate boxes on the top shelf of his wardrobe. I shouldn't think he'd mind if we use those, especially if he gets a big one."

At different times, the three of them pored over the Sears catalog and sent off their orders. Hallie told Jackie he could spend eight dollars on presents—he had earned it by helping in the cookshack. He and Meg ordered Shaft a quality meerschaum pipe with a "genuine imported amber mouthpiece" in a silk-lined case with his name imprinted in gold.

"Let's not have Milov Hurok on it," Meg said. "Let's just ask them to print 'Shaft' in the biggest letters they have."

Jackie bounced in agreement and turned pages rapidly to the section he knew best; toys and games. "Let's get toys for Rusty's kids. They're gonna feel bad that he's not there."

As Jackie would miss his own father? Though after the summer with the threshing crew, Robert Meredith's death must seem long ago, the holiday was bound to call up memories; for, though very ill, Robert had still been alive last Christmas. Since then, Jackie had lost both parents.

He had said nothing to Hallie about his mother but one day she heard him say to Meg in a puzzled way, "I thought Mama was dead. She's not. But I still feel like she is."

Meg nodded. "That's how I felt about my mother. I'm glad she never came back. There would have been no way to be sure she wouldn't leave again."

Jackie said solemnly, "Mamas hadn't ought to go off, had they? Not unless they die and can't help it, like Daddy did. Mrs. Donnelly wouldn't never, ever leave Bridgie and Kathleen. Would she?"

"Of course not, Silly Billy!"

"I'm not Billy!"

"Then," teased Meg, "of course not, Wacky Jackie!"

He collapsed in giggles. It was good that they could talk to each other about their mothers, though it made Hallie feel more than ever like an outsider. She was making out her catalog order: warm house slippers and a plaid flannel shirt for Shaft; lumberjack-style sweater jackets for Rory and Garth and Luke; a cozy bathrobe of blanket fabric for Meg and red felt ankle-high slippers with plush trim; and for Jackie a dump truck that dumped, a steam shovel that scooped up and unloaded dirt, a harmonica, a big box of crayons, and *Billy Whiskers, Puss in Boots, Robin Hood,* and several Peter Rabbit books. She also ordered him new clothes, letting him choose colors and styles.

"These aren't my Christmas presents, are they?" he asked suspiciously.

"No," Hallie assured him. "I always hated it when I got clothes for presents. Now, what kind of cap would you like?"

"One that comes down over my ears!"

"This corduroy one does. You need some mittens. And maybe you ought to have some lace-up boots for going after the mail."

"That pair has a knife! Can I have them, Hallie? Can I?"

"*May* you." The boots were $3.98—twice the cost of regular shoes—but she couldn't refuse him. Besides his birthday came just a few days before Christmas. "You'll have to promise to keep the knife folded up and in its pocket when you're not using it."

"Promise! Cross my heart and hope to die, stick a needle in my eye—"

"Jackie! Don't say things like that. It's good enough to promise—and remember. You need some other shoes, too. Let's measure your foot and send that along."

He tugged her into the front room and whispered, "I want to get Meg something nice. Do I got some money left?"

He didn't. The meerschaum pipe alone had cost six dollars. But he would learn about money soon enough. "You pick out what you think she'd like, and I'll put it on my order," Hallie said. "You can just point in the catalog, and I'll write it down. That way it'll be a surprise."

His delighted grin faded into a worried look. "Hallie, we—we forgotted, Meg and me. We forgotted to order you something!"

Hallie braced against the stabbing pang, but she couldn't check the bitter thought, *Everyone but me, when I've stayed here and taken care of her.* "Make my present," she suggested. "I'd much rather have that."

"If I have enough money, you could order you one."

She bent to kiss him. It wasn't often these days she had much chance to do that except at bedtime. "Honey, you haul kindling and coal. That's the best kind of present. But if you want to put something under the tree, draw a nice picture or make something."

"Are we gonna have a tree?"

She had supposed they would, without thinking of where it would come from. "Let's ask Meg if they usually do. But first pick out what you want to get her."

"I know!" Jackie beamed, flipping pages. "She keeps looking at this wristwatch and says she hopes her daddy gets it for her next birthday."

Hallie restrained a gasp at the price. The six-jeweled white-gold case with a gold-filled expansion bracelet cost $12.75, almost two weeks of Hallie's wages. "It's pretty expensive, honey, but we can manage if you'll let it be from both of us, and I cross off the robe and slippers I was getting her."

"I wish I could buy it all by myself."

"You could get her a necklace or perfume or—"

Jackie puckered his brow and sighed. "All right. Let's give her the watch from both of us."

The orders were mailed, and the three of them began to fill boxes with candy and sugared nuts. A five-pound box went to Luke, and Hallie sent a three-pound assortment to the MacReynoldses.

These were scarcely sent when gifts began to arrive from the crew. Henry Lowen sent a crate of winesap apples and a note hoping that Meg could walk again. He also announced his marriage to Anna and said he hoped to make the summer threshing run with the MacLeods. Baldy Tennant's gift to Hallie, Meg, and Jackie was a big box of Hershey's almond bars with a card that read DO OPEN BEFORE CHRISTMAS! From Buford Redding came a thousand-piece jigsaw-puzzle map of the world. Large packages from Rich Mondell and Jim Wyatt contained brightly wrapped individual gifts for the children and Hallie.

"These should go under the tree," said Hallie, pleased and touched at being remembered by the men. "Do you put up a Christmas tree, Meg?"

"No. We just put our presents on the table Christmas morning and open them before breakfast." For once Meg didn't sound as if the established way was best. She even looked excited. "Could we have a tree? For Jackie?"

"We'll ask the Donnellys to buy us a little evergreen that we can plant in the yard later," promised Hallie.

"And some candy canes?" Jackie asked. "Red and white ones?"

"I'll make a star for the top," Meg said. "I've been saving foil off the Hershey bars."

"We can string popcorn and cranberries," added Hallie.

The Donnellys found a pretty little pine tree at the nursery, and Mike carried it into the front room and set it on the apple crate Hallie had covered with red oilcloth. Meg arranged presents artfully to conceal the container. Jackie hung candy canes, and Hallie helped Meg fasten the foil-covered cardboard star on top. The children draped the cranberry and popcorn garlands and picked the best spots for the other foil-covered stars and bells they had made.

"It's—it's beautiful!" Meg breathed, settling back in the wheelchair to admire her work. "Oh, I hope Daddy likes it!"

He will as long as he doesn't think it was my idea, Hallie thought. She said aloud, "Now that we have the men's addresses, we can send them each a box of candy and nuts—and write thank-you notes for the things that weren't wrapped."

A few days later, Jackie puffed down the lane with a parcel that almost filled his wagon. It was from Luke and Mrs. Wells. When the children pulled away the crumpled newspapers, Meg looked puzzled. "Is it part of a tree root?"

Hallie helped lift it out. Rough outer bark had been left on a half-dome-shaped tree growth glued to a slab of rough cedar to form a sort of cavern. It was stuffed with what looked like corn shucks till Meg brought out a figure that stood about five inches high: a madonna. Her body and robe were of shucks but her sweet face was red-brown clay and the long black hair looked human. She held a cornshuck baby. His face, and those of the other figures Jackie was standing on the table, were of the same warm red clay. Joseph had gray hair and so did the crowned Wise Men and one of the shepherds. The dark-haired angels had furled wings of golden straw and harps carved from wood.

The cattle and camels were natural red clay, but the sheep had curly fleece of pale wood shavings, a pair of mules were painted gray, and there was a spotted dog, a cat, and carefully painted great horned owl and several mourning doves. A star with long rays made of straw had a slit carved for it in the roof of the cavern. The cedar-bark manager was full of fragrant hay.

"Isn't it wonderful?" Meg breathed, her eyes shining. "Look, here's a drawing from Luke on this big cardboard at the bottom! He's put the whole family on the porch of their log cabin and they've signed their names. See, here's Mrs. Wells—Vinnie—and the children. The older lady next to Luke must be his mother. It says 'Evelyn Rogers.' "

"Yes, and he's drawn the dog and cat and mules just like the clay ones!" Jackie squealed. "Can I put the owl and cat on the roof?"

"Sure," Meg said. "Luke knew we'd want to play with the people and animals; that's why he made so many of them." She perched an angel on top of the roof and fixed the star at a graceful angle. "I suppose we'd better keep it in the front room."

"The sideboard in there would be a good place," Hallie suggested. "But it's so cold that if you're going to be in there long, you'll need to put on sweaters and leave the door to the kitchen open."

It took the children the rest of the afternoon to get the manger scene arranged to their satisfaction. Jackie brought in dried grass and thistles to set under and behind the cavern. The shepherds approached from one side and the Wise Men from the other while the Rogers-Wells family smiled from the cardboard propped against the wall.

On the last day of school before Christmas, Donnellys delivered Miss Howell's pretty two-pound box of caramels and a syrup pail of almonds for the schoolchildren. On their return they brought popcorn balls and for Meg a brocade-covered autograph album from Miss Howell. All the older children had written verses or messages in it and the little ones had printed their names.

Mary Donnelly brought a tray of frosted gingerbread Santas and Christmas trees. These were put up for Christmas Day, but Hallie made hot cocoa and set out bowls of nuts and cookies. To the joyful excitement of Bridgie and Kathleen, Meg and Jackie presented the big colorful tin box of good things which Mary decreed would not be opened till Christmas Eve.

After the Donnellys left in the early dusk, Meg said fretfully, "I wish Daddy would come! What if there's a blizzard and he has to stay in Texas? I hate his being way off down there!"

"They'll be here if it's possible," Hallie tried to soothe. "You wouldn't want them traveling if the weather turns bad."

"I don't want Daddy traveling at all unless I can be with him," retorted Meg.

The day before Christmas, the pale sun was dimly visible through lowering clouds. Meg wheeled her chair to the kitchen window and anxiously watched the sky. "It's snowing!" she wailed when, in early afternoon, a few large flakes wafted to the ground.

"Angels' pinfeathers," Hallie said, trying to sound cheerful in spite of the anxiety that gripped her. "Look, the flakes are melting the instant they hit. I think I'll make a big kettle of onion-potato soup for supper. That'll be good and fast whatever time the men come."

She started a fire in the potbellied front-room stove and brought down the presents she had wrapped and kept in her room. Meg's wristwatch was the smallest gift, but by far the most expensive. Jackie had wrapped the velvet presentation case in gilt paper, and now he proudly placed it on top of all the other gifts.

"You'll be surprised!" he chanted to Meg. "Will you ever be surprised! Want to guess? Bet you can't, can't, can't!"

"I won't, won't, won't, because you can't, can't, can't keep a secret!" Meg laughed. "Don't give it away, Jackie. It's more fun to be surprised. And don't rattle your presents, goofy! You might break something."

The soup was bubbling merrily and Hallie was putting bread in the oven when Laird set up a joyful clamor. Meg wheeled swiftly into the kitchen. Jackie shot out the door. Smoky jumped up in the window to peer out.

"Oh, these dratted old crutches!" Meg swung toward the door on them. Hallie threw a coat around the girl and helped her down the steps. Now that it was twilight and colder, the snow fluffs were beginning to accumulate, but it didn't matter. The men were home safe.

The truck sputtered into the yard. Rory jumped out to open the machine shed door and Garth steered it inside. He was out of the cab in a flash and caught Meg in his arms as she shook loose of Hallie and almost leaped toward him. In the bluish light, Garth looked overwhelmingly tall and strong. Laird bounded around them, barking ecstatically.

Shaft swept Jackie to one shoulder. "Hey, here's my boy! You been takin' care of the gals and Smoky?" Smoky meowed plaintively from the steps and Shaft, balancing Jackie, bent to hoist his cat to the other shoulder.

"You've grown, too, kitty-cat!" Smoky's purr vibrated to a rumble as she pressed against her master's beard and dug in her claws to stay in place. Shaft gave Hallie a half-hug with his free arm. "Mmm-mm. If you don't smell like sugar and spice and everything nice! It sure makes it feel like comin' home, for you to be here, Hallie girl."

He got his suitcase from beneath the tarp in the backseat and set off for the house. Garth got his suitcase and followed, supporting Meg. That left Rory.

His grin faded as he watched Hallie. "I can't stand to imagine what it'd be like if you weren't here, Hallie."

"Well, I am, so——"

His hands closed on her shoulders. "When I think about you, it's—different. It's not just wanting to hold and kiss you, though heaven knows I want that till I ache. It's like a lamp shining over the plains, clear and bright and warm and wonderful. You—you're my heart's home, Hallie. You're where I can rest."

This wasn't the brash, reckless young man she knew who flirted with every pretty girl. "Rory—Rory, don't!"

He winced and let her go. "I won't crowd you. But please, Hallie, give me a chance."

"Rory—"

He placed a finger across her lips. The flash of his smile was like the old Rory. "I know you think I'm wet behind the ears, but I'm going to show you I can be a man. Your man, Hallie. Now, hurry up to the house before you freeze without a coat. I have to drape blankets over this old truck's radiator, or it could freeze and bust."

Garth shot Hallie a strange look when she entered the kitchen. Keeping her back turned to him, she washed her hands and ladled up bowls of steaming soup before slicing bread still warm from the oven.

"This soup's sure better'n mine." Shaft got up to fill his bowl a second time. "I can taste dill and cheese, and the onion makes a world of difference. I'd sure like your receipt, Hallie." That was what he called recipes.

"Is it harder cooking for railroad crews than for threshermen?" asked Hallie.

"Main difference is the old cookstove heat feels good now, and the fellas stay in the cookshack as long as they can. Sometimes I have a notion to make two troughs long enough to fit the table and just keep 'em both filled till the boys are stuffed."

Rory slathered bread with Mary Donnelly's butter. "You sayin' we're a bunch of hogs?"

" 'Course not. Hogs have better manners."

"Do you think you'll get through early, Daddy?" Meg asked.

He shook his head. Hallie had forgotten how lamplight burnished his hair, brought out gold more than silver. He and Rory were still as tanned as they had been in summer. Their strength and sun-browned faces and hands created an aura of young masculinity and vital warmth in the kitchen just as their baritones satisfied a longing for male voices that Hallie hadn't known she felt until the men's words resonated much deeper than her ears.

"We'll be home in time to get ready for the run but I don't count on any time to spare."

Meg's lip quivered. She blinked rapidly. A tear fell into her bowl. "If—if I can't drive the water wagon next summer—I'll just want to die! Daddy, I will be able to walk by then, won't I?"

The pain in Garth's face wrenched at Hallie. "Sweetheart," he said huskily, squeezing her hand, "if I could give you my legs, you know I would."

She lifted her chin. "I'm going to drive that wagon! I'll drive it if I have to get around on crutches! I—I'm not going to stay here while you go off again!"

"We'll work it out," Garth promised, but the joy of reunion was dampened by Meg's outburst. Hallie brought generous helpings of cherry cobbler and poured more coffee for the men. As well as the hot water in the range reservoir, she had filled the largest pots and kettles so the men could all bathe that night.

"Shaft!" said Jackie, tugging at his adopted grandfather. "You gotta come see what Luke sent! And our tree!"

Meg brightened. "It's so beautiful, what Luke and Mrs. Wells sent. And after Christmas, we'll plant the tree outside. We made all the decorations."

Garth flicked a glance in Hallie's direction, but his smile was for Meg. "Well, let's have a look," he said and picked her up as easily as if she'd been a small girl instead of a big one.

The lamp on the sideboard cast a mellow sheen over the red-clay faces and animals, made the straw of the star, the angels' wings, and the floor of the cavern gleam softest gold. The foil star glittered at the top of the little tree, and the ornaments reflected the red of the cranberries, white of the popcorn, and red-and-white-striped candy canes.

"Now, if that's not about the prettiest sight I ever saw," Shaft breathed. "Say, this is Christmas Eve. We've got to have a carol or two. Let me get my fiddle."

He hurried out. Rory watched Hallie in a way that made her keep her gaze on the manger. Was that something glistening in Garth's eyes as he sat on the davenport with Meg nestled against him? Hallie's own eyes smarted. It had been years since she had snuggled close to her father like that, years since she had allowed him more than the briefest hug.

If only he were still alive—if only she had let him know she loved him before he died. *Please do know it. Be happy with Mama and don't worry about Jackie. I'll take care of him.* She didn't want him to know about Felicity, how quickly she'd abandoned Jackie and married another man. Still, if there was any way the dead could know good things and not the bad, Hallie prayed it was so with her father.

Shaft tuned his wonderful old fiddle and bowed into "Joy to the World" followed by "Silent Night."

"We have to sing 'Away in a Manger,'" Meg said. "Oh, I hope Luke and Rusty's family are singing now—and aren't so sad they can't be happy some of the time!"

"They'll be happy with all the good presents we picked out!" Jackie said. "And the candy and nuts and cake!"

His face was shining. Hallie felt both relief and a stab of pain that he could forget his parents so quickly. Of course so much had happened and his life had changed so completely that his father's death must seem long ago to him, and to endure his mother's desertion, he had thought her dead, too.

Shaft finished with "Oh, Come All Ye Faithful." Looking around, Hallie made another prayer. *Let us be together next Christmas Eve and let Meg be walking. Please! I'd rather that happened than even for Garth to love me.*

Rory dried dishes as she washed and rinsed them. She wouldn't look at him but there was no way to keep from feeling the intensity of his gaze. Instead of falling for a Texas girl, he was set on her. She was fond of Rory, enjoyed his high spirits, and didn't want to hurt him. How miserable!

As soon as the kitchen was tidy, she went up to bed so the men could take turns bathing by the warmth of the range. Rory brought in the tub and started filling it while Shaft carried Jackie upstairs and Garth helped Meg.

For a long time, from across the hall, Hallie could hear the muffled voices of Garth and his daughter. If Garth ever loved a woman half as much as he did his daughter, she would be lucky indeed. No matter how much Garth loved a woman, Hallie was sure he wouldn't marry without Meg's approval, at least not while she was still at home. In the terrible event that Meg remained lame, Garth most likely would never have another woman in his life.

He may not anyway, Hallie told herself. The way he looked when you came in from outside—has Rory said anything to him? Garth *can't* think you love Rory, can he? But it would be almost as bad if he knows Rory loves you.

The muddle made Hallie's head throb. She got up and made sure that the slumbering Jackie was covered. Smoky had apparently chosen to sleep with Shaft that night, and Lambie was cuddled to the boy's cheek. She peered out the window and her heart lightened a bit to see the glow of a lamp in Shaft's little house. She had cleaned it a few days ago, filled the coal box, put on fresh sheets, and set a jar of colorful grasses and dried pods on the little table. It was a bachelor's den, yet Shaft seemed cheerful and content. His music helped a lot, and so did Smoky.

Hallie shivered. Would she be like that someday, living on the edge of other people's lives, making them her family? Her head felt ready to burst. She got two aspirin from a bottle in the dresser, washed them down with a glass of water, and got back into bed.

Garth was home. He was safe, not out on the road somewhere. He had seemed happy singing carols that night, happy to make a celebration of Christmas. She would be grateful for that, treasure every minute with him, and try not to worry about the future or Rory's disquieting confession.

XVIII

$\mathcal{A}$fter a restless night of dreams in which she tried to speak to Garth but he could not or would not hear her, Hallie dressed by lamplight in her best winter dress—a softly fitted peacock velveteen—and brushed her hair till it curved softly about her face. It wasn't long enough to catch anyone in the nets of Garth's old song, but she hoped he would like it.

First in the kitchen, she made fires in the range and front-room stove, put on coffee, and set out a plate for each person as her mother used to. Mary Donnelly's gingerbread figures, fruitcake, a heap of nuts, and some of every kind of candy and cookie made during the last weeks filled each plate.

Shaft came in cradling Smoky, and helped arrange the goodies. "Just a few inches of snow," he said. "Enough to look pretty without bein' a problem." He glanced toward the stairway and lowered his voice. "Had any trouble with Cotton or Raford?"

"No, thank goodness. And I wrote you about Felicity coming." Hallie turned to her friend. "It does seem a long time till spring, though, Shaft. Meg puts up with me because she has to, but she's taken Jackie over till I feel like I'm just a housekeeper." She sounded so self-pitying and Shaft looked so worried that Hallie added quickly, "The Donnellys always visit for a while when they bring the groceries and Meg's homework. We've made it through two months. We'll last till May."

"Sure you will, honey, but I wish—" Someone was coming down the stairs. Shaft broke off whatever he had meant to say. "How's about I make some of my special walnut pancakes?"

"Yippee!" Rory whooped.

"You must be tired of cooking," Hallie protested.

"Not for my family," Shaft chuckled, tying his beard out of the way. "Hallie, if you'll open up a can of applesauce and heat it with molasses, it tastes real good poured over the pancakes."

"When're we gonna open presents?" Jackie yelled. His new knife-pocket boots clopped down the stairs with a satisfying racket.

"Soon as you wrap yourself around a couple of these pancakes," Shaft called. "Say, are we celebratin' your birthday today on top of Christmas?"

Jackie nodded, hugging Smoky who meowed, as if explaining that she had wanted to sleep with Jackie last night, but Shaft had been gone a long time and needed a soft warm kitty, too. "I was six day before yesterday. But I wanted to wait for you, Shaft, and Rory and Garth. We'll have my cake today, and I bet I can blow out all the candles!"

"Bet you will," Shaft said. "All right, birthday boy, you get the first pancake. Sit down and see what you can do with it."

"Sounds like we're already having a merry Christmas," said Garth, helping Meg to the table.

Jackie finished first. Shaft helped him through the difficult wait for the others by giving him a pan of crumbs. "Scatter these for the birds, son, so they can have a Christmas breakfast, too."

As soon as Jackie came back in, the cardinals fluttered down, the male bright crimson against the snow, his mate gray brown with ruddy touches. They were joined by a host of larks and sparrows, so Jackie begged more crumbs. "Do you think they'd like some of my birthday cake?" he asked.

"I doubt that chocolate's their favorite flavor," Hallie laughed. "But we have lots of crumbs. I save them to put on top of macaroni and cheese, you know."

"And this pancake's scorched a tinch past brown," said Shaft.

So the birds had their Christmas feast outside while, inside, the humans enjoyed theirs. When Hallie started the dishes, Shaft steered her firmly into the front room. "Rory and me'll see to the dishes today—and we'll see to these *after* the presents on account of Jackie's gonna bust if we wait much longer."

Meg spun her chair smartly around by the tree. Some new presents had appeared since the caroling last night, including one very large box wrapped in brown paper with a big red bow. "Let me hand the presents to Jackie," Meg appealed to Garth. "Then he can deliver them. But he gets to open one first because he's the youngest."

Garth glanced at Hallie, who nodded, but Jackie with supreme effort said, "Let's give Smoky and Laird their presents first."

Laird wurfed jubilantly and galloped away with the bone Jackie had put in a shoebox that morning. Smoky batted a tinkling plush ball till Jackie tired of retrieving it from under the davenport and looked expectantly at Meg.

She scooted a large box forward. "This one's from me, Jackie!" The cardboard was decorated with crayoned Christmas trees and cardinals. Meg ripped at it as eagerly as Jackie and beamed when he cried out in delight.

"A train! And a track and station and a tunnel and—and—"

"The locomotive's got real piston rods," Meg pointed out. "Wind it up and it pulls the coal tender and rest of the cars. And there's a crossing signal and semaphore and railroad gate and telegraph poles!"

Shaft whistled. "Hey, Jack, if you'll let us, we'll all have some fun with that!"

"Yes, but everybody's got to get their presents first," Jackie said a bit regretfully. His excitement over handing out gifts rekindled as he turned toward the tree and picked out the small package that held Meg's watch. "Meg, you're next youngest!" He thrust the parcel into her hands. "Here! You can't guess what it is, not in a jillion, million years!"

She gasped at the shimmering white-gold bracelet and the dainty case. "Jackie! It—it's even more beautiful than I thought it could be. But it cost too much! You'll have to let me pay you for some of it."

"I didn't got quite enough money," Jackie confessed. "Hallie helped."

Meg's radiance dimmed. "Oh. Well—thank you, too, Hallie."

Stung and hurt, though she had expected nothing more, Hallie had to swallow before she could say, "I hope you'll enjoy it." She couldn't tell whether Garth's frown was for her, his daughter, or because he had intended to give Meg the watch on some future occasion.

"Ladies before men," he said, rising. "This one's for Hallie from Shaft and me, but it's too heavy for you to lift, Jack." Garth set the big box with the red bow in front of her, got out his pocketknife, opened the top, and lifted out what Hallie thought at first was a small suitcase till she saw the turning lever at the front.

Shaft hooked a footstool forward so Garth could set the case on it. "Open the lid, honey," urged Shaft, chuckling at her puzzlement.

Hallie flipped up the brass clasps and lifted the hinged lid. "A phonograph! A portable one! It's wonderful! And the top holds records!"

"It'll play ten- and twelve-inch records—two of 'em on one winding," Shaft declared proudly. "Just listen to this!" He wound up the motor, put on a record, and carefully set down the playing arm. Male voices rose merrily in "I'm Looking Over a Four-Leaf Clover."

"Will you let me wind it, Hallie?" asked her brother.

"Of course. Just don't get it too tight."

"We got you Vernon Dalhart singin' 'The Prisoner's Song' and 'Wreck of the Old 97,'" said Shaft. "And there's some mighty fancy fiddlin' from Eck Robertson and Henry Gilliland."

"You fiddle better than anyone, Shaft." Hallie squeezed his hand. "But it'll be marvelous to have music while you're away."

"This present's for Shaft, Jackie," said Meg, calling him to the gleeful task of giving Shaft the meerschaum.

"Boy howdy!" Shaft flourished the box with his name embossed in gold. "My grandpa had a meerschaum, but it didn't have such a fancy case. You kiddies shouldn't have spent so much, but I sure will take care of it and think of you when I'm enjoyin' my evenin' pipe."

Meg's gift to her father was a blue blanket bathrobe and Rory got pajamas. The brothers seemed pleased with the sweater jackets from Hallie and Jackie, and Shaft was delighted with his warm slippers and flannel shirt.

To Hallie's dismay, Rory's gift was an elegant seed-pearl necklace with a pearl and sapphire festoon. It was the gift of a lover, and Garth's eyes narrowed. Hallie thanked Rory but, to save her life, she couldn't pay the natural compliment of fastening it around her neck.

Jim Wyatt's gift to Meg was a music box. Jackie got a two-propeller biplane. For Hallie there was Coty's Muguets des Bois perfume and a note that said he would miss all of them next summer, but he'd located a good used engine he could afford so he'd be running it.

On the card with a box of handkerchiefs for Hallie, Meg had signed her name and Jackie's with no attempt at holiday greetings. The girl flushed when Hallie thanked her as pleasantly as if the gift had required much thought and effort. Jackie must have asked the Donnellys to get him a long piece of paper; for on a four-foot strip of pink butcher paper, he had drawn dinosaurs roaming amidst palm trees and belching volcanos while great winged creatures flew overhead.

"I love it, Jackie," she said truthfully, giving him a hug. "I'll get a frame made for it and keep it for always."

Meg shrieked happily over the Ouija board Rich Mondell sent her. Jackie was thrilled with a jointed crocodile that meandered over the floor when wound up, opening and shutting its jaws. Hallie's present was *The Congo and Other Poems* by Vachel Lindsay. *"Lindsay is America's troubadour. Read these poems to Jackie, and he'll soon be chanting them along with you. Lindsay wrote a poem about harvesting wheat in Kansas. I wish he could have tasted your cooking, Hallie!"*

Jackie was thrilled with his gifts from Hallie, his ukulele from Shaft, fire truck from Garth, and bow and arrows from Rory, but he couldn't keep his eyes off the train set.

"All right, lad." Garth gave him a pat on the shoulder. "You've held out just fine, but Shaft'll help you fix your railroad while Rory and I bring in Meg's last present." He grinned. "We'll call it Meg's, but we'll all enjoy it."

Meg caught his sleeve. "What is it, Daddy? I was getting scared you'd forgot me!"

"You know I'd never do that. You're going to have to figure out where to put it, because once it's installed, you can't be scooting it around."

"What *is* it?" Meg implored. Her father and uncle hurried out of the room and she turned to Shaft. "Do you know? Tell me! I'll see it in a minute anyway."

"So you just wait that minute, girlie. Hmm, Jack, I guess this piece of curved track joins to the straight like this—"

Garth and Rory brought in a polished wooden cabinet and set it down near Meg. "Open that top door," Garth said.

For a moment Meg just stared at the handsome mahogany with the latticed scrollwork over a frieze-covered upper panel. "A—radio! Oh, Daddy!"

The MacReynoldses had bought a five-tube table model the last year Hallie lived with them. The first commercial radio station began broadcasting from Pittsburgh in 1920, with the results of the November election when Harding and Coolidge defeated the Democrats. Since then, stations had sprung up all around the country. Farmers who could afford radios got them for market and weather reports. The music, news, educational programs, and other features had been a lot of company for Mrs. MacReynolds, and Hallie had enjoyed them, too.

Radios were expensive, though. Her glimpse at them in the catalog before she riffled swiftly by gave prices of close to $100 for similar consoles.

Of course there were "easy payments," about $15 down and the same amount each month till paid, with interest. After the bank failure that ruined her father, Hallie was afraid of debt. Had she aspired to such a luxury, she would have saved till she could pay cash. She hoped Garth had though she understood his wish to make up for being away from his crippled daughter.

Meg's fingers trembled as she pulled down the carved door to reveal knobs that turned the set on and controlled volume and tone. As everyone gazed at what still seemed near magic, Garth said, "It won't work till we set up the aerial, so you have to decide whether you want it here or in the kitchen. I vote for the kitchen since it's where we are most of the time we're indoors."

"It'll get dirty in there," Meg protested.

"But it's *cold* in here when the stove's not going," Jackie whimpered.

"I can polish it every day with furniture oil," Hallie offered.

Shaft absentmindedly stroked Smoky, who had draped herself from shoulder to shoulder with her chin hooked above Shaft's collarbone.

"Why not move that little table at the foot of the stairs and put the radio there? That way you can hear it in the kitchen and the front room, too, when the door's open."

"Let's try it," Garth said.

Shaft got to his feet, still caressing Smoky. "You figger out the directions and tubes and stuff while Rory and me redd up the dishes."

Meg gazed longingly at the phonograph. Hallie started to tell her she could play it all she wished but checked herself. It might not hurt to let Meg ask for something. Hallie smoothed and folded the reusable paper and ribbons, storing them in a box for next year.

Next year. Would she be here then? She didn't think so. Not if Meg was still so difficult. Not if Garth were so mistrustful. But taking Jackie away from Meg whom he adored— Even if Shaft came with them, it would be terribly hard on the little boy. Why, *why* couldn't they all be a family? Last night, singing carols, it had almost seemed they were.

It still looked that way, Jackie absorbed in his train, Meg closing her eyes to move the Ouija marker, the men talking about detector-amplifier storage battery tubes, voltmeters, battery testers, and aerials. But while Hallie was delighted with the phonograph and Jackie's mural and touched at being remembered by Jim Wyatt and Rich, she was troubled by Rory's expensive gift and oppressed by Garth's coolness.

What she wanted more than any lavish present was for Garth's eyes to glow as they sometimes had, for that sweet wildness to flow between them, for him to smile and act as if he liked to be with her. Instead he behaved as if it were an ordeal.

Hallie put the wrapping box in the sideboard and started for the kitchen. As if the words were jerked from her, Meg blurted, "Is it all right if I play your phonograph?"

"Use it all you like." Hallie smiled. Somehow, after all the rebuffs, she still hoped that sometime Meg would smile back freely and happily. "After all, we'll soon be listening to your radio."

"Yes," said Meg, winding the motor, "but phonographs are still nice because you can play what you want to hear."

The strains of "Bye-bye, Blackbird" followed Hallie into the kitchen. Garth had gone outside to see about where to run the aerial.

Rory caught her wrist. "Aren't you going to put on your necklace?"

She freed herself and began making cranberry sauce. "I'm going to save that necklace for you, Rory, till you find someone as special as it is."

"I already have."

"No, Rory."

"I can wait."

Shaft grunted. "You've never waited long. Now are you dryin' dishes or lollygaggin'?"

As soon as the two men finished the dishes, they joined Garth in working with the radio. Jackie made his wish and blew out his candles to strains of Christmas music and the new apparatus was kept on the rest of the afternoon. It was Shaft's fiddle they listened to that night, though, and sang more carols as he played and Jackie strummed his ukulele.

This is good, Hallie thought as she looked around in the mellow lamplight. This is happy. This is what I'll save to remember all the months and weeks till spring. Whatever happens, I'll remember this and be grateful.

Garth's eyes met hers, held. Just for the pause of a heartbeat, a surge of achingly sweet awareness seemed to pulse between them. Then he looked away.

Had she imagined it? Had the feeling been only hers? "I'm plumb fiddled out," Shaft said with a last sweep of his bow. "You want any more music, you'll have to get it from the phonograph or the radio."

"We'd all better turn in," said Garth, rising. "We need an early start tomorrow."

"Do you have to go tomorrow, Daddy?" Meg asked.

" 'Fraid so, sweetheart. But spring'll be here before you know it."

"It won't! It'll seem like—like forever!" Meg's glance touched the manger. Did she think of those who had made it, who really wouldn't see Rusty again on this earth? Whatever went through her mind, Meg straightened. "The radio will help a lot, Daddy. And I'll be walking when you come back."

"Sure, honey." He helped her out of the chair. "I'm going to need my water monkey!"

As she did before bedtime every night, Hallie supported Meg down the steps and waited for her outside the privy. The thin layer of snow was luminous blue in the starlight and crunched beneath their feet.

"Are you going to marry Uncle Rory?" Meg asked.

Too startled to consider her words, Hallie said, "Goodness, no! I don't love him."

"I wish you did. It'd be sort of nice if you married him. There'd be more—more family."

So you'd like me for an aunt, but not a stepmother. I guess that's some improvement. "Families are wonderful," Hallie said. Gracious, on the way back from the privy on a freezing winter night, they were almost having a friendly conversation! "Especially at Christmas." Hallie hesitated and then decided to risk the truth. "I'm glad Jackie and I were here with all of you instead of by ourselves."

Meg shivered. "Oh, that would be lonesome! It helps to be with people, doesn't it? Like Luke and Rusty's wife and her mother and the kids must make each other feel better. Maybe when one's real sad, the others talk and get them cheered up."

"I'm sure that's how it works. Laughing's better with others and so is crying."

"Men don't cry."

"Maybe they should. They certainly must feel like it."

They went up the steps. It was the closest Hallie had ever come to Meg's thoughts but when they entered the kitchen, Meg said a careless general good night to everyone except Jackie. She bent on her crutches for his hug and kiss and then let her father help her up the stairs while Shaft carried Jackie, his locomotive, and a dump truck.

Not wishing to be alone with Rory, Hallie wished him a hasty good night and followed hot on the heels of the others. After Jackie was tucked in, Hallie heard Shaft go downstairs and Garth a few minutes later.

The outside door shut. Shaft must be going to his place. A little muffled conversation passed between the brothers. Then one of them came up and entered their shared room. Because of the rapid footfalls, Hallie thought it was Rory. Garth moved more silently and slowly.

He must be downstairs alone. She halted with her fingers on the buttons at her throat. What if she went down? Would he immediately go up or would he talk with her a while?

Nothing ventured, nothing gained. As well hang for a sheep as a lamb. Better to have loved and lost— Hallie broke off the chain of proverbs and buttoned her collar. If he played Great Stone Face, she'd fuss in the cupboard a minute as if she had forgotten something and retreat.

What she wished she had the gall—or courage—to say was, "I love you, Garth MacLeod. When our eyes meet and my bones melt, don't you feel anything at all?" But she knew she couldn't do that unless he gave a sign.

She was going down, though, to give him that chance. Her hand was on the doorknob when she heard a vehicle coming down the lane. Who could it be at this hour?

Surely not the Donnellys. Raford? Hallie could see the back yard from the window. She tugged the edge of the curtain aside and tried vainly to peer through the frost-sculptures on the pane. All she could see was the haloed lights that went off as the engine stopped.

If it were Raford, he wouldn't try to hurt Garth, would he? Should she go down? Nothing in her room would serve as a weapon, but there were all kinds of deadly objects in the kitchen, from carving knives to the fire poker. Hallie's hand was on the knob again when she heard a female voice, one she hadn't heard in months but recognized at once.

Sophie Brockett! What was she doing here? Hallie couldn't hear what the woman was saying but she heard Garth's answer so clearly that she thought he must be close to the stairs and probably, in exasperation, speaking louder than usual.

"No, Sophie, I can't hire you. We got Shaft a helper down in Texas. He does a good job and needs the money."

An indecipherable plaint. Garth again: "If you don't like the way Raford treats you, go back to your folks."

Another murmured appeal. "I'm sorry." Garth's rough tone showed his distress. "I can't take you on, Sophie. If you need some money till you find another job—"

Sophie must have come close to him, for this time her voice carried. "You're going to need all the money you can beg or borrow by the time Quent Raford gets through with you! He's going to have this farm and plow that mess along the creek. If you have any sense, you'll sell out while you can!"

"He send you to say that?"

Sophie faltered. "N–no. But it's true!"

"We'll see. Would you mind leaving so I can get some sleep?"

There was a hissing intake of breath. "You deserve whatever comes to you, Garth MacLeod! I gave you a chance—"

"Thanks. Good night, Sophie."

The door slammed, and then the screen. Car lights glared through the curtain, then arced and faded. Hallie stood shivering, and not just from the cold. Was Sophie making wild threats, or was she sure that Raford was still intent on destroying Garth? Hallie had hoped that Raford was so involved in his election to the legislature and preparing for going to Topeka that he'd have no energy for harassing Garth.

Garth's tread on the stairs was heavier, wearier, than his brother's. Hallie couldn't bear it. She stepped into the hall. "Garth," she said softly into the darkness. "I—I heard. Maybe Sophie was just being spiteful."

"Maybe." Hallie couldn't see his face but she could feel his nearness. "But I doubt it. He tried to get me fired off my job in Texas— told a friend of his on the railroad's board of directors that I was dangerous and irresponsible—mentioned the accident."

"Oh, how awful!"

"It was a good thing the man who hired me had done some checking on my reputation around here and was able to convince the board that Raford, as road commissioner, hadn't fixed the bridge properly and that I had planked it."

"So you think he's still after you?"

"I'm sure of it."

"Maybe when he gets busy in the legislature—"

"If he's busy promoting the KKK, that won't be much of an improvement." She could imagine Garth's shrug. His tone deepened. Some of the fatigue left it. "Hallie, thank you for staying with Meg. I know it hasn't been easy." He hesitated. "Thank you for Christmas. It's the first real one we've had in—well, it must be the first one Meg can remember."

She was glad he couldn't see the tears that filled her eyes. "It was Shaft's playing and the carols and Luke's and Vinnie Wells's manger that made it special."

"And the little tree decorated with handmade pretties and the plates of candy and cookies and all. *You* made this Christmas, Hallie." His voice, warm and smiling, changed abruptly. She could almost feel him drawing back. "Whatever happens, I'll never forget it. And I'll always thank you."

Before she could speak or move, he was past her and turning into his room. If Rory hadn't been there, she would have followed, asked what was the matter.

Staring after him, glad of his appreciation yet distressed at the change in his manner, Hallie stood in the drafty hall till the cold made her shake uncontrollably. Closing the door and burrowing under quilts and blankets, she heard Sophie's threat again and the sudden remoteness of Garth's last words. Long after her body warmed, she felt chilled around her heart.

*H*allie wanted to send the men off with a good hot breakfast, so she was first downstairs again. By the time Shaft came in with Smoky cuddled inside his jacket, the aroma of coffee filled the kitchen, biscuits were in the oven, and Hallie was stirring raisins into the bubbling oatmeal.

"Sure wish we didn't have to go." Shaft poured coffee for both of them and splashed in the Borden's. "This job is keeping Garth afloat, though, so we'd better not grumble." He looked at her keenly. "Who came in that car last night? They tore out of here pretty reckless."

Hallie told him what she had heard. He shook his head. "Maybe that gal was just blowin' smoke, but I'm mighty afraid she wasn't. Guess we'll just have to wait till threshing season and see what new tricks Raford has figgered."

"We can hope he gets so busy at the state capital that he won't have time for us," Hallie said.

Garth brought Meg down and Rory followed with Jackie on his

shoulder. "Saltin' the calf to catch the cow," Shaft muttered, dishing up the oats while Hallie scrambled eggs. "Beggin' your pardon, Hallie. It's an old backwoods sayin'."

By the time the last biscuit was gone and Hallie had packed a big box lunch, dawn streaked the sky and showed the icicles hanging in front of the windows. Shaft eyed them and laughed.

"Bat Masterson wrote once that rich and poor folks get about the same amount of ice, the difference bein' that rich ones have it in the summer and poor ones in the winter. Wouldn't we like some of them icicles in our lemonade 'long about next July?"

"Right now this coffee hits the spot," Rory said. "Shaft, you stay here, and we'll take Hallie with us. She can cook and look pretty at the same time."

"For that, you get slumgullion while the other boys stuff on beef-steak and fixin's," retorted Shaft.

All too soon, the brothers brought down their suitcases. Shaft's was on the porch. "Stay in where it's warm," Garth told Meg as they embraced.

"No! I want to wave till the truck turns onto the main road and I can't see you anymore!"

"I wanna wave, too!" cried Jackie.

So did Hallie. "Let me get the blame thing running first then," Garth surrendered. He bent to shake hands with Jackie. "You keep on looking after our womenfolk, lad."

"I will," Jackie promised. He buried his face against Shaft's beard as the man scooped him up. "Oh, Shaft—"

"Take care of my ornery cat," Shaft told him. "And send me a picture sometimes in your sister's letters."

"Do you like them?"

Shaft nodded. "I show 'em to those Texicans and brag on my grandboy. Hey, sounds like Garth has the old wreck runnin'! We better jump in before it stops."

Hallie got Meg and Jackie into their coats that hung on pegs on the porch and tugged on her own old jacket. Rory followed as she helped Meg down the steps to the where the truck shuddered and belched vapor. Meg resumed her crutches and limped forward to give her father a last kiss. Shaft tucked his suitcase under the tarp with the others and hoisted Jackie for a final hug and whisper.

Hallie didn't know Rory was at her side till he swung her around and kissed her, much as he had when they left in November. Only this time he knew she didn't love him, knew she wasn't going to wear his necklace.

She shoved at him, but he had already stepped back and was climbing into the truck. "So long, angel!" he called. "If you dream, be sure you dream of me!"

"Rory!" she shouted. "You *know*—"

But the truck veered sharply toward the lane. She caught a glimpse of Garth's face, cold as a winter dawn. He waved till the truck turned at the corner, but Hallie knew the farewell was to his daughter.

Damn Rory! Damn him! Had he told Garth lies? He wouldn't have to lie, just act the way he had. Now that she thought about it, Garth had been outside working on the aerial when she told Rory she was saving the festoon for his serious sweetheart.

Should she try to explain to Garth by letter? That would be awkward. She could ask Shaft to try to set things straight and when the men came back, she'd make her feelings about Rory clear to Garth even if it cost considerable pride. What if Garth couldn't care less, saw her only as a caretaker for Meg?

She'd run that risk.

Jackie was sobbing. Before Hallie could comfort him, Meg, in spite of her crutches, managed to draw him close. "I—I'd rather have Shaft stay than have my train!" he wept.

"I know, Jackie. Like we'd both rather have Daddy than a radio—or anything. But they'll be back. Come inside and you can wind the phonograph and play your ukulele like you were part of the orchestra."

"Yes, and I'll pet Smoky and tell her Shaft'll be back."

"You can draw thank-you pictures for Jim and Rich," Hallie said, automatically supporting Meg up the steps. "We all should write to Luke and Vinnie Wells and tell them how wonderful the manger is."

The kitchen, bereft of bantering male voices, seemed chilly and lonesome. Hallie stirred up the coals, added more fuel, and went to fetch the phonograph. There was room for it in the kitchen now. Too much room.

XIX

$\mathscr{E}$arly in the morning of New Year's Day, Hallie was making beds when she heard the kitchen door close. She thought it was Jackie either on his way to the outhouse or to scatter crumbs for the birds. In a moment, the door opened and Jackie yelled, "Hallie! Hallie! Meg—she falled down the steps!"

Heart in her mouth, Hallie pelted downstairs and through the porch. At least Meg wasn't lying unconscious. Her face twisted with pain and outrage, she was trying to raise herself by pushing up from the steps.

"Why won't my legs work?" she sobbed wrathfully. "Why can't I walk? Don't howl like a banshee, Jackie! I'm all right."

"Are you sure? Did you bump your head or hurt yourself some new way when you fell?" Hallie asked, helping Meg up. At least the mud was gone from the thaw that had melted the Christmas snow so Meg hadn't suffered the further indignity of being muddy and wet.

"My dumb stupid awful legs just wouldn't hold me!"

"You should have called me."

"I'm tired of calling you!" Meg scrubbed at her eyes ferociously. "It's New Year's! I didn't want to start it out by asking someone to help me to the outhouse!"

That must be humiliating. It struck Hallie with sudden force how much Meg must hate being forced to ask five or six times a day for aid in taking care of her most private physical needs. Handing Meg the crutches, Hallie tried to think of an alternative.

A handrail! Garth must not have thought of fixing one on the steps because no one had suspected that it would be so long before Meg walked. Making accommodations for an invalid put a seal of permanency on the condition. Hallie shrank from thinking that Meg might never get better, but it was time to do anything that would give her more independence.

"Maybe we could put up sort of a rail from the house to the privy," Hallie said as they moved back up the steps. "You could probably manage then."

The flash of hope on Meg's face ebbed quickly. "The ground's hard. You can't make a lot of postholes."

"I can make a start. And I'll bet Mike Donnelly will finish what I can't and buy and set the posts."

As soon as her morning tasks were done, Hallie located a mattock and shovel in the machine shed and began digging. The ground was frozen beneath the first three or four inches, defying the shovel, and her shoulders soon ached from lifting and swinging the heavy mattock.

Well, then, she'd just start the holes. Mike could tell better than she how many were needed. She was wielding the mattock on the third hole when she heard a motor. A long shiny black automobile jounced down the lane and stopped beside her.

Raford had a new car, she thought inanely. Did he think a Cadillac went better with being a state legislator? It was too late to take refuge in the house, but with a mattock in her hands, she wasn't afraid of him. Not physically, at least.

"What on earth are you doing?" he demanded, coming out of the auto like an unwound spring.

"Digging postholes. Not that it's any of your business."

He threw back his head and laughed. "Hallie, my sweet! Hallie, my brave, strong, ridiculous darling! Don't you know there are posthole diggers?"

"I didn't know it was a special trade, but anyway—"

"A tool, Hallie. A contraption with two narrow shovels. It makes a nice deep hole—not a wide one that, begging your pardon, looks like the beginning of a hog wallow."

"Oh." It made sense that the snugger the rigid sides of the hole fitted the post before it was filled in with loose earth tamped down, the steadier the post would be. Maybe Mike Donnelly had a posthole digger but Hallie didn't want Raford to know how helpful the Donnellys were just in case he might do them some meanness. She picked up the tools and started for the shed.

"I'll send over a posthole digger tool and man to go with it," Raford said.

"I don't want your tool or your man or you here, either."

The sun was dull and shrouded, but his eyes suddenly glowed gold-green. "I suppose if I wanted a New Year's kiss, you'd try to hit me with the shovel."

Hallie dropped the shovel and fixed both hands on the more potentially vicious mattock. "No, I'd hit you with this."

He smiled. "That kind of wooing doesn't interest me. I'll have my kisses when you get tired of slaving for MacLeod." He moved lazily to the Cadillac. "Call me superstitious, but I wanted to be the first man you saw on New Year's Day. Next year I hope to be the only one."

"You won't be. Not ever."

"I came for another reason." His glance brushed her bare hands. "I know the MacLeods and that old derelict were home for Christmas."

"How did you know?"

"From the road, or even my upper window, you'd be surprised what I can see with binoculars. I've watched you hang out the laundry, help that crippled kid to the privy, seen you prime the pump when it's frozen, and wear your arm out pumping water. You're a fool, Hallie!"

Her spine chilled at the notion of his being able to see her when she was outside. Now she'd always be afraid he might be watching. Thank goodness for the curtains in her bedroom and kitchen!

Raford's eyes told her that he was amused by her alarm, that being able to intrude on her privacy gave him a sense of power and control. She was glad she hadn't known about the binoculars before. It would have been hard not to tell Garth. That would have led to a confrontation, and she was positive that Raford didn't fight fair.

He said deliberately, "I wanted to be sure that neither MacLeod—man or cub—left an engagement ring on your finger."

Hallie's spine grew colder. "What if one of them had?"

Raford brushed a speck off his black fur-collared overcoat. "He wouldn't come back from Texas."

"You have the nerve to tell me that?"

"Why not? Since you're not engaged, nothing will happen."

"Did you send Sophie to ask Garth for a job?"

The hard mouth turned down. "You don't think she'd do anything without my orders?"

"You wanted a—a spy!"

"Nothing so picturesque. But if she could get herself pregnant by Garth—or anyone—and claim the child was his—"

"You really hate him, don't you?"

"I don't let anyone keep what I want. Land or a woman." Raford got in the sleek, powerful automobile. The engine purred at his touch. "I promise you this, Hallie. This day next year you won't be alone with a couple of brats on an out-of-date farm trying to dig postholes."

The Cadillac swung away. When she was able to move again, Hallie put up the implements, hugged her arms about herself to stop her shivering, and gazed south past the barren trees along the creek, south toward her love. She'd have to warn Garth that in spite of Raford's election to the legislature, his enmity hadn't waned. But it was best for Garth not to know about Raford's spying.

After all, Raford had watched for almost two months without doing anything. Garth needed to earn his pay from the railroad, not feel that he had to come back here and challenge Raford. She hated it, being under Raford's surveillance, but he'd soon be leaving for Topeka. She prayed fervently that he'd get so involved with politics and state and national issues that he would get over his obsession to possess her, control Garth, and plow the prairie border which even in this depth of winter was alive with gossiping crows and blackbirds.

Deliver us from evil, she prayed, seeking for help and strength beyond this world. *Deliver us from evil.*

Like an answer, a dazzling shaft of sunlight slanted from the banked, suddenly glorious clouds, transforming the skeleton trees, the sere grass, but most of all the sky. Enraptured, Hallie gazed. No longer trembling, she opened her arms to sun and wind that cleansed her of fear, filled her with praise and joy. *Thank You for letting me be alive. Thank You for the beautiful world. Thank You for the sky no man can reach and use and sell.*

The light faded, but she carried the radiance with her back into the house. The Donnellys came to visit that afternoon. Mike did have a posthole digger and thought he might even have enough posts and some pipe for railing. He promised to put in the handrail next day after he took the girls to school.

"I guess you're tired of helping me out to the privy," Meg said after the Donnellys left.

Hallie winced. A great wave of fatigue overwhelmed her. "I guess you can't—won't—believe I want to make things easier for you."

Meg's eyes widened. After a moment, she said grudgingly, "It will be a lot nicer to be able to go in and out by myself."

If that was the best Meg could do for a palm leaf, Hallie wasn't going to wave it. "Let's finish up our thank-yous so we can mail them tomorrow," she said. "Jackie, have you drawn all your pictures?"

*T*he handrail improved Meg's spirits so much that Hallie berated herself for not thinking of it earlier. She benefited from it, too. Knowing how much Meg hated to hold on to her had made the service an unpleasant duty. When it snowed, Hallie cleaned off the rails first thing in the morning, shoveled off the steps, and cleared a path to the outhouse. During storms, sometimes she had to do this several times.

They were in the heart of winter, with the worst and longest storms, but slowly the days were lengthening. On bright days, the sun smiled closer to the earth. Buried seeds would soon begin to sprout, only it was best that didn't happen till the deep freezes were over. When weather warmed enough to encourage early growth, a late freeze could destroy the tender plants. Winterkill, it was called. Sometimes Hallie wondered whether her love for Garth would be like that;

frozen before it had a chance to flourish in the open. But this secret feeling had rooted itself so deeply and inexorably in her being that she couldn't believe it would die before she did, though it might well be mutilated, chopped off at the surface, and forced to grow gnarled and misshapen without the blessing of open air and sunlight.

Hallie was pumping water for the wash one bright frosty morning late in January when she heard a faint, curious sound, repeated over and over. It sounded like a number of people blowing across the open tops of bottles.

"Oh, it's the prairie chickens," Meg cried when Hallie described it. "They have a booming ground at the edge of the Old Prairie. Daddy curved the field away from it. He said the birds used it long before he was born and will be using it after we're gone, as long as it's not plowed up."

"Booming?" Jackie asked. "Boom-boom?"

"Not that kind," said Meg, laughing. "You've got to see it! The males, dozens of them, strut and show off for the hens. They raise their eyebrows, open their tails like fans, stick up the feathers on the backs of their necks, and blow up the big reddish air sacs on their throats that they boom with. They're just starting now but by spring they'll be at it before dawn every day and again in the evening."

"Can we watch 'em?" begged Jackie.

"Sure." Then Meg remembered. She glanced with loathing from her quilt-covered legs to Jackie's eager face. "It's a long way on crutches, but I can stop and rest."

"I'll bring a stool for you," Hallie offered. "That way you can watch till the booming stops."

Meg looked as if she wanted to refuse, but common sense prevailed. She said grudgingly, "You'll enjoy watching it, too."

"I won't stay long. I need to get back to the washing. But when I don't hear any booming for a while, I'll come to carry the stool home."

The sun sparkled on the frosted earth of the planted field and then on the brown grass and dried sunflower and thistle stalks of the Old Prairie. Meadowlarks rose singing.

"Shaft says they're calling, 'I'll eat your wheat, young man!,' " said Meg. "I'm glad they stay and sing all year. Summer birds are nice but it would be awful if there weren't any that stayed through the winter."

"Looky! There's a bur-bur-burrowin' owl!" Jackie cried.

"It's got long legs for such a little owl," giggled Meg. Hallie put the stool down and Meg eased herself onto it. "Oh, there's another one peeking out! Look how that white V curves down between their big yellow eyes! This one looks like he's wearing a high-collared white vest with a black ribbon necktie!"

"They got a big mess outside their hole," Jackie observed. Near the entrance to the tunnel was a scattered heap of bits of bone, hair, parts of unlucky insects and rodents and owl pellets. He wrinkled his nose. "Luke says they line their bur-burrows with dry cow or horse manure."

"The man Daddy bought this place from said there used to be a great huge prairie-dog town that ran from here to about where the house is. There were hundreds of mounds. Snakes and burrowing owls lived in tunnels the prairie dogs didn't use anymore. I guess the snakes ate eggs and owls and baby dogs sometimes, and the owls ate little dogs, but the town was home to a lot of creatures. The man plowed it up."

Jackie's eyes got big. "What—what happened to the owls and dogs?" he asked as if he didn't really want to know.

"I hope a lot of them got away and started a new town somewhere else. But prairie dogs dive into their holes when there's danger. I'm afraid plenty of them were killed by the plow." Meg swallowed and her eyes glistened as she got back up on her crutches. "Daddy wouldn't have plowed up their homes. I'm glad these owls—or their great-great-great-great grandparents—didn't lose their burrow."

It didn't seem the time to say that if someone hadn't got rid of the prairie dogs, the little animals would have feasted on the MacLeod grain. Getting humans for neighbors—at least the kind that settled in one place—must be as disastrous for wildlife as war was for people.

This realization made Hallie especially glad that Garth had left this stretch of wildland along the creek. She prayed for the birds' and animals' sakes that it would always stay like this, that whatever happened to people, the prairie chickens would still be booming hundreds of years from now.

The booming sounded now like the lower notes of dozens of ocarinas. "Let's stop behind that sandhill plum thicket," Meg whispered. "That way we can watch without scaring them."

Crouching, Hallie fixed the stool firmly behind the bushes and hunkered down at the side. The males were too intent on making themselves look big and handsome to pay much attention to anything except another male that came too close.

Erecting tall feathers that grew on the sides and backs of their necks into ruffs that looked like Indian warbonnets, the cocks not only boomed from their reddish air sacs, but cackled and clucked as they patted their feet and strutted around their chosen territory. Now and then one male challenged another. Air sacs deflated, wings lowered, they advanced with outstretched necks and flew at each other like roosters with much beating of wings.

More noise than damage, Hallie decided, as several flurries subsided. If a hen pecked her way among the males, they boomed and pranced even more frenziedly. Sometimes, somehow, a hen showed willingness to accept one of the parading gallants, and there was another flurry either on the booming ground or off in the grass.

It was fascinating, but Hallie had water heating on the range and a pile of sheets and clothing to wash. "I'll come back after they stop booming," she murmured to Meg. "Or you can start home when you're ready, and I'll fetch the stool later."

"Maybe we could leave the stool here," Meg suggested. Her cheeks were rosy and her eyes glowed. "Then Jackie and I could come whenever we wanted to."

"We shouldn't leave the stool outside, but there are some apple crates in the shed. I could put one here and another where you could stop and watch the owls."

Meg gave her a suspicious look but finally said, "That would be handy. Thank you."

As she might thank a servant. But it was good for her to be outside, to get interested in the world beyond the house. And good for Jackie, too. Both owls were perched on their burrow as Hallie passed by. They stared at her solemnly, without the slightest fear.

"I'm glad you live here," she said. "Don't let your cousin, that great horned owl down by the creek, catch you! I heard him hoo-

hoo-hoot last night, and I suppose it won't be long till he has a family to feed."

Meg and Jackie spent hours that day on a letter to Luke that had drawings of the owls and prairie chickens and told him about them. After that, they all listened for the booming which happened more frequently as February wore on. Most "boom" mornings found a bundled-up Meg and Jackie making their way to the grounds, where they spent an hour or so watching.

Much as Hallie yearned for winter's end and Garth's return, she marked off the days with mounting anxiety. Meg seemed no closer to walking than right after the accident. When the Donnellys stopped by with valentines from Meg's schoolmates and Miss Howell, Mary said hesitantly, "Meg, dear, Miss Howell wonders if you can't come back to your classes. She'll help you when you need it, and so will the other children—"

"No! I won't go back till I can walk." Patches of scarlet burned on Meg's cheeks. "I won't have them making fun or treating me like a cripple!"

"But honey, you're missing so much school—"

"I'm getting A-pluses on all my papers."

"Yes, but—" Mary floundered and Mike added, "You need to be learning alongside other kids, Meg, hearing what they think and deciding whether you agree with it or not. There's a sight more to education than knowing what's in the books."

Meg hunched her shoulders. "I'll catch up with all of that when I can walk." Her gaze was defiant but Hallie caught a hint of dread beneath the girl's bravado. "Prob'ly I can start back by Easter."

Leaning forward, Mary took Meg's hands. "Darling girl, I hate to say this, but what if—well, what if you can't ever get along without your crutches?"

Meg wrenched loose and violently wheeled her chair around. "I won't be a cripple!" she wailed. "I won't! I won't!" She couldn't maneuver the chair past the radio to reach the front room. Sobbing, she had to halt at the stairs.

Mary gave Hallie a helpless, frightened look before she followed

Meg and bent to put an arm around her. "Meg, we all want to see you walking—running. I'm sorry I upset you. But Miss Howell—"

"Tell her I'll come to school when I can." Meg's voice was muffled against her sleeve. "The valentines I made for her and the kids are with my homework right there on top of the radio."

Cottonwoods and willows budded along the creek. Bright blades of wheat sprang from dormancy and tinted fields a hopeful fresh green. Wild geese gabbled and honked and gossiped as they flew overhead in twinkling skeins and warming, lengthening days painted the gentle slopes of the Old Prairie with masses of white, pink, and blue and purple locoweeds, vetches and wood betony, a pretty purple plant known by the unpretty name of lousewort. Creamy wild indigo and perky blue-eyed grass sprang up to catch the eye while bird's-foot violets grew close to the earth. Soon there were Easter daisies, snowy beardstongue, and purple-red sweetpealike blooms of crazyweed rising from silvery pointed leaves.

The Donnellys were in the MacLeod kitchen when the radio news proclaimed that "Ma" Ferguson, governor of Texas, was trying to squelch the KKK by banning the wearing of masks in public.

"It'll take more than that to cure the rascals," growled Mike. "But at least it's a step in the right direction. Those speeches Quent Raford makes up in Topeka! They sound all fine and patriotic, but if you listen close, he's talking against Catholics and Jews and Indians and black folks and conscientious objectors, 'specially the ones like the Mennonites that speak German."

"Some people around here agree with him." Mary's happy, open face clouded.

Mike closed his big hand over hers. "Aw, sweetheart, I don't think Mrs. Brockett saw you coming out of the mercantile the other day."

"She didn't want to, that's for certain. I had to get right in front of her before she'd speak. And Shirley MacAfee! We brought the treats for the valentine party, remember? I heard her telling Miss Howell that she should be teaching the children how dangerous it was to have the Pope in Rome telling American Catholics what to do."

"Just talk," Mike said.

"The Klan's done more than talk in a lot of places." Mary shivered.

"I'm sure glad our place is paid for. Look at all the Mennonites and Catholics and folks with foreign names that Raford's foreclosed on this past year!"

Mike sighed and spread his hands. "He's keeping most of those farms for himself, but when he does sell, it's to folks like that weaselly Cotton Harris."

Hallie stiffened. "Cotton Harris bought a farm here?"

"Between Rafords' and town," Mike snorted. "Though it don't sound like he aims to grow much but trouble. He's always speech-ifyin' to one bunch or another, blamin' low wheat prices on every-thing but what *does* cause 'em."

"It all started with the war," Mary said. "Folks over the ocean couldn't grow their own grain during the war, and our farmers were supposed to feed the world. They broke a lot of virgin sod that they knew wouldn't produce very well and went in debt on machinery to farm every acre they could with a shortage of hands."

"Some of that machinery wore out before it was paid for," Mike continued. "But us farmers have a hard time gettin' it through our heads that the boom's over. Europe's growin' its own food again. Even Americans don't eat as much bread and cereal as they did before townfolks got worried about stayin' thin."

"The price of wheat is half what it was in the good years," Mary said. "So farmers plant more to make the same money—and the more wheat there is, the more the price drops."

Mike got to his feet and gave Mary a hug. "We're healthy, eatin', wearin' shoes in the winter, and our place is paid for." He chuckled and kissed the freckles on her nose, bringing the little girls into the family embrace. "You know, Mrs. Donnelly, I wouldn't trade what we've got for everything Quent Raford has or ever hopes to have!"

It would take a strange person indeed not to want to be part of a family like theirs. Hallie tried to imagine Garth putting his arms around her like that, tried to imagine what their children would look like. She gave it up. She couldn't picture Garth so relaxed with a woman, so happily confident.

He was like someone burned so badly that he would rather freeze than get close enough to a fire for warmth. Would he ever get over his pain, or would the winter in his heart blight the roots of love in her own, the love that yearned to break through the secret darkness and flourish in the sun?

*J*ackie reported that he could see the tufts of the great horned owl sticking above the nest in the biggest cottonwood. Her mate brought food for their young and took care of them while she went hunting, a very different arrangement from that of the prairie chickens. The hens alone watched over and fed the fluffy, openmouthed results of early spring's clamorous booming. The burrowing owls hadn't brought their babies outside yet, but hurried in and out of their burrow with insects and tiny birds and mice.

"Those burrowin' owls go 'Coo-coo Coo-coo,' " Jackie said. "I sat down to watch 'em, and you know what?" He gave an excited wriggle. "I could *feel* things growing, I could almost hear the roots and things shoving up through the ground!"

"Wacky Jackie!" Meg teased, but she gave him a fond hug.

Mike Donnelly brought over his team and plowed the weeds out of the wheat. Garth paid him to do this every year since as much as the MacLeods were gone, it wasn't practical for them to keep horses. Garth's fields were across the creek from the Donnellys', and there were several places where a team could easily ford the shallow stream; so Mike went back and forth through the fields rather than come the long way around by the road and bridge.

Hallie spring-cleaned the house from top to bottom, scrubbing woodwork, washing windows and curtains and quilts, and waxing the floors again. She welcomed any excuse to be outside as the buffalo grass turned green, the wheat waved waist high, and the Old Prairie bloomed now with daisies, tall larkspur, purple coneflower, and wild roses.

One day after Jackie trundled the mail home in his wagon. Meg whooped and waved the letter she had just opened. "Daddy says they'll be through with their work on the railroad in a few days! They'll head straight home and get ready for the threshing run!"

The joy on Meg's face was followed by one of fear. She got up from her wheelchair, took one step, and went down in a scramble of arms and legs.

"Meg!" Heart in her mouth, Hallie helped the girl sit up. "Thank goodness, it looks like you're all right!"

"I'm not all right! I—I'm a cripple! I won't be able to go on the run!"

"Maybe we can think of something," Hallie said.

"What?" Meg scorned. "I might drive the water wagon, but I can't fill up the tank or pump it out."

"I know it's not what you'd like," Hallie ventured, "but you can sit down to do quite a lot of cookshack chores—"

"I don't want to—to peel potatoes and stir gravy and—and—that kind of dumb stuff!" Meg interrupted.

"You'd be helping just as much as if you were pitching spikes."

Meg spun her chair so her back was to Hallie, but Hallie saw tears glint as they fell. Trying to cheer her as much as she could realistically, Hallie said, "If you want to travel with the crew, Meg, and it doesn't hurt you to ride in someone's flivver, I imagine your father would prefer that to leaving you here."

"No one should be with a crew if they aren't going to work," Meg snuffled after a few minutes. "I—I'll peel potatoes!"

You're growing up, Hallie applauded silently, but knew Meg would resent her saying so. "Maybe Shaft will teach you how to make his burnt-sugar cake that Luke liked so much," Hallie suggested. "You can practice a light touch with piecrusts and—"

Meg gave her such a pained, ferocious look that Hallie didn't finish her attempt at consolation.

X X

$\mathcal{T}$he house was shining. Two ap-
plesauce walnut cakes mellowed on the top pantry shelf beside oatmeal cookies and a crock of gingerbread men Meg and Jackie had
decorated. In case the men came home between meals, Hallie made
slaw, potato salad, and three-bean salad fresh each day after Garth's
letter came. Early that spring she had planted hollyhock and four-
o'clock seeds that Mary Donnelly gave her. Watered daily, the hollyhocks spiked higher than Jackie's head and should bloom before
long. Even now, their large green leaves softened the unpainted
wood.

She had ordered three everyday dresses that spring when she ordered new coveralls and socks for Jackie. Now she began to wear the
pretty, practical outfits with her new strap sandals. There was a ruffled
blue-and-white baby-check gingham apron to wear with the linen-
finish blue-green chambray, a dusty green apron for the leaf-print
cotton pongee, and a striped ticking apron to go over the slate blue
dimity. A day in the cookshack would wilt any clothes, but at least she
would start out looking nice—and could hope Garth would notice.

When Hallie spread clean sheets on Garth's bed and plumped the
pillows, she pressed them to her face. Soon his bright head would rest
on them. Soon, soon, she would see him every day. Overwhelmed

with a tide of joyful hope, she closed her eyes and thought she could draw in his faint salt masculine scent.

Her love for him wasn't winter-killed. It had waited in her depths to burst out of darkness at his return, like the seeds that now were fruiting into grain. Would he care?

The fourth day after the letter, it was almost bedtime. Jackie begged to hear the rest of a cowboy music program on the radio and it was the end of the yodeling of some lone cowboy that let the distant whistle of a steam engine reach their ears. Outside, Laird set up a jubilant barking as he sped up the lane to welcome his master.

"They're coming!" Meg got almost to her feet before her legs gave way and she reached for her crutches. Jackie ran ahead to hold the doors for her.

Smoky mewed protests at the commotion and jumped up on the radio where she could watch without getting trampled. Hallie lit a lamp, her hands trembling so that it took three matches to catch the wick. She set it on the table beside the washing machine so that it cast light on the steps and yard, showed Meg gripping the rail, Jackie close beside her.

The truck rattled into the yard, lights flickering at every jounce, and stopped so close to the children that Garth needed just one long step to hold his daughter close while Laird tore off in ecstatic circles. Shaft swung Jackie to his shoulder and held out his free arm to Hallie.

They were laughing a lot, crying a little, and talking all at once, when the steam engine gave a resounding blast and rumbled to a stop by the machine shed. Afraid of how Rory might greet her, Hallie hurried inside, put on coffee, and began to heat up the beans and cornbread left from supper.

Garth was home! She glowed with it, feeling as if elation radiated from her. Winter was over. He was home. She would see him every day!

Quick footfalls sounded on the steps. Rory? Of no mind to be swept into an embrace disguised as homecoming exuberance, Hallie filled the teakettle, shielding herself with it, but Shaft ducked past Rory to plant Jackie on the floor. He gave Hallie a hug and his beard tickled her cheek as he kissed her.

"It's twice as nice to come home 'cause you're here, honey!" He stood so Rory couldn't reach her without shoving him aside. "Is that one of your cherry pies I smell?"

"Two of them," she laughed. "Hi, Rory. We were glad to hear your whistle."

"Not as glad as I was to blow it." Moving beyond Shaft, he tilted his head, looked at her as if appraising every detail, and grinned. "That's a pretty apron and dress. Matches your eyes. If you have to get your hair cut before the run, Hallie, don't let Shaft whack it off. Go to a beauty parlor where they know how to make it look stylish."

Shaft's eyebrows wriggled in protest. "I thought it looked just dandy!"

"It suited me, and the price is right." Rory's intense blue gaze made her uncomfortable. It told her, plainer than words, that he hadn't found a Texas girl. She turned her back and gave the beans a vigorous stir. "Your supper's almost ready. Hurry and wash up."

Garth eased Meg into her chair and paused beside the stove. "That rail's a good idea," he said. "Should've thought of it myself. Thanks, Hallie."

How she had hungered for the sight of him! Now she couldn't look up, anymore than she dared to look directly at the sun. She felt his closeness. The edge of her vision caught the rise and fall of his chest, his tangible presence, flesh, blood, and bone. After days, weeks, and months of trying to picture him, of trying to summon up the angles of his face, his downcurved mouth, the deep gray of his eyes, he was here, he was real, ineffably more than all her imaginings.

Shaken by his physical nearness, feeling as if her spine and knees were melting, she escaped to set the table. "Mike Donnelly dug the holes, set the posts, and made the rails." Never in this world would she tell Garth that Raford had offered to have that done. "Mike and Mary have been wonderful. I don't know how we'd have managed without them."

Jackie nodded. "They didn't just bring us groc'ries and Meg's lessons. They broughted us Kathleen and Bridgie and—and lots of laughin'!"

"Sounds like Mike's due a free threshing," Garth said.

"You've helped them plenty," Rory said from the stairs.

"Threshed on credit, lent them seed wheat. If we're going to stay in business against Raford, big brother, you've got to act like this is a business."

"If I get foreclosed on, little brother, you can run an engine for someone else."

The brothers went upstairs with their suitcases, and Shaft went to his place, Smoky purring audibly on his shoulder. Hallie set out butter and filled a tureen with steaming spicy beans, giving thanks that the men were home safe and sound.

A tremendous weight rolled off her with that realization. She felt dizzying relief that she was no longer solely responsible for the children and the household. Even with Jackie, her brother and ward, Shaft would help.

It was sad that Meg still couldn't walk, but at least she was no worse. She had kept up her schoolwork and was considerably more independent, thanks to the handrails. It hurt that Meg still resented and distrusted her, but Hallie was sure the girl would have felt the same about any woman put in charge of her and the house.

Shaft came in. The brothers came down the stairs in a rush. For a moment, they stood close together, gold head next to silver gold, long-limbed, the same height, Rory not yet filled out to a man's size.

Undeniably brothers, they were so handsome, well made, and strong that Hallie thought they must be born of a man and woman who had loved each other greatly; those parents, both dead, buried across the ocean. No wonder Garth felt bound to look after his impetuous younger brother, almost as if he were trying to fill their parents' place. And of course, he had to be both parents to Meg.

Who wanted only him, her wise, strong, wonderful good-looking father. Was his daughter the only woman he would ever allow himself to love?

Garth held out a parcel. "Here, Hallie. Something you'll need for the new run."

"May I open it?"

"Sure." His eyes danced and her blood effervesced with delight in him. "But you won't need it in the kitchen."

She snapped the string and pulled up the piece of paper. Something crimson . . . She picked it up by its lavishly ruffled front, let the long broad ties dangle. "A sunbonnet!" She had often regretted that gift of his that Meg had tossed in the separator when the men threw in their battered straw hats. "Oh, it's beautiful, Garth!" She pressed it to her heart. "This one isn't going in the separator next fall no matter how faded it is!"

"Steam-engine red!" Rory said. "Just the thing for a lady engineer." He balled a fist to hit his brother's shoulder and gave Hallie an embossed gilt box. "Why didn't I think of a bonnet?" he grumbled. "I just brought chocolates."

"We'll enjoy 'em for dessert, lad," Garth teased. He positioned his chair close to Meg's and gave her a smile so loving that Hallie's heart contracted.

"Oh, Daddy!" Meg squeezed his hand and pressed it to her face. If she wasn't pleased about the bonnet, she hid it well. "It's grand to have you home!"

"Yeah!" Jackie wriggled up beside Shaft and sighed with bliss. Then he thought of a way to improve the moment and opened his shining eyes. "Hallie! Could Meg and me have more pie? And maybe some hot choc'late?"

"With marshmallows!" Hallie promised. "This is a celebration!"

"It sure is!" Shaft ruffled Jackie's hair and smoothed Smoky's fur. Meg nodded, her eyes fixed on Garth. Rory smiled with his lips though his eyes did not and toasted Hallie with his coffee cup. Hallie stole a look at Garth as she went to make the chocolate.

Maybe they all celebrated something different but they celebrated together—and that alone was wonderful.

*G*arth had replaced all the separator teeth and made the other repairs before shedding it for the winter but it had to be checked over, greased, and painted. For days the men came in for meals smelling of paint, linseed oil, pine rosin, or kerosene.

The engine was what took time. It was necessary to replace the boiler flues which were so coated with lime and rust scale that all forty-six of them had to be laboriously and carefully removed with a tube cutter, hammer, and chisel. The tube plates were cleaned thoroughly before inserting the new flues and expanding the ends to fit tightly in the holes. The protruding rim of the flue was curled over the tube plate with a tool that looked like forked chisel and deftly hammered to lock it tight.

New main bearings had to be poured, which meant that the flywheel and clutch assembly had to be taken out. The bearings were poured from molten babbitt metal—mostly tin with a little copper and antimony—heated on Shaft's small forge.

It was amazing what Shaft could do with a piece of iron or steel, a chisel, hacksaw, and a few tools. Hallie's head whirled as she tried to make sense of the men's talk of replacing injector jets and the crosshead, repacking shut-off valves, and repairing other mysteries such as the sliding valves in the steam chest.

Hallie had a project of her own. She had given Mike Donnelly money to buy a large bucket of white paint and a small one of blue. In addition to fixing three big meals a day and keeping up with heaps of stained work clothes and towels, she put on her old overalls and gave the weathered old cookshack two coats of paint inside and out. The first soaked in fast but the second left a proudly gleaming surface set off by blue window and door frames and porch rails.

"Swell-elegant!" Shaft whistled. "Almost makes me want to start cookin', though I'm sure enjoyin' your grub, Hallie."

"I didn't see the paint on your expense list," said Garth. There was no way of telling whether he approved of her undertaking.

"I bought it myself." Hallie couldn't keep defensiveness from edging into her voice. "I—I just think it's worth it to have a clean-looking place to work."

"I'll pay you back," he said in a tone that allowed no argument. "Why didn't you wear your bonnet? That scarf tied over your hair can't keep you from getting sunburned."

"The bonnet would get in my way," she muttered. Catch her admitting to him that she had wanted to protect it from paint!

The crew had assembled by the time Rory had painted the engine blazing red, the tank and coal wagons sparkled dark green, and the cookshack boasted a new screen door. Buford Redding had collected Henry and Luke and Dan Rogers, a husky, dark eighteen-year-old cousin of Luke's. Garth hired him on the spot and was still short a man, but Rich Mondell arrived in a new Ford with Steve Hartman, one of his students, who had worked the year before with a threshing outfit in eastern Kansas. Baldy Tennant came to Hollister on the train and hitched a ride to the farm with Mr. Crutchfield.

Luke, topping six feet the year before, had gained no height, but his shoulders were broader, and the boyish softness of his face had firmed. He brought Hallie a jar of chipped reddish-brown sassafras bark. "Grandmother says this tones winter blood for summer," he said.

Turning to Meg, he produced a large bottle, a smaller one, and a paper sack that rustled. "My grandmother is a healer. This camphor-weed liniment will help if you ache. The tonic is wintergreen and other herbs to cure inflammation of the nerves. And the sack holds elderflowers and leaves to put in your bathwater. Grandmother says you should soak in a tub of water as hot as you can stand it several times a day. And if there's any place to swim, it would be good for you to try, to move your legs as much as you can."

Meg gazed at him. He looked at her in sudden shock as if seeing her for the first time. Indeed, with waving dark hair grown to her shoulders, fresh and pretty in her white-collared dress of tiny white polka dots on a red ground—Meg, too, had ordered some clothes that spring, and not just overalls—she looked more young woman than girl, a far cry from the tomboy of last summer.

"Your grandmother's really kind to want to help me, Luke. Does she think any of these things might—might—" Her voice trailed off, but her heart was in her eyes.

"She doesn't know," Luke said regretfully. "But they should keep you from aching and make it easier to move." He smiled at her and tried to joke. "We'll have to find you a swimming hole at every farm we thresh."

"I don't know if I can move my legs enough to stay afloat."

"You won't sink. I'll hold you. Is there a swimming hole in this creek?"

"There's a place by the horned owl's tree where you can usually paddle around."

"Maybe Dan and I can dig it out a little." He hesitated, then decided to say what was on his mind. "We'd have sent the medicine a long time ago, Meg, but Grandmother—she loved Uncle Rusty as much as if he'd been her son, not a son-in-law—went off somewhere in her head when we brought him home. It was just this spring she came back to us and started remembering things. When she remembered about Uncle Rusty and her mind still stayed with us, we asked her what might help you."

Hallie couldn't keep back tears. Meg bowed her head. "Oh, Luke! It's so good of her! Of you—"

"You're my friend," he said. "You're all my friends. Now, Jack, I made you some moccasins. Let's see how they fit."

After the Rogers men had gone out, Hallie looked at Meg. "Shall we try that hot soak?"

"It's a lot of bother. Maybe Daddy—"

"He'll be tired when he comes in. Let's get it done now, while the men are all busy outside."

Hallie pumped enough water to fill the biggest kettles and set them to heat. Just in case a male creature wandered in, she put the round tub down on a rag rug in the front room and laid out several towels.

"I wonder how his grandmother knew," Meg wondered as Hallie helped settle into the tub with its aroma of elder. To keep flowers and leaves from sticking to Meg, Hallie had crushed several handsful in a square of cheesecloth and knotted it so it could be swished through the water. "Goll-ee!" Meg breathed. "This is hot, but it feels kind of nice. My back *does* ache a lot. Sometimes I can't get to sleep at night."

"Why didn't you tell me? I could give you some aspirin."

Meg made a face. "I hate to ask you to do more things."

"That's why your father pays me." Hallie tried to hide her hurt with a smile. "You want to be sure he gets his money's worth."

"I don't want to turn into a dope fiend."

"Dope? A few aspirin aren't dope."

"Close enough," Meg shrugged. "Indian medicine, though—Cherokee medicine, that's different!"

If enthusiasm and faith had any effect, Meg should get better. "Twenty minutes is about as long as the water'll stay hot enough to do you any good," Hallie said. "I'll help you out then. When the water cools, I'll pour it on the flowers. They're really going to enjoy your baths!"

Meg giggled. Why couldn't it always be that way between them? Twenty minutes later, Meg sighed with drowsy well-being as she rubbed her rosy skin even pinker with the towel and began to dress. "My back feels all loosened up, and the good things from the elder-flowers and leaves just soaked into me! It sounds silly in the middle of the afternoon, but I feel like going to sleep."

"Well, there's the davenport. A nap can't hurt."

Meg hoisted her legs to the couch and lay back. "Luke didn't treat me like a cripple."

"Of course he didn't. He treated you like *you*."

"He's still my friend. He wants to help me swim. He wants me to get better. Even if I don't, as long as he likes me, it won't be quite so awful."

"If someone cares, nothing's ever quite as bad."

Meg's eyes closed. Long dark lashes rested on her smooth flushed cheek. A half-smile sweetened the mouth that was so often pouty. Her small breasts curved gently beneath her dress. Child merging into woman, she looked so young and vulnerable that Hallie yearned over her and realized with considerable amazement that she loved the girl, that compassion and the seeds of duty and responsibility had grown through the winter to blossom as almost the kind of half-sisterly, half-motherly love she had for Jackie. Hallie, remembering her own motherless young womanhood, longed to be to Meg what she herself had missed. But would Meg ever allow it?

*M*arriage agreed with Henry Lowen. He smiled even more of the time, and his frame was filling out. When greetings were over, he opened a box and set out an immense domed cake. "My Anna sends you this special almond-ginger cake," he beamed. "You will find it tasty."

Rich Mondell brought a thrillingly illustrated *Treasure Island* for Jackie, Hallie got another volume of Vachel Lindsay, and the young professor smiled as he handed Meg a book with a pencil attached. "Everyone's doing crosswords since a publisher came out with a book of them last year. Some experts say they cause mental illness, but others say they sharpen intelligence and calm the spirit. Let's see what you think."

Having the crew back was like a family reunion, but Hallie fought back tears when she thought of Rusty. At least his Vinnie and the children were well, getting some income from the cows and mules. "Jess Champlin owns the settlement store and raises horses," Luke said that first night at supper. "He and my sister kept company before she married Rusty. Jess is still a bachelor, but I reckon he won't be a year or two from now."

Over coffee and a slice of Anna Lowen's spicy cake, Rich spoke indignantly of the "monkey trial" going on in Tennessee. "John Scopes is a biology teacher. Of course he taught the theory of evolution! If Tennessee doesn't want anything taught that doesn't fit with the biblical six-day Creation, then the state had better forget science altogether."

"I believe in the six days," said Henry earnestly. "It is the Bible."

"It's your right to believe it." Rich calmed down because he liked Henry. "But you aren't setting up to be a scientist."

"Science cannot make people happy or good."

"It doesn't make them bad or unhappy, either, Henry. It is knowledge, what we can find out about the world we live in."

"All we need to know is in the Bible."

Steve Hartman, Mondell's student, started to protest but Rich checked him with a look. "That may be true for a farmer, Henry. But the world is changing fast. In another generation, there'll be many more people making their livings in cities in jobs created by science."

"Yeah, new inventions are sure changing farms," said Baldy, glancing around at the other men. "These combines coming on the market can cut wheat and thresh it at the same time. Instead of hiring harvest hands and later a threshing outfit, a farmer'll be able to handle his crop with just a couple of men."

"When are we going to buy a combine, Garth?" Rory asked.

"When the mortgage on the place is paid off and we can pay cash," Garth replied rather shortly.

"I would never want such a machine," Henry said.

"Mennonites don't use any power but horses?" Buford asked.

Henry shrugged. "Some congregations believe that machines are all right. Others don't. Me, I like horses. They don't break down like machines—"

"They can get heatstroke or run away or something," Rory argued.

"Of course. But if they are treated and fed well, horses are more reliable than any machine. No machine ever tried harder because it wanted to please you. And horses make more of their own kind, so you are not going to the dealer for a new one about the time the old is paid for. They put strength back into the earth with their manure." He shrugged and smiled. "Besides, horses are strong and handsome, and I like to see them."

"Machines don't eat their heads off when they aren't working," retorted Rory.

"No," Henry retorted with perfect good nature. "They just rust in the shed and eat up interest. Anyway, the men who will be put out of work by farm machinery—will they be happier and healthier, do you think, working in a factory?"

"That's a question folks have been chewing on since handloom weavers and nail makers lost out to manufacturers," Rich said. "I don't know the answers, Henry. But I could go for another slice of your Anna's cake."

"So could I," Rory said.

X X I

$\mathcal{G}$arth checked the wheat every day to see when it was just right for harvest. One evening he came to the house with a head of golden grain. He rubbed it in his palm, then showed Hallie the hard brown kernels, freed of their husks. "It's ripe and ready!"

Thrilled that he had come to show her, Hallie wondered whether love would ever ripen for them. But that wistful thought was overwhelmed by wonderment as she looked at the grain, tiny yet so lifegivingly important.

In his hand, Garth held the miracle of seeds that could nourish people and beasts or be planted to bring forth more grain. Without grain, without planting and reaping, humans would go back to a sparse existence of hunting and gathering or roaming with their flocks. Growing food was magic like that of conception and birth.

O all ye Green Things upon the Earth, bless ye the Lord . . . She touched the grain reverently and wished she dare close her hand over his. "It will be a good crop?"

"Looks that way," he said with the caution of those whose livlihood depends on the whims of nature. "We'll start cutting in the morning."

Because the MacLeods used the steam engine to pull the header and stacker header barge in tandem, the work needed only Rory on the engine, Garth and Shaft in the stacker wagon, Baldy with the coal, and young Dan Rogers with the water tanker.

These last two wagons were drawn by horses borrowed from George Halstead, who had already harvested his bundled wheat. "Wheat can be cut by a binder while it's a little green, several weeks before it's dry enough for a header," Shaft explained. "Halstead comes from eastern Kansas, where it rains more and binding's usual. Out on the plains, most farmers use headers."

"Doesn't waiting several more weeks for the wheat to ripen make it more likely that a crop will be rained or hailed out?" Hallie asked.

"Sure, but heading works better here in the long run. Get better wheat, more of it, and a stacker wagon like the one Garth rigged up saves a lot work."

"It's handy, but I didn't figure it out," Garth admitted. "Farmer over by Dodge City named Winifred Jacobs tinkered around and came up with it about ten years ago. What it does is form the stack in the wagon with the help of a couple of men who fork the heads around and tromp them down. When the wagon's full, they open the rear gate and drop four skids to the ground. Then they drive a stake behind the wagon and tie a rope to it that's run around and under the load of wheat. The engine pulls ahead, then, and leaves a nice stack that's piled high in the center to shed rain and that'll keep well till it can be threshed. The stacker's a great thing for us. Cuts out the work of pitching off the header barge and building the stack on the ground."

The rest of the threshing crew went to help Mike Donnelly and Harry Crutchfield with their harvest. Then they would come help thresh Garth's crop and start on the summer run. "At least no more of my customers have switched to Raford," Garth said. "With any luck, we'll make expenses and a little over, though we'll have travel a long way to do it."

"Yeah," frowned Rory, "but how long can we tough it out without some real profits? We're going to need a new engine and separator in a couple of years."

"We've got to take extra-good care of the ones we've got," said Garth. "And hope Raford gets tired of losing money. Now he can wheel and deal in the legislature, I doubt he'll care so much about running me out of business."

Hallie felt a stab of guilt. Raford's wanting her must aggravate his rancor against Garth. Would it help if she left? She didn't think so. By now, the rivalry and hostility between the two was so great that she didn't think it could be resolved by anything but death or the complete crushing of one or the other.

"Don't bet on Raford forgettin' you, son," warned Shaft. "He's not used to men standin' up to him. An' when he's home, that strip of prairie you left along the creek must be like a red flag to a bull."

Garth looked weary. Hallie fiercely, protectively, wished she could smooth the furrows knitting his sun-bleached eyebrows together. "We'll just have to do our work the best we can and try to handle whatever Raford throws at us. So far we've managed."

"I want to do better than manage," Rory burst out.

"You get your engineer's share," Garth said quietly.

He didn't add what Shaft had told Hallie; that all Garth's share had gone toward the mortgage. His share from shelling corn had paid her wages and supplied household money till he could send part of his railroad earnings. Rory liked being a partner, but he didn't assume a partner's responsibilities. Some of that was Garth's fault. So much older and charged by their mother with Rory's well-being, Garth probably indulged Rory more than was good for either of them.

$\mathcal{N}$ow look at the difference, Henry," Rory said, as all the men ate a hearty breakfast before dawn on the first day of harvest. "Mike Donnelly supplies one-header and two-header barges. Crutchfield does the same. Each outfit needs a header puncher, a driver for each barge, one man in the barge, and a stacker."

"Yup." Henry buttered another biscuit. "Six men for each crew, maybe a scratcher to help the man on the stack."

"Well, with the engine and stacker wagon, three of us can do the same work."

"Yup. But you got to have water and coal. That takes two more men."

Crestfallen, Rory brightened at his next thought. "Then look at the horses!" Rory ticked them off on his fingers. "Six to push each header, and each barge needs two. That's ten horses for each header outfit, and they have to be fed and curried and rested and watered and harnessed."

"Yup." Henry sloshed catsup over his fried potatoes. "Ten horses."

"Coming at it another way," Rory pursued, "Mary Donnelly's got to feed twelve to fourteen men for a week while Hallie here cooks for five."

"Yup. But that's two header crews instead of one," Henry countered. "The main difference I see is that you use your engine instead of horses, and I am not so sure that it takes more time to take care of them than it does to take care of your engine. Anyway, my mother and our sisters all help each other cook at harvest, and they like it—working together to feed their hungry men. There are more than enough men for our family farm's headers and barges and stacks, so some of us, like me, go away to work for money wages." He nodded contentedly. "That money is shared by the family, just as Anna and I get our share of grain."

"Sounds like what those communists over in Russia are trying," said Baldy. "Maybe it works with some families, 'specially religious ones like you Mennonites who don't get too grabby over worldly goods, but I reckon it's built into human nature to want more and better than your neighbors have got."

"It's an exciting thing they're trying in Russia after centuries of all-powerful czars whose will was backed completely by the church," Rich said. "And there's China with Chiang Kai-shek, still trying to forge a republic after the revolution." His eagerness faded and he shook his head. "Going the other way, there's Mussolini in Italy and President Hindenburg of Germany favoring a monarchy though I'll bet that beer-hall rabble-rouser, Adolf Hitler, who just got out of jail, is going to cause a lot of woe before he's locked up for good."

"Wars and rumors of wars," said Henry. "Thank the good God there is peace now for our country and we can harvest the fine ripe wheat." He chuckled. "However it is we do it."

$\mathcal{H}$allie wasn't cooking for a regular harvest crew; but the men still needed three big meals a day, as well as morning and afternoon lunch which she and Jackie took to them in the field. Thus she was grateful for Meg's help with peeling potatoes, picking over beans, and all the other tasks that could be done while sitting. Shaft designed a special wide board that clamped over the wheelchair arms to make a table at a convenient height for working.

Meg made no open complaint, but it wrenched Hallie's heart to see the girl pause by the railings sometimes to gaze across the fields toward the smoke of the engine. "I expect Dan's a better water monkey than me," Hallie heard her tell Jackie. "He's bigger and can pump faster. But oh, I wish—"

Busy as she was, three times a day Hallie pumped and heated water to fill the tub. "I don't like you going to all this work," Meg said ungraciously. "It makes me feel like—like I'll owe you too much."

"You help me a lot," Hallie reminded her. "Anyway, doesn't the soaking make you move easier?"

"My back doesn't hurt as much," Meg admitted. She rubbed at the tears gleaming in her eyes. "But when I try to put weight on my legs and walk, they just go out from under me like rotten old sticks!"

"It's something not to hurt as much."

Meg glared. "It's not enough!"

"Meg—"

"Don't! Don't tell me it could be worse!" The fury in Meg's eyes and voice hardened to a calm that was much more alarming. "If I know—when I know—I'll never walk, I'll just fall down the stairs or do something Daddy will think was an accident."

"Oh, Meg, don't even think that. Didn't you say that if Luke would stay your friend, you could stand this better?"

"I don't want him feeling sorry for me, hanging around a cripple in a wheelchair when he could be having fun."

Meg was still a child but wasn't it possible that she was dreaming of when she wouldn't be? And that dream, now, must often turn into despairing questions: Could she marry? Could she have babies? And if she could, would it be fair to a man she loved?

Hallie asked briskly, "If Luke were in the chair, wouldn't you still want to be with him?"

"Of course I would, but—"

"Remember that. Try to give him—and other people—credit for feeling the way you would if things were the other way around."

Meg stared at Hallie, half-gratefully, half-resentfully. "I almost wish you were crippled for a while!" As Hallie gasped, Meg hurried on, "So you'd know how I feel—and so I could take care of you—heat your soak water, massage you, and think up things like the railings."

Hallie stifled a sigh and saw with bitter clarity that, even leaving Garth out of it, until Meg could pay the debt she thought she owed, there was no chance of friendship between them.

"I'll try not to break a leg till you can take care of me," Hallie tried to joke. "Now, could you make sandwiches for the men's afternoon lunch while I finish baking?"

*S*tacks of headed golden grain awaited threshing as soon as the full crew assembled at the MacLeod farm. Mike Donnelly and Harry Crutchfield would bring their teams and wagons to receive the wheat and haul it to the elevators in Hollister. Garth went over the separator again, checking, tightening, greasing, oiling.

"You need to give the engine a good going-over," he said to Rory at dinner. "I noticed one of the hand holes is leaking. You need to drain the boiler and replace that hand-hole gasket. And if you don't chip off those clinkers that are building up on the grate, you'll not only have a slow, smoky fire but you'll burn out the grates—"

Rory went red to the tips of his ears. "I'll take care of it, for Pete's sake! If you weren't always poking around, trying to find something to gripe about—"

"That's not hard to do. You're going to ruin the frogs on the hand-hole bolts if you don't quit forcing them. You let the ash pan fill up and touch the grates. You—"

Rory shoved back his chair. "To cut a long song to a chorus, big brother, you don't think I'm much of an engineer!"

"You're good when you're not careless." Garth paused, met Rory's glare steadily, and said more gently, "Probably this shouldn't have come up at the table, laddie. But"—he floundered—"you don't seem to hear me unless I make you mad."

Shaft interposed, "The wheat looks good to me. Fullest, fattest heads I've ever seen. What do you think, Garth?"

Both brothers relaxed. "Looks like forty bushels to an acre." Garth spoke cautiously, but his smile betrayed his satisfaction.

"Forty! Make it fifty—even sixty in the south field," Rory exulted. "If half the farmers we thresh have wheat as good, I'm going to have enough money at the end of the run to—to—"

His shining blue eyes swung to Hallie as if he couldn't help himself. Garth's face closed. "Guess I'll get back to work," he said, rising.

"Don't you want your pie?" called Hallie.

"Thanks, don't feel like I could stomach anything sweet."

Baldy and Dan Rogers divided the rejected peach pie blissfully, but Hallie still felt slapped. As standoffish as Garth was, he had no business sulking because Rory persisted in his foolishness, eyeing them grimly when Rory dried dishes for her after supper.

For heaven's sake, young Dan Rogers dried, too, and at the end of the day, very glad she had been for their help! Apart from wistful glances and an occasional brush of hands that might have been accidental, Rory hadn't flirted. She'd even begun to hope that his infatuation was subsiding. His half-voiced thought and the way he had looked at her just now forced Hallie to realize—painfully, for who would not be fond of Rory—that he hadn't gotten over his crush.

After dinner, he took over Hallie's chore of pumping and heating water for Meg's tub and then dried the dishes. After Meg was ensconced in the fragrant-smelling water, Hallie came back to the kitchen to finish the dishes.

Through the window, Meg saw Dan helping Baldy fix a wheel on the coal wagon. Jackie must have gone out with Shaft to inspect the cookshack. Uneasy at being alone with Rory, Hallie hurried with the dishes and talked rather desperately to avoid a silence.

"The elderflower soak does seem to be easing Meg's back pain.

And Meg's taking the idea of helping in the cook shack instead of driving the water wagon a whole lot better than I thought she would, thanks to Luke's promising to find places they can swim. I think—"

Rory tossed the dish towel over the rack. He turned to Hallie. "What do you think about us?"

She prayed he would not touch her. She didn't want to get into a struggle, repulse him physically, or hurt his young male pride. They were friends. They had shared last summer's run. He had patiently taught her how to run the engine. He was so handsome, strong, and likable that she might well have cared for him—if it hadn't been for Garth.

"Rory," she stumbled. "I—I wish you were my brother."

His eyes dilated. Pulses throbbed in his throat and temples. He reached for her, then locked his hands into fists at his sides. "You wish I was *my* brother, don't you?" he said in a tight hard voice. "Even if he's twelve years older than you, can't trust women, and has a bratty daughter who may be on his hands for the rest of his life?"

"Rory!"

"You think I'm just a kid! Well, there are women who know better! I'm going to town and find one of them!"

Before she could say anything—and what was there to say?—he stalked out. The door banged. In a few minutes, she heard Garth's angry voice, Rory's furious retort, and then the truck started.

*H*enry, Luke, Rich, and Steve drove up in time for supper. They said Mike Donnelly and Harry Crutchfield would be there with their wagons in the morning.

"Where's Rory?" Henry asked with a blue-eyed twinkle. "Is he ready to fire up in the morning and show me how much better his engine is than horses?"

"He had to run into town." Garth's tone was careless, but Hallie saw the tightening of his lips. "Must've had trouble with the truck or something."

"Want Steve and me to drive towards Hollister and see if he's broken down beside the road?" Rich offered.

"Oh, let's give him a while," Garth said. "The engine needs a few things fixed, though. Maybe I'd better take care of them tonight so we won't be slow getting up steam in the morning."

"Please let me help. I like the engine!" Luke's green eyes shone in his dark face. The young beauty of the graceful Cherokee was firming into maturity. No wonder Meg watched him as if she were thirsty and he were cool, clean water.

"Won't hurt you to learn how to take care of hand holes and flues." Garth smiled at Luke's cousin. "Dan, you want to hold a lantern for us?"

Dan was as eager as Luke. Their enthusiasm—such a change from Rory's grudging attention to details—seemed to put spring into Garth's step as he rose from the table. "Well, lads, let's get after it, then!"

Since the crew would set up cots or spread bedrolls on the porch or in the yard or shed, except for morning and afternoon lunch, they would have meals at the house and use the flivvers to go back and forth from the more distant fields. Shaft, once more in charge of the kitchen, planned the next day's menu while Hallie washed dishes and Meg dried.

"Say, Hallie, girl, you've baked bread for tomorrow, and that's a mighty good row of pies on the shelf, not to mention that crock of oatmeal cookies! Gets us off to a good start."

"Mary Donnelly sent eggs and butter and some wonderful new potatoes and peas," said Hallie, resolving that when she had a home, she would certainly grow vegetables. "And radishes, tomatoes, green onions, and gorgeous yellow summer squash."

"That kind of garden stuff is larrupin' good," Shaft approved. "We'll eat it while it's fresh. No pinto beans tomorrow! Bake a ham, and we're all set."

Shaft fussed around, though, discovering and rearranging things like any cook assuming command of a kitchen after someone else has used it. When Meg was having her soak in the front room, Shaft frowned at Hallie.

"I saw Rory stomp out of here after dinner, honey. He yelled at Garth that he was goin' to town, and Garth hollered that he'd better do the engine repairs first. Rory just went foggin' off." Shaft cleared his throat. "I'm not trying to nose into your business, but did that young hothead say anything to make you think he might not be back?"

The notion dumbfounded Hallie. She gazed at Shaft in dismay.

"We—we had kind of a falling out, but he didn't say he was leaving for good. Oh, Shaft, do you think—"

"I don't know what to think. Some ways, it might be better for Garth and Rory both if they split up till Rory learns what it's like not to be the boss's kid brother and Garth quits treating him that way." Shaft looked at her with sad wisdom. "And until you decide which one you want and t'other's got used to it."

Hallie flushed. "As far as Garth's concerned, what I decide doesn't seem to matter, except to me."

Shaft heaved a sigh. "Honey, Rory kind of hinted to Garth that there was something between you. Never said it right out but kind of bore down on a word here and there or put on a cat-ate-the-cream smile."

"How could Garth believe that? And when could it happen, for heaven's sake?"

"When a man's in love, 'specially when he's scared to be, he's seldom noted for good judgment and horse sense."

Hallie caught her breath. "You *do* think he loves me, Shaft?"

"I'd stake my head on it, includin' my beard. But whether he'll ever risk lettin' you in on the secret"—Shaft's tufted brows pulled together—"I don't know, Hallie, even if you waited till Meg's grown up."

"Meg may always have to live at home now."

"Yeah. There's that, too. Hark! There's some kind of vehicle comin' down the lane."

Hallie listened intently. "It doesn't sound like the truck. And it's not Donnelly's flivver."

They looked at each other uneasily. With Raford up the road and Cotton Harris a few miles farther, the sound of an unfamiliar motor could be a warning. "Maybe the truck broke down and someone's givin' Rory a lift. Let's go see."

Out by the shed, Dan held a lantern while Garth and Luke worked on the engine. A gleaming automobile pulled up beside them. Shaft whistled. "That's a new Lincoln V-8!"

"But the same Sophie Brockett," Hallie breathed. "What does she want?"

Sophie's bobbed blond hair caught the lantern light as she got out of the swank bottle-green Lincoln. Raford must be pleased with her to supply such a luxury auto. Her shrill nasal voice carried to Hallie and Shaft as they stood on the shadowed porch.

"I came to tell you, Garth MacLeod, that your kid brother's going to be engineer for Quent Raford's threshing crew. I've come to get his clothes."

"Why didn't *he* come?" Garth's tone was quiet, but it sounded like a cry of pain.

The woman lifted her bare plump shoulders in a shrug. The beaded fringes on her black dress glittered above her knees. "He smashed up your truck."

"Is he hurt?"

"Bruised and cut a little. Doctor says nothing's broke. The hangover he'll have tomorrow's probably going to be worse than anything he got when he turned the truck over in a ditch."

Garth strode toward the gloating woman. She shrank away and he halted. "Did you sell him the bootleg, Sophie?"

"What if I did?"

"The law—"

"The sheriff's paid off," she jeered. "Call in the feds if you want, but it could wind up with your curly-headed brother in the pen. I let him sell a couple of pints of booze just to make things cozy."

"You got him drunk. You set him up to bootleg. You got him to hire on with Quent Raford. What else did you do, Sophie?"

She laughed and moved her body suggestively. "Can't you guess?"

"Where is he?"

"In my suite at the hotel, of course."

"I'm coming to see him."

"He doesn't want to see you."

"Maybe not, but he's going to."

"His things—"

"*I'll* bring them. You just head for town, Sophie. I want the door to that suite unlocked when I get there, and you out of the way. Understand?"

"All right, you big fool, you can hear it from him! Just don't break the furniture or kick up a row. I manage a high-class hotel."

"Sounds more like something else."

Garth stood as if dazed and blind while Sophie got into her Lincoln and spun away. Slowly, with visible effort, he turned to Dan and Luke. "Let's finish with the engine, lads."

Rich came out of the shed where he had set up his cot. "I'll drive you in, Garth."

"I'd be obliged."

Leaving the porch, Hallie came up to Garth who was already working on a flue. "Shall I pack Rory's clothes?"

"Guess you'd better."

"I'll come with you. I might be able to talk to him——"

Garth looked around as if stung. "I have a notion you've already talked to him too much."

"Garth, please——"

"You had a fuss after dinner, didn't you, and that's why he drove off like the devil was chasing him. You'll stay here and leave my brother to me."

Hurt and offended, Hallie went inside. She helped Meg from the tub, upstairs to bed, and then entered the brothers' room. Open on chairs, their suitcases were already nearly packed for the summer run. Feeling almost as bad as if he were dead, Hallie collected Rory's toothbrush, comb, shaving things, and the few unpacked clothes.

It wasn't hard to imagine what had happened. Rory had gone looking for a woman. Sophie, taking advantage of the chance to wound Garth and ingratiate herself with Raford, doubtless beguiled the young man with both her body and whiskey.

Perhaps by asking him to do her a favor and deliver a few packages, she had made him a bootlegger. It was even possible that someone had tinkered with the truck so that a crash was almost assured.

Neither Sophie nor Raford would care if Rory were killed or seriously injured. Even drunk, he would be so ashamed of wrecking the truck that it wouldn't be hard to persuade him to work for Raford.

And what a triumph that was for the banker; what a defeat for Garth!

"It's a mess!" Shaft lamented. "If Rory won't come back, Garth's going to take this durned near as hard as he did his wife's runnin' out on him and Meg. On top of that, it leaves us without an engineer."

"Garth can run the engine, can't he?"

"Sure. But no one else can run the separator. That takes a heap of practice and know-how."

Hallie scarcely knew she was going to say it till she heard herself. "I can run the engine."

Shaft blinked. Then a smile turned up the corners of the mouth half-hidden in his beard. "By grannies, you can! Baldy can do the firin' up and help you keep the fire and boiler goin' right. Garth can help you check the flues and valves and take care of what you can't." He stared at her in sudden dismay. "But who's gonna help me feed this bunch?"

"Meg can do a lot. And maybe we can find a girl in town—"

Shaft stroked Smoky, who had jumped to his shoulder when Shaft bent for the suitcase. "Jackie likes to set and clear the table and likes to fetch stuff for me. Reckon we can manage. And some of the farmers we thresh have girls of an age to like to earn some money. If we find out I need more help, we can prob'ly hire one of them for the rest of the run."

"I'll miss helping you, Shaft."

He grinned. "Maybe I'll get you back next summer. Young Luke's crazy about the engine." The grin faded. "If Rory don't come back by then, I'll bet Garth trains Luke on the engine."

"That'll be fine with me," Hallie said. "I'm glad I can run the engine and make a set and all, but I'd really rather cook." She winced to remember Garth's stinging words and made a decision that emerged painfully but firmly from months of yearning in which hope alternated with frustrated disappointment. "I'm not going to work for Garth after the run, Shaft. Not if he blames me for Rory's leaving. Not if he's always going to find some reason to shut me out."

"But Meg—"

"I know. And I really do care about her, even though she shuts me out, too." Hallie swallowed and brushed her sleeve across her eyes so she could see to go down the stairs. "I hate to take Jackie away, but I can't—and won't—put up with Garth's blaming me for everything that's gone wrong in his life! I hope he finds someone who'll suit him and Meg better, but I really can't worry about that."

"If you and Jack go, I'm goin' with you. If you'll have me."

"Oh, Shaft! Of course we will! You're our family." A pang of regret tainted her relief that Jackie—and she—wouldn't lose this gruff, kind man who was like a grandfather or special uncle. "But Meg and Garth will miss you."

"Well, let's not worry about it now." Shaft paused before he went outside with the suitcase. "Lots can happen before the run's over." He shrugged away future worries and chuckled. "Say, now, won't you be a picture up there on the engine with your bright red bonnet? Don't see how any young fella could keep from fallin' deep in love with you!"

"I know one who doesn't seem to find it hard!"

"Bought you the bonnet, didn't he?" Shaft went out fast to keep the host of winged insects on the screen from flying in. Hallie picked up her prayer book and sat down by the lamp.

The beautiful, timeless words of the Morning Prayer gradually calmed her, helped her believe there was peace, power, and love immutable beyond this human strife and pain, that her father and mother and Rusty were in that peace. *"O ye Winds of God, bless ye the Lord: praise him and magnify him for ever . . . O ye Lightnings and Clouds . . . O all ye Green Things upon the Earth . . . O ye Whales, and all that move in the Waters . . . O all ye Fowls of the Air . . . O all ye Beasts and Cattle, bless ye the Lord: praise him and magnify him for ever . . . As it was in the beginning, is now, and ever shall be: world without end . . ."*

Rapt in the calming, joyful words, she heard no sound till a deep voice invaded her ears. "Why is it, Hallie, that I always find you praying?"

XXII

$\mathscr{H}$e had come through the front door—had probably left his car parked up the lane after Garth and Rich drove out. After her first rush of dread, she remembered she wasn't alone, that Shaft and the others were out back. All the same, the solid menace of his body, the taut expectancy in his hazel eyes, made her feel trapped by a huge cat. Instinctively, Hallie shielded herself with the prayer book.

"You give me plenty of reason to pray, Mr. Raford. This trick you've pulled with Rory—"

"The young fool did it himself."

"You made the most of it. I'll bet you hired someone to tamper with the truck."

"It doesn't matter. Rory MacLeod's going to be my engineer." Raford's white teeth flashed. "Garth will have a hard time finding one."

"*I'm* going to run his engine."

The dark pupils of Raford's eyes swelled to cover all but a thin rim of the golden green. "You?"

"Rory taught me last summer. We'll manage."

"I doubt that." Raford regained his composure. "Quite a few people around here don't like Garth's hiring Indians, draft dodgers, Wobblies, and Bolsheviks."

"Bolsheviks?"

"That atheist college professor and the pup he brought along this summer."

"It's none of your business—or anybody else's—whom Garth hires."

"Cotton Harris doesn't agree with you."

A chill shot down Hallie's spine. "Are you saying the Ku Klux Klan may get mixed up in this?"

"Just a neighborly warning." He came a step closer. "Hallie—"

"Isn't stealing Rory enough for you?"

"Not by any means. I want two things."

"Heaven and earth!"

He laughed. "Hell, too, maybe. No, seriously, my dear, I want to break Garth MacLeod. Almost above all things, I'd like to watch him bow his head to me and plow that strip of old prairie." Raford paused, then spoke softly and deliberately, "Above all things, I want you."

"Why?" she asked in baffled amazement.

"Why, indeed?" The irony in his voice changed to exasperation. "You can't guess how often I've asked myself that over this past year, especially after I got a house in Topeka and could—amuse myself. Is it because you're like the women I loved and lost, my mother and grandmother? Because you wave that prayer book at me? Or is it because you're Garth's?"

"I'm not!"

His eyes searched her. Blood surged to her face. Raford's jaw hardened. "I didn't mean anything so crude as that he'd been in your bed, Hallie. Knowing you, I wouldn't believe that could happen without a wedding ring."

"Then—"

"I mean," he said relentlessly, "that you want him in spite of all the reasons why you shouldn't. You belong to him sure as that stretch of prairie does."

"And you're bound to take over anything of Garth's. You want to destroy him."

"I'd rather not have him dead. Much more gratifying to have him beg me for work, beg me not to put him off his land."

"You can't do that as long as he meets his mortgage payments."

"How long can he do that if bad things happen to his crews and men get scared to work for him?"

Hallie despaired. Becoming a legislator hadn't lessened Raford's obsession with defeating Garth, or, apparently, possessing her. She'd never be Raford's woman. But she couldn't doubt that, with his power and money, he could eventually ruin Garth's business.

"You may take everything Garth has," she said. "You've taken his brother, and last year you stole a lot of his customers. But he'll never beg you for anything. He'll never plow that strip of the Old Prairie."

"He will. For his daughter's sake."

That was true. To care for Meg, especially now that she was crippled and needed certain comforts, Garth would sacrifice his pride and even the cherished land along the creek.

"So, my very dear," said Raford, smiling, "Do you love Garth MacLeod enough to spare him all of that?"

She stared, unable to speak. "You and your brother would be very comfortable in my Topeka mansion," Raford went on. "You'll be my hostess and confidential secretary with a generous salary."

"You're crazy!"

"No, I'm utterly sane. We'll have a contract. If your feelings don't change after a reasonable time, you'll be free to go, with enough cash to buy a house or set up a little business. Try it for a year, Hallie." His gaze roamed over her like a physical caress. She flinched, and he laughed beneath his breath. "If you don't want me by then as much as I want you, I wouldn't keep you for worlds."

But she would have served his purpose, if he was right about Garth's caring for her. Anyway, she couldn't go with Raford, couldn't endure his touch. Not if he held a gun to her head.

"You must know I can't do it."

Languorous warmth vanished from his eyes, leaving them hard. "Then, Hallie love, I'll grind MacLeod until he crawls. And you'll suffer, won't you, because you'll know you could have saved him."

With a mocking nod, he was gone. Hallie began to shake. Grateful that at least she hadn't trembled while Raford could see, she sank into the chair and lay her head on the table to stop its swimming.

What would Raford do? Garth—any farmer—was vulnerable in so many ways. A match tossed in the stacks, machinery that could be wrecked or tampered with . . . And there was Raford's threat to the crew.

With a sense of shock, when she considered them as strangers might, applying labels, instead of thinking of them as the individuals and friends they were, Hallie realized that, except for Baldy, they could all be targets for hate-blinded men like Cotton. Buford Redding was a Wobbly; Dan and Luke were indisputably Indians; Henry was a German-speaking Mennonite conscientious objector; Rich had hopes for the Russian Revolution, and Steve was his admiring pupil. Even Shaft could be called a bohunk bootlegger who had escaped the law.

It was awful! Putting scary names on people was what Cotton did in bigoted ignorance and Raford in calculated malice. She suspected that Garth's mission tonight would be futile and he wouldn't want to talk to anyone—her least of all—when he came home. His accusation—that she had sparked Rory's desertion—still rankled, but she had to warn him.

And tell him she could run the engine. Hallie started some coffee. Then she opened the prayer book and read aloud, *"Help us not to fear the terrors and dangers of this night."* But she was afraid. For all of them, but especially for Garth.

As time crawled, in spite of her anxiety, weariness blurred the words on the page. Several times she snapped awake as her head started to droop forward.

What was taking Garth so long? She hoped that at least he and his brother wouldn't use their fists on each other. Coffee revived her for a little while, but she was nodding again when a motor roused her. It stopped outside. She heard Garth thank Rich and tell him good night. Rubbing sleep from her eyes, she jumped up and had a cup of coffee poured when Garth walked in.

"Thanks," he said.

From the hurt anger that smoldered in his eyes, she didn't need to ask what had happened. "I hunted around for another engineer or separator man," he said. "Couldn't find either one, what with threshing already started. Rich'll drive me to Dodge City tomorrow. Maybe we'll find someone there."

"Garth, I can run the engine." Annoyed that he hadn't thought of her even in his desperation, and more annoyed at his incredulous stare, Hallie said firmly, "I can't do a lot of the maintenance, and I'd want you to help get up steam a few times, but Baldy could help me with the firing. I know how to use the injector, make a set, and belt up. You've seen me."

A spark of hope flickered and died in his eyes. "Who'll help Shaft?"

"Meg can do a lot. Jackie loves to fetch and carry. If Baldy and you can get up steam of a morning, I can help with breakfast and get dinner started. Shaft thinks you can surely find a girl who'd like to hire on somewhere along the way."

"So Shaft thinks this could work?"

"Yes." She couldn't keep the acid from her tone. "So do I, or I wouldn't offer."

A reluctant smile tugged at the corners of the mouth she longed to feel hard and sweet on hers. "Guess it's a good thing you learned, daft as it seemed last summer."

"I wouldn't have tried if you hadn't thought I couldn't do it."

"It's not so much I thought you couldn't. More I thought you shouldn't."

"Why?"

"Too dangerous."

"It's dangerous for men, too."

"Sure, but—" He made a helpless gesture.

"The way you feel about women, I'd think you'd be glad to get rid of at least one of us."

His hands clamped tight on her upper arms. "Don't say that!"

Their eyes battled. A wild tingling sweetness flowed through her, dissolving her strength. Her lips parted, waited for his as blood drummed in her ears.

He released her abruptly. She almost fell, had to steady herself against the table. Why had he drawn back as if her flesh burned him?

"All right," he said roughly. "You can have a try at the engine till we come across a man who can either run it or the separator. Baldy and I'll fire it up in the morning while you help Shaft get breakfast. Then it'll be all yours."

Suppressing her baffled disappointment, Hallie said, "There's something you'd better know." She told him about Raford and his sneering remarks about the crew. "I wouldn't put it past him to sic Cotton and the Klan on us."

"You're not afraid?"

"Well, of course I am! Not for myself as much as for Luke and Dan and Henry and Buford."

Garth pondered. "I'm not going to drag them out of bed to talk about this," he said after a moment. "But I'll tell them at breakfast and let them decide whether they want to stay with me."

"I think they'll stay. But if they don't——"

"Reckon I'll have to go to town and wait for hoboes to hop off the freight cars." He shrugged. Incredibly, he flashed her a grin. "If you're going to be our engineer tomorrow, you better get to sleep."

"So had you, if you're going to fire up."

"Go up the stairs, Hallie. I'll blow out the lamp."

How she wished they were going up together, arms around each other, close in the darkness. "Good night, Garth," she said, and went up alone.

$\mathcal{M}$eg and Jackie were such good help at breakfast that Hallie was able to pop three pies in the oven before she sat down with the crew. That was a funny feeling; eating with the crew, being one of them now, rather than a cook. Garth had the engine up to steam so Baldy was watching it while Garth came in to eat and explain to the men about Hallie's new job and Raford's threats.

"If any of you would rather get another job, I'll sure understand," Garth said. "I don't think Raford would hound you if you weren't helping me."

"We'd still be Indians," Luke said. Dan nodded.

"I'd still be a Mennonite," Henry said.

"How could I teach my students about being responsible citizens if I caved in to that red-necked Cotton?" Rich asked.

"Wobblies did some bad things sometimes," Buford admitted. "But nothin' as bad as the government framing Joe Hill for murder and shooting him dead or John D. Rockefeller's hired gunmen setting fire to the striking miners' camp at Ludlow in Colorado and killing women and kids along with the men. I still think the IWW had the right idea, and I'm just sorry the war broke the union. I aim to be buried with my red card."

Garth looked around, studying each man in turn for some hint of misgiving. They met his gaze. Luke said, "Dan and I appreciate your hiring us when plenty wouldn't on account of our skins. We're with you, Garth, as long as you want us."

Into the chorus of affirmation, Garth said, "All right, boys. If that's how you feel, let's start our threshing."

*G*arth gave Hallie a quick but thorough summing up of her duties. "Keep an eye on the water glass. That crown sheet's got to keep covered or the whole things blows. Now turn on the injector."

Hallie was tense at first, but Rory's persistent drilling echoed in her mind, and as water glass and steam gauge responded to her actions, she began to feel confident and excited at the power she controlled.

She glanced up to find Garth watching her with an expression that made her heart leap before he said, "Okay, engineer! Make your set!"

Hallie steered the engine to where it could be hooked up to the separator, and away they chugged to the first field. At Garth's signal, she pulled the separator between some stacks so it faced the prevailing south wind.

She drove away from the unhitched separator and swung around to face it, careful not to make her half-circle too wide. To her thankful jubilation, with the men all watching and cheering, she lined the engine up with the separator which the men had leveled swiftly. Henry and Buford stretched the belt from the drive pulley of the separator while the other men pulled the extension feeder into position.

It hurt to remember how Rory had taught her to let the engine creep toward the belt, hurt to remember how, last summer, Rusty had usually been the one to shove the belt over the big wheel on the right side of the engine as Henry was doing now.

Moving the reverse gear as if it were fine china, Hallie backed cautiously away as the belt drew tight. Buford blocked an engine wheel, saluted Hallie, and grabbed his pitchfork. He and the other spike pitchers took running jumps up the stacks, working their way up with pitchforks.

Garth gave a final squirt with the oilcan and climbed up on the platform of the separator so he could keep an eye on everything—including Hallie. Hallie tooted the whistle. It made an exuberant sound, and she drew in a breath of sparkling air before, as the first loads of grain struck the feeder, she pulled the bandanna over her nose.

The summer's run had started—and the engineer was a slender woman in a bright red bonnet.

*A*veraged out fifty bushels per acre," Garth said at supper the day they finished threshing his wheat. "Hope everyone gets that good a yield."

"If they do, it'll pay some mortgages," Baldy said. "Do we head for Brocketts' in the morning, boss?"

Garth's face tightened. "No. He sent word that Raford's outfit will do his threshing. First place we thresh will be George Halstead's. On his way home tonight, Mike Donnelly's going to stop and tell George we'll be there bright and early tomorrow."

There was an awkward silence. Everyone knew Rory would be on Raford's engine, cutting his own brother out of work. It was a relief when Baldy covered a yawn and chased his final bite of apple pie with a last swig of coffee. "So I need to fire up 'way before it's bright." He scraped back his chair. "Good supper, Shaft. Already lookin' forward to breakfast."

"So'm I," retorted Shaft, "but not perzactly in the same way." When Hallie started clearing the table, he tried to shoo her away. "I'll do that, honey. Engineers don't do dishes."

Rory had. Stabbed by remembering how they had laughed together, Hallie felt for Garth, who must ache constantly at his brother's defection. "I don't do all the things an engineer does," she said, forcing a smile. "So it's fair enough to help you when I can. Besides, running the engine doesn't make me as tired as standing up all day to cook."

"I'll still wash and you dry," Shaft insisted.

He got a good start while Hallie filled Meg's tub and settled her for a soak. These treatments were going to be hard to manage once the outfit moved away from the house, but maybe the swimming Luke promised would serve almost as well to loosen whatever was wrong with Meg's spine.

As if reading Hallie's mind, Meg said, "It's funny. My back doesn't hurt much anymore. It feels like I should be able to walk, but when I try without my crutches, something sort of locks. If there was just some kind of key—"

"Maybe we'll find it," Hallie encouraged her. "Anyway, if you don't hurt as much, that's wonderful."

Meg snorted. "What would be wonderful would be to run the engine like you—or even the water wagon!"

"You're helping Shaft, and that's mighty important."

Meg only scowled, and Hallie retreated. After all these months together, after all she'd done for Meg, the girl still resented her. Could it ever be different?

I'll last out this threshing run if it kills me, Hallie vowed. But then, if these stubborn MacLeods still treat me like Typhoid Mary, I'm taking Jackie and finding other work. Then Jackie would hate her for taking him away from his adored Meg, but Hallie knew there was no way she could endure much more of being close to the man she loved and yet so far away.

"Afraid some folks lost their harvests last night," Garth said heavily when he came in for breakfast.

"Yeah." Baldy nodded. "It was still pretty dark when we started firing up, but there was smoke all around off at a distance."

"Too far for there to be any use in our trying to help," Garth said. "Looked too far away to be Donnellys', Halsteads', or Crutchfields', but it may have got Brocketts', Jonas MacAfee's, and just about all the fields around there."

"Last night there was no lightning." Henry frowned.

"No, and hands aren't supposed to smoke in the fields," Garth said. "But every now and then someone gets careless. Doesn't take much of a spark to set stubble or stacked wheat blazing."

Baldy scratched his hairless skull. "Don't see how fires spread out like that could start from one place and all be going at about the same time. An' it would sure be peculiar for that many smokers to all get careless at once."

"Don't look my way." Buford gave a wry grin. "Wobblies used to get blamed for settin' fields on fire, and maybe a few did, but I don't hold with burnin' up good wheat."

Baldy persisted between bites of fried potatoes and eggs. "What is doggone peculiar, boss, is that it looks like there weren't any fires at the farms you're aimin' to thresh."

"It's peculiar, all right, but that is how it looked," Garth conceded. "I'm sorry. Wouldn't wish it on anyone to lose their crop."

Buford shook his head. "I don't like this, boss. Those farmers who lost their wheat are goin' to be lookin' for someone to blame."

Garth stared. "What are you getting at, lad?" he asked slowly.

"See it the way the farmers may," Buford urged. "Your wheat didn't burn. It's safe in the elevator at Hollister. Donnelly, Halstead, Crutchfield, Thomas—the ones you're goin' to thresh—looks like they're okay. But those that burned quit you for Raford. To top it all, he's got your brother on his engine. Think it over, Garth. How's that goin' to look to a bunch of farmers who've seen their year's work and profit go up in smoke?"

As if he couldn't take it in, Garth looked around the table. "You mean someone set the fires so they could blame us? Raford . . ."

Garth's voice trailed off. Would Raford order such a thing? With a sick all-gone feeling, Hallie knew he would; knew Cotton would gleefully harm people he had no quarrel with if that could destroy Garth and the crew Cotton had come to hate, including her.

Into the shocked silence, Shaft spoke gruffly. "Garth, if Raford's behind this, it's you he wants."

Rich Mondell nodded. "You better take my flivver, Garth. Pile in

Dan and Luke and Henry and head for town—or farther—till this gets straightened out. Buford, maybe you ought to make tracks, too." He grinned even in that tense moment. "Wobs do have a reputation as firebugs."

"Anyone can go who wants to." Garth finished his coffee and got to his feet. "Luke, I reckon maybe you and Dan and Henry should in case Cotton brings the Klan down on us. Hallie, you take Meg and Jackie and go with them. Me, I'm due at Halsteads' in a couple of hours. I mean to be there."

Luke rose, dark and graceful, his heavier-built cousin beside him. "We're going with you, Garth."

"So will I," said Henry, though he was pale beneath his tan.

Rich shot Steve a question. The college boy grinned. "This beats studying."

"You're out of your head, boss." Buford shrugged. "But I always did like crazy guys."

"Me, too," Baldy said.

Garth looked around at his crew. He must have felt the painful contrast between their loyalty and Rory's betrayal. "I appreciate this, lads, more than I can say. We'll go about our work like the innocent men we are. But Hallie, you and Meg—"

"I'm going with you, Daddy!" Meg glared at him. "I can't walk, but I can do that."

"You need an engineer," Hallie said and went to get her bonnet.

XXIII

$\mathscr{H}$alf an hour later, Hallie sounded the whistle and steered the engine out of the yard. While Shaft and Meg did dishes and tidied the kitchen, Hallie had driven to the separator and the men had hooked it to the engine, followed by the caravan of cookshack, water, and coal wagons. The men got into the Model Ts or perched on the seats of the wagons.

This was how the outfit had looked last summer, when Hallie first saw it, except there were so many changes. Rusty Wells lay in the soft, ancient earth of his native hills; Jim Wyatt was running his own engine again up in Saskatchewan; Cotton Harris and Pat O'Malley had been replaced with Dan and Steve; instead of Meg, Lefty Halstead would be driving the water wagon—and laughing, golden-haired Rory wasn't saluting Hallie with smart little toots of the whistle.

She would never have dreamed that *she* could control the engine. But though that had turned out to be important, far more significant things had happened in these past twelve months. She and Jackie had found a kind of family, one that he chose over going back to his mother. Hallie's smoldering hurt and anger at what she had considered her father's desertion, and the guilt she'd felt when he died, had gradually faded as she assumed responsibility for Jackie, learned more about life and people, and came to love Garth. Maybe that was growing up; to care about others and work for their good rather than concentrating so much on your own griefs and desires. Not that she didn't need Garth and hope for his love with all her heart.

The procession reached the main road and turned toward the bridge—the fateful bridge where she had joined the crew last year and where, in the autumn, Rusty died and Meg was crippled. Dust roiled high and yellow brown on the road across the creek, churned up by what looked like a dozen trucks and flivvers. The smell of charred grain carried on the breeze from fields still smoking at Brocketts' and farther away. Hallie's mouth went dry. Her eyes stung with dust. And fear.

Above the sound of the engine and the roaring motors across the creek came vengeful, gloating shouts. "Here comes that bunch of Wobs and Indians that burned Ernie Brockett!"

Dear God! Ernie, the gawky boy whose shirt and overalls had been Hallie's first threshing attire? Had he been caught in a wheat fire? Dizzy and nauseated, Hallie broke into clammy sweat as louder shouts rose above the din.

"That damned Garth MacLeod burned us out! *His* grain's safe—but he ain't!"

"We'll burn his threshin' outfit an' him with it!"

"I want the yellow-bellied Dutch draft dodger!"

"We'll teach that Bolshevik perfessor things he never learned at college!"

No escape. Not for the slow-moving engine. But Hallie could block the bridge with it, stop the motorized rabble. With luck, most of the crew could reach Hollister in the Model Ts.

It took all her will, all her love for Garth to break the paralysis that gripped her and edge the engine onto the bridge, but her brain and perceptions operated with detached clarity. The water glass! The level was dangerously low. Relying on Garth and Baldy to have checked it, she hadn't looked at it that morning, but she was sure they had.

There must be a leak. She couldn't see the crown sheet but, from past experience, she knew the crown sheet couldn't be covered by that critical inch of water, might not be wet at all. It could already be glowing a dull red . . .

Frantically, she tried to remember Rory's warning. *The quickest way to die is to inject water on a red-hot crown sheet. Open the safety valve. Close the draft and dump your fire. Stay put and try to cool off that boiler or the whole shebang will explode and blow you to kingdom come.*

Hallie halted the engine as Raford's sleek black Cadillac veered around the other vehicles, sped onto the bridge and braked scant yards away. She started to open the safety valve and close the draft but stopped. The engine was a gigantic bomb. It was also Garth's way of making a living; but if the angry farmers reached him—and Dan and Luke and Buford and Rich, that wouldn't matter. She'd better get down and run back to tell the men to swing the Model Ts around and head for town as fast as they could.

All this shot through Hallie's mind in the second that it took for Raford and Rory to get out of the Cadillac. Rory! He was furious at Garth, but to come along with Raford like this at the head of a howling mob! Hallie could scarcely believe her eyes.

Raford squeezed by the engine and caught her wrist. "Get down from there, Hallie!"

"Garth didn't burn that wheat!"

"The burned-out parties think he did." Raford laughed, but his eyes burned. "You fool, is there anything you won't do for that damned Garth? Come on, you're going to stay safe in my auto while I clean up here."

Hallie fought him, but he clamped her in arms of steel and carried her toward the Cadillac. "Bring this engine across, Rory!" he commanded. "Get it off the bridge so Cotton can bring the men over."

"Sure, boss." Rory truckling to his brother's worst enemy! He climbed up on the platform and took his familiar place. "Better move your car a good way off the bridge and let the flivvers come first. You're in the legislature. It'll look better if you come along after—"

After the lynching's over? Surely, when it came to the last minute, Rory would try to save Garth and the others. But even if he was a traitor, she couldn't let Rory—once her friend and so beloved by Garth—be blown to bits.

"The crown sheet, Rory!" Hallie shouted as Raford forced her in the auto.

Rory flourished his hat and waved. "It's all right, Hallie! You'll be just fine!"

He turned to call something to Garth and the crew who had abandoned the safety of the flivvers and were running forward. Hallie couldn't hear what he said, but the men turned and ran back to the Fords.

Except for Garth. He sprinted toward the engine. Hallie wailed in animal fear for him. Raford misread her. "No one'll hurt you. In a year, you'll be glad!"

He ripped the ties off her bonnet and lashed her wrists together before he backed from the bridge and pulled well off the road beneath a cottonwood. The engine bellowed like a great monster, belching smoke as it started to inch across the bridge.

Locked together, Rory and Garth struggled, silhouetted for an endless moment against the rising sun. Then Rory, with frenzied strength, lifted Garth bodily and sent him flying backward and sideways. He fell out of sight down the embankment.

Raford climbed out and signaled to Cotton, who was in the first truck with Sophie beside him. "Go as soon as the bridge is clear. Haul MacLeod out of the creek and hang him on the best limb you can find."

Cotton's rabbit teeth showed. "Can't we burn him?"

Raford shrugged. "Don't hurt the kids."

Sophie got out of the truck and hurried to Raford. She sobbed out incoherent words and tried to catch his arm, but he pushed her away, intent on the engine.

Hallie twisted against her bonds till her wrists bled, but the knots held. They were going to kill Garth and at least some of the others— men who were like her family—and there was nothing she could do.

She thought she would faint with the horror of it. Then thunder blasted her ears, rocked the earth. Chunks of metal thudded onto the Cadillac. Raford went down, his triumphant laugh changing to a grimace, as a flying rod tore through his center and took him to the ground. Still on her feet, Sophie rubbed blood from her cheek. Then she dropped to her knees at Raford's side, screaming at him, shaking him as if she could make him hear in death what he had ignored in life.

One shriek—cut off abruptly—had torn from Cotton as the fly-wheel hurtled against the truck, crushing the front against the back like a tin can. Her wrists still tied, Hallie managed to open the door and ran to the bank to look for Garth.

He was bowed over what was left of Rory. A wing of bright gold hair. The rest was blood and shards of bone. The uproar behind Cotton's truck brought Hallie around to face seething confusion as a score of men swarmed out of their vehicles, many with shotguns and rifles. A great slab of steel had flattened the top of one flivver and whoever was inside. Smashed by what looked like the boiler, a man had lifted his hand before it dropped against the metal.

Doors, tops, and hoods were torn or dented. One man dragged his leg. Another had a shoulder that drooped crazily. Blood ran or dripped from wounds made by the hail of steel and iron shards.

Hallie knew a few of them—wispy little Ed Brockett, Jonas Mac-Afee, and Chuck Martin, but she suspected that most were KKK members brought in by Cotton. Dazed and leaderless, they tended their hurts or those of friends, but it was only a question of time till they remembered why they were here and came after Garth and his men with redoubled hatred.

If the crew's flivvers weren't disabled, they might get away. Hallie started for the bridge. Sophie rose from Raford's body with his revolver in her hand. Her father was coming toward her. She backed away.

"Daddy! Cotton and his bunch set fire to the other fields, but I burned ours. I—I was trying to show Quent how much I loved him. I didn't dream Ernie was sleeping in a stack. I hope someday you and Mama can forgive me—"

Brockett passed his hand over his eyes. "*You* did it, Sophie? Garth MacLeod never fired the stacks?"

"I did it." She whirled on Hallie, and her face twisted. "But I wouldn't have if it weren't for her! She's the one Quent really wanted. No matter what I did—I'll go to hell, but she'll come with me!"

Sophie leveled the gun with both hands. "Sophie!" Garth was scrambling up the bank. Shaft, Luke, and the others pelted across the bridge. *I'll be dead by the time they get here,* Hallie thought with frozen calm.

Still, she wouldn't be executed like a sheep. She lunged for Sophie, but a slender body hurtled past and knocked Sophie to the ground as the revolver roared. The bullet struck Raford's body and made it jerk as if it were still alive.

"Meg!" Hallie gasped. "You ran! Your legs work!"

Hallie stretched down her pinioned hands to help the girl up, but Luke lifted Meg while Garth and Ed Brockett raised Sophie. She collapsed, weeping, against her father. As if he didn't know what else to do, he put his arms around her.

"There, girl, there. It's an awful thing you've done, and your brother dead and wheat burned all over this country—but that Quent Raford, he fooled us all. Guess it's no wonder he made you kind of crazy. Come on. I'll take you home to your mother."

Sophie was taller than he was, but he supported her as he faced the would-be vigilantes and raised his hand for silence. "Reckon you heard my daughter. Quent Raford got Cotton to burn the stacks so's we'd blame Garth and his crew. I'll come back soon as I take Sophie home. We'll clean up here as best we can."

Jonas MacAfee took charge. "Chuck, you go for the sheriff and take in anyone who needs a doctor. The rest of you can pitch in and help here."

Tough little Ed Brockett turned to Garth. He held out a shaking work-gnarled hand. "I'm sorry, MacLeod. And mighty sorry about your kid brother."

Garth hesitated only a second before he grasped Brockett's hand. "Rory knew what he was doing. He yelled at us to run for cover and injected water on a red-hot crown sheet."

Brockett nodded. "It sure stopped us. Worse'n a bomb. But you've lost your engine. And your brother." He went off with a hysterically weeping Sophie, shaking his head and trying to soothe his daughter.

Garth took out his pocketknife and cut the bloody bonnet ties from Hallie's wrists as Meg ran to him. He enfolded them both in his arms as Jackie ran up and burrowed in between the women.

"My girls," Garth said in a voice that broke. "My brave girls . . . And Meggie-love! You ran like a prize filly!" Stepping back, he looked at her anxiously. "Is it all right? It doesn't hurt to move?"

"It doesn't hurt a bit." She smiled at Luke. "That elderflower soak has made me so much better! But I needed something to unlock my legs. When I saw Sophie aim that gun at Hallie . . ."

Tears made her gray eyes brilliant. She squeezed Hallie's hand. "I knew how awful it would be if anything happened to you—and—and

I just started running!" She bent to hug Jackie who returned her embrace but still held on to Hallie's skirt. "Daddy!" Meg looked up in her old imperious way. "If you married Hallie, she and Jackie would never go away! They'd be our family."

"I'd kind of figgered that out." Garth looked at Hallie. "Rory didn't just yell at us to take cover. He said you weren't his girl—never had been, though that's what he made me think. He said I shouldn't let you get away."

"I don't want to," Hallie said.

The joy, the delight would come later. Now there was unspeakable thankfulness mixed with grief as she put her arms around Meg while Garth went to help his men carry Rory up the bank. When they reached level ground, the men moved away while Garth sank down and held his brother for what seemed a very long time. Then Shaft, Luke, and Henry brought a blanket, wrapped Rory in it, and carried him to a flivver.

*I*n spite of fire, death, and disaster, threshing had to be done before hail or rain ruined the crop. As if obeying Rory's last command, the exploding engine had destroyed three of the mob's vehicles and damaged more, but had done comparatively little harm to the threshing outfit. Garth had the separator almost ready to work again. A hole torn in the cookshack roof had been patched, and a gash in the water tank was thoroughly soldered. But all that was no use without an engine.

The night before Rory's funeral, Garth looked around the supper table at his crew. "I've saved most of my railroad-building wages, and there's money from this year's grain. Doesn't add up to enough to buy a good used engine, but I'll see if I can get a loan from the bank. I've never been late on a mortgage payment. With Raford gone, there's no reason why I shouldn't get enough cash together to be back in business."

Shaft cleared his throat. "Garth, I've got some cash hid away in a sock. Couple hunderd bucks. I'd a durn sight rather invest with you than the bank."

"Great idea, Shaft," Rich Mondell said. "I can chip in a few hundred and not draw my share till we finish the run."

"I, too, would like to do that," Henry said.

"Count me in," chorused Buford and Baldy.

Luke and Dan glanced at each other and smiled in agreement. "If we could draw half our shares to send home each payday," said Luke, "we'd like to put the rest in on the engine—except for enough to go to a movie sometimes and stop for a soda."

"I've got two dimeses and three nickels," Jackie offered.

"I don't need any pay," Hallie said. "Because—"

She broke off, coloring, but Garth reached for her hand and announced to the not-very-surprised circle, "Because, even if it may not be a good bargain, everything I have is going to be yours, too, as soon as we can get married."

She blushed even more hotly. "Garth MacLeod, are you proposing in the middle of supper in front of the whole crew?"

"Yes," he said simply, his eyes caressing her. "I can't get up the nerve to do it when we're alone."

"Oh, Daddy!" Meg scolded. "Don't you know anything about women?"

"Not much, but I'm going to learn." He gave Hallie's hand a slow warm pressure that made her pulse leap before he released her and nodded his thanks to the men. "All right, partners! We'll draw up an agreement, legal and fair and proper and when"—he broke off and swallowed—"when we've said good-bye to Rory, I'll start hunting an engine."

He dried dishes for her that night. They sat up long after everyone else had gone to bed and poured out their hearts to each other. How he had been afraid to love her, how Rory had hinted that she was engaged to him. How hard it had been with Meg and Jackie that winter, how she had resolved to leave after the threshing run if he still wouldn't trust her . . .

"We'll have bumps ahead," he warned. "I've spoiled Meg, and I don't know how to talk to a woman I love—"

"I'll teach you," Hallie said. But the kiss she began needed no words, and he was a swift learner of when to kiss her gently and when to cast off restraint.

After a long time, he said, "I'd like to drag a J.P. out of bed and marry you tonight, sweetheart. But it doesn't seem right with Rory just gone—"

Hallie burned and ached for Garth, but she also felt it was too soon. "We'll wait," she whispered. "We need to have our minds on running the separator and engine. But we don't have to wait for this . . . or this. . . ." She melted in his arms.

*T*hey buried Rory near a mass of wild roses on the Old Prairie not far from the burrowing owls. Hallie read from *The Book of Common Prayer* and Shaft played a beautiful, haunting requiem before the crew and neighbors recited The Lord's Prayer and The Shepherd's Psalm. "He leadeth me beside the still waters . . ."

"The owls will keep Rory company," Jackie said as they started home. "Won't they, Hallie?"

Was he remembering his father? "Of course they will. And the great horned owls and blackbirds and meadowlarks. But we'll come visit him, too."

Back at the house, Mary Donnelly and Mrs. Halstead had organized the bountiful dinner of covered dishes brought by the neighbors, including some rather shamefaced ones who had been in the mob. Only the Brocketts weren't there. It was whispered that Sophie had suffered a complete nervous breakdown and was in the Hospital for the Insane at Larned.

As the neighbor women were collecting children and dishes, leaving the MacLeod household enough food for several days, Ed Brockett drove up. He joined the men on the porch, nodded, and stated his mission.

"You know what we agreed, boys," he said to his neighbors. "That we'd each put what we could toward gettin' MacLeod another engine and he could pay us back by threshin' for us—those who've got any wheat left this year and all of us next year, God willin'." His Adam's apple bobbed in his scrawny throat; but, after a moment, he went on sturdily. "After I took Sophie to Larned, I stopped at every town on the way back and asked if anyone had an engine for sale. Found a good sixty-horsepower Case about twenty miles north of Hollister for $1,800." He turned to Garth. "Would you like to check it over, MacLeod? If you like it—and if our proposition suits you—I've told the owner to let you take it, and I'll send him a check."

"I like your proposition just fine." Garth looked around at his neighbors. "My partners and I have done some arithmetic, and we won't have to borrow more than about eight hundred from you, but that'll save wrangling over a bank loan. We'll sign an agreement, but I want to shake your hands."

He smiled proudly at Hallie and brought her forward. "I want you all to know that Hallie's promised to marry me as soon as the run's over. We decided we'd better not mix honeymooning and threshing."

What he didn't say but what everyone understood was that they owed this respect to Rory, who had loved her, too, and had given his life to try to right the wrong he had done. Besides, tired as they would be after a day's threshing, it would be sweet to sit in the darkness and talk and get used to being in love—if that was possible. Sweet to have a courtship and discover new things about each other. But when they came home next fall—when they came home . . .

The women hugged Hallie while the men slapped Garth on the back and shook hands with him and the crew. Mike Donnelly hugged Hallie, too, and gave her a hearty kiss on the cheek. "We'll give you the biggest, happiest charivari ever seen in Kansas," he vowed. "Shaft, you'll be head fiddler, and we'll dance all night!"

Mary Donnelly laughed. "It'll be quite a wedding. Can't remember one where the separator man married the engineer!"

"And the water monkey was bridesmaid," Meg put in.

"Will I be your real brother then?" Jackie asked her.

"Wacky Jackie!" she crooned, stooping to gather him into her arms. "You already are!"

Three days later, Hallie, in a new red sunbonnet, steered the procession past the Old Prairie. She pulled the whistle in a long, trilling salute to Rory. Then she blew Garth a kiss over her shoulder and sounded the two long, two short that meant they were on the road.